FIRST IMPRESSIONS

Jesse rose, stubbed out his cigarette in a glass dish on the colonel's desk, and stepped toward Mattie. He held out his hand. "Mrs. Hunter, it's an honor to meet you. Mr. Goodnight speaks of you often."

Mattie smiled uncertainly. "Thank you, Mr. McDade."

Jesse's eyes locked with hers, and he felt a stab of desire. Her eyes were gold. Like a cougar's. And so was her hair. He bowed over her hand and kissed it, feeling his nostrils flare as he smelled a faint scent of lilac water and rose petals. And woman.

He released her hand and stepped back, his face as impassive as he was capable of making it. "You're welcome, Mrs. Hunter."

Samuel Hunter would not be a problem, he thought.

Mattie Hunter would be the problem.

Coming soon by
D. R. Meredith

The Reckoning

Published by
HarperPaperbacks

ATTENTION: ORGANIZATIONS AND CORPORATIONS

Most HarperPaperbacks are available at special quantity discounts for bulk purchases for sales promotions, premiums, or fund-raising. For information, please call or write:
**Special Markets Department, HarperCollins Publishers,
10 East 53rd Street, New York, N.Y. 10022.
Telephone: (212) 207-7528. Fax: (212) 207-7222.**

A TIME TOO LATE

D.R. MEREDITH

HarperPaperbacks
A Division of HarperCollinsPublishers

If you purchased this book without a cover, you should be aware that this book is stolen property. It was reported as "unsold and destroyed" to the publisher and neither the author nor the publisher has received any payment for this "stripped book."

This is a work of fiction. The characters, incidents, and dialogues are products of the author's imagination and are not to be construed as real. Any resemblance to actual events or persons, living or dead, is entirely coincidental.

HarperPaperbacks *A Division of* HarperCollins*Publishers*
10 East 53rd Street, New York, N.Y. 10022

Copyright © 1993 by D. R. Meredith
All rights reserved. No part of this book may be used or reproduced in any manner whatsoever without written permission of the publisher, except in the case of brief quotations embodied in critical articles and reviews. For information address HarperCollins*Publishers,*
10 East 53rd Street, New York, N.Y. 10022.

Cover illustration by Peter Fiore

First Printing: January 1993

Printed in the United States of America

HarperPaperbacks and colophon are trademarks of HarperCollins*Publishers*

❖ 10 9 8 7 6 5 4 3 2 1

To the various cowboys, ranchers, and sons and daughters of pioneer settlers who used to linger in my bookstore telling me stories of the old days when the range was free, the cattle herds vast, and men and women stood tall and cast long shadows.

Acknowledgments

Claire R. Kuehn, archivist-librarian at the Panhandle-Plains Museum, Canyon, Texas, who willingly and with infinite patience provided files, photographs, books, unpublished manuscripts, charts, maps, minutes of meetings held over a hundred years ago, newspapers, and who furthermore answered questions without once asking what possible use I might make of the information.

Noreen I. Riffe, librarian of the Western History Collection, McClelland Library, Pueblo, Colorado, who went far beyond her job description to introduce a Texan to the Pueblo of 1875.

Bert Clifton, director of the Tumbleweed Museum, Moore County, Texas, who used to talk of the drift fence.

Any errors are solely the responsibility of the author and made despite the best efforts of her mentors.

Author's Note

It is the duty of the writer of historical fiction to put imaginary toads in real gardens. Based upon photographs, journals, personal memoirs, and contemporary newspaper accounts, my garden—the Texas Panhandle between 1877 and 1882—is as real as I can make it. The weather, the condition of the range, the epidemic of Texas fever, the rustling, and the prairie fires are based on newspaper accounts. The Panhandle Stock Association, building the drift fence, Billy the Kid, and the Winchester quarantine are all real events. Many of the characters are real, too. Charles and Mary Ann Goodnight, W.M.D. Lee, Bates and Beals, Judge Dubbs, Hank Cresswell, and numerous others are historical characters. All ranches mentioned except Mattie's Bar H and Jesse's Flying MJ existed, and in some cases still exist today.

My imaginary toads, all my characters who live on the Hunter Ranch or in the Colonel's Pueblo home, are not intended to resemble any persons actually living, and if they do so, it is entirely coincidental. Their actions while in my real garden are a figment of my imagination and are meant for the enjoyment of the reader.

CHAPTER 1

PUEBLO, COLORADO TERRITORY—1875

Colonel Andrew Corley, late of the Confederate army, professed himself to be a happy man. He had a ready supply of Cuba's finest cigars in his humidor, a number of bottles of Kentucky's best bourbon stored in his cellar, the biggest house in Pueblo, Colorado Territory, and a circle of friends who were reasonably honest and, more important, accepted the Colonel at his own face value. If any wondered how an officer of a defeated army, a man disenfranchised by the war, his plantation home burned, his slaves freed, his land endangered by the tax collector, all of which the Colonel did not hesitate to describe in fierce and bitter detail, managed to amass a fortune on a raw frontier ten years and more than a thousand miles from his birthright, their curiosity remained unsatisfied. For all his garrulous nature, the Colonel was not a forthright man.

"Jubilee," he said, his mouth twisting so that the

black body servant might trim the silky white mustache that he wore paired with a short beard in imitation of Robert E. Lee. If his resemblance to that honorable gentleman was less striking than he wished, and if it often failed to influence his character, he allowed neither fact to distress him unduly. A hero, after all, had to live up to standards from which the average man might upon occasion claim exemption. Not that the Colonel felt himself to be either dishonest or dishonorable, but he had learned that both honesty and honor were subject to interpretation. Within limits, of course, and most of his limits were as rigid as his spine. Others shifted more rapidly than a surveyor could mark them.

"Jubilee," he continued. "A man has corners in his life where no one has a right to poke, especially some of these damn Yankees calling themselves eastern industrialists. I met one today at the bank, a disgusting example of the lower orders in spite of his fine clothes. He didn't know who his family was any further back than his grandmother on his father's side, but he has the gall to sit in my office and ask me the source of my financial contentment. As if my capital is tainted! As if my bank is a financial brothel! Such behavior shows a lack of breeding. If I weren't a gentleman, I would have called him out." The Colonel slapped his chair arm for emphasis.

Jubilee poured the pan of shaving water into the chamber pot. "I suspects being a gentleman didn't have nothing to do with it. You can't hit the broad side of a barn with a gun, and I suspects that's what made up your mind. You the worst shot of any white gentleman I ever seen. I allus figured that any Yankees you shot was 'cause they walked into your bullet."

The Colonel wiped his face and smoothed his mustache. "You are uppity, Jubilee. Emancipation has eroded your respect for your betters. I'll have you know that I enjoyed the admiration of my men during the war."

"I 'spect you did. Weren't no better man with a saber than you. I remembers one Christmas you was home, musta been Sixty-two 'cause Miss Mattie was barely talking, and the field hands hadn't up and run off yet, and you was riding that old gray gelding down the fence rows and whacking dummies off the posts. It was a sight, Colonel, your saber flashing in the sun and the pickaninnies chasing after you."

The Colonel closed his eyes as he remembered. It had been a glorious Christmas for dreaming. A time before the defeat he'd anticipated, a time when, to an adoring wife and tiny daughter, to the hundreds and thousands of wives and daughters who had never dragged a gut-shot boy off a battlefield and watched him die, who'd never seen blood from a thousand dead puddle on the ground like rainwater, a man with a saber and honor might yet win the day.

He smiled bitterly and opened his eyes to meet those of Jubilee. "Now, if the Yankees had just been gentlemen and fought with sabers, Jubilee, you'd still be a slave, and I'd own some Yankee's dirty factory, and then where would we both be?"

Jubilee held up a clean linen shirt with heavily starched collar and cuffs. "I 'spect I'd still be uppity, and you'd still be a bad shot."

The Colonel leaned his head back and laughed. "I suspect you'd be right, Jubilee. Pour us a glass of that fine bourbon, and we'll drink to change and to that highway robbery you commit every month when you draw your salary."

The black man carefully hung the shirt over the back of a chair and poured a generous measure of liquor into two glasses and set the decanter back on the bureau. "It ain't highway robbery. I is free."

The Colonel took his glass and studied the other

man, noticing the gray that twisted through the black hair, the lines that crinkled around his eyes, and felt his own approaching age reflected in Jubilee's face. "None of us are free. Some men just design their own cages while others must take what is given them. I've known very few who escape. I, for example, am a southern gentleman, a man of family and breeding and honor. I have antecedents, and a sense of what is fitting."

"Then how come you drinking with me? That ain't fitting where we come from."

"You have an annoying habit of interrupting my philosophical discourses, Jubilee. I was about to say that you are an ex-slave, and we are both locked into our separate identities tighter than a hog in a pen. The world we grew up in is gone, yet we cling to what we remember, act out our roles as if the play had not been canceled. Why do you suppose we do that?" asked the Colonel, sipping his bourbon.

"We likes to fool people, Colonel," answered Jubilee, draining his glass. "You rode off to war in that gray uniform, looking real jaunty with your saber and a feather in your hat, but you never turned over all your money like the rest of the white gentlemen did. Shipped your cotton to England in sixty, sixty-one, and sixty-two. Never said a word to nobody about what you was doing, just held that cotton in them English warehouses until after Marse Lee surrendered. Some folks might say you cheated the Confederacy."

The Colonel felt a quiver of shame. But only a quiver, and that only in the deepest part of his soul, where a man keeps his love of lost causes. "And what do you say, Jubilee?"

The ex-slave set his glass down and picked up the starched white shirt again. "I says you was smarter than the rest of the gentlemen. We never went hungry after the war like most folks did."

"I always hedge my bets, Jubilee. My heart was in the war, but my cotton wasn't." He took a last sip of bourbon, set his glass down, and stood up to be helped into his shirt. "But I'm still a southerner. I just don't happen to be a bankrupt southerner."

Jubilee handed him a black, broadcloth waistcoat, ignoring his grimace of distaste. The Colonel still disliked the new style of matching waistcoat with frock coat, often saying such unrelieved black reminded him of undertakers. "And I's still your body servant. I just don't happen to be a slave no more. But we pretends like nothing changed 'cause there ain't no place in this world where we can be what we is."

The Colonel buttoned his waistcoat without moving his eyes away from the other man. "And who might we be?"

"If you was black, or I was white, we'd be friends, Colonel," answered Jubilee.

The Colonel turned the idea over in his mind. Since the war he'd often felt closer to Jubilee than to any white man, but if their former relationship no longer existed, some vestige of who he was—who they both had been—still remained. He glanced around the room at the flocked wallpaper, the four-poster bed, the mahogany bureau and matching highboy, the windows hung with velvet drapes over lace, the chairs, but only recognized the scarred campaign chest he'd carried with him during the war. All else seemed unfamiliar, too raw, too new, in spite of being several years old. Suddenly he longed for his gracious plantation home with its walls and furnishings mellowed by generations, and ached with a sense of tradition lost, burned to ashes and scattered by the wind.

Slowly he turned to Jubilee. "But I'm not one, and you're not the other."

"That's a fact, Colonel."

The Colonel tucked his watch into his waistcoat

pocket and hesitated, then clasped the other man's shoulder. "Jubilee, I wish . . ."

"If wishes was horses, then beggars would ride. That's what Missus Amanda was allus saying."

The Colonel gritted his teeth against another wave of aching loss at the mention of his wife. Dead of pneumonia their first winter in Pueblo, Amanda Stryker Corley had been the last and most beautiful of his traditions lost. Barely fifteen to his thirty-five when they married, she had been more child than woman, and he'd bedded her infrequently, pumping out his lust as quickly as possible, afraid he would hurt her delicate body. He often wondered if he had hurt her in spite of his care, but never asked. It was not a fitting subject to discuss with a wife. She was modest, softspoken, a gracious hostess who welcomed his friends with a maturity beyond her years, and if he'd often sat at the opposite end of the dining table, watching her bare shoulders glow in the candlelight and fantasizing about touching her naked breasts, it was his unworthy urge, and not anything she'd done to tempt him.

When Mattie was born in the early spring of 1860, he'd given Amanda a necklace of matched pearls and spared her his attentions until one night he'd caught her looking at him out of those enormous golden eyes with an expression that in any other woman might be called wanting. Sweating and nervous as a lad with his first woman, he'd entered her room and her bed to find a shy but eager lover.

They had never talked about their mutual pleasure either.

"Colonel, is you all right?"

Jubilee's voice pulled him away from the void that even yet left him feeding on his bitterness. He released the black man's shoulder and staggered to the bureau to pour more bourbon with a shaking hand. He drank the liquor in a few swallows and pointed his finger at his ex-slave. "I gave you my family name when the war was over because every free man needs two names, didn't I? Tried to leave you behind with your own people when I came west, and didn't you refuse to stay? I ruined a good suit of clothes diving into the Missouri to pull you out when you fell off the wagon while we were crossing the river, didn't I? I dug an Indian arrow out of your shoulder, bound you up like you a white man, didn't I? Put you in my own wagon with my own wife to nurse you when the infection set in? And didn't you carry me out of the mountains on your back when I broke my leg prospecting?"

He poked Jubilee's chest with his finger. "My father gave you to me when we were five years old. Fifty years we've been together. There will be no more talk of if I was another color, or you were." His voice lowered. "There will be no more talk of friends. We're a tradition, Jubilee, the only goddamn one the Yankees and death didn't take away from me."

Jubilee picked up the Colonel's frock coat and helped him into it. "They didn't take away your cotton neither."

The Colonel glanced over his shoulder at the black man. "Are you being uppity again?"

Jubilee tugged at the Colonel's coat until the shoulder seams lay straight. "Cotton a tradition, too."

The Colonel glanced through his bedroom window at the bleak mountains looming a scant distance to the west, their jagged peaks not softened by the snow that covered them. But then Colorado was not a soft land. "Cotton doesn't grow in this country, Jubilee."

"Maybe tradition don't grow too good here neither," said the black man, picking up the Colonel's soiled linen and hanging up his discarded trousers to be brushed and pressed for another day. He nodded toward the window. "Mr. Hunter's come for supper again."

The Colonel walked to the window and twitched aside the lace curtain to look down at Samuel Hunter. He ruthlessly tempered his distaste for the younger man's foppish appearance in his yellowish-brown nankeen trousers, gold-and-green waistcoat over a ruffled shirt, and a brown frock coat with velvet lapels. That Hunter's cravat was loosely tied in a bow after the style preferred by George Armstrong Custer only added to the Colonel's dislike for the young man. No respectable southerner would copy the apparel of a Yankee, particularly one whose reputation exceeded his abilities.

The Colonel considered the possibility, faint though it was, that his own sartorial standards had been compromised by his exposure to such frontier apparel as fringed buckskins, rough wool or corduroy pants, homespun cotton shirts, knotted kerchiefs, tattered remains of cavalry uniforms, and those copper-riveted, denim trousers called Levi's worn by hard-rock miners and other rough sorts.

After the stench of his own sweat and Jubilee's those years he'd spent rushing from strike to strike in these Colorado mountains, from one rough, filthy mining town to another, tunneling underground like a mole, developing a claim, then selling it before the ore played out, until he decided banking was a more fit way for a fastidious gentleman to make a living. There was a slight chance he was overly sensitive to the scent of a man's hair pomade.

On the other hand, he doubted that either his fellow citizens' rough clothing or their irregular bathing habits had seriously affected his judgment. He sighed and clapped his ex-slave on the shoulder. "The fact is, Jubilee, that Samuel Hunter looks too pretty to piss. But I would not misjudge him on that account. He has found favor in my daughter's eyes, and for that reason alone we must welcome him. At least, until her vision clears."

"I wouldn't bet no money on that, Colonel. Miss Mattie 'pears to be plumb happy being blind," said Jubilee.

"Nonsense. Mattie is a child, and a very dutiful child. She'll be guided by my firm hand and wiser head. We'll soon see the back of Mr. Samuel Hunter."

"I gots a month's wages coming this Saturday night, Colonel. I wants to bet it all on Miss Mattie."

The Colonel frowned. "I don't encourage gambling by servants, Jubilee. It is the first step toward more serious crime, such as laziness. However, in the interest of teaching you a much-needed lesson in respect for the judgment of your betters, I shall accept your wager. Just don't take on when you lose." He gave his waistcoat a final tug and walked to the door, glancing back impatiently at his body servant. "Stop dallying and open the door, Jubilee. I don't wish my daughter to spend time alone with that young nitwit."

Jubilee shuffled forward at a snail's pace. "You broke your arm, Colonel, that this poor nigger gots to open the door for you?"

The Colonel arched his bushy white eyebrows. "One of your less endearing traits, Jubilee, is your habit of acting like a put-upon servant whenever you disagree with me. Get along with you and offer Mr. Hunter a drink."

"What's you gonna be doing whiles I's in the parlor watching to see that the snake don't get in your henhouse?" asked Jubilee, holding open the door for the Colonel.

The Colonel sauntered through and waited for the black man to follow him. "I'll be waiting in my office for my own guests to arrive. I've invited Charlie Goodnight and his charming wife to supper."

"How come you ain't waiting in the parlor?"

"With Mr. Hunter?" asked the Colonel, plucking a cigar from his waistcoat pocket and inhaling its rich aroma before lighting it. "I've suffered that young man's presence in my parlor and at my table every night and twice on Sunday for a week. I need a respite. I will await reinforcements in the person of Charlie Goodnight. Even a young pup like Samuel Hunter will cease his yapping in Goodnight's presence."

He puffed a moment on his cigar, pleased with his strategy. In spite of being a Texan, Goodnight was an honest and forthright man. He could trust the cattleman to give Hunter his comeuppance, if need be, and he could enjoy his baked ham and pecan pie without having to bite his tongue a dozen times during the meal.

He squeezed Jubilee's shoulder. "Go see to our guest's needs. I'll not abuse my tradition of southern hospitality by neglecting to quench a man's thirst."

"That Mr. Hunter, he look right through me likes I wasn't there. I ends up by asking Miss Mattie what he wants, and then he tells her, and she tells me."

The Colonel felt a flash of impatience mixed with guilt. "If you dislike Mr. Hunter so much, why did you make that ridiculous wager?"

Grasping the banister and creeping down the stairs a step at a time, Jubilee continued to scowl. "Most all my life I worked for nothing, so when I sees a chance to make me some money, I takes it. But that don't mean I wants to win. It just means I ain't gonna lose, 'cause you a hard man 'cept for Miss Mattie. Yes, suh, I gonna win, but I don't likes it, just like I don't like that Mr. Hunter. Butter won't melt in that man's mouth."

"Your comments about *my* guest aren't fitting, Jubilee," said the Colonel, feeling his temper slip another notch. "You are forgetting your place."

"Yes, suh," replied Jubilee, halting at the bottom of the stairs. "Something musta got in me. I reckons I'll go take my place pourin' your fine bourbon down *your* guest's gullet."

The black man walked across the polished wooden floor of the entrance hall toward the parlor, his shoulders not quite so straight and his head slumped forward, and the Colonel felt a queer jolt inside his chest. He stopped on the bottom step of the staircase.

"Jubilee!"

The black man turned around, his head tilted slightly back to look up at the Colonel, his eyes guarded by ancient wrongs. "Yes, suh, Colonel?"

"Jubilee, I—" He snapped his lips closed. He didn't like Samuel Hunter any more than Jubilee did, but damn it all, he couldn't allow his ex-slave to criticize a white man. Nor apologize for taking him to task about it either. He shook his head. "Nothing."

Jubilee turned away, but not before the Colonel saw something flare up in his black eyes, then fade away like hope extinguished. "Then I best be seeing to Mr. Hunter's thirst if you don't want nothing."

The Colonel waved him away. Damn Jubilee anyway. Stir a man up with talk about what ought to be when he needs to be thinking about what is. "I'll be along directly, Jubilee, as soon as the Goodnights arrive."

"You'd best chew some mint before they gets here. Colonel Goodnight ain't much of a drinking man atall, and you smells like a pig that's been swilling at a trough of corn squeezings."

The Colonel glared at the back of Jubilee's head, then walked down the broad hall toward the back of the house. Maybe the cook had some dried mint.

CHAPTER 2

The Colonel helped himself to several slices of baked ham from the platter Jubilee held, then watched with amusement as the black man deftly turned the plate to offer the butt end and gristle to Samuel Hunter. The young man frowned as he awkwardly speared a piece of meat, and the Colonel smothered a chuckle behind his napkin. It never paid a man to be rude to a house nigger because he always got his own back. Besides, it was ungentlemanly.

The Colonel studied Samuel Hunter and tried to decide exactly what it was about the young man that roused his dander. His eyes were large, and to the Colonel's way of thinking, slightly protuberant, but Mattie claimed their luminous blue color combined with his white-blond hair gave him an ethereal look. Just like a young girl to confuse angels and men. He preferred men who had spirit rather than spirituality.

He sliced another piece of ham, dipped it in the redeye gravy, put it in his mouth, then returned to his clandestine observation of his daughter's guest. Fair skin, the kind that turned brick red in the sun, except Samuel Hunter didn't exhibit any evidence of a close acquaintance with that particular celestial orb. His skin was still baby fair as if he rubbed it with buttermilk every night. It wasn't natural. A man who sat a horse as well as Samuel Hunter ought to at least have wind-chapped cheeks. And calluses, thought the Colonel suddenly, his gaze falling to the young man's slender white hands. He ought to have calluses from holding the reins. Even with gloves, a man's hands developed hard pads across the tops of his palms from pulling on the reins when need be. Unless you rode some broken-down old nag, and no man with a lick of sense did that on the frontier. And Pueblo was still that, notwithstanding the *Colorado Chieftain*'s claims as far back as its establishment as the town's newspaper in 1868 that the frontier days were past. An opera house, a library association, a cornet band, and a few churches didn't necessarily mean all of Pueblo's inhabitants had left behind their free and easy ways. A man still needed a good horse under him just in case he ran into somebody who decided to free up his money the easy way at the point of a gun.

Samuel Hunter's voice was another trait that the Colonel held against him. A man's voice ought to be deep, capable of shaking rafters and commanding a respectful silence among listeners. Samuel's voice was light and a bit high-pitched, more suited to prattling to the ladies of art and literature and reciting very bad poetry, much of which the young man modestly admitted to penning himself, and all of which the Colonel considered an unconscionable waste of ink.

"I recently perused a copy of the 1871 edition of *Leaves of Grass* by Mr. Walt Whitman," Samuel said to Mrs. Goodnight and Mattie. "And while that gentleman has gained much recognition in recent years, I must confess that I found his verse patently vulgar, not at all suitable for delicate sensibilities." The Colonel couldn't imagine what else Samuel expected. After all, Whitman was a Yankee.

"Samuel is a wonderful poet himself, Mrs. Goodnight," said Mattie, sitting stiff and straight at the foot of the table, her back not touching her chair. "Samuel, recite a few verses of your 'Ode to a Dying Swan.'"

Samuel patted his mouth with his napkin. "I wouldn't want to bore anyone with my bit of doggerel, Miss Mattie."

"Please, Samuel, don't be so modest."

"If you insist, Miss Mattie," he replied, and cleared his throat before beginning.

The Colonel hastily debated whether it would be socially acceptable to stop up his ears with his napkin. He had suffered the death of that particular swan at least twice in the last week and doubted his digestion would survive another demise. Instead he tried to imagine Samuel giving orders to men in the late war, and decided had it ever happened within hearing of the Union army, the Yankees would have laughed themselves to death. Which brought up the vexatious question of why Samuel *hadn't* been in battle. He would have been fifteen in '65, old enough to carry a musket. God knows there had been boys younger than that fighting and unfortunately dying, a good many of them without any sort of medical aid to ease their passing. Why had Samuel been any different? Not that he wished the boy had been killed, he assured himself, but an emasculating wound to the groin would not have been amiss.

The Colonel took a bite of golden yams swimming in butter, his appetite in danger of being spoiled by the puzzling young man seated next to him. Damn Samuel Hunter anyway. How could the offspring of a fine southern family, bearer of a letter of introduction attesting to his name and character from so sterling a

A TIME TOO LATE
15

source as General Forrest be so *unsatisfactory*?

He laid down his fork and wiped his mouth, carefully stroking the edges of his mustache to remove any trace of his supper from its luxurious growth, and turned to his other male guest as quickly as Samuel finished the last verse of his poem. Best to change the subject before Samuel could begin another poetical creation. "Charlie, what is this I hear about your leaving Colorado?"

Colonel Charles Goodnight, former scout, Texas Ranger, trailblazer, cattleman, raised his massive head, a knife full of black-eyed peas poised in one callused hand. "I go to the supper table to eat."

Mary Ann Goodnight, called Molly by all who knew her and many who didn't, smiled at Colonel Corley. "Charlie believes in doing one thing at a time."

Samuel Hunter patted his blond mustache, an insignificant thing in the Colonel's estimation, and lifted one corner of his lip in a well-bred sneer. "Surely gracious conversation while dining is the mark of a civilized man, Mr. Goodnight."

Goodnight wiped up the last of his gravy with a biscuit, chewed it, and swallowed, all the while glaring at Samuel. "How do you make a living?"

Samuel arched his eyebrows. "I read for the law in Virginia."

"I knew an honest lawyer once," said Goodnight.

"Charlie!" said Molly Goodnight in distress. "Have you forgotten my father was a lawyer?"

"He's the one I'm talking about," replied her husband, pushing back his chair. "If the ladies will excuse me, I got to get up and move. Habit I got into on the trail. Staying at the table when I'm done eating makes my belly hurt. Andrew, I'm going to set outside on your fancy front porch and have a smoke."

"It's still winter!" exclaimed Samuel with an exaggerated shiver.

"Brisk, Mr. Hunter, brisk." He stopped at the foot of the table and his voice and eyes softened. "A good supper, Miss Mattie. Your mother would be proud of what a fine young lady you growed up to be."

Mattie Jo Corley raised her face and smiled at Goodnight, and the Colonel felt himself swell with pride that he had fathered such a beautiful child, although he recognized that she had outgrown that stage in the last year. Still, he wasn't reconciled to hearing her called a young woman. She was still his tiny daughter, the ripe bosom revealed by the tightly fitted bodice of her rose silk dress notwithstanding. In fact, he shied away from thinking of Mattie as even having a bosom. Wives had bosoms. Ladies of the evening had bosoms. Daughters were sexless creatures until such a time as they gave birth to grandchildren, when they became those equally sexless creatures known as mothers. The actual physical activity involved in that transformation was simply ignored as an unsuitable subject for any proper father to consider.

He glanced at Samuel Hunter, suddenly anxious to measure Mattie's womanhood by gauging this young man's reaction to it. He let his shoulders sag in relief when he observed Samuel's expression, admiring but respectful of Mattie's person, as well he should be. There was sufficient to admire about his daughter without entertaining impure thoughts. Her hair, for example, and her eyes. Mattie's hair was the color of minted gold and so thick she needed no false hairpieces or pads to fill out that elaborate coiffure of curls and swirls among whose strands he noticed she had tucked lace and bows and gewgaws.

Her eyes were a darker shade of gold, like that of old coins or antique jewelry, large and round and thickly fringed with dark brown lashes. Like her mother's, but more intense in some manner, almost willful, a thought the Colonel hastily dismissed. Mattie was a quiet, obedient child, respectful of her elders, mainly him, polite, and with perfect manners. A perfect lady. He smiled wryly at himself. No, he was certain that luminous intensity he'd seen in her eyes had something to do with losing Amanda just as Mattie trembled on the verge of womanhood and needed her mother's guidance the most. Such a loss would damper any youthful silliness and leave a young girl more thoughtful and mature.

Her eyes weren't the only difference between Mattie and her mother, though. Where Amanda's skin had been the pink and white so desired by both fashion and the Colonel, Mattie's was alabaster and coral, an exotic combination that seemed almost wanton. If it weren't for her full lips that seemed as vulnerable as a child's, the Colonel would be tempted to hide his daughter beneath a waist-length veil, or better yet, a canvas tent. Her coloring, her features, seemed too rare, too precious, *too intense, damn it,* to be exposed to the improper gaze, not to mention the impure thoughts, of any passing ruffian.

As he watched Mattie smile up at Goodnight he added teeth to her list of physical attributes. Unlike those of most of her contemporaries, hers were straight, white, and perfect, with no unsightly black spots that signaled bad breath and future toothaches.

She was lovely, kind, gentle, and a damn sight too good for the jackanapes sitting beside him and staring at her as if she were merely ordinary. The Colonel shoved back his chair. He was going to have a bellyache of his own if he sat at the table any longer, or else commit some social indiscretion such as dumping the remaining contents of the gravy boat over Samuel Hunter's head.

He smiled. "Charlie, if the ladies can tolerate our cigars, may I suggest we all have coffee and brandy in the parlor. This old widower doesn't get to enjoy the company of two such lovely ladies very often."

Goodnight cocked one heavy black eyebrow, then glanced at his wife and pulled a cigar from his pocket. "That so?"

Feeling his smile slip, the Colonel hastily pulled out Molly Goodnight's chair, praying that the lady's husband would for once in his forthright life practice diplomacy and keep his honest mouth shut. He'd forgotten running into Goodnight early one morning after he'd spent an enjoyable night at a local establishment that catered to a gentleman's more unmentionable needs. He had not, however, forgotten the look on the cattleman's face, nor the more vocal expression that accompanied it, one that raised the specter of the possible unpleasant physical consequences inherent in dallying with young women who entertained for wages. Catching the glint in Goodnight's eye, he was certain his guest remembered the occasion as well. Given the Texan's distaste for men who indulged in amorous encounters unblessed by the clergy, the Colonel was also reasonably certain Charlie Goodnight accepted his invitation to supper only because of the fondness he and his wife held for Mattie. Such morality was commendable, but damn tiresome. A man had to hedge his bets.

"Jubilee, bring coffee to the parlor," he told the black man, who waited silently next to a massive mahogany sideboard at the other end of the dining room, far enough away to ignore without conscious effort, but near enough to order about without raising one's voice.

"Papa, Samuel wants to talk to you," said Mattie, rising to her feet and stepping over to take the young man's arm, her silk train rustling softly over the floor.

The Colonel wasn't certain if his daughter was gazing up worshipfully at that interloper, or if she just naturally arched her neck in that fashion because all that long thick hair weighted down the back of her head. Must be the latter, he decided, since Mattie was a tall woman, standing some four inches above five feet, and he doubted that Samuel was more than three inches taller than that. A woman didn't need to tilt her head for three inches.

He frowned. "Not now, Mattie. We have guests, and I want Charlie to answer my question, the one I was so rude as to ask over supper. My apologies, Charlie. I forgot your untalkative nature during mealtime." He led them into the parlor as he spoke, catching Goodnight looking from Mattie to Samuel with an unreadable expression.

Whatever the cattleman might have thought of Mattie and her young man, he kept it to himself as he struck a match on the sole of his boot and lit a cigar. "I'm trailing a herd down to the Llano Estacado. It's got unbroken buffalo turf and grama grasses, miles of 'em, and enough waterings if a man knows where to look."

The Colonel sat down on one of those spindly-legged womanish chairs with the little round backs he hated so much, and wished he was in his office where a man could sit on either of two overstuffed leather sofas and be comfortable. "This is not the time to be leaving, Charlie. Congress is certain to vote statehood for Colorado this year, then there'll be a constitutional convention and elections. It's an opportunity for a man of vision."

Goodnight chuckled. "I heard tell of a man who said that if you put one hundred Americans anywhere in the country, they'd organize a government, lay out townships, petition for statehood, and at least twenty-five of them would run for the United States Senate. I got no use for towns, and there ain't no cattle in Washington, even though there's a hell of a lot of manure. No, Andrew, I'm going back to Texas."

"Is that where this Llano Estacado is?" asked Samuel, sitting next to Mattie on a horsehair sofa. Sitting too damn close in the Colonel's opinion, since Mattie's silk skirt brushed the young man's thighs. There was something indecent about that pink silk lying against nankeen trousers, not to mention the fact that the colors clashed.

Goodnight paced restlessly about the room, a man who could not stay still, and his eyes seemed to focus on some point beyond the walls of the room. The Colonel suddenly thought of a cougar he'd seen caught in a trap, a cougar that finally chewed off its own foot to escape. There was a lot of that cougar in Goodnight.

"The Llano Estacado is the damnedest, biggest plateau between New Mexico and Texas with the lion's share in Texas. It's got no boundaries that a man can see. Man can't see much of anything else either, not a tree or a shrub or even a goddamn weed, just space for a man to live."

Samuel Hunter shuddered. "A savage-sounding place."

"Well, it *is* in Texas," said the Colonel.

"Papa, you're rude to Mr. Goodnight," said Mattie with an apologetic glance toward the cattleman.

"Andrew, I always figured you had something caught in your craw about Texans," stated Goodnight, his extraordinary eyes gleaming under their bushy brows. "You better spit it out before you choke on it."

The Colonel struggled to avoid thinking of the father he'd last seen when he was fifteen years old. Leaving behind a wife, a son, a thriving plantation, and a note on his pillow that he'd "gone to Texas," Jason Robert Corley had simply disappeared. Rumors had floated back that he had died in some dirty adobe mission during the Texas war for independence, slaughtered like a hog by the Mexican general Santa

A TIME TOO LATE

Anna. He'd died a hero—or so the rumors said—which did nothing to soften the Colonel's attitude. The Colonel had never forgiven either his father, or the state whose reputation for unbridled freedom lured him. His hatred of Texas and most Texans was as much a part of him as his soft slurring speech and his love of fine bourbon, and he didn't intend to give up any of the three. The only good thing to be said for the state was that it fought for the Confederacy, but even that didn't excuse the generally violent, uncivilized behavior of its inhabitants. Much as he despised Yankees, he thoroughly agreed with the Union general who said that if he owned hell and Texas, he'd rent out Texas and live in hell.

"I have my reasons," he finally said to Goodnight, wondering suddenly why he exempted this man from his rule of never allowing a Texan across his threshold. Unless, of course, it was because Charlie Goodnight was a law unto himself, and a just law at that. The Colonel didn't know many such men; in fact, he wasn't sure he knew any.

"I reckon that's good enough. None of my business anyway," said Goodnight, turning suddenly to Samuel Hunter. "You settling down in Pueblo?"

Samuel crossed his legs and glanced sideways at Mattie. "I hope to. Of course, eventually I plan to move to Denver." The Colonel sat up with a jerk. It was the first time he'd heard of any such plan. He wondered if there wasn't a way he could smooth Samuel's path—as long as that path led out of Pueblo.

"Samuel is hoping to be elected a delegate to the constitutional convention," said Mattie, her eyes glowing as she looked at Samuel as if he were a fledgling Founding Father. "If Congress votes for statehood, that is. Samuel has some wonderful ideas, such as universal suffrage."

"We got universal suffrage in this country already,"

interrupted the Colonel. "We let the darkies vote."

"But not women, Papa."

The Colonel choked on his coffee. "A woman's place is not at the ballot box."

"Men stuffs them just fine without no help," muttered Jubilee, setting the coffeepot on a low table in front of Mattie.

Goodnight let out a howl of laughter and clapped Jubilee on the shoulder. "I heard an old man from down on the Brazos say that every race had at least ten percent sons of bitches unless you were talking about politicians and horse traders. Then you would be lucky to find ten percent who *weren't* sons of bitches. I reckon you must have knowed that old man, too."

Jubilee shook his head. "Ain't never been to Texas and got no reason to go. I ain't got no family there."

"Jubilee!" The Colonel wiped his brow with a handkerchief and wondered if the world had tilted on its axis or if it just seemed that way. Jubilee speaking out in front of company, Mattie mentioning women's suffrage, and his own disquieting thoughts about his daughter growing up, all were intolerable, and he didn't intend to have his domestic world disturbed in such a fashion.

"Jubilee, that will be all," he said, folding his handkerchief and tucking it in his pocket. "Mattie, you will not mention women getting the vote. It is an unseemly, unwomanly notion, and although I can't call to mind the exact verses, I'm certain the Good Book specifically forbids any such activity by the gentler sex. And Mr. Hunter?"

Samuel sat straighter, a worried frown putting two creases between his eyebrows. "Yes, sir?"

"Encouraging my daughter to entertain such unacceptable thoughts is a poor recommendation of your company."

"Colonel Corley, I certainly never meant to advocate such a radical cause. Miss Mattie misunderstood my meaning," Samuel said with a petulant glance at her. "I merely repeated a proposition that is gaining some favor, that of allowing the fair sex to vote for members of local school boards. It is an idea with a certain merit, since, as mothers, women have an abiding interest in education. On the other hand, sir, your argument that women's suffrage is unseemly, if not ungodly, is quite convincing."

"Does that mean you support giving women the vote or you don't?" demanded the Colonel.

"If I lived in hell and somebody attacked the devil, I'd fight on his side or get out, but I wouldn't claim I was just visiting," said Goodnight suddenly, not bothering to hide his impatience with Samuel.

Samuel's fair skin turned a mottled red, and the Colonel could sense his debating whether or not he should take offense at the cattleman's remark. The Colonel rather hoped he would. It would settle in anybody's mind that Samuel Hunter was a fool. Charles Goodnight was a tall man who looked as if he might tip the scales at two hundred pounds or better, most of it hard muscle layered on massive shoulders and chest. A blow from one of Goodnight's callus-toughened hands would render young Hunter uninterested in constitutional conventions, women's suffrage, and any other activity not directly related to nursing his broken jaw.

The Colonel sighed. Still, as host he had a responsibility to prevent bloodshed among his guests. And there were ladies present. Ladies had a tendency to have an attack of the vapors at the first sign of violence, he thought, conveniently forgetting the thousands of ladies who nursed the wounded and dying in the late war without fainting or weeping—at least in the presence of their patients. In the Colonel's opinion, such fortitude was admirable in certain circumstances, but not on a social occasion.

"I'm not certain I understand you, sir," said Samuel, standing up and puffing out his chest like a bantam rooster. Except the Colonel considered a bantam rooster more impressive.

Goodnight thrust his head forward. "I ain't surprised. The hardest thing a man has to do is make up his mind. Some men never learn the hang of it."

"My goodness, Charlie, look at the time," said Mary Ann Goodnight with the ease of long practice at smoothing over the effects of her husband's bluntness. "If we leave now, we'll make it home at a decent hour." Only the Colonel was in a position to see the steely look she gave her husband. Frail as the lady might be, she had courage. Not many men would face down Charles Goodnight.

Pulling her shawl more tightly around her shoulders, Mary Ann Goodnight turned to Samuel. "I'm glad to have met you, Mr. Hunter. Your conversation was stimulating." She leveled a glance at the Colonel that was every bit as daunting as the one she had given her husband. "Don't you agree, Colonel Corley?"

The Colonel was prepared to deny it since he didn't have to live with Mrs. Goodnight's displeasure, but then he caught a glimpse of the pleading expression in his daughter's eyes, and swallowed. "I guess you might put it that way, Mrs. Goodnight."

He saw Mattie's narrow shoulders sag in relief and felt a quiver of regret for calling her down before company. But just a quiver. A father couldn't let a young minx barely old enough to wear her hair up be disrespectful. Or express opinions in public. Particularly if they ran counter to his own.

Mattie rose from the sofa and trailed the Goodnights out of the parlor, looking suddenly like a very young girl who had tried her best to be a grown woman, and felt she had failed. "But I expected you to stay the night with us. I aired out a bedroom."

Mary Ann Goodnight smiled at the young girl and shook her head. "I'm surprised I got Charlie off his horse and away from the cattle long enough for supper. It's not in his nature to be an idle house guest even for a night. He's already spent longer doing nothing in the last hour than at any time in the past six years."

"A man who can't keep himself busy ain't worth a bucket of warm spit," said Goodnight as he helped his wife into her pelisse, a floor-length and fur-lined garment opening down the front that always reminded the Colonel of a monk's robe without the rope belt.

"Andrew, I'd like a word with you," said Goodnight as he ushered his wife out the front door.

It was clear and cold with the stars like tiny particles of ice thrown against a black velvet sky, and the Colonel shivered as he followed the cattleman outside and shut the door. He would never, if he lived the rest of his life in the west, understand how these Texas cattlemen could tolerate all but the coldest weather without a greatcoat. A couple of shirts and a vest, and they seemed impervious to anything less than a blizzard. Then they might pull on a waist-length blanket-lined jumper with sleeves, but more likely they'd untie their slicker from the cantle of their saddle and wear that. The Colonel shivered again. A voluminous affair with wide long skirts, and a slit and gores in the back so a man could wear it in the saddle, a slicker was the quickest way he knew to freeze to death in wet cold.

Goodnight helped his wife onto the seat of a buckboard and helped her tuck a blanket over her legs. The two horses stamped their hooves and swung their heads, as if to say they'd waited patiently at this hitching rail as long as they intended to wait, and why didn't the tall massive man climb onto the seat so they could get back to their own corral.

The Colonel stamped his own feet to keep the circulation going. "You had something to say, Charlie?"

Goodnight rested one hand on the low wooden back of the buckboard's seat. "What in the all-fired hell did you want tonight, Andrew, and don't tell me you wanted to know if I was going back to Texas. You could've asked me that this afternoon and not wasted my time sitting around in your parlor sipping coffee from them little cups with handles I couldn't get my goddamn fingers through."

"You're a prominent man in Pueblo, Charlie, a civic leader. You established an opera house, donated money for an institution of higher learning, opened a bank. You're known as a man of vision, of judgment. I couldn't ask a man like you to explain a rumor while standing in the middle of a public street. It wasn't fitting."

Goodnight took another cigar out of his pocket, and the Colonel wondered if it were true the man smoked no fewer than fifty a day. "I don't own the opera house anymore, and the bank went bust. The Panic of Seventy-three damn near wiped me out. Hell, I sold the only block in Pueblo that had a brick building on it for less than a quarter of what it was worth. So I'm not prominent anymore, and a lot of folks are saying my judgment isn't worth a good goddamn."

"Not necessarily," said the Colonel, picking his words carefully. "You still have a reputation for sizing up a man, so tell me, what was your impression of young Hunter?"

Goodnight let the cigar smoke trickle out of his mouth while his eyes glittered in the moonlight. "Never known you to be slow about making up your own mind, Andrew. What's making you cold-footed this time?"

The Colonel bristled at the term "cold-footed." "I'm no coward, Charlie, but Mattie thinks highly of the young man, and I'm afraid that in my anxiety to protect my daughter from unscrupulous suitors, I might be misjudging the man."

Goodnight climbed onto the buckboard and picked up the reins. "On short acquaintance, Andrew, he appears to be worthless as a four-card flush."

"Now, Charlie," said his wife. "Maybe young Samuel just needs to be seasoned."

Goodnight spat over the side of the buckboard. "Seasoning's for drying out wood. I never seen it change a man from what he isn't into what he ought to be. It just makes the most of what he already is, and in this particular case that ain't much. If you're asking me what I'd do, Andrew, I'd tell young Samuel to find another pasture to graze."

He nodded abruptly and turned his buckboard toward home, leaving the Colonel shivering in the late-winter air.

CHAPTER 3

Samuel Hunter scarcely waited until the vestibule door closed behind the Colonel and the Goodnights before whipping out a crisp linen handkerchief and blotting his forehead. "What a vulgar man! Eating with his knife like white trash! And mentioning his—his belly in the presence of ladies."

Mattie felt her corset pinch her waist as she drew a deep breath. "But we have them, too, Samuel."

Samuel carefully folded his handkerchief and tucked it back in his pocket while giving her a stern look of disapproval. "It is not a proper subject of conversation, Miss Mattie. I fear you have been too long away from genteel company if Mr. Goodnight's manners fail to offend you."

Mattie looked away, feeling the criticism like the brush of a stinging nettle. The same restlessness that disturbed her sleep and drove her to stand close to Samuel, to lay her hand on his arm more frequently than she should, had now led her into coarse conversation.

She glanced back up at him, but he had turned his face away from her. She stared at his profile, as pure in line as any of the drawings of Greek statues she had seen in art class at boarding school last year. She felt her cheeks grow hotter as she remembered the drawings in their entirety: taut muscular bodies—male bodies—in graceful nude poses. The art teacher had been dismissed without references, and the headmistress had lectured the entire student body on the need for modesty and pure thoughts. The drawings had been burned, and the art class had spent the rest of the school year painting flowers.

Mattie never told anyone how disturbing she had found those drawings—not because of the nudity of the statues, but because of the naturalness they represented, as if the models were free of the artifice, constraint, and uncertainty that some days threatened to suffocate her. She closed her eyes and imagined Samuel's disgust if he ever discovered that she had looked at a drawing of a naked man—and not been repulsed by it. He would think her a woman without virtue, such as those who lived in rooms above the saloons in downtown Pueblo, and whom she occasionally saw on streets in spite of Jubilee's admonition as he drove her to Mr. Thatcher's store or her father's bank that she turn her head or close her eyes lest her sensibilities be wounded.

"Why should I hide my face, Jubilee?" she had finally demanded one afternoon several weeks ago when she had ridden more than a block down Santa Fe Avenue with her eyes closed and her parasol tipped to shadow her face. "I'm not the one who leads a shameful life doing whatever it is these women do. And exactly what is it they do?" she asked, opening her eyes to stare curiously at one of the women whose red cheeks nearly matched her red hair, and Mattie suspected that neither color was natural. "Besides paint their faces and drink whiskey in the saloons?"

Jubilee's head whipped toward her, his face such a mask of outraged disapproval that Mattie flinched back against the tufted leather seat. "You hush your mouth, Miss Mattie, and close them eyes. A young lady like you ain't supposed to know nothin' about them Jezebels. You ain't even supposed to *think* about them. If you see one, you don't let on you know she there, 'cause far as you're concerned, she *ain't*."

He slapped the reins and the horse broke into a fast trot. "I taking you back home, then I'm telling the Colonel."

Mattie shivered as though she had stepped into one of the dirty snowdrifts that lay piled against the sides of the frame buildings they passed. "No, Jubilee! Don't tell Papa! He'll take on about Mama and how disappointed she would be in me. Then he'll lock himself up in his office with a bottle of whiskey and won't come out until he drinks it all."

Jubilee glanced at her, shuffling his feet against the wooden floorboard in agitation. "You ain't supposed to know about that, and effen you do, you ain't supposed to talk about it."

She drew a trembling breath. "How could I not know about it? I live in the same house and I'm not blind nor dumb. I see you helping him up the stairs."

"You ain't supposed to let on you notice, Miss Mattie. Your mama raised you better than that."

"My mama didn't raise me at all, Jubilee! You and Papa and Aunt Patty did! My mama died when I was ten. Sometimes I can't remember her at all, just what Papa tells me about her."

Jubilee's mouth tightened and he turned his attentions back to guiding the buggy down the busy street, but Mattie saw that his shoulders were hunched. "You ain't gonna get off that easy, Miss Mattie. The Colonel was tore up something fierce after your mama died, and maybe me and him and Aunt Patty was clumsy as field hands with the silver about raising you, but we done our best. And your mama done told you how to act like a lady afore she died." He glanced at her again, and Mattie quailed at the accusing look in his eyes. "I knows it, and you knows it. Your mama was a southern lady, and women like her teach their girl children how to behave right along with teaching them their letters. No, Miss Mattie, it ain't because you don't know what's right. It's something else that makes you chomp at the bit, like asking questions about them painted hussies, some wildness laying underneath your skin like a cougar on a tree limb, just waiting to pounce."

Mattie straightened her shoulders. "That's enough, Jubilee. It's not your place to criticize me."

The black man hesitated, and Mattie watched with a dull ache of shame the fear that momentarily surfaced in his eyes. He shook his head, the fear disappearing to be replaced with an expression of dogged determination. "You ain't getting by with that either, Miss Mattie. You done said yourself that I helped raise you—and I did! You couldn't be no closer if you was my own child, and I'm telling you these things for your own good. You, Miss Mattie Corley. You the Colonel's daughter, and the Colonel's an important man in Pueblo—in all of this territory. Folks expect you to act a certain way, and if you don't, they gonna talk."

Mattie could feel her heart beating under her wool bodice, long heavy strokes as if she had been running. "What does it matter, Jubilee? What can they do? Papa owns half of Pueblo. He has an interest in the Denver and Rio Grande Railroad. He owns part of the smelter. Will people stop riding the train because they don't like the way I talk? Will they stop using Papa's bank? Papa is more powerful than anybody in southern

Colorado except maybe General Palmer and John Thatcher and his brothers."

"You shore know a lot about the Colonel's business."

Mattie shrugged—another unladylike gesture, but one she felt like making in defiance of what Jubilee was saying. "Papa will talk at the supper table, Jubilee, and a *lady* is supposed to listen and appear interested when gentlemen talk. My mama did teach me that."

"But you ain't supposed to *be* interested, just look like you are," said Jubilee. "And don't you go talking about business at any of your tea parties. Folks will talk about that, too. And you is wrong if you think folks talking about you won't hurt. When you leave your calling card at Mrs. John Thatcher's, and she ain't to home no matter how many times you go visiting, and when there ain't no invitations to parties and such, you'll know you done cut off your nose to spite your face. I recollect a young lady of good family back home before you was born who acted wild—buggy rides without no family with her, and going for walks in the garden after dark with gentlemen. Her daddy had to marry her off to a storekeeper who wasn't much better than white trash 'cause no decent gentleman would offer for her. You want to be like her and break your daddy's heart and shame your mama's memory, you just keep on acting like you are, asking questions about things that don't rightly concern a lady."

He nodded his head for emphasis as if he were a black oracle pronouncing her fate in a sacred olive grove underneath a blue sky so clear and pure, it looked like glass. But this was Pueblo, Colorado, and the only groves were cottonwood trees along the banks of the Arkansas River from whose branches the settlers hanged outlaws. The smelter belched black smoke into the air, and the real oracles consulted ledgers and issued railroad bonds instead of prophecies. And Mattie Jo Corley sat in a buggy, her back held rigid by hurt pride and a whalebone corset, listening to an ex-slave lecture her on her duty as a lady. She felt as if she were choking.

"Don't get pouty on me, Miss Mattie. You know I'm telling you the truth. You gots to act like folks expect you to, or you gonna pay in misery. That's the way it's got to be. Always has been that way."

"Why?" she cried out. "Why does it have to be that way?"

"'Cause you a woman."

"I might as well be a slave if being a woman means I have to watch not to set a foot wrong."

"But ain't nobody gonna whip the skin off your bones if you do, Miss Mattie. Slave can't say that."

It was Jubilee's eyes as much as his grim tone that silenced Mattie. She realized with a queer shock that until that moment Jubilee had always looked at her as though peering from behind a mask. But not now; now his eyes were those of a stranger, a man who for the first time revealed himself as an individual separate from her father and herself. His eyes revealed something else—a world that she'd never experienced and that was almost beyond her imagination. Certainly she knew Jubilee had been her papa's slave, knew that white men had once owned black men. It was a way of life that had been, and now was not, but she had never considered its harsher realities.

"I—I didn't know," she stuttered.

"Ain't no reason you should. All you knows about the south is what your daddy tells you, and he remembers it some different than me."

She looked away, knowing she had lied and feeling the shame of it. She *had* known about the whippings, not because of anything her papa told her, but in the same way that all children learn secrets: by overhearing muttered words and half-completed sentences, and like a child too frightened of the adult world, she had locked away her knowledge in one of the secret rooms in her mind. But Jubilee's words had ripped the lock from its door, and she cowered away from what lay within. Her eyes drifted past Jubilee to the buggy whip standing upright in the whip socket, and she realized with a shudder of revulsion why she had never seen him use it.

"I'm sorry, Jubilee. I didn't mean to mock you."

Impulsively she touched his arm, felt him start, and jerked her hand back. While she might affectionately touch a close male relative in public, touching a male servant for any reason other than being helped in and out of a conveyance was a familiarity no proper young lady allowed herself.

Jubilee knew it, too. He self-consciously brushed his sleeve as though he could erase her breach of etiquette, and cleared his throat. "We is home."

He turned the horse through a wrought-iron gate and drove up to the four-story granite house, its shrubbery too recently planted to soften the massive lines. Mattie thought bitterly that her father, through a combination of charm, character, and ruthless will, could order his business affairs and his family in the way that best pleased him, but he hadn't yet managed to force the trees to grow any faster than nature intended.

"Miss Mattie," said Jubilee, holding out one hand to help her from the buggy. "I ain't planning on telling the Colonel you was asking questions 'bout them bad women."

She took his hand and stepped onto the walk, her legs feeling limp as though stuffed with cotton like a china doll's. "Thank you, Jubilee. I don't think I could suffer through another lecture. One in an afternoon is enough." She looked up at him. "I'm not curious anymore."

"That's best, Miss Mattie."

She mounted the steps onto the roofed veranda that circled the house, an expanse of polished wood fifteen feet wide that stretched between her and the massive front door with its stained-glass pane set into the upper half. She grasped the ornate brass doorknob, icy cold from the wind that blew off the snow-covered mountains, and stopped, turning her head toward her shoulder until she could see Jubilee's still figure from the corner of her eye. "Jubilee, did my father ever whip you?"

She saw him stiffen, then he was vaulting onto the veranda, striding across its width until he halted by her side, his eyes those of a stranger again. "No, Miss Mattie, the Colonel never whipped nobody that I ever heard."

"Thank you, Jubilee," she whispered.

"I didn't have no business talking about that." He wiped his hands on his trousers. "You just put it out of your mind along with them painted women. Thinking about something is liable to lead you into talking about it, and that's what gets a body into trouble, Miss Mattie."

"Don't worry, Jubilee. I won't tell Papa what you said."

"I weren't worrying about me, Miss Mattie. If the Colonel gets mad and lays his walking stick across my back, I reckon I can take it. I was worrying about you. A leopard don't change his spots, and you don't stop being curious just 'cause you say you do."

She avoided his eyes. "I promise I'll never let my thoughts reach my tongue, Jubilee." She thought she heard a sniff of disbelief as she turned the knob and stepped into the vestibule.

"Miss Mattie?"

She glanced over her shoulder at the black man

standing just outside the door. "What, Jubilee?"

He removed his hat, a high-crowned beaver one that Mattie remembered the Colonel discarding, and met her eyes. "Ain't no white person ever told me they was sorry before. I won't be forgetting that."

Mattie felt tears stinging beneath her eyelids and turned; stepping back out the door and rising up on her toes, she kissed Jubilee's wrinkled cheek. What, she wondered, would the neighbors think of that?

"If I may speak frankly, Miss Mattie," said Samuel, "I find your attitude shocking."

Mattie blinked in confusion, then flushed, mortified that she had lost track of the conversation. "What do you mean, Samuel?"

Samuel frowned at her and expelled an impatient breath. "Haven't you heard anything I've said? You've been staring at me as though you were listening to every word."

She clasped his arm with both hands and laid her head on his shoulder, anxious to reassure him that he had her complete attention. "I'm sorry. I was distracted. You were saying?"

His body went rigid and he pulled away from her. "Please, Miss Mattie. I hardly think your father would approve of your indiscreet pose, and such boldness is unbecoming." He tugged on his waistcoat and straightened his coat, brushing his sleeve as though to remove any trace of her touch. "Really, I don't understand you this evening. Overlooking Goodnight's manners and vulgar language, then clinging to me as if you were one of Pueblo's women of easy virtue. I believe your father is right. Allowing women the vote will inevitably lead to immodest behavior if even our slight conversation on the issue has encouraged you to act in so forward a manner."

A TIME TOO LATE

Mattie felt as though her cheeks were scalded, burning as they did from humiliation and a smoldering rage. "Then perhaps you should leave if my bold immodest behavior offends you."

An expression of disbelief flickered in Samuel's eyes, followed by another that Mattie was unable to read. "You're throwing me out?"

"Yes!"

Mattie turned and marched across the entrance hall, a room so large that it boasted one of the house's ten marble-and-tile fireplaces as well as several chairs and a long oak table that held a single vase of peacock feathers and a silver tray where callers might leave their cards if she or her father were not at home. Mattie thought both the feathers and the tray were shimmering from the chandelier's light until she realized it was her own tears that blurred their shapes and made them appear to glisten.

Brushing by the table, she continued toward the elegant staircase of hand-carved oak, intent only on reaching her room, where she could rip off her dress and the corset that was suffocating her, fling herself across her bed, and cry until she had no more tears. But tears wouldn't cleanse the self-disgust she felt. Jubilee was right! Wicked thoughts led to impure talk and coarse actions. Beginning with the drawings in boarding school, she had indulged in shameful speculation about matters that no decent woman would allow herself to think about, until tonight those speculations ended in brazen behavior that repulsed Samuel.

Faintly she heard Samuel call her name, but ignored him. She had no wish to talk to anyone, Samuel least of all. She had made a fool out of herself tonight and, perversely, blamed him for it. Oh, Mama, she thought. Why did you have to die? Didn't God know I would need you more at fifteen than I ever did at ten?

Seeing the staircase through her tears as a wavering, watery shape, she caught hold of the banister, the wood hard and slick and smelling of lemon oil, a solid lifeline leading upward to sanctuary. She grabbed a fistful of her skirt, not caring that she was crushing the delicate silk and exposing more of her foot than was proper. A real lady could climb a flight of stairs and reveal no more than the toe of her shoe, but then she had already proved she was an impostor.

"Mattie! My darling girl!"

Samuel brushed by her and knelt on the stairs, blocking her way. "Forgive me, Mattie. I was unkind and ungallant. Allow me to explain myself, and if you choose not to accept my apology, I'll take myself out of your sight and leave Pueblo because I couldn't stand to live in the same town and never see you."

Mattie felt dizzy, as though she were trapped on a carousel. Thoughts whirled around in her head as she gazed at Samuel's imploring face. Her only clear thought was unworthy—that Samuel must be desperate to risk soiling the knees of his trousers by kneeling on a carpet that hadn't been brushed since early this morning.

Taking a deep breath, she gripped the banister until her fingers felt bloodless, and inclined her head. "What do you wish to say?"

Samuel reached for her hand, stopping in midgesture and averting his eyes. Blushing with embarrassment, Mattie remembered that one side of her skirt was hiked up several inches above her ankle, revealing both her petticoat and silk stockings. She unclenched her fist and let her skirt fall back into place, noticing that she had indeed crushed the material.

Samuel clasped her hand between his own as carefully as though he were holding fine crystal. "I had no right to criticize your guests as I did. I'm a newcomer, but even I've heard of Mr. Goodnight. I must blame my unfamiliarity with Pueblo. It left me unprepared to accept Mr. Goodnight's frank talk. I should have followed your lead and complimented you on your good manners for ignoring his lapses. I'm ashamed of myself."

"Samuel, I understand, and . . ."

He squeezed her hand. "Please, Mattie, let me continue before I lose my courage. Self-flagellation is not in my nature, nor in any southern gentleman's nature." He took a deep breath. "I said some unforgivable things to you, practically accused you of being a—a shameless woman. That isn't true. *I* am the one who was tempted to act dishonorably, not you. Your beauty, your very presence tempts me to actions that would lead to your father's horsewhipping me. When you laid your head on my shoulder, I can't describe the passion which threatened to overwhelm me. Instead of confessing my weakness, I cast it upon you. That was not the action of a gentleman, Mattie, and I am eternally sorry. I wouldn't blame you if you did throw me out. I have no excuse except that my affection for you threatens my self-control."

He hesitated, rubbing his thumb over her knuckles. "If you forgive me, I would be honored if you allowed me to ask your father not for leave to formally court you, but for permission to marry you. I promise I shall control my weak nature and never harm you. I believe you will be my salvation, Mattie, my talisman of good fortune, and that with you by my side, I can live a happy and satisfied life."

He bowed his head and kissed her hand with a reverence such as Mattie had only seen in church, and seriously doubted she deserved. She might only be fifteen and inexperienced and motherless, but she instinctively knew that she *had* been forward, *had* been unseemly. She smiled bitterly at herself. She also knew that she would not admit it to Samuel. Even her limited observations of the ways of men and women taught her that it never paid to contradict a gentleman. Particularly when the contradiction was not to a lady's credit. If she wanted a happy married life, *if she wanted to make Samuel happy,* then she must act as he and the world expected her to act.

She took several shallow breaths in an attempt to clear her head and ease the sensation of being choked, and let go of the banister. She sank to her knees in front of Samuel. "I would be honored to be your wife, Samuel."

He grasped her shoulders, his face solemn. "Are you certain, Mattie?"

She nodded, and mentally locked away a restless spirit, resolving to never loose it again. If it screamed a mournful protest, she knew no one heard but her.

Samuel closed his eyes and tilted his head back as though giving thanks. When he opened his eyes, Mattie caught an expression of relief mixed with determination, and she wondered if Samuel had his own locked rooms. She forgot her curiosity when he bent his head and pressed her lips in what was her first kiss from a man other than her father. The scent of shaving soap and hair pomade, the sharp odor of tobacco, the musky smell of perspiration, all familiar scents to her since birth, took on an added significance because they were all part of the man known as Samuel. The man she planned to marry.

"What in the devil is going on here? Get your filthy hands off my daughter, you blackguard!"

Jerking his head up, Samuel flushed, then turned pale. He scrambled up, stepped in front of Mattie, and straightened his coat, a gesture that was so typically Samuel that she felt like smiling in exasperation. Samuel would hold up his own funeral just to make certain his waistcoat was buttoned properly. Given the ferocity of her father's expression, this might very well be that occasion.

A TIME TOO LATE
41

Mattie grabbed the banister and pulled herself up. "Papa, let me explain."

He never gave her glance, directing all his attention to Samuel. "Go to your room, Mattie. I shall deal with you later."

"Colonel Corley, I apologize for taking such a liberty—"

Mattie screamed as her father backhanded Samuel across the face, knocking the smaller man sprawling on the stairs. "That's not good enough," shouted the Colonel, reaching down to jerk Samuel up by his lapels.

His cheek crimson from the Colonel's blow, Samuel grabbed the older man's wrists. "I wish to marry Mattie, sir!"

"When I'm dead and in hell, sir!"

The Colonel backed Samuel closer to the hard oak balustrade, and Mattie knew he would hammer Samuel's body against it until the younger man's spine was crushed. Samuel knew it, too, because he suddenly went limp, then threw his arms up and dropped to his knees in a single graceful motion—and slipped out of his coat.

"You mangy bastard!" yelled the Colonel, throwing down the coat and chasing after Samuel, who was, Mattie noted with relief, on the opposite side of the oak table from her father.

"Colonel, you wants your gun?" yelled Jubilee, leaping down the backstairs from the servants' quarters in his nightshirt and one of the Colonel's old robes, a Navy Colt in his hand.

"Stop it, Papa!" screamed Mattie, jerking up her skirt and running down the stairs. "Jubilee, don't you dare give him that gun!" She grabbed her father's arm with both hands. "Papa, listen to me!"

The Colonel glared at her with an almost maniacal expression in his eyes and raised his other arm. "Go to your room, Mattie!"

"Would you hit me, Papa?" she asked, hardly able to hear her own voice over the pounding of her heart, but amazed that she sounded so calm. Later, she promised herself, she would bury her head under her pillows and scream with terror. Later she would vomit up the guilt that was already churning in her belly.

The Colonel slowly lowered his arm, horror replacing the rage that had twisted his features. "My God! I would have!" He wrapped his arm around her and pressed her cheek against his shoulder. "See what you've done, young man. Because of you, I nearly struck my own daughter! Now, will you have the decency to leave—leave my home, and leave Pueblo—or shall I order Jubilee to blow a hole through your worthless hide?"

Samuel glanced from the Colonel to Jubilee and back again, his face still and pale. He licked his lips. "I meant no disrespect to Mattie, Colonel Corley. I am devoted to her, heart and soul."

"It's your more corporeal devotions that concern me. My God, man! No father appreciates catching some worthless young jackanapes kissing his daughter!"

"But it's hardly a good enough reason to try to murder Samuel," said Mattie, peeking up at her father.

The Colonel looked aghast. "I did no such of a thing!"

Mattie wiggled away from him and circled the table to stand by Samuel. "I saw your face, Papa. If Samuel hadn't escaped, you would have murdered him. And all he did was give me a perfectly proper kiss to seal his proposal."

"Ha! There's nothing proper about a young man kissing a young woman he isn't married to. It leads to further liberties that you know nothing about. And"—he shook his finger—"and any well-bred gentleman approaches a girl's father to ask his permission *before* proposing."

Exasperated, Mattie shook her head. "Perhaps in your day, Papa, that was the way it was done. But not today. Any man with gumption would at least hint to the girl that he was interested in marrying her. Otherwise how would he know she wouldn't flatly refuse him?"

"That's ridiculous, Mattie! What's to keep any penniless adventurer from turning an innocent young girl's head before her father has a chance to sort out the bad risks from the gentlemen with prospects? Then we have the spectacle of an addlepated female with no more idea of what's best for her than a Hottentot's, throwing tantrums if her father refuses a suitor. The tears and heartbreak in such a system boggle the mind. No, it's much better for the father to choose whether or not a gentleman is suitable before he is given the opportunity to approach a girl."

Mattie could almost taste her resentment like bile in her mouth. "An arranged marriage, in other words, Papa. Or as good as. Is that how you married Mama? Arranged it with Grandpa as if Mama were a mare you'd come to bid on?"

Her father's normally florid cheeks faded to a sallow color. "Hush up about your mother."

Mattie glanced away, bracing herself against the oak table so her trembling legs wouldn't suddenly give way. One never showed weakness in front of her father. He was like a hound after a rabbit if he sensed his opponent was vulnerable. She caught Jubilee's eyes—his stranger's eyes—full of sympathy. Who's a slave now? she wanted to scream.

"Colonel Corley," Samuel interjected. "You're not following your own dictates, sir. I am of good family—southern family—and I am not penniless. Since I deposited my funds in your bank, I assume you checked my account when I first called on you."

Mattie noticed an almost imperceptible glint of respect in her father's eyes. "That's true, Mr. Hunter. You are solvent."

"Then I wish you would state your objections to me, sir, other than my getting the cart before the horse and committing the impropriety of proposing to Mattie without formally speaking with you. You must have known what my intentions were. Why am I suddenly unsuitable?"

The Colonel plucked a cigar from his pocket and struck a match, observing Samuel as he lit it. He blew out the match and dropped it in the silver tray. "Because I say so, Mr. Hunter. Good night. Jubilee, show him to the door."

"Wait, Papa. Let me speak to you first."

"I think not, Mattie. I'm an old man and I'm tired. I don't believe I'm up to female histrionics. Mr. Hunter, you do know the way to the door or have you grown roots?"

"Wait, Samuel," ordered Mattie as she walked around the table and across the room to her father's office. "Papa, I will speak to you if I have to wait all night. And when have I ever indulged in histrionics? Never! But I will have my way this time."

He followed her and slammed the door, falling into his chair behind his desk. "I'll not have you defying me in front of strangers, young lady." He pointed to the chair on the other side of the desk. "Sit."

She did, and folded her hands, glad he couldn't see how badly they were shaking. "Papa, is there another southern family in Pueblo with eligible suitors my age?"

He puffed on his cigar and studied her. "There are several fine southern gentlemen, many of which fought with honor in the late war."

"I said my age, Papa. I was only a year old when the war started. All those fine gentlemen you're talking about are years older than I. Would you marry me off to an old man?"

The Colonel shifted uncomfortably. "They are mature, responsible men, well set up financially. They could support you."

"Then I could support them when they were too old to climb the stairs. Oh, Papa, do you want to see me spooning gruel in my husband's toothless mouth before I'm thirty?"

"You're exaggerating, Mattie!"

She ignored his comment. She was exaggerating, but she was not about to concede the point. "I repeat, Papa, is there another southern family in Pueblo with an eligible suitor my age?"

"Not to my knowledge. None that I would receive, at any rate."

Mattie slowly expelled a breath. The first hurdle crossed, she thought. "If you want to choose my suitor, where will you find him?"

"There are many suitable young men in Pueblo."

"But you always wanted me to marry a southern boy who understood your traditions. Of course, there are all the ex-soldiers. I see them on the streets when Jubilee drives me downtown. Perhaps one of them is from the south. But judging from their clothes, most of them appear to be penniless, and I don't know if I could marry a poor man. You didn't raise me to scrub floors, although I'm certain I could learn."

Her father slapped the desk. "Vermin! Yankee vermin, most of them. And deserters."

Mattie leaned forward. "Please, Papa, no deserters. I should hate to marry a coward."

"You'll not marry any former Yankee army riffraff, and that's final."

"I'm glad, Papa. There are so few acceptable men that I was afraid you might lower your standards."

"Never!"

Mattie tapped her fingers on the desk and tilted her head. "There are all the miners, Papa. You were a miner once. Surely you wouldn't object to one of them?"

"I was a mine *owner*, Mattie. There is a difference. I'll not give you to a hard-rock miner, or a prospector between claims either."

Mattie gazed pensively at the ornate ceiling before meeting her father's eyes. "Then I guess I'll have to marry a Texan."

The Colonel reared half out of his chair. "What!"

Mattie shrugged. "Well, a cowboy then—but most of them are Texans. Perhaps Mr. Goodnight could suggest someone suitable with good prospects of owning his own ranch. Now that I think about it, I really like the idea of marrying a Texan. They're awfully rowdy—or so I've been told—but so terribly handsome. If one marries, looks are important, don't you think? I mean, one is married forever. It must be awful to face an ugly man across the breakfast table every morning."

"You'll marry no Texan! I'll see you buried in the cemetery next to your mama first!"

Mattie rose and leaned over the desk, feeling as if she were dancing in sunlight. For the first time in her life she was making the choices for herself, even though she had to resort to chicanery rather than honest endeavor. And it felt good!

"Then who is left, Papa? A stranger from Denver or perhaps New York or Chicago? A Yankee? And how would I meet them, or rather how would *you* meet them? You have too many business interests in Pueblo to travel in search of a suitor for me. Besides, if I married a man like that, I might have to leave Colorado. Then you might only see me once a year. I had hoped to marry a local boy so I could live close to you, but I

A TIME TOO LATE

guess I can't. I'll be a spinster, and hope I can live with the gossip."

"Gossip? What gossip? I'll not have any old cats talking about you."

She lifted her chin. "You can't stop gossip, Papa. It's like smoke. There is nothing to touch. But I'll survive. I do hate to be pitied, though, and overhear people wondering what's wrong with Mattie Jo Corley that no man wanted her."

The Colonel looked at her as though examining her face feature by feature. His own face was impassive. "You think you've beaten me, don't you?"

"I don't know, Papa. Have I?" she asked, thinking that if she lost this battle, she would fight another and another with different weapons and different tactics—but she *would* win.

"Do you want to marry him so badly, Mattie, that you would ignore my reservations?"

"Why don't you like Samuel, Papa?"

The Colonel turned sideways in his chair and stretched out his legs, his face solemn and old looking, as if something had worn down inside him. "Mattie, I think you're too young to understand, but I'll tell you anyway. A man has to be a man. He has to cast a long shadow so that other men will know he is someone to be reckoned with. Otherwise he'll never be his own master. He'll always be at the mercy of other men. I don't believe that Samuel casts much of a shadow."

Mattie shook her head. "Papa, Samuel is a gentle man who loves poetry instead of banks and mines and railroads. Isn't there a place for a man like that in the world?"

"Gentle men cast shadows, too, Mattie. It is weak men who do not. They are hollow, transparent creatures who survive by leeching the strength from others. I pray to God that you don't have to provide the strength for Samuel."

Mattie rose and rounded the desk to kneel by her father's chair and clasp his hands. "Then you'll give Samuel permission to marry me?"

He studied her eyes, then raised her hands and kissed each one, keeping his head lowered while the seconds ticked by. Finally he raised his head, a hard glint in his eyes that roused unease in Mattie, as though she were walking in the dark and a precipice suddenly opened beneath her feet.

"I'll give my permission on one condition, Mattie."

She heard the clock outside in the entrance hall strike midnight and wondered if its chimes had always sounded so foreboding. "What is it, Papa?"

"You'll live here, on the third floor, while I'll stay on the second. You may choose any bedrooms you wish, and may even have rooms done over for whatever purpose. You'll eat, of course, in the dining room."

"Why, Papa?"

"Why not? It's a big house. Thirty rooms if you count the basement and the servants' quarters. Why shouldn't you and your husband live here?"

"Because I want my own home."

"This is your home, Mattie."

"But Samuel and I need to be alone." Away from you, she wanted to add.

He stroked her cheek. "And you will be, Mattie. I'll not interfere, but I will be here to help if Mr. Hunter fails to cast a shadow."

"Please leave Samuel alone, Papa."

He rose and ground out his cigar in a porcelain dish. "Accept my proposition or reject it, Mattie, but do it now, because when I walk out that door, it is to either throw Mr. Hunter out on his elegantly clad backside, or to welcome him to the family. Which will it be?"

"You're a devil, Papa," she whispered.

"And I drive a devil's bargain."

CHAPTER 4

The Colonel stripped off his formal coat, untied and jerked his cravat from around his neck, loosened his collar, and flung himself down in a chair. He laced his fingers together behind his head, gazed up at the ceiling, and frowned at the garlands of roses painted around its borders. Sissy things, roses, to be on a man's ceiling. He'd told Mattie so, but she had insisted. Plain ceilings weren't fashionable, she'd said. All the most formal new homes in Denver had fancy ceilings, and he mustn't be backward. He wondered how Mattie knew what constituted a fancy ceiling. All those ladies' magazines that cluttered up his post office box—*Harper's Bazaar* and *Godey's Lady's Book* and other such journalism calculated to make a woman dissatisfied with her lot and to take money from a man's pocket, he supposed. Or did these notions of what was fashionable float in the air like filaments of a spider's web, and a woman only had to step out of doors to be bound up in a new enthusiasm? An interesting idea, and as good an explanation as any for what was in fact inexplicable. Women simply *knew* these things. Even women as young as Mattie. And men must occasionally indulge their foibles, bless every fragile bone in their soft little bodies, particularly their foible for believing that they could manage men, a harmless delusion unless carried too far.

Mattie had nearly carried it too far.

He rubbed his belly where a cramp tightened its fist on his guts. To be honest, though, he had to admit that his daughter had been very clever in her campaign to win him over to her desire for marriage. A lesser man might have been managed and never even been aware of it. He was not a lesser man, and he had been very much aware of her tactics, although he had been shaken almost into surrender by her mention of Texans. But that was not why he had capitulated and agreed to the marriage. No, not at all.

He lit a cigar and blew smoke toward the ceiling, again contemplating its flowery design. He supposed roses were better than cherubs. He balked at the idea of fat, dimpled babies' behinds on his ceiling, not to mention the fact that a cherub's simpering expression reminded him of Samuel Hunter.

Abruptly he straightened and slapped his hands on the chair arms. "Jubilee, pour the bourbon to drown our sorrows and celebrate my daughter's new estate."

Jubilee paused in the act of hanging the Colonel's coat from one of the brass hooks in the closet. "Yes, suh."

"Do it, man, and leave the clothes. I don't plan to wear them again anyway."

Jubilee shuffled toward the highboy and the decanter of bourbon. "What's you wants me to do with them?"

"Burn them, Jubilee."

"What do want to do a thing like that for, Colonel? That ain't the act of a normal man."

A TIME TOO LATE
The Colonel rubbed his hands over his face and felt how cold his skin was. "Because I don't ever want to be reminded of my daughter's wedding day."

Jubilee poured one tumbler full to the brim while barely covering the bottom of the other. Just as well, thought the Colonel, because someone was going to have to pull off his shoes and roll him into bed when he drank himself into insensibility. Provided there was enough bourbon left in the house after the prodigious amounts Samuel had drunk during the day. He must admit the boy could hold his liquor, but what right or *need* did a man have to consume so much alcohol when he had just taken a young maiden to wife? A man needed his wits clear and his capacities up to snuff at such a time. The Colonel thought of the use to which his new son-in-law's capabilities would be put tonight and balled his hand into a fist.

Jubilee handed him his drink. "Why did you do it, Colonel? Why did you give Miss Mattie to him? And I don't believe your story about how there wasn't nobody else 'cept Yankees and miners and Texans, so don't be telling me that."

The Colonel took a long swallow of bourbon, felt it burn down his throat and into his belly, easing the chill that had settled there. "I thought of many ways to get rid of the bastard, Jubilee. Don't think I gave in easily. I thought of giving him money, but he has a sizable account in the bank, and I do give him credit for enough honor to refuse a bribe. I even thought of paying some ruffian to murder him. I thought of doing it myself. But Mattie would never have believed that I was innocent if Mr. Hunter had turned up dead along the riverbank, no matter how carefully I might have arranged things. I'm afraid I gave myself away the night I agreed to the marriage. I should never have lost my temper and laid hands on the young man. All I accomplished was to convince Mattie that I intended to harm Mr. Hunter at the first opportunity. And I would have, but there was no way to do it without losing Mattie. I didn't want to lose my daughter, Jubilee, even if it meant sharing her with that worthless hound."

Jubilee shook his head, his lower lip stuck out stubbornly. "I don't believe that Miss Mattie would done have run off with Mr. Hunter. I don't think she'd set herself against you like that."

The Colonel drained his glass and handed it to Jubilee, motioning him toward the decanter. "I wasn't certain of what Mattie might do. In the war, just before Atlanta fell, when that damned Texan General Hood was sending troops against Yankee positions, I had a young boy from Virginia Military Institute in my command. He wasn't even shaving yet, Jubilee, just had soft down on his cheeks like a girl's. But he wanted to kill Yankees and be a hero. The rest of us just wanted to do our duty without getting our goddamn backsides shot off so we could go home to see if the Yankees had left us anything but ashes and hungry families. We weren't interested in being heroes. Besides, we already were. Anybody who fought in that war and didn't run when the shooting started and the bodies began falling was a hero. We didn't need to run uphill into Yankee artillery to prove it."

He took the glass of whiskey from Jubilee and drank, then gazed at the black man. "But that's what the young boy did, ran up the hill, and the Yankees blew him to pieces. We buried what we could find of him." He sipped his drink, not tasting the liquor. "That boy always had a look in his eyes, as if he was blind to everything but that one purpose, and whatever it took to accomplish it, he was prepared to give. For just a second, less time than a heartbeat, I thought I saw that same look in Mattie's eyes, and I was afraid. So I gave in. But I, by God, hedged my bet, Jubilee.

They'll live in this house, where I can keep my eye on Mr. Samuel Hunter."

"Yes, suh."

The Colonel took several more swallows of his drink until his sense of unease began to recede into a golden haze. One should never underestimate the restorative power of fine Kentucky bourbon. "Mattie was a beautiful bride, wasn't she?"

"Yes, suh."

"I think nearly all of Pueblo witnessed the ceremony—except the gamblers, prostitutes, miners, ex-soldiers, and Texans, of course."

"Yes, suh."

"It was generous of General Palmer to loan his private railroad car for their trip to Denver."

"Yes, suh."

The Colonel pulled his watch from his waistcoat pocket and snapped open its hunting case. "Nearly three o'clock in the morning. They will have arrived in Denver several hours ago. It is a short, comfortable trip these days, not like when we drove the wagons from Denver to Pueblo back in Seventy."

"Yes, suh."

"Goddamn it, Jubilee, is that all you've got to say? Yes, suh? Yes, suh? Your face is enough to sour milk. If I can put up a good front and accept this marriage, then by all that's holy, so can you."

"You done hitched up your Thoroughbred with a spavined mule, Colonel, and—"

"That's enough, Jubilee! I am not the first father whose daughter has married well, but poorly, and I will not have servants criticizing Samuel. He is family now, and I am behooved to defend him." However distasteful I find the task, he thought, feeling his unease return along with irritation at Jubilee's persistence in forgetting his place. Goddamn Abe Lincoln and emancipation.

Jubilee turned away to pick the Colonel's discarded cravat. "If you says so."

The Colonel sat up, disturbed by the black man's muffled voice, and even more disturbed by the suspicious sheen in his eyes. "Jubilee, are you weeping?"

The black man kept his back turned. "What if I is? I is free."

The Colonel threw his glass across the room to shatter against the marble-and-tile fireplace, and vaulted out of his chair to grab his servant's arm and jerk him around. "Goddamn it, Jubilee!"

Jubilee met his glare without flinching. "Yes, suh?"

The Colonel followed the slick tracks of tears down Jubilee's black face and swallowed. And swallowed again. "Don't do this, Jubilee. I could face seeing my daughter in a white wedding gown, face listening to the preacher pronounce her married to that mealy-mouthed young jackass. I could face standing in that reception line shaking hands and lying through my teeth about how proud I was that my Mattie was marrying such a fine young man. I could even face Samuel Hunter clinging to my hand like a slug—his palms were moist, did you know that, Jubilee?—and twaddling on in that girlish voice of his about how *glad* he was that we had solved our differences. Even that I could face with gentlemanly fortitude, but what I can't face is seeing you weep."

The Colonel took a deep breath, felt it catch in his throat, and surrendered. He felt the tears seep from his eyes and roll down his face to catch on his mustache. "After fifty years, Jubilee, we're like two old hound dogs raised in the same kennel. When one bays at the moon, the other follows suit. As long as you didn't weep, I didn't. But like those hound dogs can't change the path of the moon by their baying, we can't change what's happened by our weeping. It's done. Mattie is Mrs. Samuel Hunter."

A TIME TOO LATE

* * *

Mattie lay without moving, almost without breathing, until she heard Samuel's drunken snoring settle into a rhythm, then crept out of bed. She felt her way to the commode and as quietly as possible poured water into washbowl. Setting the pitcher down, she took a cloth hanging from the brass rod on the side of the commode, dipped it in the basin of water, and wrung it out, all the while wishing Samuel had returned to his adjoining bedroom so she could have lit the lamp. As it was, she didn't dare do so. If he woke up and saw her holding up her nightgown and washing herself between the legs, the humiliation would be worse than what she suffered an hour ago. She would have to do the best she could in the dark, but she could not, *could not,* wait until morning to cleanse herself.

She flinched at the touch of the cold, wet cloth and for a moment thought she might cry. She blinked back the tears and drew a deep breath. If she hadn't cried when she lost her maidenhead, she wasn't about to cry because she had to wash in cold water. She could survive one such washing. According to Mrs. Goodnight, she would only bleed once. Thank God for Mrs. Goodnight, she thought. Had the lady not talked to her before the wedding, Mattie knew she would have most probably gone into hysterics or fought Samuel. She wasn't certain which would have been worse. As it was, she had been curious, wondering how such a joining would feel—after the initial pain, of course. Now she knew. She could add the marriage bed to her list of other natural functions that were unpleasant, but inevitable, such as her monthlies and wearing a corset.

Leaving the cloth in the washbowl, she walked back toward the bed, but stopped abruptly, bending over with such a wave of nausea she feared she would vomit where she stood. Breathing shallowly, she straightened and veered toward the door to the other bedroom. She would light a lamp and sit awhile until she felt better. Her queasiness must be a result of the champagne and oysters she and Samuel had eaten when they shared a late supper. She wasn't accustomed to champagne, never having drunk anything stronger than a small glass of watered wine at Christmas, but knew from observing her father that strong drink often made one ill. She wondered if Samuel would awaken suffering with what the Colonel called a "head."

She closed the door behind her, thankful there was hardly a click. Samuel's drapes were open, and a full moon shone through the lace curtains, enabling her to see well enough to lift the globe from the coal-oil lamp sitting on the small table next to the bed. Hesitantly she turned up the wick. She hoped she hadn't turned it too high, or the flame would shoot up. She had seen one of the servant girls at home singe her eyelashes that way. She found a tin of matches lying next to the lamp and made a silent note to herself to thank the hotel manager for providing such a luxury for his guests, since matches were still not such a commonplace item in parts of Colorado as to be taken for granted. She wrinkled her nose at the phosphorus smell as she struck a match. Heart pounding, she lit the wick and felt inordinately proud of herself at the resulting steady flame. She blew out the match and replaced the globe on the lamp, careful not to tilt it so the flame didn't touch the sides and leave a sooty streak.

It wasn't that she had never lit a lamp before, but she hadn't lit many. It was a chore ordinarily left to servants along with emptying the chamber pots. Why she felt such a sense of accomplishment from a task any illiterate darkie could do faster, she didn't understand. Unless it was because lighting a lamp proved she could do something right. She sank down on the edge of the bed and clenched her teeth together until her jaws hurt and her ears ached from the strain of not crying. She had hoped to please Samuel by moving to embrace him when he slipped into bed. Perhaps she had misinterpreted what Mrs. Goodnight meant by "welcoming her husband." At any rate, Samuel had recoiled as if the touch of her body burned him.

"Why is it that you women must twine yourselves about a man like ivy climbing a wall?"

Mattie cringed, suddenly shivering from a chill that had nothing to do with the hot, stuffy air in the room. "Samuel, I didn't—"

"Quiet! I cannot stand any more of your prattle. You've nearly driven me insane today. Like all useless members of your sex, you chatter until your shrill voice drowns out all sensible male conversation. Now you paw me as though you would usurp my male function." He seized her jaw, squeezing until she knew she would have finger-sized bruises on her cheeks in the morning. "Tell me, do you know the way of this already?"

"The way of what, Samuel? What are you talking about? Why are you hurting me?" Never in her life had anyone dared touch her in such a manner, and that Samuel should do so held her rigid with shock.

He released her and rolled away. "No, of course you don't, and now I've made you afraid. I'm sorry, Mattie. Forgive me. You can't help being what you are."

She rose on one elbow and reached out to touch him, but jerked her hand back. "Samuel, I don't understand. What is wrong with me?"

"Nothing, Mattie," he said, reaching for her hand and rubbing his cheek against it. "Forgive me."

She stared into the darkness and wondered what other choice she had. She was Mrs. Samuel Hunter for better or for worse, and if it was worse, still nothing changed. She couldn't take back her vows and become Mattie Jo Corley again. "I forgive you, Samuel, but don't hurt me again."

He kissed her hand, and she felt nothing. "Thank you, Mattie." With a rustle of bedclothes, he moved over her. "Don't be afraid."

"No, Samuel."

Her answer to him had been honest, Mattie decided as she wiped her eyes on the hem of her nightgown. She hadn't felt much of anything beyond physical discomfort, certainly nothing that resembled real feelings. At least his use of her body had been short, for which she had been grateful. She supposed she could tolerate his husbandly duties as long as she remembered never to touch him. Maybe then he would be kinder and they could make do with each other. She wondered how many other brides had awakened the next morning to find the man they had married was not the same one with whom they had exchanged rings. Perhaps every man was really two men, and every woman learned to live with one and survive the other.

She wrapped her arms around her legs and rested her forehead on her raised knees. If that were the case, she would die before admitting it. In less than twenty-four hours she had lost her girlhood, her innocence, the gentle man she thought she had married, and most of her illusions. Be damned if she would lose her pride, too. She would never tell her father she had married a changeling.

CHAPTER 5

The Colonel glared first at the single setting on the long mahogany table, then at the silent man standing behind his chair ready to serve him. "Jubilee! Where is my family?"

Jubilee looked at a point over the Colonel's shoulder. "Mr. Leon, he in his crib in his mama's room. I 'spects he sound asleep."

"I was *not* referring to my grandson, Jubilee. A year-old child, no matter how precocious, does not join the adults for supper until he is able to eat without drooling. I was referring to Mattie and my son-in-law."

"Miss Mattie in her room. I done took her up a tray. She's wore out down to a frazzle."

The Colonel smoothed his mustache while he studied the other man. He suspected Jubilee was telling the exact truth—but no more. "Explain to me how my daughter can be 'worn to a frazzle' when she neither spins nor toils, when any of nine servants will drop whatever they're doing to entertain my grandson, when the most exhausting thing she does is fancy needlework. I'll admit, though, she does enough of that. She's re-covered every chair in this house with needlepoint. She even worked me a pair of suspenders. I expect her to needlepoint my unmentionables next. But that's no excuse for not coming to supper. Damn it, I don't *like* to eat alone. Makes me feel like a leper and spoils my appetite. Go tell her to join her papa for supper."

"She feelin' poorly, Colonel."

"She's seventeen years old. What excuse does she have to feel poorly? Unless"—he looked up at Jubilee—"she's in the family way again? That sometimes puts a woman off her feed. I recall that her mother couldn't tolerate the smell of ham baking. Remember that? We did without pork for nine months. Other men passed out cigars when their first child was born. I ordered a hog butchered. What about it, Jubilee? Did Cook bake a ham today?"

"It ain't that, Colonel. She had herself another spell."

"A spell? One of those fainting fits? That's no reason not to come to supper. It's the fault of those corsets women wear, Jubilee. They are the invention of the devil. Or at least the Spanish Inquisition. If a woman laces herself so tightly that her eyes bug out, what can she expect but to faint? You know yourself that every dance sees several ladies ministered to with a bottle of smelling salts. If this country ever suffered a shortage of smelling salts, the parlors and ballrooms of America would be carpeted with the bodies of unconscious ladies. Tell Mattie to put on one of those tea gowns or whatever they're called—she needn't wear a corset with one of those—but leave off the silly cap that *Harper's Bazaar* or whoever says is essential to complete a lady's toilette. The damn things make her look like a maid ready to dust the furniture."

A TIME TOO LATE

He pulled a handkerchief out of his pocket and blotted his forehead as the sense of Jubilee's words refused to be talked away. He pulled out the nearest chair and sat down. "What do you mean 'another' spell? How many has she had?"

Jubilee's face reminded the Colonel of a carved mask. On second thought he decided it didn't. A mask had more expression. "She had several the last three or four months."

"What does she do—besides faint?"

"She don't faint. She turns all white except around her eyes, where she turn dark, like her eyes 'bout to sink into her head. Her head start to hurt something awful, and she stagger when she walks. Aunt Patty put her to bed with wet rags on her head and she feel some better by the next morning."

"My God, Jubilee, we must call the doctor. I can't let my daughter suffer like that. Why didn't my son-in-law do something about this? Why wasn't *I* told?"

"She seen the doctor. Dr. Christie seen her two or three times."

"Dr. Christie? A fine physician, Jubilee. He hails originally from Virginia, I believe. Fought for the Confederacy, naturally. Well, don't just stand there like a block of wood. What did the good doctor say?"

"He tell her high-strung ladies sometimes suffer with the headaches. He give her drops, but she throw them away. Said she'd rather her head hurt than her thoughts be fuzzy. Mr. Hunter, he don't know about her spells, and she don't want you to know neither."

"High-strung? My Mattie's never been high-strung, jumping at every sound like a nervous Nellie. In fact, she's been so quiet and settled since her marriage, I almost feel kindly toward young Samuel. He calmed her willfulness—and Jubilee, I'll confess she was a bit willful—and gave her Leon. I never gave him credit of being capable of either feat. I was wrong. He's good for something after all. But Samuel's neither here nor there—"

"He sure ain't here," said Jubilee, snapping the words off as if he were snapping beans.

"Where is he then?"

"He out carousing and playing cards at one of them saloons downtown." Jubilee's features had gone from expressionless to outraged disapproval.

"Jubilee, you will persist in criticizing Samuel. I won't have it! If he is spending a night or two away from home in a friendly poker game, I'm willing to overlook it. Sometimes it does a marriage good if the husband doesn't dance attendance on his wife every night. Makes her appreciate him more and gives him the opportunity for male conversation. You must admit, Jubilee, gentlemen do have to watch their tongues around the ladies. A man needs to rip loose occasionally. If Mattie is having spells because Samuel's playing poker, that's unreasonable and unseemly, and I'll have to speak to her about it. A wife who is any kind of a lady at all doesn't begrudge a man a friendly game of chance—unless he loses the family home. Otherwise she should overlook it."

"He gone more than that."

"Of course he isn't. He's at the supper table almost every night—which is more than I can say for Mattie."

"Most nights he eat supper and go upstairs, then down the backstairs and out the door to the carriage house, saddle a horse, and leave. You don't know nothing about it, but I do. And Miss Mattie do."

"So Samuel slipped out to play poker tonight, and Mattie had a spell?" asked the Colonel, his own head beginning to pound with the same kind of rage he had always felt right before a cavalry charge when he needed rage to overcome his common sense and natural repugnance against riding into a situation likely to result in his being killed or maimed. But the only repugnance he felt tonight was that against washing his family's dirty linen in public, but then Samuel's behavior had already shamed them all.

"Miss Mattie more of a lady than that, Colonel. She knows what she not supposed to notice. It the lying what makes her sick."

"She needn't worry about that. I plan to see to it that young Samuel doesn't lie to her again."

"It ain't his lying, it's hers!" said Jubilee. "You remember how when she was just a little bitty thing and told you a fib, she couldn't eat no supper till she told the truth. Never seen such an honest child. Half the time I think she so quiet so she won't have to tell a lie."

"So what brought on this spell?"

"Some of her lady friends come over this afternoon to sew for the orphans' home—Miss Mattie feels mighty strongly about the orphans, Colonel—and they got to talking about the party on Saturday night over in that big room above Mr. Thatcher's store. Well, Miss Mattie, she wants to go in the worst way and had a new dress made—mighty pretty, too—but Mr. Samuel, he tell her he got business on Saturday night, and she gonna have to stay home or go with you. Now that ain't fitting, Colonel, for you to take her when she got a husband in town who ain't crippled or dead. But she tell those ladies all about her dress and how excited Mr. Hunter is about going. I was serving tea, and I heard her. It was right after that I seen her get real pale and sick looking."

"That bastard!" exclaimed the Colonel. "I know about that party, too. How in God's good name did he expect to get around me?"

"He ain't. Miss Mattie is. I figure she gonna take to her bed on Saturday night like she real sick. You think Mr. Hunter staying home with her, so you makes their excuses, and he rides downtown."

"And he told her to do this? He's turning my daughter into a liar and a sneak?" The Colonel could taste his rage now, like bile in his mouth.

"He don't have to. Miss Mattie covers up for him 'cause she too proud for you to know. And Mr. Hunter good to her sometimes, too—brings her flowers and such things. He keeps her all twisted up so she don't know the straight of him. So long as she didn't have to lie much, everything was all right. But it's got so she thinks every breath she takes is a lie, and it making her sick. She don't know that I know 'bout all this, but Mr. Hunter, he don't always notice me, and he never notice Aunt Patty. He don't pay no attention to the darkies what sweep out the saloons, either, but I knows them from church, and—"

"Don't tell me! If the network of spies that attend the African Methodist Church in Pueblo, Colorado, had worked for Abe Lincoln, he would have won the war in half the time. I don't think there is any event or scandal in town that escapes you darkies."

Jubilee smiled modestly. "There surely ain't much, Colonel."

"As soon as I settle Mr. Hunter's hash, I shall investigate my own network of informants. That I remained in ignorance of the situation in my own household is inexcusable. Someone, either on my payroll or beholden to me, should have told me."

"You wouldn't have thanked them, Colonel, 'cept maybe with your walking stick. You don't allow nobody to say nothing against Mr. Hunter, and if anybody tries, you just go deaf. Take a braver man than most folks in Pueblo to tell you something you don't want to hear."

The Colonel kicked back his chair as he rose. "I'm hearing it now, Jubilee. Saddle two horses and bring them around front. And bring the buggy whip."

Jubilee looked alarmed. "Lordy, Colonel, what you planning to do?"

The Colonel raised his eyebrows. "Horsewhip a worthless cur, Jubilee. It should serve to restore my digestion as well as my good name as a man not to be trifled with—not even by my son-in-law."

Without waiting to see if Jubilee would follow orders, he stalked out of the room and climbed the stairs to Mattie's room on the third floor. After getting no response to his knock, he opened the door and entered. His daughter lay asleep on the massive oak bed, her face as pale as the mother-of-pearl designs on the headboard. All of Mattie's furniture was handcrafted and all inlaid with mother-of-pearl. Even the fireplace had the same matching design on its oak mantel. It had been his special welcome-home present when she had returned from her honeymoon. Instead he should have greeted her at the front door with his saber and removed her husband's head from his shoulders.

He walked to the bed and stood looking down at Mattie. Her eyes did appear sunken, as Jubilee had said, but that was only an illusion created by the faint blue shadows underneath each eye. She was wearing only a plain cotton nightgown instead of a dress bulky with flounces and overskirt, and ribbons and gewgaws, and her thinness struck the Colonel for the first time. Her arms, pale shadows inside the long sleeves of her nightgown, looked slender enough to snap between a man's fingers, and the Colonel admitted that "bony" best described her shoulders.

He reached out to stroke her hair, but satisfied himself by tucking the covers around her instead. He didn't want to awaken her. Tomorrow was soon enough for her to discover that he had broken his promise and interfered in her marriage. At the very least Mattie would be angry. She might even hate him. But she wouldn't have to lie anymore.

God damn Samuel Hunter, thought the Colonel as he closed Mattie's door and walked down the hall toward the staircase. A man shouldn't treat a dog like Samuel was treating Mattie. And a man damn sure shouldn't hide behind a woman's skirts the way Samuel was doing. The Colonel felt his hands start to shake with the force of the rage he felt. By God, he would straighten out the young man if he had to widow Mattie to do it.

He walked across the veranda, shivering as the cold wind whipped round the corners of the house and tugged at the tails of his frock coat. He grabbed his gelding's reins from Jubilee and mounted. "According to your spies at the African Methodist Church, where are we likely to find Samuel?"

Jubilee mounted his horse like a man more comfortable driving horses than riding them. Still, the Colonel had to admit that Jubilee rode well for a man who had seldom done it at all until after the war, riding not being one of a house slave's required duties. "I reckon he be down on Santa Fe Avenue, Colonel."

The Colonel nudged his horse into a trot down Tenth Street. "That is hardly an answer, since Santa Fe Avenue boasts a number of saloons, gambling establishments, hotels, and combinations thereof. A man can gamble, drink, sleep, and take care of less respectable needs without taking more than ten steps in any direction."

"I hear he think mighty highly of the Capitol Saloon and the Assembly Saloon."

"Can't that son of a bitch even show enough respect for his family to pick a decent saloon?" demanded the Colonel, kicking his horse into a gallop. "Those vile dens sell liquor that cuts like a three-sided file going down, and burns like fire coming out. They cater to ruffians, Texans, and women who call themselves widows and have no visible means of support. A gentleman hesitates to show his face in either establishment."

"Yes, suh."

The Colonel noticed Jubilee's carefully neutral tone and debated calling him to task, but decided against it. His ex-slave might be uppity enough to mention the fact that this particular gentleman had on occasion stepped into both saloons to imbibe their brand of "Taos Lightning." A man occasionally needed the relief from respectability that patronizing two such low establishments afforded—but that did not excuse Samuel. His frequent patronage indicated a complete loss of respectability.

The Colonel turned his horse down Santa Fe Avenue, Pueblo's first and still premier business district, and felt a sense of pride. While its original buildings were frame or adobe, its newer ones were fine brick edifices that any city would be proud of. There was even talk of installing cobblestone gutters to prevent runoff from rain and the waste water from the numerous irrigation ditches from flooding the streets and leaving mud holes that inconvenienced both pedestrian and wagon traffic. The Colonel decided to try once more to persuade the city council to appoint a competent street supervisor, and to argue in favor of bricking at least Santa Fe Avenue. It was downright shameful for a city as progressive as Pueblo to suffer unpaved streets.

Tonight, however, the street was reasonably dry and the moon bright enough for a man to avoid the worst of the rough spots. It was also bright enough to reveal the jostling crowds of Texas cowboys loosed upon Pueblo after driving cattle up the Goodnight-Loving Trail, employees of any of the city's four railroads, smelter workers eager to spend whatever little was left of their pay packets after paying rent and whatever bills were owed to local merchants, and a miscellany of other men whose employment was less regular and frequently less respectable. Pueblo was not any less busy at night than during regular business hours. It was considerably more noisy, however, as though the darkness released inhibitions. Voices that were moderate during the day turned raucous and argumentive; language that was guarded in daylight out of respect for decent women who ventured onto the avenue to shop became profane; insults and slights left unspoken during working hours erupted from tongues loosened by an unending river of alcohol.

The Colonel loved it.

A little vice was a necessary thing, in the Colonel's opinion. Occasionally indulging in vice made virtue bearable—if such indulgence did not threaten financial security or the sanctity of family life. He knew that Samuel had violated the latter, and he resolved to investigate the extent of his son-in-law's dereliction in respect to the former. That Samuel's cash resources were reduced, he never doubted. Gambling four or five nights a week depleted any man's capital—unless he was a professional, a possibility that horrified the Colonel and sent rage pounding through his skull again.

He reined in his horse at the sight of his son-in-law's gray being held, along with several others, by an ill-clad urchin of ten or so. Dismounting, the Colonel tossed his reins and a half-dollar to the boy. "Watch my horse, boy, and there's another half-dollar if you can tell me where the owner of that gray is."

"Yes, sir!" exclaimed the boy, almost dancing with eagerness to please, as the Colonel knew he would be. A dollar to hold two horses and impart information was an unheard-of salary for a youngster. "He's in the Capitol, sir!"

A TIME TOO LATE

"Thank you, son," said the Colonel, tossing the boy another coin. "Get off your horse, Jubilee, and come along. I want to get this business over with before Cook turns my supper into warmed-over buffalo chips. Where's the buggy whip?"

Jubilee handed his reins to the boy and stepped onto the board sidewalk, his features twisted into an expression of stubbornness. "I didn't bring no buggy whip, Colonel. Miss Mattie gonna be shamed enough without you whipping her husband through the streets. I didn't bring no gun neither. Bad a shot as you is, you'd kill somebody might not need killing."

"I'll thank you not to mind my business for me, Jubilee."

"I'm not. I'm minding my own. I goes in there with you, and you starts laying into Mr. Hunter with a buggy whip or a gun, it's gonna start a fight just 'cause folks like to fight when they're liquored up. Somebody gonna land in the calaboose and it sure ain't gonna be a city councilman like you. It's gonna be me 'cause I was with you and I'm a nigger. I heard tell that jail's got lice bigger than you and me, and stinks besides."

"Nonsense. That jail was whitewashed inside just last year, but if you're going to be so stiff-necked about this, you wait outside."

The Capitol Saloon occupied a modest white frame building next to John Pyle's Jewelry Shop and Drugstore. No oil paintings of naked ladies done by itinerant artists in payment for drinks adorned its walls since the proprietor operated on a cash-only basis; besides, he didn't see the necessity of providing his customers with canvas nudes when there were so many women willing, for a small consideration, to pose the same way in the flesh. The suggestion that a man might prefer the fleshy perfection of the dream to the well-used parts of the reality would be greeted with a hoot of disbelief from the proprietor, promptly followed by the suspicion that such a man was unnatural and not to be trusted around animals and young children.

The Capitol's bar was chest high, moderately carved, with a brass footrest already splattered with spilled whiskey and tobacco juice, where customers had missed their mouths with one and the spittoons with the other. A potbellied stove stood on a square of bricks at one end of the bar, close enough for the bartender to stoke it without taking his eye off the cash drawer, but enough out of the way that the odd fight or two didn't knock it over.

What the Capitol lacked in fancy furnishing it made up for in atmosphere, which this evening was gray with tobacco smoke, loud with drunken voices, and rich with the acrid odor associated with flannel long johns donned at the first cold snap and worn until late spring, and the scent of professional women who often looked and smelled, in the Colonel's estimation, as though they had been rode hard and put away wet. The Colonel was sorry he was sober. A gentleman's tolerance of an establishment such as the Capitol was in direct proportion to his degree of inebriation.

He peered through the yellow gloom cast by coal-oil lamps suspended from the ceiling and saw Mattie's husband sitting at a round table near the back of the saloon dealing a round of cards. His companions ran the gambit from a flashily dressed man who the Colonel suspected was either a professional gambler or a pimp, a cowboy duded out in his best shirt and vest, a prospector with the mud of his claim still clinging to his boots, and two Pueblo businessmen whose preeminence in the community was not matched by their respectability.

The Colonel walked up behind Samuel, pulled him out of his chair by his coat collar, flipped up the tails of his flock coat, and grabbed him by the seat of his pants, jerking straight up as hard as he could. The resulting gagging sound from Samuel was all the Colonel could have hoped for. "Gentleman, Mr. Hunter regrets that he must settle up for this evening, but he has suddenly remembered a previous engagement. Isn't that right, Samuel?"

Samuel's gagging noise turned into a most satisfying gobbling as he stretched up on his toes in an attempt to relieve the pressure on his testicles exerted by the Colonel's tight grip on his trousers.

The Colonel shook his head in reproof. "He does take on when he has to leave such genial company. I trust you *are* genial company." He eyed the two businessmen, who nodded in agreement, prompted, the Colonel had no doubt, more by their fear of a powerful banker than by any innate gentility.

The prospector and the cowboy reached for the pot to retrieve their ante, both with the expressions of drunken relief common to men who were about to lose all their money before having an opportunity either to get drunk enough to hold them until their next trip to town, or to enjoy the dubious charms of whatever sporting lady was free to accept their wooing and their money. Before their callused fingers could touch the pile of assorted greenbacks and silver dollars, the gambler briskly threw out one arm, thus snapping a tiny derringer holdout gun down into his hand. "No gentleman leaves in the middle of a hand. Let Mr. Hunter go, sir, before anyone is harmed."

The Colonel stared into the gambler's eyes, their green-brown color reminding him of river-bottom scum, and did not doubt that the man would as soon shoot him as not. He had seen eyes like the gambler's before, always hungry for someone else's pain. He glanced around quickly. The denizens of the Capitol had fallen silent, watching the frozen tableau with excited eyes, waiting for violence to erupt and someone's blood to spill. The Colonel was very much afraid it might be his.

"Shooting an unarmed man is murder, sir," he said, seeing the bartender reaching under the bar for what the Colonel hoped was a gun and not an ax handle. While useful for dispersing unarmed brawlers, an ax handle lacked the necessary range in this instance.

The gambler smiled. "But I am defending a gentleman who is being assaulted and abducted against his will. I'm certain Mr. Hunter would testify on my behalf in case I'm forced to kill you."

The Colonel was certain of it, too, which only made him more enraged. "Damn it, I'm not assaulting him! I'm his father-in-law!"

An expression the Colonel couldn't quite read surfaced from the muddy depths of the gambler's eyes. "Release him, Colonel."

The Colonel saw that the bartender did have a gun, a Winchester Model 1873 rifle, and tensed himself to drop to the floor, thus giving the man a clear range of fire, when a black hand holding a full bottle of whiskey appeared just above and behind the gambler's head. The Colonel never regretted the waste of fine Kentucky bourbon when Jubilee closed the distance between the gambler's skull and the whiskey bottle. The gambler's legs folded up and he dropped across the table on top of the money.

The Colonel cleared his throat and motioned to the other players, all of whom looked considerably more sober than a few minutes before. "Roll him on the floor and split the pot, gentlemen. Jubilee, shall we go? Cook is waiting supper."

CHAPTER 6

The dress had looked so elegant when the dressmaker delivered it, a confection of ivory, pale yellow, and deep gold; sunshine in silk of three different textures: ribbed silk faille, silk Sicilienne, and velvetlike silk chenille. The colors were not favored by the most fashionable modistes, grays and various hues of purple from plum to violet to prune being more popular, but Mattie had ignored the dressmaker's hand wringing. She *wanted* the yellows; she *needed* the yellows; besides she looked feverish in prune-colored silk.

But the gown's princess basque fit tightly as a corset, the square neck exposed her throat and the tops of her breasts, the shoulder straps formed miniscule sleeves edged in white lace that bared her slender arms. Mattie suddenly felt like a scrawny alley cat. The garlands of leaves embroidered around the neck and the edges of the square court train were not enough to distract the eye from features that appeared almost gaunt. Even the fact that the narrow gold faille skirt was draped diagonally and an ivory Sicilienne scarf was pleated around the hips, its ends hidden under the train and held there by a spay of forget-me-nots, did not disguise the fact that her hips and thighs were too thin.

"I look like a mop dressed in a ball gown, Aunt Patty," she said, feeling another headache begin to throb along the right side of her head.

"Better than looking like a sofa pillow stuffed in a corset and wrapped up in gray twill like some I could mention," answered the old woman, busily pinning Mattie's thick hair into a disciplined pompadour of curls.

Mattie smiled at the bony old woman, but didn't reply. It wouldn't have done any good. Since the day her parents had found her burying the last of her children in a shallow grave along the road to Independence, Aunt Patty had been a woman with her own opinions, beginning with the brusque statement in answer to the Colonel's offer to fill in the grave for her.

"I bury my own, mister, but thank you just the same."

"My dear woman," said the Colonel. "A grieving mother should not watch her own child's face being forever shut away from the light, much less have to be the instrument responsible."

"Fancy talk, mister, but no woman ought to turn away from what needs doing." She stopped and leaned on the shovel, looking into the distance with pale blue eyes. "It was the cholera. First it took my man. That didn't surprise me none. He was still weak from the war, couldn't fight it off. Then it took my oldest girl. Near twenty she was. Hoping to find a man to marry up with who wasn't sick and bitter and missing a leg or an arm. Then it was the baby. She was six. Then my

A TIME TOO LATE
75

middle daughter and son. This was my last child, and a strapping boy he was. Never figured he'd die of it." She faced the Colonel. "That's my story, mister. Left a string of dead family that stretches all the way back to Tennessee. Got nobody left but myself, my wagon, and a team of mules."

The Colonel cleared his throat. "You would be welcome to follow along with us to Independence. We plan to cross the river there and continue on to Colorado."

Aunt Patty shoveled more dirt in the grave and patted it down. Finally, she turned back to the Colonel. "Colorado sounds good to me. See you have a wife and a youn'un with no one to tend to them 'cept you and that nigger. I'll go along with you. You pay me what you can till we put down roots, then we'll talk about what's fair."

"My good woman, I am not in the market for a ladies' maid."

"That's good, 'cause you ain't getting one. You're getting me. I can cook over a campfire and wash clothes in the river. I know what plants are pizen, and which one helps a lady when she's down bad with her monthlies."

Mattie remembered her mother's gasping at Aunt Patty's frankness while her father had blustered, his face as red as the old mountain woman's hair. "Madam, I insist you watch your language. There are ladies present."

Aunt Patty, her freckles standing out like dabs of brown paint against a sun-blistered skin, shook her head. "I know that. I can see your wife, and I also see that she's not used to this kind of life. Some of us are, and some of us never will be. Ain't no reflection on anybody. Just the way things are. So I figure I can help your wife. Your gal, I don't know. She may be strong and outgrow me, and she might not. Hard to tell right now." She put her hands on her hips. "What's it going to be, mister. Do I hitch my mules on to the back of the nigger's wagon, or don't I?"

The Colonel surrendered. "His name is Jubilee."

Aunt Patty had walked up to the wagon and looked hard at Jubilee. Finally she nodded her head. "You look to be a good man, Jubilee. My name's Aunt Patty." She held out her hand. "You look after man's business and I'll look after woman's business, and I reckon we'll argue about the rest."

And that had been pretty much that for the last ten years, thought Mattie. Aunt Patty wore unpatched calico dresses instead of ragged ones, put up her thinning red hair in a braided coronet instead of wearing it in a knot at the back of her neck, and didn't dip snuff in public anymore, but otherwise she was the same skinny, outspoken mountain woman her father had hired on the road to Independence.

Aunt Patty stuck a white heron's feather aigrette and a cluster of forget-me-nots in Mattie's hair, and stood back, tilting her head from side to side as she studied the younger woman. "You're done, honey. Put on that black velvet dog collar with the topaz pendant and your gloves, and you are ready to dance holes in your shoes."

Mattie fastened the dog collar on and studied her reflection again. "I'm still so thin, Aunt Patty."

"Eat more, and wean that young'un. He's more than a year old, and he's got teeth. You don't need to be nursing him anymore. It ain't like you're doing it to keep from getting caught again. That man of yours got to hang his britches on the bedpost more than he does for that to happen."

Mattie slammed down a bottle of perfume, shattering it into aromatic shards. "That's enough, Aunt Patty. I won't listen to your crude remarks about my husband or my marriage. Samuel can't draw a breath without you or Papa jumping on him. No wonder he goes out every night. At least he finds some peace away from your harping and Papa's criticism."

She pulled on her white kid gloves, glad they were cut in the new style without buttons at the wrists, because her hands were shaking too badly to fight the tiny loops over equally tiny buttons. She had never quarreled with Aunt Patty before, and she felt as if she had sliced into her own heart. But she could not listen to her talk in that fashion about Samuel. He was her husband. She owed him her loyalty.

For better or for worse.

She looked into the mirror again, lifted her chin, then slipped on wide gold bands over her gloves. She would not cry tonight. Or have another headache. She drew a deep breath, picked up her grosgrain evening bag, and stood up. "Fetch my brocaded velvet cloak, Aunt Patty. It's still chilly outside this time of year."

"Supposed to be. It ain't summer yet," muttered the other woman, stepping inside Mattie's dressing room to get the cloak.

Mattie walked across the room and stepped behind a Chinese screen to lean over Leon's crib. Gently she touched the sleeping baby's cheek and smoothed the wispy hair that had lately begun to darken to her gold color. He had inherited Samuel's brilliant blue eyes, but the shape of his face and chin were hers. He was a quiet baby, almost somber, and studied every adult with wide, curious eyes as if debating whether or not to admit that person into his confidence. If he decided yes, then he would toddle back and forth between his toy chest and his confidant, sharing his toys and babbling quietly in a language of his own. If he decided no, then he simply walked away, content in his private world without feeling obliged to share it with someone he did not like. No one ever got a second chance with Leon.

Except Samuel.

Leon would offer Samuel a toy, then offer it to him again if he was rebuffed. Mattie decided that Leon knew Samuel was part of him, and was determined not to give up until Samuel joined that intimate circle of adults whose lives revolved around the year-old baby. She wondered how long Leon would try before he gave up. Dear God, how long does a son crave his father's attention?

She was still wondering as Samuel whirled her around the room above the Thatcher Bros. Mercantile Company to the accompaniment of fiddle music. For that matter, how long did a wife crave a husband's attention before her heart broke or she tired of waiting and turned to—what? Her children? She only had one, and even if she spent all of his waking hours with him, there were still hours left over. Perhaps if she had more children—but that, in Aunt Patty's words, required Samuel's pants hanging on her bedpost, and that particular item of her husband's wardrobe had been conspicuously absent from her bedpost, her chaise longue, her chair, her floor, or anywhere else in her bedroom. And she didn't know how to entice, seduce, or even flirt with her own husband. Like Leon, she was never sure of her welcome.

If she could not occupy herself with children, what else was left? Headaches and needlepoint? She was determined to overcome her headaches, and she was infernally tired of needlepoint. She supposed she could take up painting or gardening, both respectable pastimes for ladies. But she had no gift for art, and her father had a full-time gardener. There were always good works, of course. She could visit the sick, comfort the bereaved, organize benefits to raise money for worthwhile projects such as the library association. She could be Pueblo's angel of mercy and goodwill. She smiled wryly to herself. At the risk of seeming uncharitable, she thought she might prefer needlepoint.

She pursed her lips and glanced over Samuel's shoulder at the line of gentlemen waiting for the dance to end so they might claim the ladies for the next one. Men still outnumbered respectable women in Pueblo, and no woman, married or single, no matter how elderly or homely, ever lacked a dance partner. Indeed, they were forced to turn down invitations. Mattie noticed several of the gentlemen watching her, most with an almost indecent gleam of admiration in their eyes, and knew that she would be surrounded as soon as the music ended. She wondered why she was attractive to every man but her own husband.

Samuel's restless eyes darted about the room, never lighting on one person or thing for very long, as though he knew whatever he was seeking was not to be found. "Mattie, you're looking lovely tonight, rather like a buttercup in a dung heap."

She stumbled and trod on his foot. "W-what did you say?"

"I likened you to a flower, my dear. Rather recklessly, I am afraid. I was referring to Pueblo as a dung heap, not you, although I am not certain your father will appreciate the distinction when you repeat my words to him."

"I don't carry tales to my father, Samuel," she said, thinking how like Samuel it was to make two-headed compliments.

"You don't have to. You only have to whine to him of how inattentive and *absent* your husband is, and your father descends upon me in a rage." He squeezed her waist, his fingers exerting pressure on an area where the whalebone stays in her corset already inflicted enough discomfort. She flinched away, and he quickly eased his grip. "My apologies, Mattie, and for God's sake, smile. Everyone is looking, and thanks to your father, Pueblo has enough to talk about without your cowering away from me."

She parted her lips in what she hoped was a passable smile and nodded pleasantly to the small group of men clustered around the punch bowl with her father. Samuel was right; they were staring at him with expressions ranging from barely concealed curiosity to outright disapproval.

Mattie raised her chin and stared back, feeling a confidence she had not felt before. Whatever the latest disagreement between Samuel and her father was, it was none of anyone else's business. "What did my father do?"

Samuel's face twisted into such a mask of hatred and desperation that Mattie fought her natural inclination to cringe. "As if you didn't know, my innocent little wife. He dragged me out of the Capitol Saloon last night with the whole town watching. He humiliated me in front of my friends, threatened to whip me if I didn't dance attendance on you like a lapdog." He whirled her around again. "Well, here I am, Mattie, a gibbering, slobbering, mindless lapdog. I'm not good for much else. Your father has seen to that."

Mattie felt as breathless as though his words were bands squeezing all the air from her body. "I didn't know, Samuel."

He studied her, his face still twisted in the same terrible way that ripped at her heart. Finally he looked away, his expression changing to one of smiling enjoyment. If capable of nothing else, Samuel was a master of social pretense. "I believe you, Mattie. You wouldn't turn so pale if you had known. You had better pinch your cheeks or whatever you women do to give yourselves color. Otherwise your father may accuse me of beating you, and God knows what he might do then. Throttle me probably."

"I wouldn't have let him shame you if I had known."

Samuel lowered his head as if whispering a lover's secret in her ear. "How would you have stopped him, Mattie? Thrown yourself in front of his horse? Cut out the servants' tongues? Because if it wasn't you, then it must have been your nigger or that white-trash woman that carried tales. Damn them and damn you for encouraging them to act above themselves."

Her face began to ache from the effort of holding her smile. "I did not encourage them. Whatever they did was because they love me and they're loyal to Papa."

"That's one affliction I'm not cursed with!"

Mattie felt cold and hollow. She didn't dare ask him whether the affliction he spoke of was love or loyalty. She was seventeen years old, neither homely nor infirm, and she was afraid her husband didn't love her anymore.

If he ever had.

But she couldn't allow herself to think that; otherwise her marriage would be make-believe, and she wasn't certain how long she could pretend without going mad. There was one reality she could face, though. Samuel was wilting in her father's shadow like a plant that lacked sunshine.

"Colonel Corley?"

The Colonel turned at the sound of the man's voice. "Officer Bilby, the strong right arm of the law. Have you stopped by to sample the punch and perhaps cut in on one of the gentlemen monopolizing our ladies on the dance floor?"

"Not exactly, sir," the officer began, looking from the Colonel to the other men, all of whom were listening while appearing not to.

The Colonel laid his arm across the shoulders of the shorter man. "Surely you don't think you can fool me,

Officer. You heard that the table would be laden with all kinds of delicacies made by the hands of our lovely ladies. I know what a sweet tooth you have. Come with me and fill your plate." He led the officer to the table and lowered his voice to just above a whisper. "What did you do with the gambler, Bilby?"

Bilby scratched his head. "Well, Colonel, we rightly should have had him up on charges, what with his drawing down on you and all—"

The Colonel shoved a plate in his hand. "Try some of those little cookies, Officer Bilby. They are delicious." He continued in a whisper. "And lower your voice, damn it. I don't want the whole town knowing my business."

Bilby swallowed, his Adam's apple sliding up and down his skinny throat. "Sorry, Colonel."

The Colonel cut the officer a piece of cake. "You didn't throw him in that sorry excuse for a jail, did you? If two felons as lacking in intelligence as those two who knocked a hole in the jail-house wall with a flatiron could escape, a ruffian as bright as the gambler would be out practically before you lock the door. I want him out of Pueblo, but without resorting to Judge Lynch."

Officer Bilby looked alarmed. "Now, Colonel. We ain't lynched anybody in a while."

"Smile, damn it, and fill your plate." The Colonel glanced surreptitiously around the room, then continued. "You misunderstood me. I don't want the man lynched. What kind of a savage do you think I am?"

Officer Bilby balanced his plate in one hand and pulled out a handkerchief with the other. He swabbed his face, which the Colonel noticed with satisfaction was sweating. "I don't know, sir." He gulped as he realized what he had said. "I mean, sir, I didn't rightly know what to do, so me and another officer dumped him in a freight car heading east." He grinned and tucked his handkerchief back in his pocket. "It was half-full of cattle at the time, Colonel, and we told him that if we caught him in Pueblo again, we'd throw him in a freight car *full* of cattle. Last we seen of him, he was dancing around pretty fancy trying to stay out of the way of the cow shit and horns."

The Colonel laughed and clapped the officer on the back. "Very imaginative, Bilby. I knew I could depend on you. Now, enjoy the food, and if you can fight your way through the crowd of men, ask my daughter for a dance. She's the belle of the ball tonight."

The officer's eyes took on an expression of yearning. "She's a fine-looking woman, Colonel. Makes you wonder, don't it?" He stopped abruptly and shifted his plate from hand to hand. "I mean, makes you wonder how I'm gonna get through that crowd of galoots."

The Colonel smiled. "I know what you meant, Bilby, and I agree. It does make you wonder why a man would prefer spending his time in low company instead of enjoying the rewards to be found in home and family."

"I wouldn't presume to be thinking any such thing, Colonel," Bilby assured him.

"I can't control what you think, Bilby, but I trust you will be more discreet about expressing your thoughts. I would take it amiss if you did not."

"I won't open my mouth, Colonel."

The Colonel nodded as he watched Mattie accept an invitation to dance with one of Pueblo's physicians. "See that you don't, Bilby." He saw Samuel walk off the dance floor and raised his voice to its normal volume. "Excuse me, Officer. I must have a word with my son-in-law."

He walked toward Samuel. Much as it gave him a bellyache to think about it, he had to act as if last night never happened. He could depend on the business community and the respectable people to follow his lead out of good manners; the other inhabitants out of fear. He was too powerful a man for anyone to thwart. What Pueblo thought in private was another matter. He only hoped no one thought badly of Mattie. He didn't give a damn what they thought about Samuel—as long as no one said anything aloud. In the meantime, to confuse both friends and enemies alike, he would treat Samuel with respect and affection, and hope the young bastard might someday deserve both.

About the time hell froze over.

"Samuel," he called jovially. "Come join the crowd of leftover men. Once the ladies select their partners, we are what is left over."

Samuel looked both confused and wary. "I thought I might step outside to smoke, Colonel."

The Colonel threw his arm around the smaller man's shoulders. "Don't even think about leaving this room," he warned softly, leading him toward a cluster of men. He raised his voice to hail a short, heavyset man. "John Thatcher, what have you heard from Charlie Goodnight lately?"

Reputed to have the sweetest nature and the sharpest mind in Pueblo, John Thatcher was almost constitutionally unable to say a bad word about anyone, a trait the Colonel counted on to ensure that Samuel would be treated civilly and invited to join in the general conversation. Such uncritical acceptance by Pueblo's most respectable and respected citizen would go far toward quieting any disapproval his own reputation might fail to quash. He had no illusions that he was held in as high esteem as John Thatcher. No one ever claimed that Colonel Andrew Corley had a sweet nature.

The Colonel met Thatcher's eyes, knew the banker and merchant had already heard about the fracas at the Capitol, and almost regretted placing the kindly man in such an untenable position. Almost.

John Thatcher cleared his throat. "Charlie left for Texas in February. He hadn't heard from his men in the Panhandle most of the winter, and he was afraid outlaws might have killed them and taken his cattle."

"Not unless the outlaws are interested in meeting their Maker at the end of a rope," remarked the Colonel. "Not that I've ever heard of Goodnight hanging anybody, but I wouldn't care to tempt him either."

John Thatcher laughed, another attractive trait of his, thought the Colonel. He was a man who liked to laugh. "I suspect you're right, Colonel. At any rate, Charlie found his men and property in good order and came back to Pueblo long enough to change horses and check on his slaughter pens down at Las Animas, then back to Texas."

"The man must sleep on horseback," said the Colonel.

"He must," said Thatcher, "because he had hardly arrived back in Texas when he received a letter from his wife, who has been visiting cousins in California, that either he come back to civilization, or she would join him in Texas, and he was to meet her in Denver. So far as I know now, that's where he is, picking up Molly and meeting with John Adair."

"Adair?" asked the Colonel. "The Britisher who owns the brokerage firm in Denver? The muddlehead who went on the buffalo hunt in Kansas in Seventy-four and didn't manage to shoot a damn thing except his own horse?"

"I believe Mr. Adair didn't prove to be much of a buffalo hunter," said Thatcher in a mild voice.

"That is putting the best face on it, John. So why is Charlie meeting with Adair?"

"Mr. Adair expressed an interest in investing in a cattle operation and was informed that Charlie Goodnight had forgotten more about running cattle than most people hoped to learn. They'll be traveling to Texas together, to visit Charlie's ranch in the Palo Duro, and making plans to become business partners."

"Why would Charlie Goodnight want to take in a man as partner who can't even manage to get his rifle up high enough not to shoot his own horse through the head? Seems to me Mr. Adair might prove to be hard on livestock."

"I believe finance is the principal consideration, Colonel. Goodnight plans to establish an extensive operation, and he needs capital. Not having any interests in ranching, you might not be aware of the amount of capital required. After the Panic of Seventy-three, Charlie had nothing left except his place near Pueblo and sixteen hundred head of cattle. He needs money to buy more cattle, to negotiate to buy up more land. The Panhandle is all public land owned by Texas, and in order to ensure his success, he needs title to it rather than just grazing his cattle on free grassland. Otherwise he might find farmers and small ranchers laying claims to bits and pieces of his range. With backing, Charlie Goodnight could well end up with a ranching empire."

"And Adair believes there is money to be made ranching?" asked the Colonel.

"I'm not certain Mr. Adair's interest is solely in making money. There is the romantic element involved in controlling a vast ranch, in fighting the elements, in nurturing the land."

"If one enjoys wading knee-deep in cow dung and building up calluses on one's behind from riding horseback for hours herding animals that in my observation have less sense than a chicken, but with the added disadvantage of having horns and hooves. No, John, my interest in cattle is limited to the Sunday roast."

"You may be missing an investment opportunity, Colonel," said Thatcher. "There is much interest being shown by the English and the Scots in Texas cattle operations. I predict that within the next two years we'll see vast amounts of money invested in Charlie Goodnight's Texas by our English cousins."

"Our so-called English cousins will have an advantage, won't they?" asked the Colonel. "They can hire men like Goodnight to manage their property and will not have to live in that benighted state themselves."

"You have never softened your harsh opinion of Texas, have you, Colonel?" asked Thatcher. "Personally I think the state has much to commend it—not the least of which is its caliber of men. There is no finer man than Charles Goodnight, and I have been favorably impressed with many other Texans. As a general rule, I like them."

"As a general rule, you like everybody, John, but I will hold with my own opinion. It would take an act of God to make me set foot in Texas."

CHAPTER 7

"Texas!" shouted the Colonel the following week.

Mattie winced. "Papa, please don't shout."

The Colonel's face was puce, and Mattie was certain that she could hear him grinding his teeth together. "I'll shout if I wish, young woman. This is my office in my home, and I don't allow anyone to tell me how to behave in it. Not even my daughter. Particularly my daughter. I am your father, Mattie, and you will show me respect."

Mattie lowered her eyes. She had seldom seen her father so angry—not even when he had caught Samuel kissing her the night she accepted his proposal. "Yes, Papa."

"That's better!" He turned his head toward the room's other occupant, and Mattie saw Samuel clench his shaking hands around the chair's wooden arms. "Now, young man, suppose you repeat that preposterous statement you made. I surely did not hear you correctly."

A TIME TOO LATE

Samuel cleared his throat, and Mattie surreptitiously pressed one of his whiteknuckled hands while praying that her husband had imbibed enough Dutch courage in her bedroom to stand up to her father. "I said, sir, that I will be following Charles Goodnight's lead and establishing a ranch on the Texas plains. I spoke at length with Mr. Thatcher about the possibilities. As Goodnight's friend and as owner of his own ranching operation near Pueblo, Mr. Thatcher seemed the best person to consult about my prospects. I believe that given time and adequate capital, I can become a successful rancher."

"In a pig's eye, you fool! You don't know any more about running a cattle operation than a Chinaman."

"But Samuel can learn, Papa."

"Don't interrupt, Mattie," ordered her father. "Young man, you put such notions out of your mind and bend your mind toward your job at the bank. I don't want to hear any more talk of ranching in Texas."

"Sir, I am determined," said Samuel.

"Determined to make an ass out of yourself," said the Colonel, pounding his desk. "I will not countenance any move to Texas nor any such endeavor. This discussion is ended."

"No, it isn't, Papa," said Mattie. "Samuel wants to ranch in Texas, and I support him. It is a wonderful opportunity."

"Your wifely support of your husband is noted, Mattie. Now put such foolishness away and go tend to your son."

"No!"

The Colonel rose out of his chair and leaned over his desk, staring at her. "What did you say?"

Mattie swallowed but refused to lower her eyes. This was Samuel's only chance to develop into a strong, independent man, something he could not do in her father's shadow. She had little knowledge of ranching in Texas and suspected that Samuel's was minimal, but she knew he would embark on any kind of a venture as long as it removed him from the vicinity of his father-in-law. And this particular venture happened to be the only one that guaranteed that. Her father would rather be drawn and quartered than set foot in Texas. Samuel would finally be free of Colonel Andrew Corley, and pioneering in Texas would provide him a challenge. He would have his chance, and her father could go hang.

"I said no, Papa. I will not be sent from the room like a child. I am Samuel's wife and I will follow him."

"You will not! I forbid it!"

"You do not have that right, Papa. A husband's wishes take precedence over a parent's. It says so in the Bible."

The Colonel made several attempts to speak before he managed to bring what Mattie knew was a truly formidable rage under control. "I will stop you. I won't have you trailing after this young idiot while he chases some will-o'-the-wisp."

"I would follow him to hell, Papa. I certainly would accompany him to Texas."

The Colonel sat down, folded his hands, and smiled. Mattie braced herself and squeezed Samuel's hand again. Her father was most dangerous when he smiled in that conciliatory manner. "Now, Mattie, Samuel, I'm certain that in the flush of enthusiasm you have not considered the practicalities. For example, in order to establish a cattle ranch, you will need cattle. I haven't glanced out my window in the last few minutes, but I doubt I will see a herd of the bovines grazing on my lawn.

Where do you propose to obtain these beasts?"

Samuel sat up straighter. "I propose to buy them at Mr. Iliff's ranch on the North Platt east of Denver. According to Mr. Thatcher, that gentleman is the 'cattle king' of Colorado. Three thousand head should be a goodly number."

"With what do you propose to buy these cattle?"

Samuel patted his forehead with his handkerchief, and Mattie felt her stomach churn with a premonition of approaching disaster, but didn't understand from which direction it was coming. She ignored her premonition as a too-generous dinner and a too-tight corset, and lifted her chin. "Really, Papa. Who is being foolish now? Samuel had a substantial bank account when we married, and you've paid him a generous salary since then. Living with you, we have few expenses beyond clothes and incidentals. Why would you believe Samuel would have difficulty buying cattle?"

The Colonel smiled again, and Mattie's stomach felt as if she had swallowed a block of ice. "I took the opportunity of examining young Samuel's bank account. Thanks to his profligate gambling, he is somewhat financially embarrassed. Isn't that true, Samuel?"

Samuel nodded and licked his lips.

"So there it is, Mattie," said the Colonel with a pleased expression. "With no cattle, it is difficult to establish a cattle ranch. Now, I trust I will hear no more of this nonsense."

"I can borrow the necessary money by pledging the cattle as collateral," said Samuel, his voice holding a note of determination and stubbornness. "I have discussed the possibility with John Thatcher."

"I'll have a word with John Thatcher," said the Colonel. "Point out to him the error of his thinking. He may be a kind, generous man, but he's no fool. A gambler and a drunk like you is not a good business risk."

Mattie stood up and laid her hand on her husband's shoulder. "Then I will sell my jewelry, we will buy what cattle we can, and go to Texas anyway. You can't stop us, Papa, so don't create another scandal by trying." She smiled at her father, feeling rage and triumph and guilt mixed together. "Don't look so shocked. Did you think I wouldn't find out what happened at the Capitol Saloon? Did you think I wouldn't find out how you treated Samuel?"

The Colonel had the decency to look ashamed, Mattie noticed. "I did it to protect you. I see now that my methods were wrong. But just because I embarrassed Samuel is no reason for the two of you to throw common sense to the winds and risk bankruptcy in this farfetched scheme. Samuel, think of what you are doing. You are not a stockman or a cowboy. You don't know the country. How will you manage?"

"Samuel will manage. He will hire cowboys."

The Colonel leaned his head back against his chair and contemplated the ceiling. Mattie felt her stomach churning again. He lifted his head and stared at her. "Is there no way I can dissuade you, Mattie? Is there no way I can convince you that neither of you is suited to what you are proposing? Texas is a hard land, and any man who challenges it must be equally hard. He must cast a long shadow, else the land will be his undoing. And a woman"—he swallowed and rubbed his eyes—"a woman has no chance at all."

Mattie closed her eyes. She could almost hear her father saying these very same things when he tried to persuade her not to marry Samuel. She had not wished to listen then, and she would not listen now. She opened her eyes. "Papa, it is already too late for such talk."

She reached for Samuel's hand, and for once felt him grasp hers as firmly as she could have wished. "We are going, Papa."

The Colonel nodded and shaded his eyes with one hand. Mattie felt as if she were being ripped in two as she watched the white-haired man who had raised her, teased her, spoiled her, but most of all, loved her. Or rather, loved who he wanted her to be.

She blinked her eyes and tightened her lips to keep them from trembling, then glanced down at Samuel, who she wasn't certain loved her at all, and wondered why, at seventeen, she felt so old.

The Colonel finally lowered his hand. "If you are determined to go through with this ill-conceived notion, then there are certain things that can be done to ensure some chance of success. I have a proposal, Samuel."

"No, Papa! No more devil's bargains!"

His eyes were free of subterfuge. On the contrary, her father looked very much the banker: calm, dispassionate, and very, very detached. "Mattie, this is strictly a business discussion, no devil's bargain. I give you my word, and you know I have never gone back on my word to you."

"That's true."

"Then go upstairs, or sit quietly. Samuel and I need to discuss practical financial arrangements, and you wouldn't understand."

She stood frozen by indecision. She did not altogether trust her father, but neither did she want to anger him further. Finance was man's business, and Samuel was both a lawyer—at least, he had read law—and a banker, if not as astute as her father. If she was to trust Samuel to care for her and protect her in the wilds of Texas, then she must trust him now.

She leaned over and kissed Samuel's cheek, noticing

that he flinched less than usual. Perhaps he was already gaining more confidence. She hoped so. He would need confidence to negotiate with her father, who she suspected could trick the devil out of hell. Fortunately this negotiation involved Texas, and the Colonel often said he'd rather take hell.

"I'll go upstairs, then, and let you two arrange the details. Samuel, don't let Papa flummox you."

Samuel looked up at her. "Really, Mattie, that is not a proper thing to say. It casts doubt upon my business sense, and hints of misconduct by your father."

"Yes, Samuel," she said in as contrite a voice as she could manage while she itched to scream. She had forgotten for the moment how much Samuel's habit of deferring to her father's opinion irritated her. It was an unattractive trait, and a useless tactic. She suspected that Colonel Andrew Corley couldn't care less whether Samuel agreed with him or not. She looked up to see her father watching her with a speculative expression, and wondered what her own face revealed. Nothing, she hoped.

She smiled at both men and left.

The Colonel felt his tense stomach relax as Mattie closed the door. He wondered what had occasioned her brief expression of rage when she had answered Samuel. In fact, he was still a little shaken by her behavior in general this evening. From a quiet, dutiful daughter and wife, she had turned into a defiant termagant. Most unattractive and unseemly, not to mention the fact that angered him the most: she had displayed all that temper and willfulness and spirit on behalf of her weakling husband and against her own father. Samuel did not deserve such a devoted advocate. The fact that

Mattie was his wife was beside the point.

He examined Samuel from underneath lowered brows and wondered not for the first time what kind of a marriage his daughter had with her husband. Not the same kind that he had enjoyed with Amanda; he would bet his last penny on that. In spite of being wedded and bedded, there was an untouched air about Mattie. For a brief second the word "virginal" occurred to him, but he blanked it out immediately; in fact, pushed the subject of his daughter's marital relations out of his mind. Speculating about such matters was not only improper, but possibly unnatural.

He cleared his throat and bent his mind toward the matter at hand: how to hedge his bet. "Samuel, I have no desire to see my daughter at the mercy of uncertain economic events, so I propose to fund your venture. I will advance monies to buy cattle, to pay wages, to invest in land and in whatever equipment is required to set up a cattle operation, and to generally assure that my daughter might live in that wilderness with a minimum of discomfort. In return for my investment, I will hold the deed to the property for a period of five years. I will, of course, examine the books each of those years. At the end of that time, you will repay my monies at an interest rate of, oh, say nine percent."

"Nine percent!"

The Colonel waved his hand. "You may, of course, repay the loan sooner with no penalty. Whenever the loan is repaid, I will turn over the deed to you and Mattie."

"Mattie!"

"Surely you did not think I would turn over the property solely to you. I may not be a believer in women's suffrage, you young ass, but I have no intention of investing my money in a venture in which my daughter does not have a share. I would sooner sow the ground with salt. Of course, if you do not repay the loan within the five-year period, I will own it outright, which means it will pass to Mattie on my death, and you will be out in the cold. And lest you plan to mistreat Mattie in this matter after my death, let me inform you that I have appointed the Thatcher brothers, John and Mahlon, banker and lawyer, as executors of my estate. It will be a cold day in hell before you play ducks and drakes, or rather faro and poker, with my daughter's wealth. The Thatchers will see to it."

"This is outrageous!"

"Nonsense. It is a straightforward business arrangement. I will be risking a sizable sum of money on a very uncertain proposition. No reputable banker would offer you any more liberal terms, and the disreputable ones would bankrupt you."

"And you won't?" screamed Samuel, his face almost purple with temper.

"Not if you seriously intend to pursue this idea with as much enthusiasm as you have for gambling."

He sat back and watched Samuel gnaw his lip and glare at him in glassy-eyed hatred. For a moment he felt guilty, as if he had kicked a helpless animal, but only for a moment, and then the rage he had felt for the past week came flooding back to wash away the guilt. The little prick deserved it.

He leaned forward again. "Let me assure you that I have no desire to see you fail because I have no desire to be permanently saddled with a ranch in Texas. Therefore I propose hiring a trail boss to drive this herd of soon-to-be-purchased cattle to Texas, and afterward to manage the ranch. It is the only sensible arrangement. Much as I dislike you, Samuel, and I believe the feeling is mutual, I will not allow you to degrade yourself to the level of a common herdsman. I believe fifty dollars a month will hire us a competent man who will enjoy the dubious rewards of tending cattle."

Samuel reared back in his chair. "I can manage my own ranch. There cannot be that much to it if an uncultured lout such as Goodnight can do it."

"You are confusing culture with competence, Samuel," remarked the Colonel dryly. "An error many a better man than you has made. You will be settling in what I understand is a mostly uninhabited land with which you are totally unfamiliar. You will not know the location of the water holes, rather essential information if you do not want three thousand cattle dying of thirst. I doubt that you would even know what constitutes a good range, or how often to move the cattle to prevent overgrazing. I doubt that you can swing a rope, a skill that I understand every trail boss and cowboy must master."

"I thought you were ignorant of ranching," said Samuel in a petulant voice.

"Ah, you misunderstood me. I never said I was ignorant, merely uninterested."

"I still don't want some unwashed lout running my ranch for me under your orders."

The Colonel raised his eyebrows. "I misunderstood you, Samuel. I did not realize you *wanted* to fail—which you will surely do without help. I did not realize that you did not want to own your own property independent of me. And I certainly did not realize you expected me to interfere with your endeavor. I shall try to accommodate you, but Pueblo is, I believe, some three hundred miles from where you will be. How I shall manage to order your every breath, I don't know. No railroads, no telegraph, no stage lines, not even a road of any description. I fear you are setting me an impossible task."

He watched Samuel mull over his words. Were it

not that he had given his word to Mattie, he would have ended this conversation long before now. As it was, he was driving a hard bargain, but not a devil's bargain. There was the faint, very faint, possibility that Samuel would succeed. Not that he had any intention of allowing Samuel authority over whomever he hired as ranch manager. This whim of his daughter's to encourage Samuel's insanity would entail no little expense, and he had no intention of losing money. On the other hand, he did not expect Samuel *or* Mattie to last more than six months, so he would require a good man to build up the operation so he might sell it at a good profit. There were more ways than raising cattle to make money out of a ranch.

"After thinking about it carefully, I have decided that your suggestion of hiring a ranch manager is a good one, Colonel. I am a neophyte cattleman, and an experienced man might be of some little help to me."

Samuel's voice was as prim as a spinster's and it surprised the Colonel how very much he disliked the mealymouth agreeing with him. A real man would have consigned him to the devil long before this. "I'm pleased you agree."

"Of course," continued Samuel, "the man would have to understand that he is accountable to me."

The Colonel grimaced. Any man that would agree to be accountable to Samuel would not be worth hiring even at fifty dollars a month. He would merely tell the man to pay lip service to Samuel, then do as he thought best. "I am certain any man hired would understand who was in charge."

Samuel scooted to the edge of his chair. "I think I should immediately find a competent trail driver. I shall ask Mr. Thatcher for recommendations. As a banker and a rancher, he should know of a good man."

The Colonel felt a brief alarm. "I don't know that I

A TIME TOO LATE

agree, Samuel. John Thatcher is a Colorado rancher, and he does not engage in trail drives. I think we need the advice of a Texan. In fact, I think we need the advice of the best stockman in this part of the country. I shall wire Charlie Goodnight for a recommendation, preferably the name of a man who already knows this Llano Estacado, or Staked Plains."

"But Mr. Goodnight is such a crude man," said Samuel. "How do I know that he won't recommend some equally crude man whose language and manners would offend Mattie?"

"Have you lost your mind, man? What cause would Mattie have to even be within hearing distance of a cowboy? She will have a home to look after and little Leon."

"Of course," said Samuel quickly. "I certainly did not mean to insinuate that I would allow my wife to actually socialize with cowboys, but I assumed that the manager might have occasion to report to me. I could, of course, send Mattie out of the room."

"That would be best, Samuel. We men must protect women against the rougher sorts." The Colonel stood up. "Then I take it we are in agreement? I will provide the capital, the ranch manager, whoever he is, will provide the expertise, and you will provide the supervision." At least until you come running back to Pueblo with your tail between your legs, bringing my daughter with you, added the Colonel to himself.

Samuel rose and held out his hand. "I believe we can shake hands on it like two southern gentlemen, Colonel."

The Colonel grasped his son-in-law's hand, felt the moist palm, and shook it quickly. "Then it is final. I will have the papers drawn up for our signatures and wire Goodnight at John Adair's office in Denver. If we are lucky, he will not have left for Texas yet and will reply immediately. When I hear, we will talk again. In the meantime go reassure my daughter that her Papa has played fair."

"Certainly, sir," said Samuel, hurrying to the door as if he were a boy just released from school.

The Colonel clipped the end off a cigar and lit it, satisfied with the way the conversation had gone. After all, hedging one's bets was not the same thing as being unfair. He pulled a piece of stationery from his desk drawer and began to compose a telegram. He had lied to Samuel only once that counted. He planned to pay the trail boss more than fifty dollars a month. Anyone fool enough to work for that kind of wage was too much of a fool for him to hire. He would offer seventy-five. That was a princely salary for a Texan. He should stay bought for that.

It was not until he received a reply from Goodnight some three days later, hand-carried by Goodnight's recommended trail boss, that he realized he might have miscalculated his payroll.

"Colonel," said Jubilee, poking his head around the office door. "There's a man here, says he come from Mr. Goodnight. He give me this letter. Says it's to you from Mr. Goodnight.

The Colonel took the letter and slit the envelope, puffing contentedly on his cigar. He unfolded the sheet of paper and began to read, nodding to himself.

Colonel Corley—

I read your telegram twice as I thought I had mistaken your words. They were the same the second time I read them. I told Molly you were pulling my leg, but she read the telegram and said you were serious. You are planning to invest in a ranch in the Llano Estacado to be owned by Samuel Hunter, and you wish to hire an experienced trail boss and manager. If Samuel Hunter is not planning to live on the ranch, your salary is generous and I can name several men. If Mr. Hunter plans to take an active part in the operation, you will have to offer more to keep a good man. I have sent you a good man. Jesse McDade is a former Indian fighter and Texas Ranger as well as the best trail boss in Texas. I will be sorry to lose him, although I might not. If you meet his demands, you will not regret a penny. If you do not, Jesse will continue working for me. I told him of your needs because Jesse is one of the squarest men I have known, and deserves an opportunity to earn enough money to set up his own outfit—which I am in no position to pay him. If you turn him down, anybody else you sign on will be second best. Good luck to you in your operation.

*Your Friend,
Charles Goodnight*

The Colonel laid the letter on his desk and chuckled. "Jubilee, that Charlie Goodnight is a smart old bastard."

"Yes, suh. I always thought he was a right smart man."

"Send in Mr. McDade, Jubilee, and call Mr. Hunter. Let's see how our two roosters will get along."

Jubilee frowned as he turned toward the door. "I don't know what Mr. Goodnight told you in his letter, but that Mr. McDade sure ain't no rooster."

The Colonel expelled a cloud of smoke toward his rose-wreathed ceiling. "Then what would you call him, Jubilee?"

"I'd call him a hawk, Colonel," replied Jubilee as he shuffled out.

The Colonel chuckled again. Darkies had lively imaginations.

"Colonel Corley? I'm Jesse McDade."

The Colonel jerked around, startled by the deep,

slow voice. The man walked like an Indian, so quiet he hadn't heard him step in the room. Disconcerted for the first time in years, the Colonel rose from his chair and held out his hand. "Mr. McDade, I'm pleased you could come on such short notice."

"If I hire on with you, Colonel Corley, I thought I'd best do it fast. If you want to trail a herd into the Llano Estacado, we need to start it moving by May. The grass is greening up and the rains will keep the waterings full. If we wait until June or later, it'll be harder on the cattle. Where we'll be going, it doesn't rain much, if at all, in the summer. The playa lakes will dry up. A thirsty herd can be more trouble than a pack of starving hounds after a single jackrabbit."

"I see you've already decided to work for me, Mr. McDade."

Jesse sat down in the chair in front of the Colonel's desk and crossed his legs, dropping his wide-brimmed hat over his knee. The Colonel noticed it was a Stetson and looked made-to-order at a cost of perhaps thirty-five dollars. Expensive headgear for a cowboy. "I said if, Colonel. I haven't sized up the situation yet."

"A cautious man, I see," said the Colonel, doing a little sizing up of his own. Jesse McDade was a tall man, at least six feet without his square-toed, high-heeled boots, and broad through the shoulders, tapering to a narrow waist and slim hips. He wore a plain blue pullover work shirt, three-button variety, with a round, fold-over collar, and a plain black vest. His big kerchief was also black and tied loosely around his neck. The Colonel noticed with disapproval that he wore a pair of those indigo-blue Levi's trousers but no suspenders. The four brass suspender buttons on the front of the trousers seemed to wink obscenely in the lamplight. The Colonel tried to remember if such a state of incomplete dress was common to Texans, but having spent his life ignoring them as much as possible, he couldn't recall.

A Colt .44-40-caliber pistol, preferred by many cowboys because it fired the same shell as the Winchester Model '73, nestled in an open holster. He really did not approve of an armed man in the house, but he sensed this man would sooner strip off his trousers than his gun. In fact, Jesse McDade seemed a mite too comfortable with his gun. It must be a holdover from his days as a Texas Ranger, since most cowboys the Colonel had observed wore their weapons as a necessity, but not as if their pistols were part and parcel of the whole man.

Jubilee was right; this man was no rooster.

The Colonel locked glances with the trail boss and felt a jolt of surprise. The man had silver eyes. Ridiculous, he thought. No one had silver eyes; they were gray. A pale, pale gray so luminous they looked almost like pearls against his sun-darkened skin. They were also amused, as if the man minded not at all being studied. His nerves must be made of the same grade steel as his pistol. Or else he was the most confident, mostcomfortable-with-himself man the Colonel had ever met.

And, the Colonel suspected, one of the most dangerous, because of that very self-confidence. When he decided to act, his judgment would not be clouded by self-doubt. This was a man with a shadow as goddamn long as Charles Goodnight's.

He was damn disconcerting!

Jesse smiled. Perfect teeth, the Colonel noticed. "Do I pass muster, Colonel?"

The Colonel flushed for the first time since '69 when Amanda had caught him with his britches off and the flap of his union suit undone. "Your hair is too long. It hangs down to your collar and over your ears. Is there a shortage of barbers in Denver?"

Jesse's smile disappeared, and the Colonel discovered just how cold gray eyes could be. Cold as a frozen stream in the winter. "You've not worked much on the plains, have you, Colonel, or you would know that hair protects the back of the neck and the ears when it's cold, and the damn wind feels like it's blowing straight off the ice. At least I don't wear it to my shoulders like Custer."

"Didn't give him much protection," snapped the Colonel.

"He cut his hair before Little Big Horn, Colonel. Maybe he lost his judgment with his hair."

The Colonel fell into a brooding silence as he stared at the man's curly black hair. A man with hair that curly ought to look sissy. Why didn't this man?

"Colonel, Jubilee said you wanted me." Samuel walked into the room, his eyes focusing immediately on Jesse.

"Yes, yes, Samuel," said the Colonel in a hardy voice that immediately embarrassed him. Damn McDade! Putting him out of countenance like that. "Mr. Goodnight has sent us a trail boss. This is my son-in-law, Samuel Hunter. Samuel, Mr. Jesse McDade."

Jesse rose with the grace of a man confident that his body would perform flawlessly whatever was asked of it. "Mr. Hunter, I'm pleased to meet you." He held out his hand.

Samuel ignored it, and Jesse's eyes flashed, like the sun reflecting off a frozen pond. Damn that little bastard, and Samuel did look smaller than usual next to Jesse, thought the Colonel. He's going to offend the best man for a thankless job, and Jesse McDade would take his valuable knowledge back to Goodnight. And he would lose money. The Colonel felt the sweat break out above his mustache.

"Have you told McDade what his duties are?"

asked Samuel as if all six feet plus inches of Jesse was not sitting less than two feet away.

"No, he hasn't," said Jesse in a slow drawl. "Why don't you enlighten me?"

Samuel looked surprised at hearing a word of more than one syllable coming from Jesse's mouth. "I expect you to drive a herd to Texas, three thousand head or so. I have already arranged to buy them from Mr. Iliff from Denver."

"You what!" yelped the Colonel.

"I have already arranged to buy the cattle," repeated Samuel. "I have not been cooling my heels since we last talked, Colonel. I have been busy. And my arrangements with Mr. Iliff's man were most satisfactory. Nearly half the herd are already carrying calves."

Jesse listened, his face expressionless, and held up his hand to stop Samuel. "A mixed herd is trouble, Mr. Hunter. The calves cannot keep up." He looked at the Colonel. "We have a choice. I can commission wagons built to carry the newborn calves. For that size herd, I will need at least forty wagons, especially reinforced to hold the calves. That means extra men to drive the wagons and load and unload calves for feeding, men I will not need when we arrive in Texas. Yours costs will be substantial, Colonel."

The Colonel blotted his forehead and silently cursed Samuel. "What is my other choice, Mr. McDade?"

"We cull out the cows due to calf in the next four months, sell them, and buy others. Or"—he hesitated, an expression of distaste on his face—"we shoot the calves on the bedding grounds. It goes against my grain to shoot calves. The mothers bellow until they're hoarse, and none of the cowboys feel too good either. There's always a certain amount of it to be done when you're driving a breeding herd anyway, because of the calves dropped prematurely. They can't survive, and we can't leave them for the coyotes and wolves to kill, so we do it ourselves. But nobody likes it, and I for damn sure don't want to make a practice of killing healthy calves. I push for culling the herd. Find somebody in the market for cows ready to calf. If you can. Arkansas River Valley's been overgrazed. Might not be anyone too interested in increasing their herd."

The Colonel looked over at Samuel, but spoke to Jesse. "Cull the herd, then. Your decision. And Samuel, we will defer to Mr. McDade on any further purchases. *Of anything!*"

"I haven't said I'm taking the job, Colonel Corley. I haven't finished listening to Mr. Hunter's list of my duties."

Samuel was pale, his vanity pricked. He cleared his throat. "You will be responsible for setting up our headquarters, build pens and barns and so on. Then we'll need to build the house, of course. Nothing large, six or eight rooms will be sufficient for the first year."

An expression of disbelief flashed across Jesse's face, but disappeared so quickly the Colonel wasn't certain he had even seen it. Jesse uncrossed his legs and leaned forward. "Mr. Hunter, the first duty of a ranch manager is to the cattle. All of our energy and money"—there was a slight emphasis on the word—"are spent on increasing the herd. We build enough of a shelter to eat and sleep in. If you are forced to sell up because you're losing money on the operation, nobody is going to pay a plugged nickel for a fancy house. Provided cowboys were carpenters in the first place, and trees were plentiful, which they aren't where we're going."

"Just a moment, Mr. McDade," said the Colonel. "I don't expect my daughter to live in a rough shelter with a crowd of lewd cowboys."

A TIME TOO LATE
107

Jesse's look made the Colonel feel as if he was pinned to his chair. "Your daughter? Mr. Goodnight never mentioned a woman."

"Then you advise against it?" asked the Colonel, his mood improving considerably. This was excellent. He would get rid of Samuel, but Mattie would stay home where she belonged. And there was always the chance Samuel would be trampled in a stampede.

"I guess you've heard it said before, but Texas is hell on horses and women. Takes a hardy woman to survive. Is your daughter hardy?"

"She is the finest example of young southern womanhood, gently raised and a credit to her family."

"That doesn't necessarily mean she's not hardy," said Jesse. "I'll size her up when I meet her."

"There will be no need for that, Mr. McDade. After listening to you, I have decided Mattie will not go to Texas. Do you agree, Samuel?" asked the Colonel, rubbing his hands together. Without Mattie to worry about providing for, he intended to scale down his investment in this enterprise considerably. And without his golden-eyed daughter sticking her pretty nose where it didn't belong, he could get by with it. No need to provide more than the bare necessities for survival. Mr. McDade obviously didn't expect it, and Samuel would have to learn to do without expensive luxuries. Might be the making of him. Although the Colonel doubted it.

Samuel hesitated, his blue eyes holding a speculative expression that put the Colonel on his guard. "I want my wife with me. We'll meet the challenges of Texas together. And I'm sure she would never consent to staying behind."

The Colonel ground his teeth together in frustration. He had underestimated Samuel. Weak and ineffectual and generally unsatisfactory as the younger man might be, he was not stupid. He knew that without Mattie along, he would be at the Colonel's mercy. He was right.

And Samuel was right in another respect. Mattie would never consent to stay behind. His only hope was that Jesse McDade would refuse to take her.

CHAPTER 8

The Colonel raised his voice. "Jubilee! Ask Miss Mattie to join us."

Jesse pulled out his bag of Bull Durham tobacco and papers and rolled a cigarette while he wondered about the exchange between the Colonel and Hunter. Goodnight had told him there were hard feelings between the two men, but he decided the stock grower had understated the case. Colonel Andrew Corley detested his son-in-law, and Hunter returned the favor. Jesse suspected that Corley also dismissed the other man as less than he was. Not that Samuel Hunter had demonstrated any common sense, good breeding, manners, or higher-than-average intelligence in the short time since Jesse had met him, but he sensed that the foppish young man possessed a chameleon personality and a streak of petty cruelty that the Colonel either overlooked or ignored. In the years since reaching manhood, Jesse had met many men like Samuel: weak, but with a tenacious desire to survive, gratify their desires, and see to their own comfort.

They were the toadies, the gamblers, the drunks, the sneak thieves, the bushwhackers, the liars, the cheats of the world.

Sometimes such men were more dangerous than the overtly evil.

Jesse had killed several such men.

He let smoke trickle out his nostrils and considered the problem of Samuel Hunter. He thought he could handle the man without resorting to thrashing him.

He wondered why in the hell Colonel Corley had given his daughter in marriage to Samuel Hunter in the first place. Surely a man with his wealth and reputation for shrewdness could have done better selecting a husband for his only daughter. The girl must be ugly as a mud fence.

"Papa? Jubilee said you wanted to see me."

Jesus, Joseph, and Mary! Jesse felt all the blood in his body rush to his groin and broke into a sweat controlling the strongest jolt of lust he had felt since he was a young boy fighting a penis that seemed to have a mind of its own whenever he saw an attractive woman. He grinned unwillingly. At thirteen, attractiveness wasn't a criterion. Woman was enough.

But he was twenty-eight and felt anger curl in his gut at his loss of self-control. And disgust with himself for his inexcusable reaction to a respectable woman. And a mother, he added as he noticed a toddler peeking from behind Mattie's skirts.

But she was most definitely not ugly.

"Mr. McDade, may I introduce my daughter, Mrs. Mattie Hunter."

Jesse heard the Colonel's words as if they were coming from a great distance, and he cursed himself again for his inexplicable vulnerability as he rose, stubbed out his cigarette in a glass dish on the Colonel's desk,

A TIME TOO LATE
111

and stepped toward Mattie. He held out his hand. "Mrs. Hunter, it's an honor to meet you. Mr. Goodnight speaks of you often." Actually what Goodnight had said was that Mattie Hunter was a "sweet little thing," which proved that either Goodnight was blind to the girl's more obvious attributes or that Jesse had been too long on the trail without release for the sexual passion he knew was as much a part of him as his gray eyes.

Mattie smiled uncertainly and held out her hand. "Thank you, Mr. McDade."

Jesse's eyes locked with hers, and he felt another stab of that damnable desire. Her eyes were gold. Like a cougar's. And so was her hair. He saw her catch her breath and frown slightly as if she had just recognized someone she had never expected to see. He bowed over her hand and kissed it, felt his nostrils flare as he smelled a faint scent of lilac water and rose petals. And woman. He resisted the impulse to open his mouth and touch her with his tongue.

He released her hand and stepped back, his face as impassive as he was capable of making it. "You're welcome, Mrs. Hunter."

Samuel Hunter would not be a problem, he thought.

Mattie Hunter would be the problem.

"Mr. McDade is Charles Goodnight's man," explained the Colonel. "He and I are discussing the possibility of his hiring on as trail boss and ranch manager."

Mattie smiled at Jesse. "If Mr. Goodnight recommends Mr. McDade, then I think we should hire him, Papa."

"Mattie! Your father and I will make that decision," said Samuel. "You have no inkling of what kind of a man we require."

Perhaps not, thought Jesse, watching Mattie's cheeks turn red with embarrassment at Samuel's reprimand, but she had sense enough to trust Goodnight's judgment, which was more than her husband and father seemed to do.

"You can see, Mr. McDade, that my daughter is unsuited to the rough life in Texas. She's far too delicate to survive its harsh demands," said the Colonel. "Besides, she has been ill and is under the treatment of a physician."

"You look healthy enough, Mrs. Hunter," said Jesse, refusing to speak of Mattie as if she was not present, and wondering why her father did.

Mattie's cheeks were even redder, and Jesse hoped the heightened color was due to anger. "I was recently plagued by headaches, Mr. McDade, but I assure you that I am fully recovered." She turned toward her father, but not before Jesse saw a flash of resentment in those golden eyes. "Papa, it was unfair of you to worry Mr. McDade with visions of being a nursemaid to a sickly woman. And you did give me your word to be fair."

Her father's jaw tightened. "My bargain with Samuel does not include risking your life on a cattle trail. It's out of the question. Not to mention how improper it would be for you to be alone on a trail in men's company. You would invite unwelcome attentions from the men."

"Not unless they want to be hanged," said Jesse.

"What did you say?" demanded the Colonel.

"I make my men sign an agreement before I ever move the cattle out. If any man shoots another over a falling-out, I stop the herd, hold a trial, and hang the survivor. Any man who approaches Mrs. Hunter with any motive other than the purest respect will be hanged." Mattie's face lost its color, and Jesse shrugged. "The men would expect it, Mrs. Hunter."

"It's horrible," Mattie said, closing her eyes for a second.

"A trail drive is not a Sunday-school picnic, Mrs. Hunter."

"She sees now how impossible her presence would be," remarked the Colonel.

"She can stay inside the wagon, Colonel," said Samuel. "There is no need for her to tempt the men."

Jesse felt the blood drain from his face again—but not to his groin. To his body. Which tingled with the need to beat Samuel Hunter, and yes, Corley, too. Until that moment he had been undecided whether to accept responsibility for Mattie Hunter or not. He doubted she could even imagine such a life of loneliness and hardship as she would endure for several years. But now he knew that he would turn down the job before he would leave this woman behind. At least on the drive and on the ranch she would have the one thing that neither her father nor her husband seemed able to give her in spite of their easy use of the word. She would have respect.

"Mrs. Hunter will come to Texas with us, Colonel Corley," announced Jesse, looking at Mattie. "And Mr. Hunter, she will be driving a wagon. Every able-bodied person on a drive works." He heard the Colonel's exclamation of protest, and a prissy murmur of triumph from Samuel, but he saw only Mattie Hunter's mouth curved in a smile, and sensed he had just taken the first step along a path from which it was even now too late to turn back.

He turned away to pick up his hat from his chair and saw the Negro servant standing unobtrusively against the wall staring directly at him. Jesse was surprised. Negroes seldom looked white men in the face and even less seldom made eye contact. He guessed no one had ever told Jubilee that because the man was doing both. He saw Jubilee glance from Mattie back to him, and realized the black servant was the only one in the room who had sensed his reaction to

Mattie and stood ready to protect her. Imperceptibly Jesse nodded, aware that he wanted this old man's understanding far more than he wanted the Colonel's, and Jubilee relaxed and raised his eyes to look over Jesse's head.

"Mr. McDade, I am not at all pleased with your decision," said the Colonel.

Jesse picked up his hat and turned it around and around while looking at Corley, whose angry expression bothered him not at all. "But you did say it was *my* decision to make. Now, if Mr. Hunter has finished listing my duties, at Mr. Goodnight's suggestion I'd like to have a minute of your time, Colonel Corley. As the principal investor in this enterprise, you have, I assume, the authority to discuss my terms of employment."

"The salary is fifty dollars a month," announced Samuel.

Jesse cocked an eyebrow. "Mr. Hunter, I don't saddle my horse for fifty dollars a month. A laborer is worth his hire, and I am worth a good deal more than that."

"I don't allow arrogance from the help," said Samuel. "Perhaps you should understand that at the outset."

"But I am not the 'help' yet, Mr. Hunter."

The Colonel got up, nearly knocking his chair over in his haste. "Samuel, escort Mattie and Leon upstairs, and wait for us in the parlor. Mr. McDade, would you care to join us for supper?"

"Colonel, I don't think we need to keep McDade that long," said Samuel.

"Thank you, Colonel Corley. I'd be glad to stay for supper. I haven't had a meal that didn't feature beans as the main course in a while." Jesse took perverse pleasure in thwarting Hunter.

"Samuel, Mr. McDade and I will see you at supper.

Mattie, you better put that baby to bed before he annoys Mr. McDade."

Jesse hunkered down to face the tiny boy, who had been tugging on his trousers. He took Leon's hand and shook it gently. "Hello, Master Hunter. Have you come to sign on as a cowboy? You might have to grow a little."

Mattie swooped down and picked up the baby. "I'm sorry, Mr. McDade. I hope Leon didn't soil your, er, clothes. Babies always seem to have sticky hands."

"No harm done, Mrs. Hunter." He smiled at Leon, who smiled back, showing six pearly teeth. "Oh, Mrs. Hunter," he said to Mattie's back as she turned away. "Get the boy some trousers. They're more practical on the trail than those dress-looking outfits womenfolk seem to think little boys ought to wear. And have several pairs of shoes made for him in varying sizes. We won't be near any boot makers where we're going."

"Aren't there any at the nearest town?" asked Mattie.

Jesse pulled out his tobacco and proceeded to roll another cigarette to hide his surprise. Evidently no one had bothered to tell Mattie Hunter anything about what she would be facing. "Fort Elliot is a hundred twenty or thirty miles away, and the nearest town worth calling that is two hundred or more, and we won't go there but every six months or so." He took no satisfaction in her look of shock.

"Jubilee, pour Mr. McDade and me some bourbon. Negotiating business is dry work," said the Colonel as soon as the door closed behind Mattie and Samuel. "You'll have to excuse my son-in-law. His enthusiasm for stock growing has gone to his head. He's a mite uncivil at times because of it."

Jesse sat down again and stretched out his legs, crossing them at the ankles. "Colonel Corley, I work around bullshit every day. I've learned to recognize it.

Mr. Hunter reminds me of a man whose daddy didn't take him to the woodshed often enough when he was a youngster. I'll tell you straight that I won't take orders from a man like that, and you won't find a cowboy worth his salt who will, even if you offer a hundred dollars a month. You want a ranch established in the Panhandle, and you want it to make money. I can do that for you, but I want a free hand. I hire my own men, and I fire them when I need to. No one questions my orders, and no one questions my decisions. That's hard country, and it needs a hard man. I'm a hard man. I may guess wrong once in a while, but I'll take the responsibility for it." He pulled a folded paper out of his pocket. "Here is a contract stating my terms of employment. You pay me twenty-five hundred dollars a year in salary, and a bonus equal to half the value of the ranch I help establish at the end of five years."

"That's outrageous!" yelled the Colonel, slamming his fist on the desk. "I can hire Goodnight himself at that price."

Jesse shook his head. "No, Charlie would take a third of the land and throw Mr. Hunter off the ranch in the bargain. I'll handle Mr. Hunter, and I won't shame him in front of the men unless he forces me to, but he will sign the same agreement about fights and liquor and gambling on the drive that all my other hands do. A man can cuss all he wants to, but I don't want any drunks and no gambling, at least not for money. Both cause trouble on a trail drive, and Mr. Hunter's pregnant herd will cause enough without any help from John Barleycorn."

The Colonel toyed with an inkwell, then looked up at Jesse. "I'll pay you your first year's salary, buy the herd and all the supplies, plus twenty-five thousand acres. After the first year, your salary and all operating expenses comes out of the proceeds. If you don't make money, Mr. McDade, you don't get paid, but you still abide by the five-year contract."

"Twenty-five thousand acres isn't enough, Colonel Corley, not if you want to safeguard your investment. I recommend you buy one hundred fifty thousand acres and get an option on another one hundred fifty thousand to be bought the next year. And you authorize *me* to contract with the surveyors and the speculators that hold the certificates on the public land. I'll buy up all the water and any odd piece of land that some two-bit outfit might want to stake a claim on in the middle of the range we control."

Jesse thought Corley's eyes were literally bugging out of his head. "Good God Almighty, McDade. I don't want to buy the whole goddamn state."

"There'll be plenty of Texas left over."

"All I want is a decent-sized ranch I can sell at a profit when my son-in-law gets tired of this latest idea of his."

"In other words, you will hold the title to the ranch?" asked Jesse.

"My financial arrangements with my son-in-law do not fall into the scope of your responsibilities, Mr. McDade."

"I'm proposing to spend five years of my life working for you, Colonel. I don't intend to do so if you're planning to sell up the minute Mr. Hunter decides he prefers the city to the ranch. So suppose you lay out your cards and tell me what your contract with your son-in-law is. It may be in conflict with my best interests, in which case I'll finish my drink and catch the train back to Denver."

"Just a minute, Mr. McDade. Don't be so hasty. I'll tell you my arrangements with Samuel so you'll see that they will not injure you in any way."

Jesse listened and decided the Colonel was diabolical. Five years to pay off an investment at nine percent. Those were harsh terms. Meeting the terms would keep a ranching operation strapped for cash at a time it was most needed. Either Samuel Hunter was a fool for accepting such terms, or he had no choice. There was more behind this venture than Samuel Hunter's urge to be a cattle baron, and Jesse wondered what it was. Not that he could let it matter. Working for the Colonel was his best chance to accumulate enough capital to start his own operation without going into debt to bankers.

He let smoke trickle out his nostrils while he considered. "I will check with Mahlon Thatcher tomorrow, Colonel, but I believe that you must pay me half the market value of the ranch regardless of whether it has earned enough profit to pay back your investment or not. My bonus is independent of your arrangement with Mr. Hunter. However, I will add a clause stating that if you sell before the end of the five years, I still get my bonus regardless of what is still owed you on the venture. However, as I see it, Colonel Corley, it is in your best interest to stick it out for five years whatever Mr. Hunter does or does not do. I will endeavor to earn back your investment in the five years, but not before. I do not intend to work for Mr. Hunter, bonus or not, contract or not. Are these terms agreeable to you?"

The Colonel nodded. "Have you ever read for the law, Mr. McDade?"

"I always preferred honest work, Colonel Corley, although my father was a lawyer and he provided me with the knowledge to protect myself against his fellow professionals before my education and his life was ended by the war."

"And now you're a cowboy?" said the Colonel with a rising inflection that turned the statement into a question that asked more than the words implied. It was a suitable compromise between the southern tradition that demanded to know a man's family history, and the western code that held a man's past to be his own business.

Jesse deliberately ignored the Colonel's invitation to explain himself. The idealistic, ragged sixteen-year-old boy who pushed a wheelbarrow loaded with the only possessions the carpetbagging tax collector would allow him and his grandmother to take from the plantation his grandfather had built in East Texas had died somewhere along the road to survival, and Jesse McDade, Indian fighter, Texas Ranger, and now trail boss, had risen from his grave. It was a common enough story in Texas after the war, but it was his own story and he didn't intend sharing—particularly with a man he suspected had jettisoned even more idealism on his own path to survival than Jesse had. At least the man that sixteen-year-old boy had become had kept his honor, even though it was threadbare in places and patched in others. The price of survival was the loss of innocence. Jesse could live with that.

"Now, shall we return to the matter of how much land to buy?"

"Shall we go directly to the point instead, Mr. McDade? How much is this empire going to cost me?"

Jesse closed one eye and appeared to do some mental arithmetic for the Colonel's benefit. Actually he had already calculated the minimum capital required. "The land is going for anywhere from twenty cents an acre to a dollar and a quarter, depending on what a man can negotiate. Let's figure on one hundred thousand dollars, Colonel, not including the price of Mr. Hunter's cattle, which, by the way, I am certain he paid too much for. Mr. Iliff is a square shooter and so are his men, but I suspect Mr. Hunter paid the first price quoted instead of bargaining. I'm only guessing, of course. I could be wrong."

"I doubt it, Mr. McDade," said the Colonel, swabbing his face with a now-damp handkerchief. "One hundred thousand dollars. That is an immense sum of money."

"I heard you paid forty thousand—in cash—to build this house and another fifty thousand to furnish it. All you have to show for all that money is one house on one city block."

"This is a damn fine house!" shouted the Colonel.

"So it is, Colonel. But wouldn't you like to build something that matters, something that grows and flourishes—and turns a profit—instead of owning a pile of rock that's good only for other folks to admire? Wouldn't you like to create something where there was nothing before?"

The Colonel looked over Jesse's shoulder, and the younger man could sense the challenge pulling at him. Finally he nodded. "You'll have your hundred thousand, Mr. McDade, and I'll take every penny out of your hide if you cross me."

"Fair enough. And if you cross me, I'll kill you." Jesse put out his cigarette and accepted a drink from Corley's servant. "Thank you—Jubilee, isn't it?"

"Yes, suh. When is you all planning to leave for this here place?"

"Jubilee, goddamn it, that's none of your business," said the Colonel, his face still a little pale from the effect of Jesse's words.

"As close to the middle of May as I can make it," replied Jesse. He lifted his glass in a toast. "God willing and the creek don't rise."

"Jubilee, bring the decanter over here, then go hurry the cook along. You keep listening to Mr. McDade here, and you'll be thinking you're worth more money, too."

The old man shuffled out, but not before he cast Jesse another direct look that the younger man would swear was one of admiration.

"So do we have a bargain, Mr. McDade?" asked the

Colonel, pouring himself another drink, then offering the decanter to Jesse.

Jesse put his hand over his glass. "I spent too many years on the trail where a clear head made the difference between waking up in the morning or being buried in a shallow grave with rocks piled on top to keep the scavengers from digging you up. Moderation has become a habit."

"Have you no vices, Mr. McDade? Does nothing tempt you?"

Jesse thought of Mattie. "Yes, but I resist."

"About my daughter, Mr. McDade."

Jesse controlled his urge to stiffen and carefully kept his face bland. "Yes, Colonel Corley?"

"Why did you agree to take her?"

"Because a woman is a gentling influence, and gives a man something to work for besides himself. And I thought her presence might moderate her husband's behavior." And I felt sorry for her, he could have added, because the only person in this whole damn too-big, too-cold house who really seemed to care about her was an old Negro servant. And a hardcase trail boss named Jesse McDade, who ought to know better.

"Why did you agree to let her come?" he asked curiously.

The Colonel hesitated, his eyes focusing on something Jesse sensed wasn't really there. "Let's just say I don't want Mattie to be a hero and leave it at that." He kicked back his chair. "Shall we see what's holding up supper?"

Jesse had been in bigger dining rooms, but he had never been in one so luxurious. He was certain that the furniture had been custom-made for that particular room and no other because each piece matched not only other every other piece, but also the woodwork. A huge silver-plate chandelier hung over the middle of the table, and Jesse pitied the servant whose duty it was to polish it. The table settings reminded him of endless afternoons spent with his grandmother while she patiently explained the uses of eight different pieces of silver to an impatient and uninterested ten-year-old. He was glad now for her etiquette lessons, since apparently Samuel Hunter had expected him to eat peas with his knife and make a bib of his napkin. He wondered how Samuel would take to eating beans from a tin plate and sopping up the juice with a sourdough biscuit.

"Samuel, when will we be leaving? I need to set the servants to packing. I thought they could begin with the silver and china and linens while I decide what clothing we will need immediately and what Papa can send later. The furniture, of course, will be the last thing. Papa, I think I'd best leave my piano. It's so heavy and awkward, and would probably be out of tune after such a trip."

Jesse dropped his fork and chipped the bone-china plate. "Furniture?"

Startled, Mattie looked at him. "Yes, Mr. McDade. Furnishing a small home in the wilderness requires careful planning. I will need to know the size of the rooms, though, in order to know which pieces to take. I hate overcrowded rooms. Samuel, will you have time to order the wagons, or shall I ask Papa to do it? I think fifteen should be enough."

Jesse looked across the table at Samuel. "Didn't you tell her?"

Samuel's face took on a sullen expression. "I don't intend to live in a one-room log cabin."

"You won't," said Jesse. "Because there aren't any trees. Or not very damn many, except along the Canadian River, and my cowboys won't be wasting their time chopping them down and hauling them out of the river bottom. You and Mrs. Hunter will live in a dugout until we get settled enough to waste time building a house with a parlor."

Samuel's sullen expression changed to one of horror. "A dugout? A hole in the ground?"

"A one-room hole in the ground, about ten by fourteen feet if I think we can spare the time to dig one that large. Remember, I have to build shelter for my cowboys, too," said Jesse. "And Mrs. Hunter, forget your fancy furniture. The blistering heat in the summer and the freezing winds in the winter will ruin it, and you can forget your silk dresses while you're at it. You'll have no place to wear them. You and Molly Goodnight will be the only white women in the entire Panhandle. And you can forget your fifteen wagons. My cowboys are needed for herding cattle, not driving wagons full of gewgaws. We will take four wagons. You may have two, provided you and Mr. Hunter drive them."

"I won't live in a hole in the ground!" repeated Samuel in a shrill voice.

"Samuel and I can't live in one room!" exclaimed Mattie. "Our beds won't fit."

"Your baby's crib won't take up much room," Jesse pointed out.

"I mean Samuel's and my beds," explained Mattie.

Jesse cocked one eyebrow. So the Hunters didn't sleep together, and judging by his expression, it was a custom Samuel didn't care to change. The man must have no blood in his veins. If Mattie Hunter was *his* wife . . .

"One bed, Mrs. Hunter, a table to eat on and prepare food, some chairs, one of those kitchen safes with the bin for storing flour, a small cabinet for dishes, and a cook stove. Although you could do with less and survive, I think we could manage to haul at least that much in two wagons along with whatever personal items you think you can't live without. The rest of the space will be filled with a year's supply of staples—flour, coffee, and such like—extra clothes, and tools."

"See here, Mr. McDade," said the Colonel, rousing himself from his brooding silence. "I don't think you understand. Mattie is a lady."

"Hush, Papa. This is a disagreement between Mr. McDade and myself."

Her eyes were brilliant with anger, and Jesse felt himself respond in kind. "A disagreement is a difference of opinion, Mrs. Hunter, and Texas does not care about your opinion. The land will not change to fit your conclusions about its nature. And neither will I. I have told you what you may expect, and why it will be impossible to provide you with anything better. A tantrum will not change anything." He dropped his napkin on the table and pushed back his chair. "Colonel, thank you for supper, and now I'd better find a room and turn in. I want to check Mr. Hunter's cattle tomorrow and start hiring men, beginning with a cook. Good food keeps down trouble."

He walked out of the room, carrying a disturbing picture of Mattie Hunter's angry, panicked eyes.

He was halfway across the entrance hall when a low voice stopped him.

"Mr. McDade, suh?"

He turned around to see Jubilee step out of a hall that he supposed led to the kitchen. "Yes?"

"If you is looking to hire a good cook, I'm a good cook. I took care of the Colonel's needs plenty of times when we was prospecting, 'fore he decided there was more money in selling supplies to other prospectors and holding their pokes for them."

"I don't think Colonel Corley would appreciate my hiring his servant behind his back, Jubilee," said Jesse, ready to dismiss the idea out of hand.

"It don't matter what the Colonel thinks," said

Jubilee with that same direct look Jesse had seen before. "I is free. I can hire myself to anybody I wants to. I'm going to Texas with you, and if you don't hire me, I'll trail along behind you. Either way the Colonel's gonna have a conniption fit, so you might as well have a good cook."

Jesse rolled a cigarette while he thought about the old man's offer. "Why are you so determined to go to Texas, and how did you know I needed a camp cook?"

"I listened behind the door," said Jubilee. "I needs to keep up with what goes on in this here house, and sometimes listening at doors is the only way I have."

"That answered one question, but not the most important one: Why do you want to go to Texas?"

Jubilee lifted his chin. "Somebody gots to look out after Miss Mattie."

"Miss Mattie!" exclaimed Jesse.

Jubilee nodded. "Yes, suh. That husband of hers too busy looking after himself to worry none about her, and her daddy don't see what's as plain as the nose on your face."

"And what would that be, Jubilee?"

"She ain't no china doll to be sit on the shelf until it's time for folks to see her. One of these days she gonna find that out for herself, and I 'spects I better be there to keep her from hurting herself when she does."

Jesse lit his cigarette and blew out the match, dropping it in his pocket out of habit. A man didn't take chances starting a prairie fire. "Let her find out, Jubilee, even if she hurts herself in the process. I don't have the time to bother with a china doll, and neither does Texas. And I can't spare my camp cook to play nursemaid to a spoiled girl nor cater to her myself."

"You're a hard man, Mr. McDade."

"And your Miss Mattie had better turn into a hard woman, Jubilee, or she won't survive."

Jubilee shook his head. "Folks don't like hard women."

"Where we're going, it doesn't matter. There aren't any folks except a few Mexican sheepherders." Jesse stopped as an idea occurred to him. There might be a way to cater to Miss Mattie and get himself a ranch headquarters better than a dugout at the same time. Of course, it would cost the Colonel a little more money, and it might give Miss Mattie Hunter the idea she had won an argument. So he wouldn't tell her yet. Let her prepare for the worst—because the worst was generally what you got in the Panhandle.

CHAPTER 9

Looking from the trunks and boxes that stood with lids and tops gaping open like tiny birds waiting to be fed, to the piles of folded undergarments, bed linens, towels, toilet articles, shoes, and dresses that still remained to be packed made Mattie's shoulders and back ache and her breath short. Perhaps she should accept Aunt Patty's suggestion that she leave off her constricting corset and wear a wrapper. But there was something so decadent about wearing such loose clothing in the late afternoon that she had shied away from taking the servant's advice.

"Did you pack your sewing kit?"

"Yes, Aunt Patty, I packed a sewing kit."

"You got enough needles and thread?"

"Yes, Aunt Patty. I have enough needles and thread to sew uniforms for the entire Confederate army. I have *two* thimbles and *two* pairs of scissors, pins, extra buttons, dress patterns for dresses I refuse to make. I won't wear those ugly, shapeless Mother Hubbard things."

"Considerin' you ain't never made a dress in your life, I figured you needed to start with something simple. And practical. You don't need no corset or bustle, and you'd look like a fish out of water wearing them things in a dugout anyway. And you better take the trains off them dresses you're packing 'cause dragging a train across a dirt floor is just gonna make it filthy."

Mattie stared at the other woman as though she had suddenly taken leave of her senses. "Leave off my corset? No lady appears outside her front door without a corset. It isn't decent!"

Aunt Patty tucked a bolt of yellow-flowered calico in a trunk. "Long as you got on your chemise and drawers and maybe a petticoat, you're decent."

Still reeling from Aunt Patty's suggestion that a corset was not the underpinning of basic morality and shield against loose behavior, Mattie pointed to the bolt of material. "And I won't wear calico."

"Then make your husband's shirts out of it."

Mattie gasped. "Samuel would never wear calico shirts! He wears linen."

"The time may come when he's glad to have a shirt, never mind what it's made from. Now, I packed you bolts of calico, gingham, wool challis, printed cotton, flannel for the winter, cambric for collars, muslin for lining your bodices, except you can use your scraps for lining if you have to." She ticked items off on her fingers. "Now, did you throw in that darning egg I give you?"

"Yes, but I've never darned socks."

"Don't matter. I figure you'll learn when the time comes. It ain't hard. Plenty of women not as quick as you have learned it. Now, what's slipped my mind?"

Mattie sank down on the stool in front of her dressing table. "A seamstress? A maid?"

Aunt Patty gave her sharp look. "Don't you be snippy with me, Miss Mattie. You'll be thankful enough one day for all these things I'm telling you." She snapped her fingers. "Aprons! I knew I was forgetting something. I made you some aprons, plain ones for everyday, and a fancy gingham with cross-stitch around the hem for Sunday best. Lady needs to dress special on Sunday even if there's nobody special coming for dinner and the nearest church is a hundred miles away."

"Aprons?" asked Mattie, her mind grappling with the idea of wearing a garment she associated with maids and cooks. She didn't believe she had actually worn one since she put her hair up and her skirts down. An image of herself in a silk dinner dress and covered up in Aunt Patty's gingham apron slowly took shape in her mind, and she started laughing. It was that or cry, and if she allowed herself to start crying, she might not be able to stop.

"I'm not funning with you, Miss Mattie. A woman needs to gussy herself up on Sunday."

Mattie stopped laughing. "Do you think God will care in a dugout?"

"Ain't just for God. It's for you, too. Reminds you that you're good for something besides cooking and scrubbing and wiping a youn'un's nose."

"Maybe I had better dress as if it was Sunday everyday. I'm good at that. It's the other six days that frighten me." Her hands started to shake, and she clasped them together in her lap. "I can't cook except to make a lemon pie, and cook always cleaned up when I finished. I've never scrubbed anything. I direct the maids to do it. Ever since you started packing house goods, I've been trying to remember if I've ever even used a broom. I don't think I have. I'm like the girl in the nursery rhyme, Aunt Patty, I can sit on a cushion and sew a fine seam—provided it's fancy embroidery or needlepoint—but I can't make myself a dress."

She leaped up and began pacing. "All my life I've known exactly what was expected of a lady of my station. I've known what was appropriate dress for the afternoon sewing circle. I've known never to wear my rings over my gloves. I can write a polite thank-you note or an invitation, keep the household accounts, select the week's menus, spy dust on the furniture or tarnish on the silver and reprimand the proper person, count the linen in the closet and jars of spiced peaches in the pantry, but the most ignorant darkie can polish the floor, and I don't know if I can."

She paused by the trunk to finger the bolt of calico. "When I was a little girl, my mother did for me. After she died, you did for me, you and the nine servants that work in this house. I knew when I woke up in the morning what each day would bring. I knew to put on a morning dress, then change into an afternoon dress in case of visitors. I poured tea and asked whether my guests preferred one lump or two. I listened to Papa in the evening and entertained his guests at the piano. I attended church on Sunday and discussed the minister's sermon on Monday."

She plucked a dress pattern out of the trunk. "Now I'm told that I am not to be the Mattie Jo Hunter I've always been, that I was raised to be, that I know how to be. Now I'm to be a leathery woman in a shapeless dress who lives in a house with a dirt floor and wipes her baby's nose with the hem of her apron. 'Don't bother to pack your silver tea service, Mrs. Hunter. No one will be coming to tea. You can't bring your writing desk, Mrs. Hunter. There is no room in the wagon. No silk dresses, Mrs. Hunter. There will be no one to see them.'" She dropped the pattern back into the trunk and faced Aunt Patty. "If I hear one more word from Mr. Jesse McDade about what I cannot do or cannot bring or cannot expect, I shall slap his face. I shall wear silk if I wish. I shall hold fast to what I've been taught, to what I am. I see no reason to lower my standards just because I'm moving to a rough shelter."

Aunt Patty smoothed a scraggly lock of hair behind her ear. "So that's why you're having this fit."

Mattie whirled to face her. "I am *not* having a fit!"

Aunt Patty tucked the pattern back where it belonged. "Don't know what else you'd call it. You been as snappish as an old dog with a sore paw, fighting with McDade every chance you get. If you ain't arguing over that dugout, it's something else. The fact is, he don't treat you like every man you've ever knowed does, and you don't know how to handle it. He don't act like you'll break like your daddy does, and he don't think you're worthless like your husband does. He tells you how the cow ate the cabbage, then stands back to let you figure out how to cook the cabbage and milk the cow, and you're scared you can't do it, so you hang on to acting like a lady in the parlor 'cause that way if you fail, you figure you'll have an excuse. Mr. McDade don't appear to me to be the type of man to let you get by with that."

"You planning to drive that team of mules holding a parasol, Mrs. Hunter?" asked Jesse, cupping his hands around a match to light his cigarette.

"Are you objecting, Mr. McDade?" asked Mattie, tilting the object in question to peer at the trail boss. He sat astride his sorrel gelding with the grace of a man who, if not born on a horse, took up riding shortly thereafter. It was not enough to say that he seemed part of the horse, she thought; it was more as if the horse was part of him, a Pegasus of the range.

Jesse blew out his match and dropped it in his pocket. "No objections at all, Mrs. Hunter—as long as you don't hold up the trail drive by wrecking the wagon and killing yourself because you can't control the team. Funerals take time and leave a pall on the spirit." He grinned. "Wouldn't do much for your spirits either. That is, if you didn't die right away. Lingering wears on a person."

Mattie swallowed. "I—I'm certain that won't happen. You're just trying to frighten me. This is a well-trained team of mules. Papa bought them because they were particularly gentle."

Jesse arched one eyebrow and looked at her father. "That true, Colonel?"

Mattie saw her father shift uncomfortably on the hard wooden wagon seat. He cleared his throat. "The gentleman who sold them to me assured me that a lady would have no trouble with this team."

Jesse dismounted, dropping the reins so they hung loosely to the ground in what Mattie knew was a ground hitch, something only a man supremely confident of his mastery over an animal would do. He sauntered over to the team and examined the lead mule's mouth, then ran his hand down the backs of the other five animals. He stepped back, his face that cold impassive mask that Mattie had learned to hate because she was never sure what thoughts it concealed.

Jesse readjusted his Stetson to a slight tilt over his right eye. "Your lead mule has a mouth like leather, and the others have healed scars under their winter coat. This was a freighter's team, and a hard-used one at that. I'll trade it for the team pulling the supply wagon. I bought them. Mrs. Hunter will at least have a fighting chance controlling them." He looked up at Mattie. "But not with the parasol. If you lose the reins trying to hang on to that bit of silk, you lose the team.

A TIME TOO LATE

If you lose the parasol and it blows near the cattle, it might frighten them."

"And we can't have that, can we, Mr. McDade?" asked Mattie, feeling more and more ignorant, useless, and foolish.

He shook his head. "No, ma'am. Frightened cattle stampede and somebody is liable to get hurt—perhaps you." Jesse turned to look at the milling cattle that covered at least a half mile of valley floor like a loosely woven carpet of multicolored hide. "You see, Mrs. Hunter, in spite of their sizable horns and mostly spotted hides, these cattle are not pure-bred Texas longhorns. They have a strain of shorthorn in them which makes for better beef cattle and a sweeter disposition. But they may have lost certain traits that make longhorns for all their cantankerousness a good breed to trail. A longhorn has a strong sense of self-preservation. A longhorn will turn aside to avoid running over a wagon or a rider. These mixed-blood cattle may not. They may run right over your wagon and scatter pieces of it and you all over the trail." He turned back and looked at her from those piercing gray eyes. "Get rid of the parasol, Mrs. Hunter. Or I will."

"See here, McDade," said the Colonel as he looped the team's reins around the brake lever and climbed off the wagon. "I've had enough of your high-handed remarks. My daughter's a lady. You must make some concessions for her delicate disposition."

"Better your daughter's nose be blistered than be smashed by a hoof, Colonel Corley," said Jesse, his voice as brutal as his words. He dropped his cigarette and ground it under his heel, his eyes never moving from the other man's. "Perhaps I failed to make my position clear. A trail boss is a tyrant. He has to be. He is responsible for the safety and well-being of several men and several thousand animals. What he says, goes. He is the final authority, and to steal a term from the legal profession, there are no appeals of his rulings. If you were trailing along on this drive, Colonel, you would be subject to my orders just as surely as the horse wrangler is. The fact that you owned the cattle would make no difference."

Jesse turned toward the herd again, his face taking on a brooding, dark expression. "This is not the boardroom or the drawing room. It's a trail drive. When we move out the herd tomorrow, we leave all the written laws behind and ride into a world of our own making. It's harsh and dangerous, makes no compromises, no exceptions, and it doesn't give a damn about delicate dispositions."

He gathered his reins and mounted the sorrel with the smooth bunching of muscles that left Mattie with a hollow feeling inside. She closed her eyes, and images of nude, muscular bodies of Greek gods and heroes from her long-ago art class took on shadowy life and danced against her closed eyelids. They all looked like Jesse McDade.

Jesse turned his horse and pointed toward the far side of the herd. "You and Mr. Hunter pull your wagons over there by Jubilee's. And stay at least a half mile from the herd. I don't want you spooking them."

"Damn Jubilee!" exclaimed the Colonel, a queer note of hurt in his voice. "Leaving me like that after fifty years. And damn you, McDade, for hiring him behind my back."

Jesse rested a gloved hand on his thigh and held his reins loosely in the other, the lazy pose of a man not inclined to defend himself or seeing the necessity of doing so. "He asked for a job and convinced me he was qualified. I hired him. And I tend to think that fifty years at the beck and call of another man is long enough. Maybe Jubilee thought so, too. Besides"—he cast a quick glance at Mattie—"I think he's as worried about Mrs. Hunter's delicate disposition as you are. I'm willing to allow him to watch out for her—as long as it doesn't interfere with his duties." He tipped his hat toward Mattie. "Mrs. Hunter, I'll see you at supper tonight unless you're planning to cook your own meals for yourself and Mr. Hunter."

Mattie managed a polite smile in spite of her panic and wondered how long she could conceal her inability to cook. She hoped long enough to pick up at least the rudiments from watching Jubilee. "My husband and I will join the others for supper, Mr. McDade. We wouldn't want to be an exception."

Jesse's mouth quivered as though he were about to smile, and Mattie felt disappointment all out of proportion to its cause when he didn't. "You are welcome, Mrs. Hunter. Colonel, I'll give you the final tally of the herd at supper, go over our final arrangements, and obtain Mr. Hunter's signature agreeing to my rules on the trail."

"Don't you want my signature?" asked Mattie. "I wouldn't want to *disobey* your orders out of ignorance."

Jesse's mouth quivered again. "As a gentleman, Mrs. Hunter, I'll accept your word that you won't drink, fight, or gamble for money. You may curse if you feel the need and it doesn't violate your notions of how a lady should behave."

"Mr. McDade! A lady never uses profane language under any circumstances."

"A *lady* doesn't often have occasion to drive a mule team, Mrs. Hunter." He nudged his horse into a lope and rode away, trailing soft laughter behind him.

Mattie snapped her parasol closed and threw it into the back of the wagon, narrowly missing the pallet where Leon lay napping away the fatigue of the five-mile drive from Pueblo. "He is the most vexatious man, Papa. I don't know how I shall tolerate his ungentlemanly behavior."

The Colonel lit a cigar, blew out his match, started

to toss it on the ground, hesitated, and tucked it in his waistcoat pocket instead. "Then forget all this nonsense about going to Texas and come back home with me tomorrow morning. Let Samuel go. A trail drive is no place for a woman. You're as useless as a fifth wheel on a wagon. Samuel likely is, too, but at least he is a man and better able to live in such immodest company. He lacks the special needs of a lady." He blushed and avoided her eyes as he climbed back on the wagon, unwound the reins, and slapped them on the mules' backs.

Mattie blushed, too, and looked straight ahead, horribly embarrassed by her father's oblique references to certain unmentioned and unmentionable topics. Ladies had to fight skirts and petticoats and drawers to sit when answering nature's call; gentlemen faced none of those encumbrances and had the freedom of standing—at least for their most frequent needs. There were also her monthlies. Aunt Patty had packed a plentiful supply of the soft white cloths needed, but there remained the problem of washing them and hanging them out to dry without the men observing and guessing their function. Mattie shuddered at even the possibility of that occurring and thought of the beautiful home she was leaving behind, where such tasks were relegated to other hands.

The Colonel slapped the reins again. "What do you say, Mattie? Shall I tell McDade I'm taking you home?"

Mattie looked across the half mile that separated her from Jesse McDade. A haze of dust from the hooves of three thousand cattle was beginning to dissipate as the animals stood quietly on their bedding ground, and she had no difficulty picking Jesse's form out of the several riders surrounding him. Just as she did he shifted and looked back at her wagon. She felt his glance as though he had touched her breast.

"I won't be going back home, Papa. It's too late."

"Samuel can live without your holding his hand, Mattie. Might even do him some good." He slapped the reins again and cursed. "That damn McDade was right about these mules."

Mattie silently blessed the stubborn animals. Without their recalcitrant behavior demanding her father's attention, he might have noticed her face lose all its color when it suddenly occurred to her that she had not thought of Samuel at all when deciding not to go home.

The following morning, her eyes gritty from too little sleep and her stomach unsettled by Jubilee's breakfast of salt pork, sourdough biscuits, dried prunes, and coffee, Mattie clutched Leon and fought her urge to succumb to an attack of the vapors. Sinking gracefully into oblivion would at least allow her to escape, if only for a little while, from the noise of bellowing cattle, the pungent smell of fresh manure and the thousands of flies it attracted, the rising puffs of dust, the confusion, and her own sense that her life was a garment slowly unraveling. Already she felt the seams parting to reveal parts of herself she could not explain. She felt as though the Mattie Jo Hunter she knew would soon stand naked, clutching tatters of cloth about her and fearing to examine her own heart.

"Mattie?"

Startled, she looked around to see her father mopping his face, then the inside of his planter's hat with a white linen handkerchief. His trousers were dusty and one leg bore the unmistakable hoof print of a mule. "Yes, Papa?"

"I have your misbegotten mules hitched up, although I doubt the wisdom of your driving a team of such spawns of the devil."

"I shall manage, Papa."

"Don't talk foolishness, Mattie. Of course, you cannot manage. I spoke to McDade about it this morning," the Colonel continued. "But he refused to release one of his cowboys and further refused to delay until I could hire a driver. It seems the herd has grazed out this area and must be pushed on. Were it not that I foolishly signed a contract with the young man, I would withdraw my support of this enterprise. As it is, I find myself in the position of continuing or losing my investment. However, I shall get around Mr. McDade. When he realizes the impossibility of a woman like you driving a team of mules, he will be forced to provide for you. He will have no other choice. In fact, I suspect he has already planned for such a contingency. I doubt that he has any more confidence in your abilities than I do."

"He said that?" asked Mattie, shifting Leon to her other hip and suddenly wondering why Jesse McDade's opinion mattered more than her father's.

The Colonel evaded her eyes. "Not in so many words."

"I believe I said that you wouldn't last an hour in that getup, Mrs. Hunter."

Mattie whirled around at the sound of Jesse's slow drawl. The trail boss sat on his horse, casually rolling a cigarette and watching her from those expressionless silver eyes. She felt a childish urge to scratch them out. "My 'getup' is my business, Mr. McDade, and it is most ungentlemanly for you to mention it."

"You interrupted a private conversation, McDade," added the Colonel.

Jesse ignored the Colonel. "I am certain your attire is suitable for riding a Pullman car to Denver for a few days' shopping, Mrs. Hunter, but your bonnet fails to protect you from the sun, and that train on your dress will only catch on all manner of objects. I suggest you adopt a garment our Texas women have found most suitable. I believe it's called a Mother Hubbard."

"I will dress according to my station," replied Mattie, her face turning hot with embarrassment. Never did she imagine she would be discussing clothes with a man not her husband, and certainly not in public.

Jesse shrugged. "Suit yourself, Mrs. Hunter. Some people have to learn the hard way." He turned his attention toward her glowering father. "Colonel, I have arranged for Squinty to take care of Mrs. Hunter's mules."

"The man driving the supply wagon?" asked the Colonel. "What good will a man with only one leg be to my daughter? I fail to see why you hired him in the first place. You need able-bodied men."

"Squinty lost his leg in the war, Colonel. He didn't lose his usefulness. He manages better with that wooden leg than most men do with two good ones." Jesse tipped his hat. "Say good-bye to your daughter. We're ready to leave. Mrs. Hunter, follow Jubilee." He rode away without looking back—as if he were so confident of his orders being followed that he didn't think it was necessary to check.

The Colonel's chin quivered for a second, and Mattie saw his eyes tear before he wrapped his arms around her and Leon. The little boy patted his grandfather's cheeks and smiled. Mattie rubbed her forehead against her father's waistcoat and fought to swallow the sobs that seemed lodged in her throat. Her chest filled with a black emptiness, as though part of her had passed out of her body, leaving space to be filled.

"Papa, I'll be all right. I'll manage."

"Yes, suh, Miss Mattie will be fine, Colonel," said Jubilee, walking up, an unfamiliar figure in his denim pants, a dark flannel shirt, and boots very much like Jesse McDade's. But unlike the trail boss, Jubilee didn't look at home in his clothes. He looked like an impostor, Mattie thought suddenly. Just as she and Samuel did. They were all pretenders traveling to a land that had no use for pretense. She shivered as she wondered what would happen to them all when the game of make-believe ended.

The Colonel kissed Leon, then blew his nose on his sweat-stained handkerchief. "Don't talk to me, you worthless, disloyal darkie. To think I gave you my name only to have you run away to Texas."

Jubilee looked at the Colonel with that straightforward expression in his eyes that Mattie had first noticed so long ago. "I'm going to Texas 'cause now I gots family there."

"What family?" scoffed the Colonel.

"I reckon if my name's Corley, then I got Miss Mattie."

Mattie felt her father's hand shake as he stroked her hair. "Get out of here then, and good riddance. I never could stand an uppity nigger." He kissed Mattie and abruptly turned away to mount his horse.

Mattie thrust Leon into Jubilee's arms and hurried toward father. "Papa," she began, but stopped at the sight of his face. Colonel Andrew Corley had aged in the space of a few seconds. Lines and grooves she had never noticed before scored his cheeks and the area around his eyes, and he appeared shrunken, as though some part of him had disappeared.

Her chest and throat began to burn again with tears. "Papa, I—I'm so sorry. I wish I could stay, but I can't."

The Colonel leaned down from his horse and kissed her cheek, then straightened to look at Jubilee. Mattie saw the master and his ex-slave lock glances for one long eternity until the Colonel finally looked away, an expression of grief in his eyes. "God damn Texas! What the war didn't wrest away from me, that godforsaken state has."

He wheeled his horse around and rode back toward Pueblo.

CHAPTER 10

Mattie wiped her eyes and tucked her handkerchief in her pocket, glanced over her shoulder to make sure Leon was playing happily in the back of the wagon, and picked up the reins. Her corset dug into her belly and she felt her tight-fitting bodice bind underneath her arms. She ignored both. A lady was used to discomfort. Clothes, after all, were designed for style and to flatter one's figure, not for comfort.

She slapped the reins as she had watched her father do. Other than wiggling one ear, the lead mule ignored her. She slapped the reins harder and once more was ignored. She felt a trickle of sweat roll down her forehead and her hands inside her buckskin gloves were moist and sticky. Carefully she laid the reins down beside her, retrieved her handkerchief, and blotted her forehead again. She yanked her bonnet forward to shield as much of her face as possible from the newly risen sun, and picked up the reins again. She saw Jesse waving his hat to signal the cowboys to start the herd moving, saw the chuck wagon with Jubilee sitting comfortably on its seat jerk forward, and felt a rising desperation.

"Please!" she called to her mules, and slapped the reins. The lead mule flicked his tail at a fly, but otherwise didn't move. She saw Jesse looking toward her and felt tears blur her eyes. She would *not* let him see her defeated by a bunch of four-legged animals.

Looping the reins around the brake lever, she scrambled off the high wagon seat. She felt her train catch before she heard the ominous rip. She tumbled to the ground, landing on her belly and knocking herself breathless. Gritting her teeth, she controlled her urge to writhe on the ground like a snake, and lay facedown until she could draw a breath. Before she could push herself up on her knees, a pair of hands grabbed her under the arms and pulled her to her feet.

"Mattie! Damn it, I told you not to wear that dress! Are you hurt?"

Even if she had not recognized the voice, slow and deep and mellow, Mattie would have known without looking up that Jesse McDade was holding her. No man she knew smelled of that particular blend of tobacco, leather, sweat, and what she thought of as "savage man" when she allowed herself to think of such personal traits at all. He smelled *clean*. Almost everyone else she knew, whether man or woman, depended on scented soaps, perfumes, colognes, and hair pomade to cover their natural odor. Sometimes, at a crowded party, Mattie would excuse herself and step outside just to breathe air untainted by the smell of perspiration soaked dresses and suits. She knew that the upper classes were not supposed to sweat, but anyone who truly believed that had never attended a dance in mid-July.

But however clean Jesse McDade smelled, he was

still a male unrelated to her and was holding her in a far too intimate fashion. "Mr. McDade, I believe you said 'suit yourself.' And you may release me. Nothing is injured but my pride, and I fear you are holding me in a most improper manner."

Jesse released her as though she had suddenly burned him. A flush stained his cheekbones. "My apologies, Mrs. Hunter. I was more concerned with your safety than with propriety."

Mattie was uncertain whether she was more embarrassed by Jesse's witnessing her ignominious landing, or by her own indelicacy of calling attention to the fact that the heels of his hands had been digging into the sides of her breasts as he gripped her under the arms.

Unable to meet his eyes, she brushed at her brown skirt, now hopelessly dusty. "It is quite all right, Mr. McDade. I appreciate your concern, but there was no need to endanger your life by riding over here so quickly. I was just climbing down to talk to the mules when I fell."

Jesse gripped her elbow and turned her around. "Let me help you back on the wagon, Mrs. Hunter, and I'll see to the mules."

Mattie twisted away. "If I am to manage, I must do my own talking, Mr. McDade." She looked up to catch him studying her with a speculative look.

His lips twitched. "Certainly, Mrs. Hunter."

Straightening her shoulders, Mattie walked by the team until she stood in front of the lead mule. Grabbing his ear, she pulled his head up. "Listen, you four-legged, misbegotten, flea-ridden, *damn* mule. When I slap the reins, I expect you to move! If you do not, I shall most probably borrow Mr. McDade's pistol and shoot you. Do you understand?"

The mule opened his mouth and brayed. Mattie swallowed hard to keep from gagging. She had not expected its breath to smell quite so foul. "Thank you very much."

She nodded her head at the mule and walked back toward Jesse, her head held at the regal angle she practiced when walking into a ballroom. She noticed her train, carefully folded, lying on the wagon seat, and felt herself turn crimson. She had not remembered that her whole backside might be exposed to Jesse McDade and the elements. She preferred the elements.

Jesse leaned against the wagon, rolling a cigarette. "Don't worry. You have no reason to feel embarrassed."

Mattie covered her cheeks with her hands and closed her eyes. She felt as if her entire body was feverish. Not only had Jesse McDade touched a part of her even Samuel had the decency not to trespass upon or even look at, but he knew entirely too much about women's clothing and he was far too intuitive about her thoughts. At least he was too much of a gentleman to mention out loud that her petticoat was now showing.

She opened her eyes and lowered her hands. "Thank you again, Mr. McDade. Now, if you will excuse me, I believe I am holding up the drive."

She turned to the wagon and grasped its side, steeling herself for the arduous climb to the seat, when she felt strong hands seize her waist and lift her up in the air. Gasping with shock and embarrassment, she awkwardly tumbled onto the seat. Taking a deep breath, she picked up the reins. "I must insist you remember yourself, Mr. McDade. Your methods of help are most improper."

"And I suggest you remember where you are, Mrs. Hunter. What is improper at one of your tea parties is likely to be practical on a drive. As you pointed out, you are holding up things. My intent was to get you back on your wagon and moving in the fastest possible manner. Lifting you up rather than allowing you to take another tumble if what is left of your train caught on the wagon seemed the best way to accomplish that. Don't read into my actions more than is there."

Mattie blushed again, wondering why she could not seem to control either her thoughts or her tongue. A proper lady would never have mentioned that she noticed Jesse's touching her, or else would have screamed and swooned. All she had managed to do was embarrass herself and offend the trail boss. She turned her head to look at him. "I apologize for implying that you were taking liberties, Mr. McDade. I have more experience with tea parties than cattle drives, and I can only plead unfamiliar circumstances."

Jesse nodded. "Perhaps you should work on sorting out the two in your mind, Mrs. Hunter." Gathering his reins, he mounted his horse. "I wouldn't care to be hanged by my men because you accused me of being disrespectful."

Mattie caught her breath at the image of his tall body turning slowly at the end of a rope. "Then perhaps my husband should see to my well-being in the future."

Jesse's mouth twisted. "Your husband saw you fall, Mrs. Hunter."

She clenched her hands more tightly around the reins. "Samuel was feeling unwell this morning. He might have felt unable to tend to me."

His tall body tensed and she felt his eyes watching her. "What was wrong with him? I noticed he ate no breakfast."

"A headache," replied Mattie, avoiding looking at him and slapping the reins. The wagon lurched ahead as the mules strained against the harness, and Mattie laughed with triumph and relief.

"I can drive a mule team after all, Mr. McDade. In spite of what you and my father thought." She turned

A TIME TOO LATE
to look at him, and caught a bemused expression in those gray eyes.

He smiled at her, and she almost gasped. She had always known he was a handsome man, but not until now had she realized he also possessed a masculine charm. She suspected the combination could be dangerous.

"Unlike your father and your husband, Mrs. Hunter, I never doubted you. I would have bet money on you against any mule team."

"Why?" asked Mattie curiously.

Jesse's smile disappeared as he studied her face. "Instinct, Mrs. Hunter—the same instinct that urges me to check on your husband's condition. Any man so ill as to fail to come to his wife's aid must be near death."

Mattie turned to stare over the mules' heads at the back of Jubilee's chuck wagon. "I don't think that will be necessary, Mr. McDade. Samuel found that the soup Jubilee fixed last night disagreed with him. I'm certain he's feeling much better." It would not do for the trail boss to discover Samuel had hidden two cases of her father's best bourbon in his wagon, and that he had drunk himself to sleep in her wagon after exercising his husbandly rights in spite of her reluctance. After avoiding her since Leon's birth, she didn't understand why he had chosen last night to break his abstinence. She had lain stiff and aching beneath him, fearful that the men sleeping near their wagon would hear his mumbled words and coarse sounds.

Afterward she had felt soiled and confused.

"The son-of-a-gun stew gave your husband a headache?" asked Jesse.

"W-what?" she asked, jerking her head to stare at him. The charming man who smiled at her was gone. In his place was the man with the hard face and eyes.

"You said your husband had a headache. Now you

say last night's supper upset him. Which is it, Mrs. Hunter? A headache or a bellyache?"

Mattie squeezed her eyes closed as a crescendo of pain hit the right side of her head for the first time since Samuel had decided to go to Texas.

"Mattie?"

Mattie opened her eyes and fought to keep from swaying. "I don't care for your personal questions, Mr. McDade. Samuel is none of your concern."

Jesse shook his head. "You are a loyal wife, Mrs. Hunter, but a very poor liar. Your husband's reputation proceeded him." He turned his horse and loped off toward Samuel's wagon.

Mattie pulled up the mules and tied the reins around the brake lever. She could not let Jesse McDade confront Samuel. Even though Samuel was in the wrong, she must protect him from such an unequal contest. It was her duty as his wife. His loyal wife.

Scrambling down from the wagon, ripping off the lace trim on one cuff in the process, she lifted her skirt above her shoe tops and began running toward Samuel's wagon. She felt what was left of her train catch on a bush and stumbled clumsily from side to side as she jerked it free. She panted for breath as her corset seemed to squeeze her lungs more tightly with every step. A catch in her side sent her to her knees in an attempt to ease the pain. A gust of wind caught her bonnet and sent it rolling across the valley floor toward the herd.

"Oh, God, no!" she screamed, staggering to her feet to chase the bit of straw and grosgrain ribbon. Her ankle twisted as she stepped on a rock hidden in a clump of grass, and she sprawled on the ground. Pushing herself to her knees, she looked up to see the bonnet tumble between the hooves of the moving cattle. She froze in terrified awe as three thousand cattle almost in a single instant became a maelstrom of deafening sound and thunderous movement. Mattie clapped her hands over her ears and cowered on the ground as the bellows and pounding hooves and clashing horns blended together in an unearthly roar like nothing she had ever heard. A dozen thunderstorms could not equal its sound. Infrequently she heard a higher-pitched scream as an animal stumbled and those behind ran over it, their sharp hooves churning it into a pulp of blood and bone and gristle. The dust billowed up until it seemed to Mattie that the haze reached as high as the clouds. In the midst of the brown pounding hell Mattie saw the cowboys, their mouths hanging open in soundless screams, riding next to the mindless, stampeding cattle, swinging coiled ropes and slowly, almost imperceptibly, turning the herd to the right. She opened her mouth to loose her own soundless scream as she realized she was crouching directly in front of the herd's new path.

And so was Leon!

Her baby was in the back of the wagon, too small to escape, and too young to know that he should. Sobbing with a fear so immense she knew she would never experience its like again, Mattie stumbled up and began running toward her wagon, staggering drunkenly as she labored to breathe. Her chest felt encased in iron as her corset became a vise that threatened to suffocate her. When another vise wrapped itself around her chest and jerked her up across a saddle, she emptied her lungs of air in a scream she could hear over the hellish thunder of the herd.

Within seconds she found herself tumbling onto her wagon seat, and immediately tried to scramble over the back of the seat to pick up a screaming, cowering Leon. She felt herself jerked back as a hand grabbed her skirt. Screaming, she kicked desperately at whoever was keeping her from her baby. She felt her foot hit something, but her blow didn't prevent her captor from flipping her around and slamming her down on the seat, imprisoning her legs with his knee and gripping both wrists.

"Mattie! Mattie, listen to me!"

She heard the voice, saw the gray eyes, now the color of thunderclouds, above the black bandanna covering his nose and mouth, but Jesse McDade was just another devil inhabiting the hell that was her world. "My baby!" she screamed. "You're keeping me from my baby."

Jesse lowered his face until his cheek touched hers and his lips behind the bandanna blew against his ear. "You may hate me tomorrow, Mattie, but if you want to save Leon's life and your own today, you must do exactly as I say. Your wagon is in the way of a stampede. I don't know if we can turn the herd in time. You have to drive the wagon straight north until you leave the herd behind."

"I can't!" she cried.

He released her hand and caught her chin, turning her face toward his until her lips brushed the bandanna. "You must!"

"I can't, Jesse. Drive me, please!"

He stilled, his only motion the gentle stroking of his thumb over her cheek. His gray eyes seemed to turn molten silver as he stared at her, so close she could count the individual eyelashes, feel his breath, hot and tobacco-scented, against her lips.

"I can't do it for you, Mattie. I have to turn the herd into a mill, a circle, or it may break and run in any direction. It may even turn north. If it does, you cannot outrun it. Your only chance to save yourself is for me to stay behind. I've turned stampedes before. I can do it again. I'm the best trail boss there is. Charlie Goodnight said so."

A TIME TOO LATE
She sensed he had smiled behind his bandanna. "But Leon. I have to hold him."

He shook his head. "You can't drive a running team and hold a baby, Mattie. Leon will have to stay in the back of the wagon. He will be frightened and unhappy, but he will survive. That's what's important. Survival." He released her and helped her sit up, then untied the reins and handed them to her. "Be careful. Keep your eyes on what lies ahead of you so you can avoid rough spots. I don't intend saving you from a stampede only to have you hurt if the wagon turns over." He jumped down and vaulted on his horse.

"Jesse, the stampede is my fault," she said, her voice quivering.

"Finding fault can wait." He lifted a coiled rope from around his saddle horn. "Hang on to those reins. I'm going to slap your lead mule where it will do the most good. He's ready to run anyway. In fact, I'm surprised he hasn't already. A stampede spooks every animal."

Jesse's arm came down and Mattie winced as his hemp rope cracked against the mule's hindquarters. With a bray of anger the gray mule broke into a run, and Mattie felt her arms almost jerked out of their sockets as the team pulled against the reins. She heard the arm seam of her bodice rip, felt the whalebone corset pinch her waist, and braced her feet against the floorboard of the wagon. She swayed from side to side as the wagon bucked and lurched behind the mules, the squeaking sound of its iron wheels swallowed up by the hellish noise behind her. Mattie held tight to the reins and prayed.

She was still praying after what seemed hours later, although she had no idea how much time actually had passed, nor did she know how far she had driven. She only knew neither she nor the mules had any strength left to run. She sat slumped on the wagon, her elbows propped on her knees, her head hanging down. Her bodice was now ripped under both arms and split down the back where the seam had given way when she had sawed on the reins to turn the team to avoid a small boulder. She felt the wind on her bare shoulders, knew her corset and the top of her chemise were exposed to anyone who might happen to ride by, and didn't care. She had lost half her hairpins, and wavy thick locks of hair tumbled over one shoulder and down to the wagon seat. Her undergarments and bodice were soaked with perspiration and she stank. Of dust, of sweat, of fear—and fear had its own smell, an acrid, unpleasant odor. Where are the tea parties now, Mattie? she wondered as she lifted her head to watch her foam-specked team lapping water from the small stream that ran close to the valley walls.

She supposed she was killing the team by driving the wagon into the stream and letting the mules drink all they could hold, but she had no other choice. She had not the strength or the knowledge to unhitch them—and they had to have water. Just as she did, she realized as she licked parched, dust-caked lips with a tongue that felt swollen to twice its size. She tied the reins to the brake lever, her fingers so stiff she could hardly bend them, and slid off the wagon into the hip-deep icy water.

Gasping and shuddering from cold, she waded to the front of the team and grasped the lead mule's bridle. "Come on, boy, time to get out before we both catch pneumonia—if mules can catch pneumonia." The mule balked, and Mattie jerked on the bridle. "Don't fight me now, you damned animal. I may strangle you with my bare hands and leave your carcass for the wolves."

Whether the mule believed her or just decided in his breed's stubborn unpredictable way that he wanted out of the stream, he started to move. Guiding the team up the shallow bank, Mattie heard a wail from Leon as the wagon's front wheels rose higher than the back ones.

"Let Mama tie up the team, Leon, and I'll take you out of the wagon," she called, her voice hoarse from dust and sobs and prayers. Once the wagon reached level ground, she ran back, loosened the reins from the brake lever, dragged them over the team's backs, and tied them to a tree in such a knot she knew she would never be able to undo it.

And still she hadn't managed to outrun the sounds of the stampede. She thought there must be no quiet anywhere in the world. The pounding, bellowing herd lay just beyond her sight, although small bunches of cattle had run past the wagon almost from the moment Jesse had slapped her lead mule.

With wet skirts slapping against her legs, Mattie walked back to the wagon and hauled herself up with arms that ached with every movement. Leon wrapped his tiny arms around her legs, his sobs jerking the frail body. Mattie sank to her knees and gathered the wet, soiled little boy into her arms and rocked back and forth, laughing and talking while the tears flowed down her cheeks.

"We're alive, Leon! We survived, just like Jesse said we must." She stopped, jerking her head up to stare blindly at the white canvas top of the wagon. She had called the trail boss Jesse. She had done it before—when she was fighting him on the wagon seat. And he had called her Mattie. The circumstances excused such lapses of propriety, of course, so this eerie sense of some boundary crossed was merely fatigue and thirst.

After gathering up towels, and a dry diaper and clean clothes for Leon, Mattie climbed out of the back of the wagon. Her own filthy garments could wait until after she saw to Leon's needs and drank half the water in the stream. Then she must wipe down the mules. Perhaps if she dried their sweaty coats, they wouldn't sicken. They might not anyway, but she had no way of knowing. Then she must feed Leon and eat something herself—perhaps some of the dried fruit that Aunt Patty had packed. Or a slice from the loaf of light bread she had brought along and had planned to add to the evening meal—a celebration of the first day on the trail. Leon would have to do with the bread and a cup of water.

By the time she had fed Leon, wiped down the mules with the tattered remnant of her train, washed her face and as much of her body as modesty allowed, since she could not remove her clothes and bathe in the stream like an unchristian savage, Mattie crawled into the wagon and collapsed onto her pallet. Exhausted from fear and sobbing, a clean and sweet-smelling Leon lay curled up asleep beside her. Mattie undid several buttons on her bodice and thought vaguely of removing it and her skirt, but knew she lacked even the minimum strength required to lift the lid of a trunk to find clean clothes. She would do it later. First she would rest.

"Cows are runnin', boss!"

Squinty's yell had ripped away Jesse's single-minded anger as if it were a lace curtain, and he had cursed himself for sparing even a moment's attention from the herd. He'd known Mattie Hunter would be trouble from the moment he first saw the golden-eyed beauty in her father's office, long before she troubled his sleep and distracted his mind. But he could no more have stopped himself from galloping to her when he saw her fall than he could stop the sun from rising in the east. She was burrowing under his skin like a sand flea, and he found himself enjoying scratching the itch. He enjoyed her prim talk and her modest, ladylike demeanor, particularly since he suspected both traits were self-imposed, defenses against a world that expected such behavior from its girl children.

Her eyes gave her away.

When she defied him, argued with him, her eyes sparkled as though sunlight was trapped in their depths, color surged beneath the honey skin, and her body quivered as if her spirit was ready to burst free. Other times, when her husband was present, her eyes were shadowed with confusion like a child trying to please. And she was still very much a child, Jesse reminded himself, still trying to fit the pieces of herself together in such a way as to please both herself and others. In Mattie's case, he doubted that was possible. He sensed a will in search of a purpose within her, and such women seldom gained the world's approval.

But at any rate, the puzzle of Mattie Hunter was causing him more trouble than he had anticipated. He should never have left his place with the herd. He knew how easily a herd spooked at the beginning of a drive, knew, too, how important it was that he set an example. He could not ask more of his men than he was prepared to give. Instead, he had rushed to a woman's side and then had intended to search her husband's wagon for the liquor he knew must be hidden there. Liquor on a cattle drive was suicide, even if the drunkard was not a cowboy. Jesse cursed himself again as he admitted he was using the liquor as an acceptable excuse to confront Samuel. His real reason was neither acceptable nor respectable. He had slept near Mattie's wagon last night, had heard Samuel commit what amounted to a rape of his wife, and wanted to beat the man senseless. Only the knowledge that marriage was sacrosanct had prevented him from bursting into the wagon and dragging Samuel out.

Jesse had no respect for a man who couldn't elicit a loving welcome from a woman, and could not imagine what joy there would be in forcing one's own wife.

Wheeling his horse, he had ridden for the front of the herd with his most experienced hands following him. As cattle stampeded, the fastest and strongest always pushed to the lead. If the cowboys could swing the leaders in an arc, the others would follow, and soon the swiftest animals would catch the slowest at the tail of the stampede, and thus throw the herd into a mill, a circling whirlpool of animals a half mile wide. It was a tactic he had seen Charlie Goodnight use, and it was one he himself had used. With luck, with good men and horses, the tactic would work this time, too, and perhaps without too many injured men and animals. At least it was daylight and the riders could see what obstacles lay ahead. Most stampedes happened at night when a cowboy might ride into ravines, gullies, boulders, or over cliffs, without ever seeing his danger. Invariably, though, someone would be trampled. Jesse had never seen a stampede that somebody's horse didn't step in a badger hole, or a gopher hole, and break its leg, throwing its rider off. A cowboy in a stampede without a horse was almost always buried afterward, or so badly injured that he might never ride the cattle trail again.

Most cowboys would rather be dead.

It was not until Jesse had succeeded in veering the leaders to the right—and he had never seen a herd circle to the left—that he'd seen Mattie rise up from the ground. Without a thought for the herd, his responsibilities, or his life, he had raced his horse past the panicked cattle and ridden Mattie down, scooping her up across his saddle with a strength he doubted he would have had if his fear had not been spurring him as hard as he spurred his gelding. He didn't regret manhandling her on the wagon seat. It was necessary because he had not the time for gentle explanations. He told himself it was also necessary to press his face against hers, that she would not have been able to hear him otherwise, but he knew he lied. He had grasped the opportunity because it was there and acceptable, given the circumstances, and he might never have the chance to be so close to her again.

That still did not excuse his almost kissing her through his bandanna, his lips so close to hers he could feel her panting breath heating his mouth. That was inexcusable, and he still cringed when he thought about it. He had shamed her and himself. If his men and Samuel Hunter ever found out what he had done, they would shoot him without thinking twice. He laughed. His men would shoot him. Samuel would not. Samuel Hunter didn't give a damn. He had even begged off riding out to search for Mattie's wagon when the stampede was over.

"I'm ill! I was ill this morning before the stampede—which I have no doubt you are responsible for. Surely you can't expect me to ride over hell and gone looking for my wife. She knows I'm ill. She wouldn't expect it."

"Don't suppose she does," remarked a young dust-streaked cowboy whose carrot-colored hair had earned him the moniker of Red. He spat out a stream of tobacco juice that barely missed Samuel's boot. "I reckon she knows which side her bread's buttered on. Probably buttered it herself. Starve to death if she waited for you."

Samuel drew himself up. "See here, cowboy, you can't talk to me like that."

Red lifted his hat and wiped his sweaty forehead on his sleeve. "I reckon I answer to Jesse. If I thought otherwise, I'd draw my pay and ride back to Pueblo."

"Give him his money, McDade," ordered Samuel. "I have no intention of permitting such disrespect."

"Catch a little sleep while you have the chance, Red. You need to relieve Mac in a couple of hours."

Red nodded. "I'll do that, Jesse. Smell's a little bad around here anyhow. I need to find a little fresh air."

Samuel grabbed Jesse's left arm. "I told you to fire him!"

Jesse drew his gun and rapped the barrel across Samuel's wrist. "Don't ever grab a man, Hunter, without giving him warning. It's a good way to get yourself killed. Get back in your wagon and quit bothering my men. I'll ride out to look for Mrs. Hunter, and you better hope I find her in good health. Otherwise . . ."

Samuel flushed. "Otherwise what, McDade? My wife is no concern of yours and you had best remember that. I saw you rush to her aid this morning like a dog sniffing after a bitch in heat."

Jesse slid his gun back in its holster and turned away, grinding his teeth together to keep from losing what little control he had left. He gathered his reins and rested his foot in his stirrup before glancing back at Samuel. "Did you ever worry, Hunter, about what will happen to you if she ever decides that her place is wherever the hell you aren't?"

Samuel smiled. "Of course not. I'm her husband. She has no choice."

Jesse swung his leg over the saddle and turned his horse toward the north. "There are always choices, Hunter. If we're willing to pay the piper." He urged his horse into a gallop while there was still light.

Jubilee caught his bridle as he rode past the chuck wagon. "Mr. McDade, let me go with you."

Jesse shook his head. "You don't ride worth a damn, Jubilee. Besides, you're the cook. The men need to be fed worse than I need the company. Don't worry. I'll find her."

"I 'spects you will, but you see to it that you gets

her back here before it gets too dark. It ain't proper for you and her to be out late."

"You must have heard Hunter's remark, but rest your mind."

Jubilee looked toward Samuel's wagon. "I heared him, and I knowed it long 'fore he saw anything. You and Miss Mattie rub up against one another the wrong way just to see the sparks fly. I don't want neither one of you to get burned."

Jesse flushed. "I would never endanger Mrs. Hunter's reputation or honor, and I entertain no improper thoughts toward her."

Jubilee chuckled. "If you got anything in them pants besides your underwear, then you got thoughts. I ain't seen a man what gets close to Miss Mattie that don't. Except the one she married and her daddy and me. But I don't worry much about thoughts. Reckon sometimes they just pop into a man's head when he don't expect them. I just worry about them thoughts leading a man into acting disrespectful. I might have to kill him if he did."

Jesse laughed reluctantly. "Are you her guardian angel?"

"Just remember what I said."

Jesse leaned over and clasped Jubilee's shoulder. "If Mattie is ever really harmed, it won't be by me. I care for her." He heard his own whispered words, admitted their truth, admitted also the shame of them, for he felt the hunger of his own passion and knew it was inseparable from his caring.

"I knows that, too, and I feels sorry for the both of you." He squeezed Jesse's hand. "You go find Miss Mattie, and if she ain't alive, I'll kill Samuel Hunter myself. I figures I'll have to do it someday anyhow."

Jesse straightened up. "Hush that kind of talk, Jubilee. A man in your situation can be hanged just for speaking of killing a man."

"I reckon so. Some folks think just being a nigger is good 'nough reason to hang a man, but that won't stop me if the time comes." He stepped back and slapped Jesse's horse on the rump. "Get along with you now. I reckon my girl child is good and scared by now, wondering if anybody's gonna find her."

CHAPTER 11

Jesse found the wagon less than five miles down the valley. He marveled that Mattie had been able to come so far. For a young girl more used to pouring tea than driving a team of mules, she was quite a woman.

"Mattie?" he called softly as he dismounted, not wanting to frighten her, and to give warning in case she was in the bushes tending to a personal need. No one answered except a mule, which raised its head and snorted. The small grove of trees by the bluff was nearly silent except for the distant thunder of the herd, now slowing and quieting as exhaustion claimed them.

"Mattie?" he repeated, drawing his gun and quietly circling the grove to read sign. The wheel ruts and muddy shoe prints told their own story, and he holstered his gun and walked to the back of the wagon to part the canvas flaps and peer in.

He saw her palms first, soft and white and brutally

blistered. Some had ruptured, leaking a mixture of clear fluid and blood that dripped down the sides of her hands as she slept.

"Dear God," he whispered, climbing into the wagon to kneel beside the exhausted sleeping woman. He saw her discarded gloves and turned them inside out to see smears of blood and tiny slivers of skin. Her blisters must have broken, re-formed, and broken again until her palms stuck to the buckskin. He swallowed at the thought of how much pain she must have suffered stripping those gloves off.

He cast the gloves aside and looked again at Mattie. She lay on her back, her arms curled limply above her head, exposing tiny swirls of golden hair underneath her arms where her sleeves had ripped almost completely loose from her dress. He stared at the tender flesh of the underside of her arms. Soft flesh. Woman flesh. No hard muscles like a man's. How had she driven a hard running team of mules nearly five miles?

He looked at her face next. It, too, was blistered. Damn woman and her silly bonnet, he thought, suddenly angry with her. Maybe next time she would listen to him. He wanted to wake her up and rave at her, wanted also to gather her up in his arms and kiss her sunburned skin. He wiped his palms on his pants and closed his eyes for a second. He had not the right to do either.

He opened his eyes and leaned closer, greedy to look at her and ashamed of himself for taking advantage of her in such a manner. She was defenseless in her sleep, and if he possessed any honor, he would climb out of the wagon and call her name until she awoke. He picked up a lock of her hair instead and wound it around and around his hand, marveling at its warmth and color until his own yearning frightened him. Drawing on a strength of character he would have sworn he did not possess, he unwound the lock and laid it gently on her breast. His eyes drifted over to the partially unbuttoned bodice and his breath wedged in his throat. The skin above her chemise was the color and texture of ivory satin. Soft, beautiful, fragile, tempting.

And forbidden.

Averting his eyes, he reached out and curled his hand over the top of her shoulder and shook her gently. "Mattie, wake up."

Her eyelids quivered and she moaned in protest. "No, don't want to."

Jesse squeezed her shoulder again. "Mattie, it's over. I came to take you back."

Her eyes opened, dull gold with shadows, confused and frightened, a child's eyes. He watched the child in her grow to the woman as confusion changed to awareness and memory. "Jesse?"

His hand moved to cup the side of her face. "Yes, it's Jesse. You're safe, Mattie. You survived."

She flinched away, jerked her arms down with a grimace of pain, rolled to her side, and tried to push herself up. She gasped when her blistered hands touched the pallet, and collapsed again, unable to stand the pain. She looked up at him, tears welling up and overflowing the corners of her eyes. "I hurt. And I can't sit up. I managed everything else, though."

"Damn it, Mattie!" Jesse exclaimed as he leaned over and slipped his arm underneath her back and raised her up to a sitting position. He hesitated, still kneeling beside her, his arm supporting her back, then with a sense of doomed inevitability, lifted her to her knees and gathered her to himself, until she rested against his chest. "I never doubted you could manage."

She gave a sob. "I did, though. I cried and screamed and prayed every minute. I was not composed. I was not dignified as a lady should be. And I was not brave."

Jesse held her tighter and laughed. "Mattie, you're the only woman I know who could do what you did today and still claim you aren't brave. You're also the only lady I know who would have the good sense to wait until the crisis was past to worry about her dignity." He cupped her chin and tilted her head back so he could see her face and those golden eyes. "You are a remarkable woman, Mattie Hunter, and I'm glad I met you."

She cried again, silently, the tears rolling down her sunburned cheeks. "You shouldn't be, Jesse. I started the stampede. The wind blew my bonnet off, and it rolled into the herd."

Rage buffeted him like a sudden gust of wind. All that waste, that gut-wrenching fear, all that death—and he still didn't know how many head had died—all because of a woman's goddamn hat. If she was a man, he would knock hell out of her.

His eyes must have revealed something of his thoughts because Mattie twisted out of his arms and scooted backward on her knees until she crouched against a pyramid of boxes. Less than three feet separated them, yet it might as well have been a river at flood stage because she was drowning before his eyes in guilt and self-contempt. And for what? Because Jesse McDade wanted someone or something to blame for what might have happened anyway for any number of inexplicable reasons?

His rage faded into shame as he observed the bedraggled and exhausted woman opposite him, and felt a need to comfort her. "It doesn't matter. A new herd is easily spooked. All those animals away from their home grazing, crowded together in a small space, anything could have frightened them. A gunshot, a saddle creaking, a cowboy striking a match to light a cigarette, even a sneeze at the wrong time, and the cattle are running."

"But it wasn't any of those things. It was my bonnet. I'm responsible."

Her sad, hopeless voice tore at his heart. "Don't be so quick to take the blame. You don't control the wind. God does, and sometimes I think God has a capricious nature."

"That's blasphemy!"

Jesse shrugged. "No doubt, but I've been too long on the plains to believe God is quite the orderly gentleman preachers talk about. Or else we misunderstand his purpose because it so often conflicts with our own. I'm a stoic, Mattie, and believe in fate and random chance because I find it preferable to believing that cattle run and cowboys die because God wills it."

Mattie jerked back, her eyes questioning. "Die? Who died?"

Jesse knew there was no way to shield Mattie from the truth, not on the cattle drive and not in Texas. Besides, to lie to her would be to diminish her.

"Bob Grimes's horse went down. He was trampled to death."

Mattie slumped against the boxes. "Oh, God, no!" She made a low, keening sound and broke into sobs.

Jesse reached for her and pulled her unresisting body back into his arms. He lowered his head to press his cheek against hers. "Death happens on the plains. Accept it, Mattie."

"I can't!"

He pulled back and grasped her shoulders. "You must, or else you'll go mad like many other women on the frontier." At her disbelieving look, he nodded. "Madness happens, Mattie, more than you know. There's even a name for the person hired to take those women back to their families in the east. He's called a homesman."

She shook her head vehemently. "I have no intention of going mad, but I understand why those women might. Perhaps it was the only way to escape the dirt and noise and loneliness. And perhaps it was the only way to escape hard men like you with your demands and orders and expectations and your casual talk of accepting death as if it was a minor inconvenience." She shoved him away and crossed her arms over her open bodice. "Who appointed you oracle of the plains and my personal guardian angel, Mr. McDade?"

Jesse almost choked on his anger. "Riding into the teeth of a stampede in order to save your stiff, ungrateful little neck gives me the right. And what the hell were you doing out of the wagon in the first place, *Mattie*?"

"You will not use such language to me, and I did not give you permission to call me by my Christian name."

"It's too late for such formality. Calling me 'Mr. McDade' will not erase what has passed between us, Mattie."

"Nothing passed between us, *Mr. McDade*."

Jesse leaned closer. "I held you in my arms while you cried, Mattie. I comforted you. That entitles me to the truth. Why did you get off the wagon?"

Mattie's eyes wavered, then fell, and he noticed her fingering the buttons on her dress. "You put a price on your comfort?"

He shook his head. "Jesse doesn't, but Mr. McDade does. He's a hard man."

Mattie's head sank lower, and her voice was muffled. "I was chasing my bonnet."

Jesse sat back on his heels. She was lying. Her guilty expression and fidgeting gave her away. Since the day he had met her, he had only known her to lie once—this morning, to protect Samuel. "You might have chased your bonnet, Mattie, but that isn't why you left the wagon. When I saw you, you were seventy-five yards *behind* your wagon instead of off to one side of it, where you would have been had the wind caught your bonnet while you were on the seat. You lost your bonnet when you were running toward Samuel's wagon to try to persuade me not to search it. Isn't that true?"

Mattie swallowed and looked up at him, her eyes a tear-washed gold. "If you had not been so stubborn, I never would have left the wagon and the wind would not have blown my bonnet into the herd. And that cowboy wouldn't have died."

"He didn't die, he was trampled. And he wasn't 'that cowboy.' His name was Bob Grimes, and I rode up from Texas with him. He was my oracle, Mattie, him and Charlie Goodnight. And he's dead because an unworthy man disobeyed my orders and you tried to protect him."

She held out her hand. "Please, Jesse."

"So I'm 'Jesse' again. I don't think so. A man has to earn the right to call me by my Christian name, and so does a woman, *Mrs. Hunter*."

Jesse was still tasting rage when he pulled the wagon up close to the cook fire. He threw the reins to Squinty and climbed off the wagon, suddenly aware of how exhausted he was.

"Miss Mattie be all right?" asked Jubilee, stepping up to Jesse.

Jesse glanced at the cowboys who had clustered around the wagon, and saw the slumped shoulders, drawn faces, and sunken eyes that spoke of tiredness that bordered on physical collapse. Yet the men had waited up long past dark when they should have been in their bedrolls. Riders were changed every two hours at night, and several of these men had passed up sleep because a woman was missing and unprotected. They had waited until she was safe.

All but one.

Jesse nodded to Jubilee. "She's alive. Get her out of the wagon and give her and Leon some food. And heat some water and find me some clean rags."

"What for, Jesse? What's wrong with Miss Mattie?"

"Her hands are all blistered up. The worst I've ever seen. I'm going to wash them and then disinfect them."

Jubilee's broad forehead wrinkled up like a washboard. "How we gonna do that, Jesse?"

"I believe Mr. Hunter has something in his wagon that will work admirably. Where is the son of a bitch anyway?"

Several cowboys shuffled their feet and looked at one another. Red finally answered. "He had sort of an accident. Tripped over my boot and landed on a case of dried prunes Jubilee had setting on the ground. He ain't hurt or nothing. Hell, everybody gets a scratch or a bump on a cattle drive. I figure his chin will be healed up in a week or so. Probably won't even have a scar. I don't know why he took on so. He didn't even have any loose teeth out of the deal. Or none he mentioned. But anyhow, he acted like he'd been mortally wounded and 'retired' to his wagon."

Jesse nodded. "I think I'll disturb Mr. Hunter's rest." He walked to Samuel's wagon, lowered the hinged back, and vaulted in.

"Who is it?" asked a querulous voice. "Who's there?"

"McDade," answered Jesse, lighting Samuel's coal-oil lamp that hung from one of the iron ribs of the wagon.

"McDade! What are you doing here? I didn't give you permission to enter." Samuel sat up on his pallet, wearing a linen nightshirt that made Jesse's lip curl.

"I brought your wife back, Hunter. Don't you want to put your pants on and go see if she's all right? Or would you rather tell me where you've hidden your liquor first? Or shall I dump everything you own on the ground until I find it?"

Samuel clawed at Jesse's leg. "You have no right!"

Jesse kicked Samuel in the belly, then leaned over and seized the writhing man's collar and tossed him out of the back of the wagon, followed by his pants. "Red," he called. "Escort Mr. Hunter to his wife. His concern is truly heartrending."

Red's grin nearly split his face in two. "You bet, Jesse." He put his hands on his hips as he watched Samuel struggling into his pants. "My, my, just look at what he's got on, boys. Looks like a lady's nightgown. Bet his wife don't wear nothing any fancier."

"Red?"

"Yeah, Jesse?"

"I don't want to hear you discussing Mrs. Hunter again."

Red's grin disappeared. "I didn't mean to give no offense."

Jesse toted two cases of bourbon to the back of the wagon, then jumped to the ground. "Well, I took offense on Mrs. Hunter's account. I might lose my temper if I have to do it again. You understand, Red?" He picked up a bottle of bourbon and smashed it against the wagon wheel.

Red licked his lips. "I understand, boss."

Samuel howled and grabbed for the case of whiskey. "You bastard!"

Jesse put his hand in the middle of Samuel's chest and shoved him back into Red's arms. "I believe Mr.

Hunter has a poor sense of direction or else he's blind. He thinks his wife is sitting on this case of whiskey. Why don't you and a couple of the boys turn him around and head him toward the campfire, Red?"

"Be glad to," said Red, watching Jesse methodically smash the rest of the bottles in the first case. "That's a downright waste of good whiskey, boss."

"No, it ain't," said Squinty, limping up to Jesse's side. "Whiskey's ruint many a good man. It ain't good for nothing."

"It's good for something," said Jesse, picking up the second case of whiskey. "It kills infection." He stopped and looked at Samuel, who was resisting the grinning cowboys' attempts to turn him toward the campfire. "Boys, peel that fancy nightshirt off Mr. Hunter. It strikes me that it would make some mighty fine bandages. You don't mind, do you, Mr. Hunter? Your wife has more use for it than you."

With the help of two other cowboys, Red stripped Samuel's nightshirt over the struggling man. The night air, cooler than usual for late April, raised chill bumps on the man's bare chest and arms and he shivered. Jesse couldn't dredge up any sympathy. He recognized that punishing Samuel in such a fashion was not the wisest course of action, but under the force of circumstances it was the only one. He could not allow Samuel alcohol while forcing the other men to abstain. Playing favorites on the drive was the quickest way he knew to undermine his authority. His men would abide by the most stringent, arbitrary rules he might devise—so long as they applied to all. Jesse knew he controlled his world through personal loyalty and force of will. If ever either weakened, he was through as trail boss and through as a man.

But he need not humiliate Samuel completely. "Red, let Mr. Hunter find a shirt. He won't wish to embarrass his wife by appearing half-undressed."

Jesse continued toward the chuck wagon and campfire, Squinty by his side. The full moon turned the landscape into a world of black and shades of gray, totally devoid of color. Even Mattie's hair had faded from sunshine to shadow.

Leon lay sleeping in the horse wrangler's arms. Danny Boone was the youngest man on the drive and held the lowliest job. Jesse thought Danny's place in the pecking order accounted for his name and his insistence that he was a descendant of Daniel Boone. Jesse doubted both name and ancestry; in the west a man changed his name for any number of reasons, the principal one usually being that his birth name might be found on wanted posters. Jesse didn't care what sins a man might have committed under another name, so long as he didn't commit any on the drive.

"Danny, take the boy to his wagon and put him to bed. There's a pallet in the back."

Mattie lifted her head. Wrapped in a heavy woolen shawl to hide her damaged bodice, she sat on an upturned crate and held a tin plate of beans and sliced roast on her lap. Jesse noticed she had buttoned her dress and wondered how she had managed to do so. Her palms and fingers were so blistered and stiff, it must have been an act of will.

Mattie fixed her eyes on his. "I can manage to put my own son to bed, Mr. McDade."

"It would be best if the boy didn't stay, Mrs. Hunter. He might wake up and be frightened when Jubilee and I clean and bandage your hands."

"I hardly think Leon would be terrified of seeing his mother washing her hands, Mr. McDade."

Jesse set the case of bourbon on the chuck wagon's tailgate and glanced at Jubilee. "Probably not, but seeing his mother in pain might not be good for him." He picked up a bottle of whiskey and pulled the cork out. "Jubilee, if Mrs. Hunter is finished eating, get the soap and hot water, and let's get this over with. The longer we wait, the greater the chance infection will set in, and I saw a man in not much worse shape than her lose his hands that way."

Jubilee caught his arm. "Lordy, Jesse, you can't do that to Miss Mattie."

Jesse clenched his teeth to keep from screaming that he'd rather cut off his own arm than hurt Mattie. "It's necessary, Jubilee, and whiskey's the best thing I know of."

Mattie stood up, letting the plate of food slide off her lap. "What are you talking about? Jubilee, what does he mean?"

Jubilee picked up a pan of water and soap and walked toward her. "Let's wash them hands, Miss Mattie, get 'em real clean, and maybe Jesse don't mean nothing."

"Don't lie to her, Jubilee. She's stronger than that," said Jesse, flinching as he saw Mattie bite her lip when she plunged her hands into the pan of water.

Jubilee gently soaped Mattie's hands, sweat popping out on his face to sparkle in the moonlight as she gasped when the harsh suds stung her raw flesh. "How strong you think she is, Jesse? How much more you going to ask her to do?"

Jesse's neck ached from holding it rigid. "No more than she has to, Jubilee."

"Mattie!"

Samuel rushed up. Jesse noticed he had taken the time to brush his hair after donning a clean linen shirt. Both actions were an improvement over his mussed locks and hairless bare chest. Jesse couldn't remember ever seeing a man who lacked even a sparse sprinkling of hair on his chest. It was unmanly, and he fought back a spasm of nausea at the thought of this hairless white slug in Mattie's bed.

Mattie looked up, and Jesse saw the wet shine of tears in her eyes. "Samuel! Oh, Samuel, I'm so glad you're here. Mr. McDade is—"

"Don't talk to me about Mr. McDade, Mattie," interrupted Samuel, turning to stare at Jesse with maniacal hatred. "He pawed through my wagon and destroyed my personal possessions. I shall deduct the damages from your wages, McDade, and inform my father-in-law of your high-handed actions."

"What did Mr. McDade do?" asked Mattie, allowing Jubilee to dry her hands with a soft cloth.

"He destroyed two cases of your father's finest Kentucky bourbon."

"Only one case," said Jesse. "The other will stay in the chuck wagon for medicinal purposes. Jubilee has my authority to deal with anyone caught stealing whiskey in whatever way he thinks fit."

"You'd let a nigger lay hands on a white man?" demanded Samuel in outrage.

"Out here, Mr. Hunter, competence counts for more than color does. Besides, next to the trail boss, the cook has the most authority on a drive. And Jubilee is the cook."

"I won't permit it!"

Jesse shrugged and hunkered down in front of Mattie. "You have a choice, Mr. Hunter. You can always take over the cooking. I doubt you'll like the hours. Jubilee starts breakfast about two-thirty in the morning and finishes his duties after dark. It makes for a long day. He also drives the chuck wagon and gathers firewood, or buffalo chips if wood is unavailable. Buffalo chips are dried dung, in case you don't know. Not a chore you would care to discuss over the supper table, but a necessary one."

"But, Samuel," said Mattie. "You did sign Mr. McDade's paper, agreeing to follow his rules."

Samuel wheeled on his wife. "It is most unseemly to interject your opinion in this discussion, Mattie." He stopped abruptly as he noticed her appearance for the first time. "You are untidy, my dear. I hope this drive does not have a detrimental effect on your character."

Mattie straightened, and for the first time Jesse saw her eyes flash at her husband. "No, but driving a mule team in a dead run does tend to have a detrimental effect on my person, Samuel." She thrust out her palms to show him.

He looked at her hands and winced. "Of course, my dear, I understand. I've been a selfish brute to be so concerned with my own problems to the exclusion of your difficulties. Forgive me." He patted her shoulder. "It has been an upsetting day. I'm sure you understand and sympathize if I seem preoccupied."

"'Difficulties' is an understatement, Samuel. Leon and I could have very easily been killed. I can't give you any sympathy tonight because I have none to spare. I need it myself."

"You are distraught, my dear. I understand. You will feel better tomorrow."

"Perhaps you would care to demonstrate a little sympathy yourself, Mr. Hunter. If you could sit by your wife while I disinfect her hands, I am certain she would appreciate your support."

"Ain't there no other way, Jesse?" asked Jubilee, his eyes nearly as shiny and wet as Mattie's.

"If there was, don't you think I'd take it? Do you think I enjoy pouring whiskey over raw wounds?"

Mattie gasped. "Oh, God, please."

"That's savagery, McDade!" exclaimed Samuel.

"It's survival, Mr. Hunter," corrected Jesse. "And sometimes they amount to the same thing." He looked at Mattie. "This is going to hurt like the very devil, but you mustn't scream. We cannot afford another stampede. I'm sure you understand that."

Mattie nodded. "I would not want another man's death on my conscience, Mr. McDade. Perhaps if you give me something to bite on, it would help."

"My God, Mattie!" exclaimed Samuel. "Surely you aren't agreeing to this." He looked around at the watching cowboys. "Are you going to permit McDade to torture my wife in this fashion? Aren't any of you going to stop him?"

Red spat. "It's gotta be done. Reckon nobody likes it, and we're plumb glad Jesse gonna be the one to do it. Takes a strong stomach, and that's why he's the boss and we ain't. You best let him alone and let him get on with it. Waiting won't change nothing, and it's hard on the lady. Sitting there dreadin' what's about to happen can't be easy."

"Hush, Samuel," said Mattie. "I really don't believe I'm up to being the object of a disagreement." Her voice quivered on the last word, and Jesse strained against his inclination to gather her into his arms.

"I can't stand to watch, Mattie," said Samuel quietly, with the first note of sincerity Jesse had ever heard in his voice. "I'm sorry. There is much about myself I would change to please you if I could, but my nature holds me fast. It's why I drink, I think, to forget." He touched her cheek briefly. "Forgive me." He turned and walked away to stand near his wagon, unable to free himself of whatever demon lived in his soul.

It was the first time Jesse had ever seen Samuel act in a manner worthy of respect.

"Mr. McDade, perhaps I could borrow one of your gloves to bite on."

"My gloves are filthy, Mrs. Hunter. Let me find you something else."

She shook her head. "No. You have suffered my various moods today. Please indulge me in another, Mr. McDade."

His eyes fixed on hers, trying to convey feelings all the more powerful for being unspoken, he pulled off his glove and placed it between her teeth, his thumb lingering a second to rub the corner of her mouth. "My name is Jesse."

CHAPTER 12

Mattie put in the last stitch, bit off the thread, carefully stuck her needle back in the pincushion, and tucked it away in her sewing box. She could not take a chance on losing a needle. In the first place, Leon might find it, and in the second place, she had no way of knowing where or when she might be able to replace it.

Holding up her sunbonnet, she laughed at its ridiculous appearance. Made from the train of her navy gingham dress, its brim was a full eight inches wide with horizonal lines stitched as casings into which Mattie had inserted thin wooden slats Jubilee had whittled for her from a crate. On either side of the brim and on the back she had sewn the curtain, a long ruffle of material that hung to the top of her shoulders and protected her neck from the sun. The back of the bonnet was a gathered circlet of material in which Mattie had sewn a drawstring to puff and shape it. She had used pink braid torn from another train to edge the bonnet.

She was quite proud of it even though her stitches were still clumsy. Her hands were healing, but it still hurt to hold a needle and force it through several thicknesses of material as she had when making the brim. Jesse had assigned Jubilee to drive her wagon while she lay incapacitated on her pallet, feverish from her severe sunburn and her suppurating palms. While she had escaped the gangrene Jesse had so feared, several of her blisters had become infected, necessitating lancing and repeated doses of her father's finest Kentucky bourbon. The first few days she had fainted during the treatment, waking to find Jesse and Jubilee leaning over her pallet. Jubilee was always crying and wringing his hands, but Jesse's face just turned harder and harder until she would have thought it carved from granite had she not seen the throbbing vein in his temple.

She never saw that vein at any other time.

She slipped on thick cotton stockings, another surprise Aunt Patty had packed in her trunk without telling her, and then stood up and stepped into her drawers. Pulling them up under her nightgown, she tied the drawstring, then slipped her arms and head out of her nightgown until it was draped like a tent over her body. Awkwardly she put on her chemise and one petticoat, then her bodice and skirt, fastening each without the difficulty she expected. She must have lost weight during the last ten days when she had felt too ill to eat because her clothes were made to fit her corseted figure, not this unfamiliar, unbound body that felt so soft and free under its clothing.

She pulled off her nightgown and folded it neatly and laid it under her pillow. After the difficulty of dressing and undressing in such a way as to preserve her modesty in case one of the men walked by or the wind should happen to blow the canvas flaps open, Mattie was almost looking forward to the dugout.

A TIME TOO LATE
Almost.

She wasn't certain how she and Samuel would handle living in a single room. She had never undressed in front of him in all their married life and had never even seen his naked chest, much less any of the rest of him without clothes. He came to her in the dark, when he came at all, and he left in the dark. All she knew of her husband's body was by feel, and that was confined to his legs and that portion of him where he was a man. She had never touched him with her hands in either place, and he had never touched her except to part her legs.

She wondered if anything would change and realized that she hoped not. She thought she might be physically ill if Samuel ever really touched her. She didn't consider what he did touching because only parts of their bodies were involved. If Samuel ever tried to hold her in his arms and press her whole body against his as Jesse had done that evening of the stampede, she thought she might go mad.

Throwing her head back, she gazed sightlessly at the canvas wagon top. She must not think about such things, must not think so about Samuel. And Jesse. Jesse was forbidden.

Sitting back on her pallet, she pulled on a pair of Samuel's old boots. They were a comfortable fit and made her feel unwomanly. It was unfashionable to possess feet so large and clumsy that a wife could wear her husband's boots without stuffing the toes with paper. But it was infinitely better to be unfeminine than to wear her own new, high-button shoes that pinched her toes and whose soles were slick as her hand mirror. She had no intention of falling in the dirt anymore, thank you.

Nor did she intend to ruin her complexion by exposing it to the sun again either, she thought as she tied her sunbonnet. Her nose and forehead were already shedding skin faster than a snake in spite of the lard that Jubilee had lathered over her face. And she had seen freckles across the bridge of her nose last night. Not many, and rather light, but very definitely freckles. And she had no lemons and no buttermilk with which to bleach them out.

She had asked Jesse about allowing Jubilee to milk a cow, but he had laughed so hard that he quite offended her.

"My God, Mattie," he had said. "It would take four ropes and five cowboys to milk one of those cows—if we managed to catch one that had calved recently enough to have milk. They are wilder than deer." Then he had studied her face. "Besides, your freckles make you look more like a wildflower and less like the hothouse rose that started this drive."

"I liked looking like a hothouse rose, thank you. It's bad enough that I will have scars on my palms without having my skin look like splotched leather."

Jesse caught the hand she waved and looked at its palm. He gently touched the red streaks that marred the skin. "They will fade in time, Mattie, and not much time at that. Don't you think, Jubilee?"

The ex-slave examined her hands with such a grave expression, Mattie thought he might be pronouncing sentence on a villain. "I believes Jesse is right, Miss Mattie. Ain't nobody gonna notice them scars in a year or so."

"That is not the point," insisted Mattie as the trail boss rhythmically rubbed his thumb over her palm. It was the first time Jesse had touched her except to treat her blisters since the stampede, and it only added to her restless, frightened mood. "I'll notice them. I'll know. My hands will never look the same again. They have changed, and I don't like it."

"These scars are a badge of honor," said Jesse, his face turning hard. "They're a symbol of survival, and out here that is more important than an unblemished complexion."

"Can't I survive without changing?" she cried.

"No! Hothouse roses die on the prairie. Only the wild kind with small, sweet blooms and thorny stems survive. Your scars are your thorns, Mattie." He released her hand and glanced at Jubilee. "The lady is sounding snappish. I think she's been too long with only our company. Why don't you join us for breakfast tomorrow, Mattie, and ride up front with Jubilee for a while."

"She ain't fit to drive, Jesse," said the Negro.

"She won't get fit either, Jubilee, as long as she stays inside this wagon resting on a pallet worrying about things that don't matter—such as scars and freckles."

Mattie jerked her hand away. "You sound like Aunt Patty, always telling me that it's what inside that counts. I'm tired of hearing of it. I won't change into one of those snuff-dipping old pioneer women with gnarled hands and leathery faces, Mr. McDade. I won't."

Jesse clinched his jaw. "So we're back to formality. The lady is angry with me, Jubilee. She only calls me 'Mr. McDade' when she's displeased."

Jubilee frowned. "She oughts to call you Mr. McDade all the time. Ain't fitting to seem too familiar. Folks will talk."

Jesse shifted restlessly as though he was impatient with the conversation. "There are no 'folks' on this drive, Jubilee, only my men, and they would not think to criticize Mattie."

"We ain't always gonna be on the trail, Jesse. We gonna run into folks sometime."

"Not anytime soon, and I would never take advantage of my position as Mattie's friend," said Jesse, standing up and tilting his head to one side to avoid bumping the canvas top. "And I would kill the man who claimed I did."

Jubilee shook his head. "It just ain't natural, a man and a woman being friends, and nobody else gonna think so either."

"Are you accusing me of taking liberties, Jubilee?" asked the trail boss, his eyes gone gray like granite. "Perhaps I should have preserved the proprieties and left Mattie to die in the stampede instead of plucking her up and throwing her across my saddle. Or let her develop gangrene rather than holding her hands and pouring whiskey over them. Or let her languish in the back of this wagon without once paying my respects as good manners dictate."

"You making me feel like a foolish old darkie," said Jubilee.

"You're talking foolishness," said Jesse, glancing from one to the other. "And so are you, Mattie."

"Must you be so hard, Jesse?" she asked. "Don't you understand that I'm frightened of what I am becoming?"

"And what is that, Mattie?" he had asked.

She only shook her head, staring up at him with all the fear and confusion she felt. His face had softened for a moment, then grown rigid, and he had climbed from the wagon followed by Jubilee, and Mattie knew he would not pay his respects again.

Even now Mattie felt ashamed and angry at the same time. She had sounded worse than foolish; she had sounded shallow, as if her mind had no room for thoughts beyond soft hands, clear skin, and tea-party manners. It wasn't true, but she was uncertain what the truth was. Except that she was afraid.

She glanced at herself in the mirror, plucked a loose patch of skin from her peeling nose, shuddered at the freckles sprinkled like cinnamon over the pale honey of her complexion, and replaced the mirror in her trunk.

After hiding for ten days in the back of the wagon without even Leon's company at night, Mattie Hunter was emerging from her cocoon. If she wasn't a butterfly, at least she wasn't a moth either. She still hadn't resorted to a calico Mother Hubbard.

She jumped lightly to the ground, pleased that Samuel's boots didn't have the same propensity to slide that her own shoes did, and strolled toward the campfire. Jesse stood up, tin cup of coffee in his hand, his gaze drifting over her with approval. She wondered if he knew she had dispensed with her corset. She felt naked all of a sudden, as if she had left off more than just that whalebone garment.

"Good morning, Jesse." She picked up a protesting Leon, who had been chewing on a biscuit while banging a pan with one of Jubilee's spoons. Leon peered under Mattie's brim, then grinned when he recognized his mother under the strange hat. Mattie noticed he had cut another tooth.

"Good morning, Mattie. That is a most attractive bonnet."

She blushed. "Thank you. Jubilee, might I have a cup of coffee, please? I suppose it is as strong as usual?"

Jubilee grinned as he wrapped a rag around his hand and lifted the hot coffeepot. "Six-shooter coffee, Miss Mattie. That's what the cowboys call it. Gots to be strong enough to float a six-shooter."

"It's a foul brew, but pour me a cup anyway," said Samuel, strolling up as if he were entering a parlor. Dressed in buckskin trousers and matching coat he had ordered from a Pueblo tailor, he should have looked as if he were a part of the landscape. But he didn't. His clothes were too clean, too well tailored, his gloves fancy with their heavily beaded and fringed gauntlets. The other men wore denim and flannel and short wrist-high roping gloves. Samuel looked like an exotic bird in the midst of sparrow hawks.

"Good morning, Mattie," he said, smiling at her as if he had visited her every day instead of only once—when he had bolted from the wagon when Jesse had removed the bandages from her hands. Leon he glanced at, then ignored.

"Good morning, Samuel." She tamped down her resentment. Samuel could not help it if he found sickness unpleasant. She must not feel this bitterness toward him. Nor should she resent the fact that he looked not one bit different today than he had in Pueblo. Perhaps his face was less pale, and his clothes a fraction more casual, but those were the only changes. While she, Mattie Hunter, cosseted and protected daughter of Pueblo's richest citizen, wore a sunbonnet, had removed the train from her skirt and the corset from her body, and had freckles on her nose and scars on her hands.

Samuel would never change.

Jubilee poured Samuel a cup of coffee, his face as hard and blank as Jesse's usually was. "Breakfast's in the skillet and biscuits are in the Dutch oven, Mr. Hunter. Help yourself. I gots to start cleaning up the plates. Be moving out in a little while." He turned his back and started busying himself.

"Mr. Hunter," said Jesse, tossing the rest of his coffee on the ground. "If you could keep up today, I would appreciate it. And if you could delay your rides to shoot at the local wildlife until we stop for the day, I would appreciate that, too. Or if you could at least manage to hunt something Jubilee could cook. Prairie dogs are not good eating."

"See here, McDade," retorted Samuel. "You're exceeding your authority again."

"Suit yourself, but I can't spare a man to hunt for you if your horse steps in a prairie-dog hole and throws you. You'll have to walk. And if your shooting

A TIME TOO LATE

spooks the herd, I'll take your fine Winchester you're so proud of."

"Your morning shooting hasn't caused a stampede yet, McDade."

Jesse frowned. "Mine can't be helped."

"What are you hunting, Jesse?" asked Mattie, sipping her coffee and chewing on one of Jubilee's sourdough biscuits. She couldn't face salt pork this morning.

Glancing at Jubilee, who had twisted around at Mattie's question, the trail boss hesitated, then shrugged. "Just taking care of business, Mattie." He walked over to his horse and mounted, riding off toward the herd strung out over a half mile.

Samuel smiled, a particularly unpleasant expression on his face. "He's shooting the calves."

Mattie dropped her biscuit and stood up, clutching Leon, who was busily playing with the ties of her bonnet. "What did you say?" Her stomach threatened to empty itself of the sourdough biscuit.

"Now, Miss Mattie," said Jubilee with one of those direct looks at Samuel. "It gots to be done. That stampede brought on lots of calves too soon. They can't keep up and they can't live, so we shoots them."

"Oh, God. Oh, merciful God. Is there no end to the evil of that stampede?" cried Mattie. She thrust Leon on Samuel's lap and turned and ran toward a saddled horse patiently waiting for its rider.

"Miss Mattie, where is you going?" shouted Jubilee, dropping a plate into his pan of water.

Mattie grabbed the reins and stuck her foot in the stirrup. "I'm going to stop him!" The horse shied, dragging Mattie several feet until she managed to throw her leg over the saddle. The horse sidestepped as it felt the unfamiliar sensation of a woman's skirts flapping against its sides. Mattie jerked on the reins.

"Stop it, you damn mangy animal. I don't like you any better than you like me."

"Miss Mattie!" Jubilee started toward her, and Mattie kicked the horse into a gallop, hanging on the saddle horn and hoping that when she fell, she wouldn't break her neck.

"Mattie!" screamed Samuel. "You are behaving most improperly. Remember yourself."

"I do!" she screamed back. And she did. She remembered the high-pitched bellows of animals trampled, the lonely mound of rocks that was Bob Grimes's grave, and her own part in all that death. She would be damned if anything else died because of her and Jesse's heartlessness.

As she drew closer to the rear of the herd, the "drag," so called because that was where the slow, the crippled, and the injured cattle that couldn't keep up were, the temperature rose. She remembered Red telling Jubilee that it was always several degrees hotter close to a herd because the moving animals generated so much heat.

The gunshots, the mournful bellowing of the mothers, the dusty grit kicked up by thousands of hooves, the rising heat only increased Mattie's impression of riding into hell.

"Jesse!"

Jesse turned, his face going taut with shock when he recognized her, then he was running toward her.

He jerked on her horse's bridle as the animal passed, hauling it to a stop, and circling Mattie's waist with his arm, pulled her off the saddle. "You damn fool, what are you doing?"

She grabbed his vest with both fists. "Don't kill those baby calves! I won't let you!" Another shot echoed through the broad valley, and she screamed.

Jesse slapped his hand over her mouth, barely flinching when she kicked his shin. "Hush, Mattie!

Screaming could set off another stampede!"

She clawed his hand away from her mouth. "Then stop him!" she exclaimed, pointing to Red, standing poised with his pistol in hand.

She saw grief flash through Jesse's eyes before they turned the opaque granite she was more used to. "I can't, Mattie. I can't risk slowing the herd for a few calves. Three thousand cattle eat a lot of grass. We have to keep it moving, or it will graze out the area. I'd start losing the weaker animals to starvation and maybe I'd lose men, too. Hungry cattle are dangerous to handle. Besides, most of these calves are premature. They couldn't survive anyway. Several were stillborn."

"But to kill them!"

He grasped her shoulders. "Do you think I like it? Do you think any of us like it? The men draw numbers out of my hat so no one man has to do it every day. I did what I could. I traded off what cows were so far along I knew they'd drop their calves during the drive. I've given calves to homesteaders we've passed. But I couldn't trade them all, and we've left the homesteads behind. My God, Mattie, do you think I'm a monster?"

"Jesse, let her alone. She don't know no better." Jubilee pulled up his horse and slid off. "Miss Mattie, you come back to camp with me. Let Jesse get on with it."

Mattie looked toward Red, who waited beside a tiny brown calf, its coat still slick from its mother's rough tongue. The mother stood on thin wobbly legs, a dumb, frightened expression in the brown eyes that looked back at her. Other cowboys with grim faces drove mothers away from their already-dead calves.

She twisted out of Jesse's grip and ran toward the tiny calf, intent on saving it. She gasped when Jesse's strong arms circled her waist, lifted her off the ground, and swung her around. His voice in her ear was harsh as the death behind her. "Give it up, Mattie. Those calves won't live, and they'll die more slowly and painfully than you can imagine. This way they don't suffer."

"It's hard to suffer when you're dead, isn't it?" she asked, slumping back against him.

She heard him curse. "I'm sorry, Mattie."

She looked again at the tiny calf. "Please, Jesse, let me save that one. He looks hardy enough to survive, given a chance. Isn't that what you've been trying to teach me all along? Survival? But I wouldn't have survived if you hadn't saved me, would I? I wasn't strong enough or wise enough. I was ignorant and terrified and thrown into a world I knew nothing about. I was as helpless as that baby calf."

His voice was as gritty as before, but she sensed a softening within him. His arms no longer held her so tightly, and the chest pressed closely against her back no longer felt so rigid.

"Damn it all, Mattie, haven't you understood anything I've said?"

She nodded, surprised that she did. "Yes, I understand, and I won't think less of you for doing what has to be done, but isn't there room for any mercy in your world? Is it all sharp edges and harsh decisions? Isn't there any room for softness and kind choices?"

"Jesse, that calf could ride in the cooney, and we could let it out to visit its mama when the herd stops to graze and at night."

Mattie looked at Jubilee. "What's a cooney?"

"It's that rawhide hammock hanging underneath the chuck wagon, Miss Mattie. Some of the cowboys call it a 'possum belly.' It ain't got nothing in there but spare wood for the fire. I reckon that baby calf ain't gonna take up much room. When he gets too big for the cooney, he'll be big enough to keep up with his mama."

Mattie felt Jesse give a sigh of resignation. "Damn it all, Jubilee, what will I do with two such foolish people?"

Jubilee scratched his head. "I guess you just have to put up with us. Us and Miss Mattie's baby calf."

CHAPTER 13

They trailed down by Two Butte to the Cimarron, passed by Robbers' Roost, the old hideout of the Coe brothers, and on toward the Canadian. The mountains lay behind them to the northwest, hidden beyond the horizon, even the memory dwarfed by the cloudless sky that rose to forever above their heads. In front and surrounding them, the harsh, featureless plain marched on mile after endless identical mile, a lush, green vastness that nourished the animals and swallowed man in its indifferent monotony. The Llano Estacado, the Staked Plain, a legendary region believed to be uninhabitable, frightened and diminished some, while others grew to cast a longer shadow upon its face.

The vast emptiness both frightened and fascinated Mattie as it wrapped her in heat that sucked away her last fashionable plumpness, and in isolation that threw her back into her own mind for company. She felt as though she was the only woman in an unfinished creation. "Did God forget the trees, Jesse?"

Jesse rolled a cigarette and looked eastward, where the rising sun painted the rim of the world rose and orange and bloodred. "He didn't forget, Mattie. I like to think He made the Llano Estacado after the Fall. He wanted to create a place where men couldn't hide, either from Him or from themselves." He lit his cigarette and exhaled a puff of smoke. "Man's original sin wasn't gaining self-knowledge, it was denying responsibility for his own nature afterward. Here, on these plains, a man stands exposed for what he is. He comes face-to-face with his own nature."

Mattie shuddered. "What if he doesn't like what he sees, Jesse?"

He turned his head to look at her, his eyes faintly amused. "I never said a man wouldn't find himself wanting in some respect or another, just that he couldn't lie to himself any longer."

Mattie picked up the reins and slapped them against the mules' backs. "I think your theology would shock Reverend Whitlow of the First Presbyterian Church in Pueblo and most other ministers of the Gospel, Mr. McDade."

Jesse grinned. "It shocked you, *Mrs. Hunter*. You might tear the trains off your skirts, leave off your corset, and wear a sunbonnet, but you still cling to being Mattie Hunter, a lady from Pueblo."

"I should hope I haven't forgotten who I am!" exclaimed Mattie, blushing at his mention of her corset. "And I'll thank you not to discuss improper subjects such as my clothes."

Jesse pinched the end of his cigarette and dropped the butt in his pocket. "Did I mention women have to face their own natures, too, Mattie? Ask yourself if you didn't lace up your mind every time you laced up your corset."

"Mr. McDade!" she gasped.

Before Mattie could find the words to express her

indignation, he tipped his hat and rode off to scout for a watering hole where the herd could stop for the night. Jesse McDade was an irreverent man. Every Christian knew that Original Sin referred to Eve's tempting Adam, and that God had established religion to teach man to deny his nature, not accept it. Mercy, what would the world be like if everyone accepted himself? A little hypocrisy, after all, was necessary for civilization.

And so was a corset.

Otherwise a woman's body might seem too easily available, might tempt a man into forgetting himself. Man, according to Reverend Whitlow, was easily tempted, and woman the eternal temptress. Mattie frowned, a spark of unexpected resentment setting fires in her mind. To be honest, she had never understood why women on the one hand were held to be vessels of purity above the sins of the flesh, while on the other hand they were held responsible for seducing men into those very sins. It seemed a contradiction to her. Was she an object of reverence or an object of desire? How could she face her own nature if she wasn't certain what it was?

Damn Jesse McDade, and damn this lonely land! She had not troubled her mind with such questions since she had locked away her wicked curiosity and restlessness after she married Samuel.

Mattie slapped the reins again and tapped her foot on the floorboard of the wagon. Leon played in the back with a calf Jubilee had carved out of tree stump he picked up before the drive left behind all vegetation higher than one's knee. Leon had named the toy Baby after the real calf. And what, Mattie wondered, did Mr. Jesse McDade think of his own nature when he'd given in and saved Baby? Was he displeased to learn he was not so hard as he supposed?

She was still wondering that night at supper as she

coaxed another spoonful of beans into Leon's mouth. "Just another bite, Leon, please. You want to grow up to be big and strong, don't you?"

Leon grinned through the mouthful of beans. "Jesse?"

Mattie jerked and spilled the plate of beans. She could sense Jesse turning toward her. "Big and strong like Daddy," she said, stressing Samuel's name.

Leon slid off Mattie's lap and ran to the trail boss, holding up his arms. "Jesse! Eat beans!"

Jesse swung the little boy up in his arms and poked his stomach. "That feels like an awfully empty belly, Leon. Do you think Jubilee might have a few dried apples to fill it up?"

Leon clapped his hands. "Apples."

Jubilee took the little boy from Jesse. "I 'spects I might have an apple or two in muh wagon iffen I know somebody might need them."

"Leon," said the boy, pointing to himself.

Danny Boone, the young horse wrangler, stood up and started searching through his pockets. "You know, I got to grind up the Arbuckles coffee this morning, and what do you reckon I found along with the coffee beans, Leon?"

The little boy laughed. "Candy!"

Mattie smiled in spite of her pounding heart caused by her son's naming Jesse rather than Samuel. All the cowboys spoiled Leon, but none so much as the horse wrangler. The cowboy who drew the chore of grinding the coffee beans every morning had first call on the stick of candy the Arbuckles company put in every package of its coffee beans. Candy, or sugar of any kind, was coveted on the trail because the cowboys rarely got any sweets. Sugar was expensive and was saved for special occasions such as when Jubilee baked a pie of dried apples or raisins. The closest substitution was molasses, which the cowboys called "lick" because they dipped their sourdough biscuits in a pan of the sweet syrup. For Danny to give his candy stick to Leon was more than a kindness; it was a sacrifice.

Leon practically leaped from Jubilee's arms into Danny's. Dried apples, after all, couldn't hold a candle to a stick of candy. When Danny gave the little boy his treat, Leon waved it in the air. "Baby! Baby! Candy!"

A soft bellow that sounded too loud for such a small animal heralded Baby's arrival. Still only the size of a large dog, the calf nudged Leon's leg. The boy leaned over Danny's arm, trying to get to the calf.

Danny hauled him back. "No, no, little feller. You ain't gonna share your candy with that flea-ridden animal tonight." He looked at Mattie and ducked his head. "I caught Leon and Baby eating the same candy stick last night, ma'am. I stopped it, of course, but neither one of 'em was very happy."

"Name of heaven, Mattie," said Samuel from the other side of the campfire. "You're being remiss in your duties. Letting Leon make a pet of that filthy animal and now he's eating after it. It's intolerable. You should have let McDade shoot it instead of interfering."

Mattie flushed. She wished Samuel would not call her down in public. It was humiliating, and she sensed the cowboys resented it on her behalf. Besides, she thought with a recurrence of the resentment that had so startled her earlier, Leon could eat coals from the fire if stopping him required Samuel to bestir himself to taking any interest in his son's activities. He was only interested now because he found Leon's behavior personally embarrassing.

She pushed her sunbonnet off her head to let it dangle down her back. "Samuel, Leon loves Baby. He tells him all his little-boy secrets, and Baby is so gentle with him."

"That's right, Mr. Hunter," said Squinty, looking

like a ruffian with his wooden leg and half-closed eye. "I ain't never seen no calf like that one. Follows your wife and boy around like he thinks he's human. Won't stay with his mama any longer than it takes him to get a full belly, then he's back to the wagons looking for Miz Hunter or Leon. Don't rightly know what she's gonna do with him when he grows into a bull and still stands around bawling for her to rub his head. No doubt about it, that's one unusual animal. Be a shame to get rid of it."

"That's too bad, because that is exactly what I plan to do."

"No, Samuel!" exclaimed Mattie.

Samuel pointed to the calf. "McDade, take it out and shoot it."

Jesse glanced at Mattie, then leaned over and scratched the small calf between the ears, concentrating on the tiny little nubs that would one day erupt into horns. "I don't shoot an animal unless it's necessary, Hunter. I certainly don't shoot an animal that asks to be petted and does no harm. I'm not so particular about shooting a man. Sooner or later a man will most likely give me a good excuse. Besides, I don't do anyone else's dirty work."

Even in the dim light of the fire and Jubilee's single coal-oil lamp, Mattie saw Samuel's face turn brick red. "Damn it, McDade, then I'll do it myself."

Mattie had never seen a man draw his gun as fast as Jesse. And never wanted to again. She jammed her knuckles against her mouth to keep from screaming and tried to think of what to do. She remembered Aunt Patty telling her that men with guns were unpredictable because their blood was up and pounding through their heads so hard, they couldn't hear it thunder, much less hear anybody trying to talk sense to them.

But Jesse didn't look as though his blood was up. In

fact, he looked so cold, she shivered. "You'll confine your shooting to the prairie dogs, Hunter," said Jesse. "I'll not have you shooting Baby."

Jubilee pushed a cup of coffee at Samuel. "I reckon that Baby will go with his mama when we gets to where we're going. He's apt to be too big by then for Leon to play with. Until then, it sure is nice the little tyke has something to pet. Sure would hate to see him get his little heart broke—especially by his daddy. Talks about you all the time, Leon does." He nodded in emphasis. "Yes, suh, thinks a lot of his daddy, that boy does."

Mattie lowered her hands and stared at Jubilee. Not all the syrup was in the molasses can. Leon never talked about his daddy anymore. Hadn't in weeks. Besides, precocious as he was, Leon still had a very limited vocabulary, and most of it centered around Baby. And Jesse.

Jesse holstered his gun with a sideways glance at Jubilee. "That's true, Hunter. I'd say it was a case of hero worship, and heroes don't shoot pets."

Samuel rubbed his chin and looked suspiciously at the two men. Mattie prayed that her husband wouldn't pick this occasion to refuse flattery.

He didn't.

"A boy should admire his father," Samuel began.

Red rode up, jerking on his reins so hard his horse half reared. "Injuns coming, Jesse! About sixty or seventy. Looks to be Comanche near as I could tell."

Mattie did scream then. And grabbed Leon out of Danny's arms.

"God damnit!" exclaimed Jesse. "Hush, Mattie! How far, Red?"

"Maybe a mile, coming this way. I'm sure sorry, Jesse, that I didn't see them any sooner."

"You ought to be," said Jesse, pulling out his gun and checking it. "It's not as if they could hide on this prairie, and the moon's so bright you could read a newspaper by it."

"I wasn't expecting no Injuns," the redheaded cowboy said. "Damn it, them devils supposed to be on the reservation in Indian Territory."

Jesse climbed on the back of the chuck wagon and stood looking across the flat landscape. "They've got their women and children with them. It's a hunting party." He jumped down. "Jubilee, close up the chuck wagon. Danny, take two men and guard the remuda. I don't want any horses stolen."

Mattie grabbed his arm with one hand while she clutched Leon with the other. "Horses! What about us? Oh, God, Jesse! It's Indians! We'll be massacred like the Utes did to the settlers at Fort Pueblo in 1854. They did terrible things to them, Jesse, and the Comanches are worse. I've heard stories."

"You and the other ladies talk about Indian atrocities at your tea parties, Mattie? How unseemly of you," said Jesse, gently freeing his arm from her grip.

"Do not laugh at me, Mr. McDade!"

He grasped her shoulders and turned her toward a crate. "I'm sorry you're frightened, Mattie, but I don't believe there is any need for concern."

Mattie twisted away from him and darted behind Samuel, her whole body shaking from terror and disbelief. Why, it had not even been a year since Colonel Custer and his men had been foully murdered and their bodies mutilated. She and several ladies of her acquaintance had sneaked the newspapers without their husbands knowing and read the lurid accounts of the Little Big Horn. And the Comanches! They were the most savage of all. She remembered whispered stories of captive whites rescued with noses and lips cut off, of women abused and beaten, of babies dashed against stones or left on the prairie to die because they cried.

And Jesse said there was no need for concern.

Samuel danced around, his face so white it looked as if it had turned to marble. "You men pull the other wagons up. Make a square. We'll hold the savages off."

Jesse ignored him. "Red, pick two other men. I want one of you at each wagon. I don't think the Hunters want all their possessions carried off. Have your guns ready, but don't use them unless they make a threatening move. The rest of you get your Winchesters and drop some spare shells in your pockets."

Samuel grasped the back of Jesse's vest and jerked him around. "Shoot them, man, for God's sake. Drop them before they get here. Use the Winchesters."

Jesse swept Samuel backward with a single motion of his arm. "You go sit by your wife and comfort her. And *don't* move. I said this looked to be a hunting party. The Indians are hungry. The army may be late issuing provisions or some damn Indian agent may have cheated them. Or else they may just have wanted to hunt. These are Comanches. They lorded over the Llano Estacado for nearly two hundred years after they either killed or chased out the other Indians. They're not used to living on a reservation yet, and they're not used to being ordered around by the white man. They lost their war just like the south did, and it doesn't set well with them any more than our loss does with us. I'll speak with this band's leader on common ground, warrior to warrior, defeated but not beaten."

"You're insane, McDade, talking about Indians as though they were our equals," said Samuel.

"Interesting you should say that, Hunter. The Comanche consider themselves superior—to the white man and to other Indians. Such arrogance is another trait they share with us."

"You admire them, don't you, Jesse! Dear God, you admire those Indians and their savage ways!" cried Mattie, shaking now with anger as well as fear.

Jesse cocked his head as though considering her accusation, then shrugged his shoulders. "I believe I said before that survival and savagery often are one and the same. To the extent that Comanche savagery springs from a need to survive, I understand it. That doesn't mean that I forgive the torture and mutilation certain of them have visited upon their captives nor do I forgive the murders of families on isolated homesteads in Texas. But every race has its share of sons of bitches, Mattie, and the Comanches are no exception. Admire their ways? I suppose I do admire some of their customs. But I'm a Texan, and the Comanche has been my blood enemy, perhaps even more than the Yankees."

"Blood brothers is more like it, Mr. McDade!" said Mattie, nearly spitting the words out. "Brothers under the skin! With all your talk of survival you'll still risk our lives out of some misguided sense of admiration for these people."

"Sit down, Mattie! And be silent!" commanded Jesse in a voice so cold, she thought her blood might freeze from its very sound. "I will kill every last one of them down to the smallest child if I think there is the least chance of their hurting you. But I know the Comanche and you don't. You must trust my judgment."

"Your damn judgment will get us all killed!" shouted Samuel, grabbing for the pistol he had begun wearing in a holster about his waist.

Jesse punched Samuel in the belly and confiscated his gun.

Mattie gasped and dropped to her knees beside her writhing husband. "Oh, God, Samuel!" She looked up at Jesse. "Damn you, Jesse McDade, I hate you!"

His only response was a darkening of his gray eyes

as if her words had hurt some part of him deep inside where she couldn't see. He turned to Jubilee and handed him Samuel's gun. "If I have misjudged and we have to fight, give him back his gun. Otherwise keep it." He glanced back at Mattie. "I will not see men killed needlessly—not even for you, Mattie."

He turned and walked toward the approaching Indians while Mattie saw the cowboys, all holding their Winchesters, standing in a circle around the camp. Every face was grim, not distrustful as much as watchful, prepared to kill if necessary but willing to find common ground with an old, familiar enemy. Mattie realized what a void of understanding separated these men from herself and Samuel. They were all Texans even though many had been born elsewhere, and all but Danny had driven herds up the Goodnight-Loving Trail while Mattie was still playing with dolls at her mother's knee. They were hardened by a life she was only now experiencing. The heat, the flies, the dust, the bone-tiring work, the stampedes had welded them into a brotherhood that stood shoulder to shoulder, ready to fight as a single man to defend the herd, her, and the tall man with the silver eyes who was one of them, yet who always stood alone.

In the silence broken only by the distant bellowing of cattle, by Samuel's panting breath, and by her own pounding heart, Mattie sensed a deeper truth behind this inexplicable behavior of Jesse and his brotherhood of cowboys. They did not want to fight the Comanches because they understood better than she that in some way the defeated Indians heralded their own end. As the white settlers, the farmers and the merchants, the miners and the railroaders, brought their own way of life to the west, the time when Comanches and cowboys might ride free and untrammeled, each in his own way, over unclaimed land, was passing. The time of the Comanche had already passed into history, and the time of the trail herd and cowboys must surely follow it into the shadows.

But Mattie's sense of witnessing a poignant moment didn't prevent her from seizing Jubilee's Bowie knife he had left by the fire and hiding it in the folds of her skirt. If she could drive a mule team, she could stab an Indian. If need be. And the devil take men and their brotherhoods and her own romantic imagination.

Crouching on the ground, shifting just enough to keep her legs from going numb, and holding Leon in one arm while her other hand remained anchored to the knife, she watched Jesse greet an Indian with long, gray-streaked braids and an impassive face. She understood little of the mixture of English, Spanish, Comanche, and sign language that passed for conversation between the two, so concentrated instead on viewing the dreaded savages about whom she had heard so much even in Pueblo.

They failed to live up to expectations.

None of the men was as tall as Jesse, for example, though most were taller than Samuel, and none wore breechclouts, which relieved her of the necessity of averting her eyes to avoid the embarrassment of bare bodies. They wore no feathered headdresses, nor were their faces streaked with paint. They did wear moccasins, pointed-toed with beadwork that featured straight lines rather than circles, but so did a few white men Mattie had seen on Pueblo streets. Their clothing was a duke's mixture of Indian and white man's fashion, with the leather garments showing wear and the heavy cotton shirts and bright calico dresses looking new. Rather than the feathered, painted, near-naked savages she had imagined, she saw a ragtag band of men, women, and children whose expressionless eyes and gaunt faces reminded her of the defeated South.

Jesse was right.

The Confederate state of Texas and the Comanche nation shared common ground.

Mattie let go of the Bowie knife.

Jesse held up four fingers. "Squinty, pass the word. Cut out four beeves, drive them a quarter mile out from the wagons. I don't care to sleep near a slaughter ground, and I don't want those cattle butchered near the herd."

"Mighty generous, Jesse," remarked Squinty, hobbling toward the remuda for a horse.

"It will keep them a few days until they find the buffalo they're looking for, if they can find a good-sized herd. The buffalo hunters have made a good living the last few years, and the gigantic herds of ten thousand animals the Comanche remember are no more. They'll be lucky to find a herd of a thousand. Another two or three years, and they won't find that many."

"That's my cattle you're feeding those savages, McDade!" exclaimed Samuel, sitting up but still holding his belly.

Jesse ignored him and continued his conversation with the Comanche leader. Finally he nodded and pointed his hand to the north, and the band of Indians silently moved away to wait for their cattle.

Mattie turned her head when the butchering started, but the wind carried the coppery scent of blood back to the camp. Holding a subdued Leon, she scooted over to lean against one of the chuck wagon's wheels and closed her eyes to wait out the night.

She felt someone tugging her hair and twisted her head away without opening her eyes. She must have slept because she could smell the morning coffee boiling on the fire and hear people moving around. Someone pulled her hair again, freeing the mass from its anchoring hairpins and it spilled over her shoulders. Feeling exhausted and out of sorts, she batted at the hand she could feel clinched in her hair, and opened her eyes to see her worst nightmare.

A Comanche squatting next to her grabbed her wrist with one hand and continued stroking her hair with the other. An ugly raised scar hugged one side of his face from chin to ear like a gray-white segmented worm, and fetid breath from a mouth full of black and rotting teeth bathed her face. He grunted something at her, twisted a long lock of hair around his one hand, and jerked her forward to smell the side of her neck where she had dabbed lilac water in a futile effort to cover her own stench. In a land where the animals had first claim on what little water was available, bathing was restricted to whatever portion of herself could be washed in a tiny basin of water drawn from the barrel strapped to the side of her wagon. But bad as she stank, the Comanche smelled worse.

Mattie clawed at his face with her one free hand and screamed. She was still screaming when the Comanche released her and bounded to his feet, grinning at her in spite of the red scratch marks down his scarred cheek. The Indian whipped a blanket off his shoulders that was so dirty she doubted it had been washed in recent memory and dropped it over her head. She heard Jesse's voice shout a curse of such a foul nature that she felt almost glad her face was hidden under the blanket so none of the men could witness her embarrassment.

Thinking of the cowboys sent her into another panic, and she tried to fight her way out of the odorous blanket. Were there any men but Jesse left alive, or had the Comanches sneaked into camp and murdered everyone? And where was Leon? If those savages had taken her baby, she would follow them to hell if necessary, and stab every one of them—beginning with that horrible scarred one.

The blanket was plucked off her head. "Lordy, Miss Mattie, is you all right?"

Mattie sucked in a breath of clean air delicately scented with dust and fresh cow manure. "Where's Leon?"

"Leon woke up early, so I took him and Baby to Danny to look after. Figured they was both safer down with the remuda than hanging around the fire with all them Indians touching everything that caught their fancy. Jesse and me and the cowboys was so busy keeping our eyes on all them Indians after they got their bellies full of the Colonel's beef, that we plumb forgot you was sleeping over here. Jesse was a mite upset when he heared you scream. Had his gun out and was fixing to shoot that ugly Injun where it would hurt the most when that pigtailed chief feller stopped him. The three of them is over by the fire jawing about something. Anyway, there's lots of hand waving and head shaking going on. Don't follow much of it myself. I never had much truck with Injuns. Had enough to do just keeping up with what the white folks was fixing to do to us niggers from one minute to the next without messing around with folks what might take your hair without asking first if it's all right."

"I'm all right, Jubilee," said Mattie, watching Jesse shake his head vigorously in reply to some inquiry by the scarred Indian. The other Comanche, the one she assumed was the chief, finally interjected several sharp words into the silent conversation, then also shook his head. Obviously disgruntled, the scarred one turned on his heel and stalked back toward Mattie.

She shrank back against the wagon wheel. "Oh, God, Jubilee!"

Pulling a pistol out of the waistband of his pants, Jubilee stepped between Mattie and the approaching Indian. "I figures you understands this gun even if you don't understand what I'm saying. You touch Miss Mattie again, and I'm gonna shoot you right up the middle till I runs out of bullets."

With a contemptuous look at Jubilee and a frustrated one at Mattie, the Indian picked up his blanket and stalked off. The chief said something to Jesse in a quiet voice, then followed the scarred Indian.

Jesse walked over to Mattie and hunkered down in front of her. "Did he harm you or just frighten you?"

"He didn't hurt me, Jesse, but what did he want?" she asked, reaching out to touch his arm.

Jesse's larger, warmer hand covered hers. "He was quite taken with you. Offered me a hundred horses in trade."

Mattie gasped. "That's horrible."

"Look at me," he ordered, and when she did, she gazed into the fierce eyes of a man who had been ready to kill for her and to count it as nothing. "Actually it's a compliment, but I told him you were married, and that I wouldn't take a thousand horses."

Mattie turned to watch the rest of the Indians drift silently back to their waiting ponies, taking with them the butchered remains of four head of cattle. And the belief that she was Jesse McDade's wife.

A few days later she discovered that the scarred brave had left her a gift. Instead of horses, he had given her lice.

CHAPTER 14

At first Mattie blamed the flies and tiny bugs Squinty called buffalo gnats that swarmed over the trail drive like the plagues of Egypt, biting and nipping at any exposed skin, for the itching that drove her and Leon into frenzies of scratching. She blamed the fierce heat and lack of opportunity to take a bath for the crawling sensations that afflicted her scalp and more unmentionable parts of her body. Drops of sweat rolling down her sides and back, scalp and neck, legs and arms, collecting dust on the way until they felt like mud balls, couldn't help but make her feel as if she was furnishing a home for tiny little animals. However unladylike it might be to admit it, she did sweat and she and Leon were often less than clean. Not until she actually found a louse in Leon's hair did it occur to her that she and her son were indeed hosting a large party of a common western parasite.

She dropped her hairbrush and tore at Leon's

clothes, stripping them off and heaving them out of the wagon. She examined every inch of his scalp and body, then grabbing her hand mirror, examined her own thick luxurious hair, gagging at each new glimpse of a "grayback." She had no doubt what she was looking at. Stories from her father, half-heard and half-understood, of the Confederates spending nearly as much time and ingenuity fighting infestations of lice as they spent fighting the Yankees bolstered her certainty. Memories of frequent admonitions from Aunt Patty and Jubilee to avoid touching or brushing against certain individuals because they looked to be lousy white trash confirmed it. She wondered what Aunt Patty would say if she knew Mattie Jo Hunter, often warned about the dangers of taking daily baths, was as filthy and lousy as any piece of white trash who ever lived. Probably tell her that she was keeping bad company.

Hugging Leon, she sank to her knees and rocked back and forth. With part of her mind she recognized that her peals of laughter were hysterical outbursts, that her intermittent sobs were the sounds of a woman very close to losing her sanity, that Jesse might very well have to find a homesman to take back to Pueblo what was left of the lady named Mattie Jo Hunter.

With all the strength that remained to her, she wrapped Leon in a sheet jerked off his pallet, and with half-buttoned basque and twisted skirt, unclad feet, and unbound hair, she climbed out of the wagon and trudged to the only person convention and her own modesty decreed was allowed to help her.

"Samuel?" she called, pulling at the canvas flaps at the back of his wagon. She ignored the curious looks of the cowboys around the chuck wagon less than fifty feet away. "Samuel, help me."

Samuel pulled aside the flaps and peered out, straight razor in one hand and his face still half-covered in lather. Unlike the cowboys, Samuel's insistence on shaving every day had nothing to do with Mattie's presence on the drive and a wish to make as handsome an appearance as possible to impress her. Samuel's beard was thin and scraggly, and he felt that allowing it to grow put him at a disadvantage next to the more hirsute members of the drive, particularly Jesse, whose whiskers at the end of the day proved him more than capable of growing a luxurious beard had he chosen to do so.

"Mattie! What do you mean by appearing in public with your person in such immodest condition. Return to your wagon immediately and see to yourself."

Mattie flinched under his well-justified criticism. Not only was she covered with lice, but she had failed to meet her own standards of propriety. She felt herself slipping away. "Samuel, please, I need your help. I don't know what to do."

A petulant frown wrinkled his brow. "If you need help dressing, I'm afraid you will have to manage yourself. It would be most unseemly for me to lace your unmentionables."

"Samuel, I haven't worn a corset for weeks!"

He frowned again. "I hadn't noticed, but I hardly think it a proper subject for conversation."

She licked her lips. "Samuel, you must listen to me. You're my husband and there is no one, *no one,* else who can help me. Leon and I"—a sob choked her, and she paused to regain her rapidly disappearing composure—"Leon and I have lice! It must have happened when that Comanche threw his blanket over me. I don't know what to do. I don't know how to get rid of them. I know I need to boil my clothes and bathe, but there's no water and I can't strip myself naked in front of men."

Samuel shrank back, his mouth working soundlessly for what seemed to Mattie like hours. "Get away! How dare you think of coming near me, of infecting me

A TIME TOO LATE
209

with your filth! My God! It makes my skin crawl just thinking about it!" He suddenly leaned over the back of the wagon and vomited.

Mattie flinched away, tugging the sheet around as much of her own body as she could without exposing Leon's nakedness. She swallowed back her own bile, too ashamed to allow even the contents of her stomach to commingle with that of Samuel's.

"Please, will you help Leon then? Will you help your son at least?"

Samuel looked at them both with hatred and revulsion. "That is your duty, though why God designated such slack-fleshed and lax creatures as women to be the vessels of life and guardians of helpless children is beyond my understanding."

Mattie fell to her knees, Samuel's words lacerating her already-feeble spirit. *Oh, God, his words will drive me mad.* "I'm sorry, Samuel, but I didn't ask to be what I am, and I didn't ask for lice. Merciful heavens! Have you no charity?"

Samuel grasped the edge of the wagon with both hands and hung his head between his stiff arms. Finally he raised his head, his face ravaged by a contempt so great Mattie knew it encompassed them both. "I'm sorry, too, Mattie, sorry for what I am and for what you are. I wish it were otherwise. There is much I admire about you and much that I shrink from. But I cannot help you, or what little chance we have to live together in some tolerable fashion would be finished. I cannot touch your verminous body or see it, else I would never to able to put it out of my mind. I would never be able to touch you again. Conquering my thoughts will be difficult enough. Would to God that you had been less strong with your father, and that we had never married. Or that I had been less weak." He put his hands over his eyes. "This damnable land! It plagues my mind with questions. Pity me, Mattie, as I pity you. It is too late for anything else."

She hitched Leon higher in her arms and turned back toward her wagon, her mind seeking refuge from shame and self-disgust. "Pity won't kill the lice, Samuel. And there is nothing else left."

Jesse drained the last of his coffee and handed Jubilee his cup, his eyes watching Mattie's stumbling progress back to her wagon from Samuel's. Her unbound hair was like a shimmery gold drapery hanging in graceful folds past her hips. He didn't know why he suddenly thought of it as a shroud. "Something's wrong, Jubilee."

The Negro turned to follow Jesse's gaze. "Lordy, it's something bad to make Miss Mattie come out in public without her hair up."

"Red," said Jesse. "You're lookout today. The Canadian River's not more than five miles ahead. Stop the herd about a mile shy of it and take them up in bunches to water. Let them graze, then trail them parallel to the river for another four or five miles. Make camp and wait for word."

"What you gonna do, Jesse?" asked Red, shoving the last piece of his biscuit in his mouth and handing his plate to Jubilee.

"I don't know yet, but it appears Mattie is unwell. I'll need to see about her." He started toward her wagon with long strides, then broke into a run, his sense of uneasiness growing to a knot in his chest.

He heard steps behind him. "I is coming, too, Jesse," panted the ex-slave.

Jesse didn't take time to answer. Reaching the wagon, he vaulted over the tailgate. The interior was dim, the sun not yet high enough for its rays to pierce the heavy canvas top, and he nearly didn't see the two figures huddled under the sheet.

"Mattie!" he exclaimed, jerking at the sheet and revealing a woman with slack face and vacant eyes that hardly resembled the golden-haired beauty that troubled his mind and turned his body to aching want. He dropped to his knees and gathered her up. "Mattie, what is it?"

"Jesse!" said Leon, throwing his small naked arms around the trail boss's neck. His eyes were filled with the confusion and fear that Jesse knew came only to the very young and the very innocent when their world turned upside down.

Jubilee climbed into the wagon. "Miss Mattie, what's troubling you?"

Mattie struggled against Jesse's hold, her eyes wide and wild and so filled with self-hatred that he clenched his jaw to keep from cursing God for not watching over her.

"Let go!" screamed Mattie. "I'll give them to you, then you can vomit."

"Give me what, Mattie?"

She stopped struggling and cringed away instead. "Lice! I'm filthy with lice. Leon and I. Don't you understand? We're unclean! Oh, God, I'm so ashamed!"

Jesse understood why Mattie had gone to Samuel's wagon when she never had before. A lady like Mattie Hunter would never think of confessing such an intimate matter to anyone but her husband unless desperation pushed her to it. In this case, desperation was named Samuel Hunter.

He brushed her hair away from her face. "There is no need to be ashamed, Mattie. I wish I had a silver dollar for every grayback I've found on my miserable hide. Every trail hand on this drive has given room to the little devils at one time or another."

"I think maybe a couple of them is carrying graybacks this drive, Jesse. Danny's been scratching like he got the measles, and I think I gots them, too."

"Probably from Leon," said Jesse. "You and Danny spend the most time holding the boy. You and he had better take a bath with lye soap and boil your clothes when you get to the Canadian. I'll take Mattie and Leon upriver from the herd and strip out the wagon and tell her what to do to clean herself. We'll join you when we're through. Might be two or three days. I want to make sure she and this wagon are cleaner than a hound's tooth."

"And I reckon I'll be going along. Squinty can cook while I is gone. I ain't have folks talking about you being alone with Miss Mattie."

"Damn it, Jubilee, look at her. She's right on the edge of losing her mind. Do you think I'd make an improper gesture and be responsible for tipping her over?"

"I don't think nothing of the kind, but folks talk even when they ain't got nothing to talk about. Besides, I figures Miss Mattie gonna need family. All this gonna be mighty embarrassing to a lady like her."

Mighty embarrassing was one of the darkie's more notable understatements, thought Jesse as he sat on the edge of the Canadian and scrubbed a wiggling Leon with lye soap, then rubbed a solution of tobacco and water through his hair. He wasn't certain exactly why tobacco juice killed lice in hair better than any other remedy, but it did. He finished by washing out the tobacco with another lathering of lye soap, then handed the slippery little boy to a scrubbed and newly shorn Jubilee.

"Let him run around buck naked until some of those wet clothes finish drying. And for God's sake, put on a hat. You practically shaved all your hair off. I don't care if you are already black as the ace of spades, the sun will boil the top of your head."

"My hat's staked out over an anthill like you told

me. I don't figure them ants gonna finish eating it clean of them varmints and their eggs for a day or so."

"Then wrap your head up in a turban, Jubilee. I don't need you passing out on me. There's too much to do."

Jubilee looked offended. "I ain't fixing to pass out. I'm gonna finish emptying out that wagon and scrubbing it down."

"Burn it!" said Mattie suddenly, her eyes glittering with an expression of comprehension and horror.

It was the first time she had spoken since they had left the herd nearly six hours ago, and Jesse felt something loosen inside. He had been afraid she would be lost inside her own mind. "We can't burn it, Mattie. You're a long way from a seamstress or a store, and you'll need your clothes and your household goods."

"I won't touch anything in that wagon again." Her voice was flat again, untouched by any emotion, and that glazed, unfocused look had returned to her eyes.

"You have no choice, Mattie," he said in as brutal a voice as he could bring himself to use. "I won't burn the wagon and neither will Jubilee. Don't talk like an empty-headed woman at a tea party."

"Jesse! There ain't no call for talking like that to Miss Mattie," said Jubilee. "She just a mite upset right now. She don't know what she's saying."

Jesse rose to his feet and grabbed the darkie's arm. "She might never know what she's saying again either, if we can't bring her back to feeling something except how dirty she thinks she is. Look at her eyes, Jubilee. Look at how she hates herself. She can't survive hating herself like that. Goddamn that bastard Hunter! He's responsible for this, him and her own upbringing that won't let her accept that dirt and lice and hardship are as much a part of life as silk dresses. You all taught her not to accept herself. You didn't respect her, goddamn it! None of you did!"

He stripped off his vest and pulled his heavy shirt over his head, felt the hot wind dry the sweat on his bare chest, then sat down and pulled off his tight-fitting boots and socks.

"Lordy, Jesse, what you think you're doing? You gonna shock whatever sense Miss Mattie got left right out of her head showing your hairy chest like that."

Jesse rolled up his pants legs as far as he could. "I hope I shock her. I hope I bring out all those drawing-room manners and that primness she hides her real nature behind so she'll call the wrath of God down on my head for not being a gentleman, because then she won't be calling it down upon herself for some imagined transgression against polite society."

He got up and, rubbing his hands on his pants, glanced at Jubilee. "It's time. You take Leon and go back to boiling clothes. And don't come running to save her if she starts screaming. You can't protect her from what needs to be done, and I won't."

Jubilee picked up Leon who had been happily making mud pies on the riverbank. He stood irresolute, an aging man who Jesse well knew had himself been raised to respect the drawing room, and watched a young woman of another race who nevertheless was the daughter of his heart. Finally he turned away, but not before Jesse saw the tears. "I gives her to you to care for 'cause I reckon you can save her."

Mattie saw Jubilee looking at her and deliberately turned her head. She wished he and Jesse would stop talking about her and go away. Then she could walk down to the river and hide among the cottonwoods that lined its banks. No one would ever have to look at her again. She pushed away considerations of how she would survive, angry that her mind persisted in bringing such matters to her attention when retaining some

Discover a World of Timeless Romance Without Leaving Home

Get
4 FREE
Historical Romances from Harper Monogram.

JOIN THE TIMELESS ROMANCE READER SERVICE AND GET FOUR OF TODAY'S MOST EXCITING HISTORICAL ROMANCES FREE, WITHOUT OBLIGATION!

Imagine getting today's very best historical romances sent directly to your home – at a total savings of at least $2.00 a month. Now you can be among the first to be swept away by the latest from Candace Camp, Constance O'Banyon, Patricia Hagan, Parris Afton Bonds or Susan Wiggs. You get all that – and that's just the beginning.

PREVIEW AT HOME WITHOUT OBLIGATION AND SAVE.

Each month, you'll receive four new romances to preview without obligation for 10 days. You'll pay the low subscriber price of just $4.00 per title – a total savings of at least $2.00 a month!

Postage and handling is absolutely free and there is no minimum number of books you must buy. You may cancel your subscription at any time with no obligation.

GET YOUR FOUR FREE BOOKS TODAY ($20.49 VALUE)

FILL IN THE ORDER FORM BELOW NOW!

YES! *I want to join the Timeless Romance Reader Service. Please send me my 4 FREE HarperMonogram historical romances. Then each month send me 4 new historical romances to preview without obligation for 10 days. I'll pay the low subscription price of $4.00 for every book I choose to keep – a total savings of at least $2.00 each month – and home delivery is free! I understand that I may return any title within 10 days without obligation and I may cancel this subscription at any time without obligation. There is no minimum number of books to purchase.*

NAME_____

ADDRESS_____

CITY_____STATE_____ZIP_____

TELEPHONE_____

SIGNATURE_____

(If under 18 parent or guardian must sign. Program, price, terms, and conditions subject to cancellation and change. Orders subject to acceptance by HarperMonogram.)

GET 4 FREE BOOKS
(A $20.49 VALUE)

TIMELESS ROMANCE READER SERVICE

120 Brighton Road
P.O. Box 5069
Clifton, NJ 07015-5069

AFFIX STAMP HERE

semblance of Mattie Jo Hunter, gentlewoman, was so much more important.

"Mattie."

She heard Jesse's voice and put her hands over her ears and closed her eyes. She didn't want any more to do with him.

He pulled her hands down. "Mattie, look at me."

She tried to free herself, but his fingers were like iron bands around her wrists. "How dare you touch me so! My husband will be most displeased."

Jesse's laugh was ugly. "Then he should be here himself. But he isn't, is he, Mattie? He refused to help you. You have lice and he refused to help you cleanse yourself."

She cried out as his words pierced the numbness in which she had wrapped herself and made her feel again. She didn't want to feel, wanted to stay just as she was, suspended in a nirvana of apathy.

"Leave me alone!" she screamed.

He jerked her to her feet, released her wrists to grab her shoulders, and shook her. "Open your eyes, Mattie!"

Enraged by his treatment, she did—and gasped. "You're naked! Dear God, you're naked! Aren't I shamed enough? Do you have to violate my modesty?"

"I took my shirt off, Mattie, because I didn't see the need of wetting more of my clothes than necessary. I have neither shamed or violated you."

She stared at him, appalled and fascinated at the same time. Curly black hair covered the upper portion of his broad chest, narrowing to a strip that vanished beneath the waistband of his trousers. The drawings of the Greek statues had shown no such hair, although the muscle and sinew that bunched and rippled with his every movement made a bas-relief sculpture of his chest similar to that of a statue of Hercules. Suddenly she realized that the drawings that had so disturbed her young girlhood pictured idealized figures that in no way compared to Jesse's raw masculinity. The Greek gods and heroes were myths that in no wise threatened her. Jesse was real and he compromised her in a way she only vaguely understood.

"But propriety is all I have left!" she cried.

His eyes didn't move, nor did his face soften. "Strip out of your clothes, Mattie, and get in the river."

She wrapped her arms around herself and cringed away, unable to decide whether she was more terrified or horrified. "No! I can't! Don't you understand? No lady removes her clothes outside the privacy of her own bedroom, and to do so in the open, in front of a man . . ." Her voice rose to a wail. "I can't!"

His eyes darkened, and she cowered back. "Do you think I am such a scoundrel as to gape at a frightened, embarrassed woman? I will turn my back until you are in the water."

She shook her head violently. He didn't understand that what he was asking violated every tenet of acceptable behavior. She even knew some women who bathed in their chemises to avoid seeing their own nakedness. "It's impossible! To expose oneself in such a way is shameful."

"It's a damn sight less shameful than refusing to rid yourself of lice because you think your body is some kind of dirty secret. You're all of a piece, Mattie. Your body is as much a part of you as your face or your hair. Now, do you strip off and jump in the river with a bar of lye soap, or do I strip you and scrub you myself?"

She crossed her arms over her breasts. "You wouldn't dare!"

"You have five minutes."

She stared at his implacable face and swallowed. He would do it, and she would be defenseless against his strength. "Let me go."

He released her and she walked to the edge of the

A TIME TOO LATE

river. "Don't stray too far from the bank, Mattie. It's a treacherous river during spring runoff, or anytime for that matter. The sand can give way under your feet. Cattle and wagons can be mired down in the blink of an eye. And so can men."

She knelt down and dipped her hand in the water. "It's the right color then, isn't it, Jesse? Red as blood."

"To the cowman, it is blood, this land's blood. It's water, Mattie, and in this country it's more precious than gold."

Sitting down, she removed Samuel's boots and her cotton stockings and garters, then stood up and methodically took off one garment after another until she was clothed only in her hair, which she pulled over her shoulders to cover her breasts. Bending over, she picked up the bar of soap and rag left by Jesse and stepped into the river, catching her breath at its icy temperature. Blood should be warm.

She waded out until the water reached her knees, then knelt down and began to wash. She was still exposed to the waist and the wind kept whipping her hair up to expose her breasts with their cold, erect nipples. The lye soap was harsh and stung her skin. It also didn't lather well, at least not to Mattie's way of thinking.

Wading out farther, she dipped her head underwater to wet it, then began to rub the bar of soap all over her hair in an attempt to work up enough lather for an adequate shampoo. It was always difficult to wash hair as long and thick as hers, and to do so with lye soap while kneeling in a cold river was nearly impossible. After repeatedly dropping the soap and having to splash after it awkwardly, Mattie finally stood up and threw it on the bank. As she did so a dollop of lather ran down her forehead and she felt as though hot coals had suddenly been pressed into her eye sockets.

She clawed at her eyes and lost her balance, falling

facedown in the Canadian River. As the icy water flooded her mouth and nose she floundered on the river bottom, felt the sand give way beneath her hand. Suddenly something jerked on her hair, pulling her head above the water, and she felt an arm circle her chest just under her breasts and lift her to her knees. Her back thudded against a broad chest, and she felt the tickling of body hair like a kitten's soft fur.

"Are you all right, Mattie?" Jesse demanded.

She coughed up water, felt more water running from her nose, and finally managed to draw breath. "Damn those ungodly, filthy Indians, and damn you, Jesse McDade, for ever letting them into camp!"

"Godliness has nothing to do with it, Mattie. There's not an Indian or a white man west of the Mississippi that hasn't kept company with a grayback or two. It has to do with sharing quarters and grub on the trail, with having no fancy bathtubs and maybe not even a creek to swim in, and what water there is goes to the cattle and horses first, and then to the men for drinking. It has to do with learning to survive our own dirt and smell, but it doesn't have a damn thing to do with whether a man is good or bad. Lice are a fact of life, and so is charity. Even if I had known that the Comanches were lousy, I wouldn't have turned them away. They were hungry and I fed them. Out here, if you're not your brother's keeper, then you're his murderer. Turn away a hurt or hungry man, and the chances are he'll die before he finds another man to help him. There are so few of us in this land, Mattie, that we have to help one another. It's a matter of survival."

She slumped over his arm, feeling sick and ashamed. "I'm sorry, Jesse. I would not let another human being starve just to save myself from possible embarrassment. I don't want you to think that of me."

"I never thought that, Mattie."

He let go of her and she felt him back away. She shivered at the loss of his warmth, then cowered down in the water in an attempt to cover her nakedness. She was uncertain which facet of her behavior horrified her most: that she had been kneeling—naked—in Jesse's arms, or that she had never spared a thought to her breach of propriety.

"Go away, Jesse. Please don't violate my modesty further."

She felt him gather her hair up, and fought to hold the wet strands over her breasts. "Dear God, what are you doing to me?"

"I have to cut your hair, Mattie, at least to your shoulders and preferably shorter. It's impractical to attempt to kill lice and their eggs in hair that hangs past your hips."

She half rose and fought to pull the heavy masses of hair from his grip. "No! Not my hair. Isn't it enough that you strip away my modesty, shame me by demanding I expose myself in a river without any thought of my feelings? Please, Jesse, my hair, any woman's hair, is so important. Please don't do this. Please leave me something of myself."

She heard him expel a breath, then started as he reached around her and gently loosened her grip from her hair. "I'm sorry, Mattie, but there are no halfway measures possible in this land. You cannot survive with one foot in the drawing room and one foot on the prairie." He withdrew one hand and when it reappeared, she saw the sharp Bowie knife. "Will you break, Mattie Hunter, or will you survive?"

She let her hands fall limply into the water, and watched the long golden strands of hair float away on the bloodred current along with the last of her girlish illusions. She, not the land, must be the one to compromise. She must bend, or she would break. And she would not break; she would survive and flourish.

She felt Jesse's hands grasp her shoulders and raised her own to lace her fingers between his. She heard him catch his breath with a groan, then pull her gently back against his chest and lean forward to rest his lips against their entwined hands. She felt time slow down, then stop, to allow them an interval uncounted and unseen by others when they might admit the chaste but forbidden bond between them.

Mattie turned her head and pressed her lips against his cheek. She and Jesse had earned this time together.

CHAPTER 15

Jesse stood at the edge of the bluff and smoked a cigarette while gazing down at the Canadian River a hundred feet below. He hated a man who boasted overmuch, but there were times for it and this was one. He had remembered this particular section of the Canadian River Valley from his one trip into the Llano Estacado with Goodnight, and without maps or guides or any directions but the stars and his own sense of seeking home, had found it again. Maybe he wasn't a trailblazer like Goodnight, but he wasn't a slouch at finding his way either.

And his way began here, in this valley of the Canadian. Tall red bluffs broken by small, spring-fed tributary streams stretched along the north banks of the river, while rolling breaks on the south banks extended for miles before gently flattening out again. Juniper, cottonwood trees, plum thickets, willow, hackberry, some mesquite, wild china, and even scrub oak and grape along some stretches would provide fuel and lumber to build corrals and pens. The small tributary valleys would provide both protection for the cattle from blizzards as well as paths to the top of the escarpment where rich, flat pastureland stretched northward farther than a man could dream. It stretched almost that far to the south, too, but Charlie Goodnight's Palo Duro Canyon lay to the south, and Jesse was too respectful to crowd him. Or not too much anyway.

He ground his cigarette beneath his heel, making sure no spark remained, and rested his hand on his gelding's withers. "It's a good land, old fellow, and whether I look north or south, the river will always be to my back." And in a land with little rain, that was important. The man who claimed the river, or rather the land up to its edge, controlled the grazing adjacent to it. While he was buying up sections for the Colonel, he would buy up some of his own, all he could afford. Along the river.

He stepped closer to the edge of the bluff. "Doesn't look like much of a river, does it? Not like the Mississippi or the Missouri or the Arkansas or even the Brazos. It's often sand-choked and sometimes doesn't look to have much water, but the riverbed is nearly three quarters of a mile wide along this stretch with a four-mile floodplain. There's more water in the Canadian than a man thinks, and on occasion when a flash flood sweeps down its channel, there's more water than a man wants."

He fell silent, gazing into the distance. He estimated the valley itself to be twenty miles wide at this point, a generous enough area to graze the cattle while he went about staking out the boundaries of Mattie's ranch. And his own, for which he was trading five years of his life to Colonel Andrew Corley.

Yes, Jesse McDade, you picked a mighty fine spot, he thought as he mounted his gelding and let it pick its way down the bluff.

When he reached the little group of wagons pulled up a quarter of a mile across the river, he caught himself grinding his teeth. The only drawback to the next five years would not be the struggle against harsh winters and blazing hot summers, or the danger of prairie fires, or screwworms in injured cattle, or tick fever in the herd caught from longhorns being trailed through the Panhandle from South Texas to pastures on the northern plains. The drawback was that in addition to whatever obstacles nature and fate might throw at him, he would have to deal with Samuel Hunter. He had kept his distance from Hunter for a week, ever since the man had refused Mattie help, because he did not trust himself not to kill him. But there was no help for it today. He had to endure the man's company. To outsiders, Samuel Hunter was the owner of the herd, Jesse's arrangements with the Colonel notwithstanding. The trail drive was over, and Jesse no longer had absolute, unquestioned authority granted by tradition. Now his authority rested on a written contract with the Colonel. But the Colonel was in Pueblo, and Samuel was in Texas. To those with whom Jesse must deal and deal quickly—the land speculators and the surveyors—Samuel was the man in charge, at least at first blush. With Samuel, the blush would quickly fade, but Jesse anticipated much more teeth-grinding frustration in the interim. On the other hand, Samuel also lacked any ability whatsoever to lead men. The cowboys would never follow his orders, so Jesse didn't fear that Samuel would be more than a pesky fly on a cow's rump as far as day-to-day operations went. But he could be a problem otherwise if he chose, or if anyone stronger encouraged him to be. Fortunately Samuel possessed such an indolent nature that he stirred himself only to see to his own comfort. Jesse would see to it that most situations requiring Samuel's nominal presence would be so fraught with discomfort that the man would avoid them like the plague.

In the meantime there was Mattie. A stronger woman had walked out of the Canadian than had walked into it, and Jesse could no longer pretend that his interest was suitable. It was not. He desired her as much as he respected her. As they had knelt together in that swirling water only his honor had persuaded him to kiss their entwined fingers rather than her naked breasts. Only his honor and her innocence kept him from her, and God help them both if either should ever fail.

He dismounted and tied his horse to the back of the chuck wagon. Samuel sat on a crate far enough away from the campfire so that he didn't feel its heat, while Mattie, her basque and skirt covered by an apron, mixed sourdough biscuits in a large pot with Leon snatching bits of dough to share with Baby.

"Now you needs a smidgen more lard and another pinch of soda, Miss Mattie," said Jubilee, leaning over her shoulder to watch. "Else you gonna end up with flat 'sinkers' instead of fluffy biscuits."

Mattie wiped her forehead with the back of her arm, then ladled another spoonful of lard out of a large can, took as much soda as she could pinch between her thumb and first finger, and dropped both ingredients into her dough. Her sunbonnet dangled down her back and her short hair brushed her collar as she concentrated her frowning attention on her work.

Jesse stepped up beside her. "Mattie, I'll have to add you to the payroll as assistant cook."

Her golden eyes flashed up at him and a faint red color tinted her face before she turned back to her biscuit making. "I'm afraid my biscuits don't hold a candle to my lemon pies, Jesse, but there aren't any lemons out here, so I guess the cowboys will never know that. I can serve up canned tomatoes as well as Jubilee, though."

A TIME TOO LATE
225

Jesse caught a faint breathless quality in her voice that told him, even if her eyes had not, that she remembered the river and was worrying it around like a dog worries a bone. He supposed that was natural. She had sloughed off part of herself that day and wasn't comfortable yet with what she had uncovered. It took longer than a week to get acquainted with a stranger.

"I guess you're wondering about when I'll build that dugout," he said finally.

"The thought had crossed my mind," she admitted with another flashing glance, this one holding unhappy resentment.

There was still a bit of the old Mattie Hunter inside her, Jesse realized. She wasn't completely reconciled to life without silk dresses and comfortable quarters.

"Maybe I won't have to build it," he said. "Maybe I can provide you with something better."

"I've been waiting for you to admit you lied, McDade," Samuel interrupted, rising to his feet and strolling toward them with a self-satisfied smirk. "You deliberately misled us. You said there were no trees when in fact there is a whole river valley full of them, enough for a city of houses. You caused needless suffering. I can't tell you the number of nights I tossed restlessly in my wagon unable to sleep because of the prospect of living in a hole in the ground like a badger."

Jesse remembered whipping the last man who called him a liar, but decided to let Samuel's remark pass, since he suspected his desire to punish the man had little to do with his insult and everything to do with Mattie. "I never denied there were trees along the Canadian. I merely said I had no intention of allowing my cowboys to chop them for the purposes of building a house. There's another way. With a persuasive tongue and some of the Colonel's funds, I propose to buy Mattie a Mexican plaza by nightfall."

"What!" exclaimed Mattie, wiping her hands on her apron.

"There are a string of plazas along the Canadian River Valley owned by Mexican sheepherders from New Mexico Territory. They graze their sheep on the free grass. Buying a plaza will provide Mattie her house and get rid of one flock of sheep at the same time. I have no desire to start a range war to clear out the sheep. Money is cheaper than blood. So saddle a horse, Mr. Hunter, and let's pay a call on Señor Alessandro Mendoza."

"I'm coming, too," said Mattie, removing her apron.

"Of course you aren't, Mattie," said Samuel. "This is business. It's not your place to come along. You wait here."

"If I'm to live in this plaza, then it is my business. I will no longer wait alone while decisions are made, and be told about them later as though I were no older than Leon."

"You will do as I say, Mattie. It is your duty as my wife."

Mattie turned to Jesse. "Will you select a gentle mount for me, or is your mind set against me, too?"

"I'll get your sidesaddle, Mattie," said Jesse, turning toward her wagon.

Samuel caught his arm. "You are interfering, McDade. This is a matter between husband and wife."

Jesse shook free of Samuel's grip. "This is a business matter, Hunter, and Mattie has a business interest."

"She's a woman! What does she know about business?" demanded Samuel angrily.

"She can learn! Being born a woman shouldn't condemn her to a lifetime of stupidity and helplessness." He walked away before Samuel could answer and

A TIME TOO LATE

dragged Mattie's sidesaddle from her wagon.

"You ain't doing Miss Mattie no favor by taking her side against her husband," said Jubilee, following Jesse to the remuda.

Jesse lassoed a chestnut gelding that was better broke than the other horses in the remuda. At least a rider didn't have to take the "pitch" out of it every morning by letting it buck a few times just to prove its independence. "Mattie is the Colonel's daughter and will own half this ranch. She needs to learn to protect her own interests against the poor judgment of her husband. I'm merely seeing to it that she has that opportunity."

The ex-slave shook his head. "That ain't why you're doing it, or leastwise not all of it. You two pairing off like wolves, but Miss Mattie ain't no wolf, and Hunter's gonna take his mad out on her."

Jesse tightened the saddle cinch. "If he ever hits her, he won't live to hit her a second time."

"He ain't gonna do nothing like that. He ain't such a fool as you thinks. But he's her husband, and he's got rights over Miss Mattie you can't do nothing about."

Jesse thought of Mattie's satiny skin under his hands, the coral-tipped breasts he had tried not to look at while he was cutting her hair, the thin, vulnerable nape of her neck, and shuddered. A woman had so many soft, tender places that a man might hurt if he were so inclined.

Jesse spat out a mouthful of bile. "Even Samuel wouldn't do her harm."

"I reckon it depends on what you calls harm." The black man looked away, his eyes focused inward toward times past. "You ain't never been a slave, Jesse, so you don't feel things like I do. But I figure Miss Mattie does. Being married to Hunter must be a lot like being a slave. Leastwise she don't belong to herself if he say she don't, and if he's in the mood to pester her, she's obliged to accept him whether she wants to or not. I figure that's as close to harm as a body's likely to get."

"God Almighty, Jubilee!"

"If He ain't interfered, Jesse, what right does you have?"

Built of adobe bricks, Alessandro Mendoza's plaza was fifty-one feet wide and forty-six feet long with its walls and partitions a full eighteen inches thick. Its roof was made of cottonwood poles, six to twelve inches in diameter, laid side by side from wall to wall and covered over first by lumber brought from New Mexico sawmills, then by a two-inch layer of adobe mud topped by another eighteen inches of dirt. Jesse claimed the lumber and hard adobe mud prevented dirt from filtering through the cottonwood ceiling, but Mattie reserved judgment. Men seldom noticed dust as much as women, and she doubted the construction was as tight as all that.

Three rooms opened off each side of a ten-foot hallway and each of the six rooms had a window with heavy wooden shutters. The house also boasted packed-earth floors and an eighty-foot corral joined to the north end by an adobe wall. Mattie also reserved judgment about the last two features. Given Leon's fondness for making mud pies, and the multitude of flies that kept company with the livestock, she wasn't certain dirt floors and a corral outside her parlor window were desirable.

A spring in back of the plaza bubbled with the first clear water Mattie had seen in weeks. It would be nice not to have to share water with fish and cattle. But it was the garden, already planted with onions, melons, sweet corn, squash, cabbage, tomatoes, beans, and green peppers, as much as the plaza that decided

Mattie. If caught between a rock and a hard place, she could live in a dugout, but she would kill for the chance to eat something besides beans, beef, and canned or dried fruit. Just looking at the tiny green peppers beginning to form made her mouth water. She could almost hear the crisp sound a pepper made as you first bit into it.

And the tomatoes. She remembered Aunt Patty sometimes frying green tomatoes and serving a squash casserole made with crisp onions, cheese, and covered with golden-brown bread crumbs. Her mouth watered again, and she licked her lips. She caught Jesse looking at her, a smile on his face as though he divined her thoughts, and felt her stomach hollow out in a way that had nothing to do with hunger.

Quickly she turned to Samuel. "It's wonderful, isn't it?"

He cocked one eyebrow and pursed his lips. "It is a mud house, Mattie, whatever kind of fancy name McDade might give it."

She tamped down a flash of irritation that urged her to scream at him. "But it is better than a dugout, Samuel. At least the roof won't leak and dirt won't fall on our heads—or not as much anyway. Jesse says the thick walls will help keep it cool in the summer and warm in the winter. And there is one of those little round fireplaces in every room. Jesse says they heat the air quite pleasantly in the winter."

"If Jesse says so, then it must be the word from on high," snapped Samuel. "Really, Mattie, your reliance on our ranch manager is most unseemly. His supervising at your delousing did not convey sainthood on him."

Mattie glanced at Alessandro Mendoza, standing with Jesse by the spring less than twenty feet away, and hoped he had not overheard Samuel's remark. The sheepman's polite but puzzled expression reminded her that he didn't speak English, or at least not enough to understand what occasioned her red face.

Jesse understood, though, but other than a slight narrowing of eyes, whose color suddenly reminded her of ashes on a hearth that were banked but still smoldering, he made no other move. She closed her own eyes briefly in thanksgiving. It was enough to be humiliated in public without being the subject of an altercation between Samuel and Jesse.

"Please, Samuel," she whispered. "Don't embarrass me so."

He smiled at her, his expression brooding. "But it's quite all right for you to embarrass me, is it, Mattie?" He reached out and grasped her wrist, squeezing it until she imagined she could hear the fragile bones grinding together. "It's quite all right to defy me in front of Jesse McDade, isn't it, Mattie?"

She held back her tears by an effort of will. "Let go of me, Samuel."

He looked down at her wrist where his fingers were digging into soft flesh and loosed his hold to observe the dark red marks he'd left on her white skin. He released her hand and stepped back, his expression sober. "I apologize, Mattie. I should not have done that, but my nature coarsens with each passing day in this rough country until I despair of restraining it. Help me, Mattie, by not provoking me, lest your defiance drives me mad one day."

She caught his plaintive tone and felt her own despair. She wanted to reassure him as she would Leon, but at the same time a cold, practical voice she had only recently begun to hear within her mind asked her why Samuel's peace should come at the price of her own. That she should always please others with never a thought of pleasing herself suddenly seemed less a virtue than a path to martyrdom.

Yet Samuel was her husband and she owed him loyalty. "We must both try harder." She took his hand and tugged him over to the row of pepper plants. "Look, Samuel, aren't those tiny peppers more beautiful than roses?"

He smiled at her. "Sometimes you're like a child, Mattie, imagining beauty in the most mundane things. I'm quite fond of you at times like this, but I must confess I prefer roses to pepper plants."

"You can't eat roses, Samuel," she replied, wondering when her life would have room again for both roses and peppers. Or if it ever would.

"Samuel, Señor Mendoza has invited us to share a glass of tequila with him while we discuss our business," said Jesse, his voice carefully neutral.

Samuel let go of Mattie's hand. "You mean you haven't already concluded the business? What were you doing, McDade, with all your blathering in Spanish with that Mexican?"

Jesse's nostrils flared as Mattie saw him draw in a deep breath. "Mendoza is not Mexican. He is Spanish and proud as Lucifer of his lineage. Don't offend him by treating him as if he were a peasant. As for our business, I only just now told him of our intentions to establish a ranch and run cattle where his sheep are grazing."

"What were you telling him before?" demanded Samuel.

Jesse shrugged. "I was admiring his plaza."

"You were flattering him, McDade!"

"I don't flatter a man I respect, Hunter, and I respect Mendoza. He has been here less than a year and accomplished more than most men would in twice that time. I only regret that he and I cannot be neighbors, but cattle and sheep don't mix, and he knows it as well as I."

Mattie followed the men into the plaza, seated herself at the table in the large kitchen, and watched the

Spaniard remove three glasses and a bottle of tequila from an elaborately carved cupboard. He turned around, saw Mattie, and snapped out a question in Spanish.

Jesse casually dropped into the chair next to Mattie's, leaned back, and answered Mendoza's question, his eyes dark and hard in contrast to his relaxed posture.

"What did he say about me?" asked Mattie, staring at Mendoza from eyes she knew were as hard as Jesse's. She was tired of men speaking of her as if she weren't present.

Jesse hesitated. "He said he was startled to see you sitting with the men."

She turned her head and glared at Jesse. "I doubt he used those words, not when he is looking at me as though I were a fly he found in his soup. What did he say exactly, and do me the honor of not prevaricating. I am not a child to be lied to."

Jesse nodded. "He asked why the yellow-eyed woman was so ill-mannered as to sit with the men while business was being discussed."

Mattie inclined her head toward the Spaniard, all the resentment and anger and confusion from years of meeting everyone's expectations and suffering disapproval when she failed bubbling over like a caldron over too hot a flame. "I am Mattie Hunter, and I've come to buy your plaza."

Mendoza set the bottle and glasses on the table with a thump, and stood looking down at Mattie. "Why should I sell you my plaza?" he asked in heavily accented English.

Mattie felt her face turn red again. If Mendoza spoke English, he'd understood Samuel's remark about lice after all. Damn Samuel and Mendoza, too. "Because you appear to be an intelligent and hardworking man, too intelligent to want to lose your investment in this plaza when I buy the land your sheep are grazing and order my cowboys to evict you from my property."

"The grass is free, Señora Hunter," said Mendoza, his voice stiff with dislike.

Mattie swallowed, aware that she had climbed out on a limb, one Mendoza might well very chop off. She knew nothing of the legal status of land in the Panhandle, knew nothing of Texas and its policy on public land. But she knew her father, and knew he would never invest a cent in any endeavor if he didn't own every bit of it—lock, stock, and barrel. Or in this case—plaza.

"The grass is free only until I buy it, Mr. Mendoza," she said.

He waved his hand as though swatting away her words. "I do not talk business with women. I will speak only to your husband."

Samuel drained a glass of tequila. "And rightly so, Mr. Mendoza. Women are useless at the subtleties of commerce."

"Samuel! Please!" exclaimed Mattie, at a loss to decide whether she was more angry at her husband for his slighting remark, or at his failure to support her argument. In his eagerness to disparage her, he threatened their mutual interests, a case of cutting off your nose to spite your face if Mattie had ever seen one.

Jesse grasped her hand under cover of the table and gently stroked the bruises left by Samuel. Stunned by his illicit caress and by her own calm acceptance of it, she barely heard his whispered words. "Never let your opponent goad you into losing your temper, Mattie."

He looked across the table at the other two men and raised his voice. "In this case Mrs. Hunter has grasped the subtleties very well, Samuel. Texas is offering Panhandle land for sale, Mendoza, and we are buying. When word gets out about the rich grazing, other cattlemen will come. Not all will buy all their land. Many will graze on public land as long as possible, but I'm a southerner, and so is Mrs. Hunter's father, whose agent I am. Any southerner who lost his property after the war is very concerned about legal possession. We don't intend to be thrown off our land again because we failed to get clear title. Of course, you may buy land, too. Then you may be in the position to evict us."

Mendoza sat down, his black eyes haughty. "The sheepmen have never paid for grass. We always graze our sheep on public land. It is our tradition."

Jesse nodded, his eyes steady on the sheepherder. "It's the cattleman's tradition, too, Mendoza, but nothing stays the same. Open range will soon pass. Too many people coming west for it to last much longer. Farmers with plows will turn over the grass and kill it, leaving the land to bleed away its topsoil between crops. It's time for us to buy what we can, preserve it for as long as we can."

Mattie heard the melancholy in Jesse's voice, saw it reflected in Mendoza's face, and felt deeply ashamed. She thought she had been threatening the sheepherder's property when instead she had been threatening his soul.

Mendoza sighed and looked away, his expression stoic. "It will be as you say, Mr. McDade, but I will follow tradition until it is no more, and perhaps it will last until my death. Some of us chose to live in a time too late. I will sell my plaza to you and that Hunter woman"—he gestured at Mattie—"who is too bold for my taste, and I will return to New Mexico, but I am not the only sheepherder on the Canadian."

He reached for the bottle of tequila and smiled, a peculiar sort of smile that sent warning tingles up Mattie's back. "Tell me, Mr. McDade, does

Goodnight know what it is you are doing? Does Goodnight know you are in the Canadian River Valley?"

"He knows I'm coming, and I'm guessing he'll soon hear I've arrived."

Mendoza poured two glasses of tequila and pushed one toward Jesse. "I'm certain of it, Mr. McDade. Then you, too, may have to make a choice you do not like."

CHAPTER 16

Late August brought unremitting heat and such hordes of flies that it was almost impossible to stand still outside without being covered with a buzzing, stinging blanket of them. Mattie closed all the shutters and stuffed rags around the cracks in an attempt to keep them from coming in the house. Jubilee kept a fire going in the kitchen stove to keep the flies from crawling down the chimney while tired, sweaty cowboys huddled around the table to eat with one hand while swatting at flies with the other. Mattie unrolled bolts of fine muslin to make tents to cover each bed so tired men might sleep without their buzzing companions. Cattle, blinded and maddened by the flies, would scatter in small stampedes or run over the edges of gullies and bluffs like lemmings. Jesse kept them loose herded to prevent their bunching up and goring one another in their frantic uneasiness, for every cut and open wound on an animal meant screwworm.

Jesse claimed the buffalo hunters were responsible

A TIME TOO LATE

because when they slaughtered the animals for their hides, they left the dead carcasses on the prairie to rot, providing breeding grounds for flies. Mattie, exhausted and plagued by the suspicion that Samuel's last visit to her bed had left her with more than a painful memory, didn't care who was responsible for the flies; she only wished them gone and prayed for an early winter.

But each day the mercury in the thermometer Jesse hung outside the backdoor hovered above one hundred, and the wind, as ever-present as the sun, died away. The leaves on the cottonwoods that shaded the spring back of the plaza hung limp and wilted, and the grass that covered the land turned yellow as hay. Mattie and Jubilee carried water for the garden and the soil drank it up and turned dry again within hours. The sun burned the men's skin to the color of mahogany and they soaked their bandannas and tied them around their faces to cool the air they breathed. Mattie left off her last petticoat in favor of a long chemise, cut off the legs of her drawers to midthigh, and made herself a Mother Hubbard out of cool, yellow-checked gingham. And Jubilee browned flour in a skillet for Leon's heat rash.

But Mattie remembered that first August in Texas for more than the heat and the flies. It was the month Jesse broke his leg, and Charles Goodnight came calling.

"Miss Mattie!"

Red burst through the front door just as Mattie lifted her head away from the chamber pot. She had ignominiously lost her lunch for the second day in a row and finally admitted missing her monthly had nothing to do with the hardships of recent life. She was in the family way and it terrified her.

"Miss Mattie!"

"What for you screaming, Red?" Mattie heard Jubilee ask the cowboy as she wearily replaced the lid on the chamber pot and pushed it under the bed. Her room smelled of sweat and vomit and heat. She'd never known until now that heat had its own odor. But it did. It smelled of dust kicked up by cattle hooves, smoke from tiny campfires, and tar. Hot weather was screwworm weather, and the cowboys would heat up what they called "smear," a loose coal-tar substance, until it became liquid, then cover the cattle's infected wounds with it. There was more to the treatment than that, but Mattie's delicate stomach forbid her thinking of the cowboys first cleaning out the larvae with their knives.

"Jesse's done broke his leg," declared Red. "Squinty and Danny are bringing him in on a travois we rigged up. Happened when we roped that big longhorn cow to treat her. Damn critter whipped her head around and cracked him right across his shin with one of her horns. We all heard it snap like a dry tree limb. The bone ain't sticking out or nothing, so we figure it's a clean enough break, but Miss Mattie sure needs to look at it."

Mattie never remembered getting off her knees and leaving her bedroom, but she found herself standing in the hall. "Close the front door, Red. The flies are particularly bad today. Jubilee, heat some water and bring it to Jesse's room. He'll likely be dirty. Then find me some rags—tear up all my old trains that you'll find in the brown steamer trunk in my room. They ought to be good for something. And take four slats out of my bed. Cut to fit his leg and padded, they'll make fine splints."

"Lordy, Miss Mattie, you don't know nothing about setting nobody's leg," said Jubilee.

"I watched the doctor set Aunt Patty's leg last winter after she tumbled down the servants' stairs. Can you do any better, Jubilee? Red?"

The cowboy shook his head. "Only broken legs I ever been around belonged to horses, and we just shoot them."

"I believe that's too extreme a remedy in Jesse's case." She walked into the bedroom opposite her own. Over Samuel's objections, Jesse lived in the plaza with the family instead of sharing one of the other two small adobe houses that stood fifty feet or so away. As ranch manager, Jesse used his room as both an office and bedroom. It held a bed, a chair, a table that he used as a desk, and a locked campaign chest Mattie knew held the ranch's ledgers and extra cash. A hand-drawn map of the Panhandle with Hunter land marked in red hung on the wall above the bed. A much smaller section was marked off in black. She wondered what it was and decided it must be land Jesse intended buying later.

"Jubilee, if Samuel is home, please ask him for a bottle of tequila. I have observed it has a quicker and more powerful influence on a man than Papa's whiskey. At least it seems to on Samuel. If he is not at home, then go in his room and find a bottle. He bought all of Mendoza's supply, and I think the sheepherder must have been planning on opening a saloon. Surely there is one left."

"Have you taken up tippling, my dear?" asked Samuel, appearing in Jesse's doorway, his eyes holding that glassy belligerent expression she knew from experience heralded one of his binges of drinking.

"Jesse broke his leg," she replied, her voice carefully neutral. "As I'm sure you heard if you have been in your room. Please bring me a bottle, Samuel. Jesse will likely have more need of it than you."

"I don't think so, my dear. McDade prides himself on being a hard man. Let him prove it."

Mattie felt a wave of dizziness sweep over her and grasped Jesse's chair to stay upright. Her stomach seemed to turn over and she bit her lip to hold back the nausea. Jesse needed her and she was sick and miserable with a baby fathered by Samuel Hunter. No, not fathered—that sounded too kind a word—forced upon her the day they had bought the plaza.

"Red, please accompany Mr. Hunter to his room," she said. "And bring me back a bottle of tequila."

"Are you defying me again, Mattie?" asked Samuel softly.

She swallowed. He was most dangerous when he spoke softly. And he would come to her again tonight if she continued to defy him. Samuel used his body to punish her. She knew that now, knew also there was nothing she could do about it. She could not refuse her own husband.

But she would have that tequila.

"Red, bring me the bottle, please," she repeated without breaking eye contact with Samuel. She sensed the cowboy hesitating and felt terror clutch her heart. With Jesse hurt, Samuel was in charge by virtue of his position and his sex. Mattie had no authority except what he chose to allow her. If Red refused to obey her, then she had no recourse. She would be at Samuel's mercy both in the daylight and after dark.

"I reckon I'll have that liquor, Mr. Hunter." Red's voice held no hint of the hired hand speaking to his boss.

She sat down in Jesse's chair before her legs gave way. "Thank you, Red."

Samuel turned toward the cowboy. "You're fired!"

Red lifted his Stetson and scratched his head, then carefully replaced his hat, tilting it slightly over his right eye. "I believe I'll quit, Mr. Hunter, and seeing as how I don't work here anymore, I'm gonna do something I've been wanting to do for a long time and didn't out of respect for Jesse and Miss Mattie."

"What might that be, cowboy?" asked Samuel, his blue eyes filled with contempt.

"This," replied Red as he smashed his fist into Samuel's chin and watched him crumple to the floor.

Mattie clapped her hands over her mouth to keep from screaming.

Red dusted off his hands and turned to Mattie. "A cowboy works for who he wants to. We're independent cusses that way. I'll get your bottle and be on my way, Miss Mattie. I apologize for upsetting you, but I ain't sorry I hit him. If I could have some beans and bacon, I'd appreciate it. It's a long way to anyplace from here and I'll need some grub, but if you say no, I'll understand. He is your husband."

Mattie folded her hands in her lap and cleared her throat. "You work for Jesse and me, Red, and neither one of us fired you. Mr. Hunter is not himself today. I must ask you to excuse him."

Red looked at the unconscious Samuel. "If you say so, Miss Mattie."

Jubilee touched his arm. "Iffen you're going after that bottle, you best be doing it. And as long as you're going in that direction, might just as well drag him along with you. Miss Mattie and me gots to tend to Jesse, and we can't be stepping over nobody to do it."

Mattie watched Red toss Samuel over his shoulder and walk out of the room. "I should not have allowed that, Jubilee. I should not have allowed my husband to be shamed."

"He shamed himself, Miss Mattie," said Jubilee.

"But I should not set myself against him so often. It's wrong."

"Is it right to let Jesse hurt?"

"No!"

"Then don't be whipping yourself. You done right even if nobody else thinks so. And I think it would be right if you stayed with Jesse tonight. He's liable to feeling mighty poorly, most likely have a fever. I'll fix you a pallet on that buffalo robe on the floor next to his bed, and I'll sleep out in the hall in front of his door. Iffen your husband comes looking for you tonight, I'll tell him you're sitting up with the sick for the next little while."

Mattie jerked her head to look at him, then flushed and glanced away. Jubilee knew! He knew that Samuel would hurt her tonight under the guise of claiming his husbandly rights, and was protecting her as best he was able.

She swallowed down her shame. "Thank you, Jubilee."

He patted her shoulder. "I'll be heating up that water, but you ain't gonna be giving Jesse no bath. It ain't proper. Folks will talk."

She waited until he left the room to cover her face and rock back and forth laughing. It wasn't proper to bathe a hurt man, but it was proper to sleep beside his bed to avoid sleeping with her own husband. She doubted anyone in polite Pueblo society would approve of Jubilee's idea of propriety. There was still a part of her that didn't approve either.

When Squinty and Danny carried Jesse into the bedroom, she forgot about propriety. "Strip off his shirt and his boots, Danny, but don't jostle his leg. I'll be right back." She walked across the hall to her bedroom and closed the door. She fumbled through her sewing basket for her scissors and turned to walk back to her door when the shaking began. She dropped the scissors and hugged herself, taking deep breaths and concentrating on an image of the Panhandle sky, deep and high and empty and clear. So must her mind be— empty of fear, clear of visions of Jesse's sweaty, dirt-streaked face with his mouth so tightly shut against pain that it appeared bloodless.

Gradually the shaking stopped, she picked up her scissors, and walked back to Jesse.

Shirtless, he sat propped against the headboard, a gun in his hand and his boots still on. "No one is cutting off my boot. It's the only pair I have and I can't walk or ride barefoot."

"God Almighty, Jesse," protested Danny, his hands held high. "We can't pull it off. No telling what it might do to your leg."

"You won't be walking or riding for a while anyway, Jesse," said Mattie, picking up his Bowie knife from the table where the cowboys had dropped it. "When you're able again, we'll worry about boots." She walked to the bed, holding the knife. "I'm cutting off your boot. If you're planning to shoot me, you'd best do it now."

"Damn you, Mattie. You know I won't shoot you," he said, easing his thumb off the hammer of his gun.

She slipped the sharp Bowie knife inside his boot between his calf and the leather. "I thought not, but so much of what I used to be certain of turns out to be either untrue or impractical, so that I sometimes feel the world shifts under my feet every day."

"You can always be certain of me," he said, dropping his gun on the floor beside the bed. "And give that knife to Squinty before you amputate my foot. Begging your pardon, Mattie, but I don't think you know how to cut off a boot. Squinty, cut the seams down both sides. Maybe that way I can lace them back together long enough to get to a boot maker."

Red pushed the bottle of tequila at him. "Drink up, Jesse, while Squinty's working on that boot. That leg's gonna hurt like a son of a bitch when Miss Mattie sets it."

Jesse handed the bottle to Red and wiped his mouth with the back of his hand. "Mattie?"

Mattie took a deep breath and hid her shaking

hands behind her back. "Of course, Jesse. I'm a southern lady, raised to nurse the sick and comfort the dying."

His eyes appeared sunken in his head, badly tarnished pieces of silver, but he inclined his head, the closest thing to a bow of which he was capable. "And much prettier than the last sawbones who worked on my carcass. You do have some experience, uh, nursing the sick, Mattie?"

Squinty eased Jesse's boot off his foot and Mattie began cutting up his pants leg. "Actually no, but at least I don't plan to shoot you like Danny does his horses. Do you trust me?"

The deep lines around his mouth eased as he smiled. "Till hell freezes over, Mattie."

Jubilee entered the room and almost dropped the pan of hot water he was carrying. "Lordy, Miss Mattie, what you doing?"

"I'm cutting Jesse's pants off," she answered, trying to ignore the hairy muscular flesh she was exposing with every snip of her scissors.

Jesse grabbed her hands, wincing at the movement. "Best let Jubilee do that, Mattie."

"I have to get these pants off so I can set your leg. Now let go of me. Why did you have to break your leg anyway? Why were you roping that stupid cow? We need you, Jesse!" Her eyes started blurring and she wiped away the tears on her sleeve. "We need you."

Jubilee took her hands and led her away. "You let me get him ready, Miss Mattie. A man don't want no woman to see him in his altogether when he's helpless as a baby."

Mattie felt hot all over. Jubilee meant Jesse wasn't wearing any unmentionables. She had not thought of that. Samuel always wore them. She had hung them on the line with the other laundry. "Then put a nightshirt on him, and let me set his leg."

She heard Jesse's muffled curse, then Jubilee's voice. "He's done passed clean out."

Mattie turned around, averted her eyes from Jesse's nude body, or at least that part of it she was most curious about. "Red, be ready with that tequila in case he wakes up. Jubilee, where are those slats?"

Jubilee gasped and tossed Jesse's shirt over his bare groin. "Miss Mattie!"

"Oh, hush up, Jubilee. Danny, find Jesse's nightshirt so Jubilee won't have a conniption fit about my modesty."

"Jesse ain't got no nightshirt, Miss Mattie," said Squinty.

Mattie swallowed. "Well, then, he'll have to do without." She rubbed her hands on her skirt and leaned over the bed to examine Jesse's right leg. It was broken halfway up the shin, and she murmured a prayer of thanks. The bone was so close to the surface, she should be able to feel it when she fit the two broken ends together properly. Gently she touched the slight bump on the shin that she believed indicated the break, and Jesse screamed, then lapsed back into unconsciousness.

Jubilee brought her the bed slats and Mattie marked where she wanted them cut. "Wrap rags around them so the wood won't rub sores." She laid out long strips of cloth, murmured another prayer, and motioned to Red and Squinty. "One of you grab his ankle and the other his leg just below the knee. Then pull while I wiggle the bone into place. Danny, you and Jubilee be ready to slap those splints in place and tie them down as tight as you can." She grasped his shin and nodded to Red and Squinty. "Now, please."

When it was over, and Jesse's leg snugly splinted and wrapped, Mattie sank down on the bed and reached for the bottle of tequila.

"He ain't come to yet, Miss Mattie. He don't need

that," said Jubilee, slipping one of his own nightshirts over Jesse's head and pulling it as gently as possible over the unconscious man's form.

"But I do, Jubilee," replied Mattie, upending the bottle. The tequila burned her mouth, her throat, her stomach, and brought tears to her eyes. Choking, she felt Jubilee take the bottle and slap her on the back.

"Goddamn it, Miss Mattie," said Red with awe. "You drank that like a man." Then he blushed to match his hair. "Pardon my tongue, ma'am."

She managed to catch her breath. "Thank you, Red, and never you mind about the language. When a man's among friends, he forgets one of those friends is a woman."

Red considered her statement for a moment, then grinned and nodded. "I reckon that's true, Miss Mattie."

"You done a fine job, Miss Mattie," said Squinty. "Ain't nobody coulda done a better one."

"We didn't have to shoot him after all," said Danny.

Mattie saw the admiration in the men's eyes and felt a warmth inside that had nothing to do with the tequila. It was the first time she could remember being admired by men for any reason other than her looks. Except for Jesse.

She still felt the glow inside when Jesse regained his senses around midnight. "Mattie?"

She leaned over him, smoothed his hair back from his forehead, and frowned. His skin felt dry and feverish. "I'm here, Jesse."

"You did it, didn't you, lady. I knew you could." He smiled at her. "You look like a sunbeam in that yellow dress, all airy and insubstantial, but you've got more grit than you know, Mattie." He looked down at himself. "What in the hell am I wearing?"

"Jubilee's nightshirt."

"It looks like a damn shroud and it's hot as hell besides." He began pulling on it and gave a muffled groan.

She grabbed his hands. "Don't, Jesse."

He looked up at her. "Where's the tequila?"

She handed him the bottle. "Drink some and try to go back to sleep."

He drank several swallows and handed it back, his eyes glittering, alive, reckless. "I'm stripping down, Mattie. You best go on to bed."

"No," she said, feeling time began to slow.

"Suit yourself," he said, pulling on the voluminous garment and managing to twist it around his chest. He fell back against the pillow, his mouth looking pinched and bloodless again. "God, but I hurt, Mattie."

She tugged the sheet up well past his waist and pulled the nightshirt over his head. "As long as you're indecent, I might as well sponge you off. I think you have a fever."

He reached for the tequila, took several more gulps, then lay back and closed his eyes. "That might not be a good idea, Mattie. I'm not myself."

She dipped a cloth in the pan of water she had replenished for just such an eventuality and gently wiped his face then washed his throat. When she reached his chest, she tilted her head and smiled as the wet cloth turned the wedge of black hair into soft, damp curls. She felt the warm glow inside her burn hotter as she looked up and met his eyes. Glowing silver eyes.

He took the cloth from her suddenly limp fingers and dropped it on the floor, then threaded the fingers of his right hand through her hair while his left arm circled her back. He held her loosely, gave her every opportunity to pull away as she knew she should, all the while his eyes fixed on her. Such lonely eyes, she thought; as lonely as hers, and as yearning and reckless. As first her breasts pressed against his damp chest, then her lips touched his, she wondered why he always made her feel reborn.

Charlie Goodnight rode into the plaza on the last day of August, two weeks after Jesse broke his leg. He sat at Jesse's desk and stared at him with brooding eyes while Mattie perched stiffly on the bed, careful to keep a modest distance from Jesse's prone body. She had not been so close to him since the night he had kissed her, and their unspoken constraint was wearing on her.

Goodnight looked from Jesse to Mattie, seeming to loom over them although he was sitting down. At six feet and two hundred pounds, he was physically intimidating, but mere size did not explain his formidable presence. Nor did his facial resemblance to President Grant, which in any case was not a desirable attribute in the formerly Confederate state of Texas nor anywhere in the country, given Grant's inability to impose his own rules of conduct on his government subordinates. Mattie could not imagine Goodnight having the same difficulty.

Goodnight commanded because he lacked self-doubt, she decided as she met his eyes and felt the jolt of his powerful will that she always experienced when she chanced to be the object of his attention. Other men trusted Goodnight because he trusted himself.

After scrutinizing Mattie, Goodnight turned his attention back to Jesse. Samuel he ignored after a single glance at the glazed, red eyes and limp form leaning against the wall.

"What are you doing on the Canadian, Jesse?" demanded Goodnight.

Jesse poured tobacco out of his bag of Bull Durham and rolled a cigarette. "We're grazing our cattle. I got our range pegged at twenty miles of river and ten miles on each side of it. It's as much as I can hold right now. Soon as the weather and the flies ease up, and my leg heals up, I'll build a permanent camp on each of the four boundaries and we'll push out from there come spring."

"You're trespassing on the sheepherders' range, Jesse. I made a pact with Casimiro Romero, the head Mexican, goddamn it. We shook hands on it. The cattlemen would stay out of the Canadian River Valley, and the sheepmen would stay off the headwaters of the Red River and out of the Palo Duro."

Jesse blew a smoke ring toward the ceiling. "I heard a rumor to that effect, Charlie, and thought it mighty high-handed of you. It's not as if either of you owned an acre of the land you were dividing up."

Goodnight pounded his fist on the table. "When the nearest courthouse is two hundred miles away, it doesn't matter if you got your name on a piece of paper so long as you got your feet on the range. When I visited with Romero, there weren't but two pairs of feet of any import in the whole damn twenty-five thousand square miles of the Panhandle, and they belonged to him and me. When there ain't no law, Jesse, a man makes his own, and makes it as fair as can be."

Jesse leaned back against his pillow, so relaxed that Mattie was awed. "That's exactly what Mattie and I did. We made our own law, and to be fair, I paid fifteen hundred dollars in gold to Mendoza for this plaza and his promise to take himself and his goddamn sheep back to New Mexico."

"You're talking out of both sides of your mouth, Jesse. Mendoza never owned a goddamn foot of ground, so your deal with him ain't worth a hill of beans. It appears to me that you are a mite high-handed yourself."

"I never said I wasn't, Charlie, but there are four

pairs of feet in the Panhandle now—yours, Romero's, Mattie's, and mine."

Goodnight's eyes flickered toward Mattie, and she saw a speculative expression in their depths. He glanced at Samuel again, his mouth tightened, and he gave a half nod as if he recognized that authority did not lie in that direction. He swung his ponderous head toward Jesse and Mattie like a bull buffalo preparing to charge. "And yours and Mattie's are planted right in the goddamn middle of the Mexicans' sheep. How long do you think the peace Romero and I made will last with every jake-leg cow operation throwing their herds on whatever grazing land strikes their fancy? Move your herds north to Palo Duro Creek or Coldwater."

Jesse stubbed out his cigarette in a tin plate Mattie had appropriated for his use as an ashtray. "Jot Gunter has already surveyed this land and I've bought up the certificates on every section with good water and grass. I even bought the certificates held by the railroad. I bought everything but the school land. The spread looks like a crazy quilt because of those school lands, but that can't be helped. We'll lease from the state what we can't buy. Should be able to get a low rent, too, since those fools in Austin still think this land is a worthless desert."

Mattie blotted her forehead with a handkerchief and tried to follow the conversation. Jesse had explained that by treaty Texas owned the public lands and to prevent large blocks from being gobbled up by individuals or organizations and to encourage as many families as possible to settle had designated alternate sections of land to the schools and the railroads. Jesse was scornful of the state's intentions since there was too little rainfall for farming, irrigation much beyond the riverbanks wasn't feasible, and a single section of pastureland wouldn't support a ranching operation.

Fortunately, he explained, land speculators such as Jot Gunter's firm of Gunter, Munson, and Summerfield out of Sherman, Texas, did a brisk business in land certificates. It was possible to obtain title and consolidate holdings, and Jesse had done it. Mattie didn't altogether understand the procedure, but she had the deeds locked up in her trunk, and that was enough to satisfy her. It was all well and good to talk of feet planted on the range, but she was a banker's daughter and knew the value of a deed.

Goodnight leaned back in his chair and lit a cigar. "I've done business with Gunter. The son of a bitch never mentioned you."

"He mentioned you, Charlie, and not always in a complimentary fashion. That's how I know you're talking through your hat. You're buying up Palo Duro Canyon as fast as John Adair will advance the money, and you ran Jot Gunter ragged surveying your own crazy quilt. We want the same thing. We want to make this cow country and hold it against the farmers that will want to chop it up and plow it under, destroy its native grass the way they did in Kansas and parts of Nebraska. Give us five years and we'll feed millions on good Texas beef and shoe them in Texas cowhide. There will be no need for a man to go without meat or a child without shoes."

"Then trade your certificates for land farther north, Jesse, where there aren't any sheep," Goodnight urged. "I aim to keep this land peaceable and that means I don't want any damn range war between you and the sheepherders."

"No!" said Mattie suddenly, fear overcoming her awe of Goodnight. If there were no sheepherders farther north, then there were no plazas to buy, and she could not tolerate living in a dugout with Samuel. "If the flies and the heat can't make me leave, your talk of sheepherders and range wars won't either."

Goodnight's eyes sharpened as he turned to her, and Mattie hesitated, frightened of her own forward behavior. "Range war is a goddamn bloody business, Mattie, and I've never seen one that did credit to either side. Some of these sheepmen used to be comancheros before the army ran the Comanches out of Texas, and they ain't worth the powder it would take to blow them to hell. But most of these folks are good people and friends of mine. If you try to run the sheepmen out of the Canadian, I won't permit any such outrage. I got more cowboys than you and Jesse, and if it's a fight you're after, then I'll give you one."

"Jesse and I plan to buy out more of the plazas next year. The smaller ones will make good line camps. But even if we didn't, I wouldn't leave. Jesse's in no shape to be moved. Besides, your pact with the sheepherders has nothing to do with us."

"It was made in good faith—" began Goodnight.

"I don't care!" interrupted Mattie. "We're here and we mean to stay. And we'll not be intimidated by anyone." She felt Jesse lay his hand against the small of her back as if to calm her. "You and Romero aren't the only two strong men in a kingdom anymore."

Goodnight drew on his cigar while he considered her answer. "And it appears there's at least one headstrong woman, Mattie. You plan to always set yourself at odds with everybody else?"

"I'll do what I have to do," said Mattie.

Goodnight got up and put his Stetson back on. "Reckon I found out what I came for, so I'll be getting back home. Come visit us, Mattie. Ain't but forty or fifty miles. Can't miss the Palo Duro Canyon. Biggest goddamn gully you ever seen."

"You're not getting away that easy, Charlie. Just what did you find out that you didn't already know? I figure you knew before you saddled your horse that you couldn't talk me into moving out of the Canadian. You also knew I wasn't a man who would cheat the Mexicans or start a war with them, so you didn't have to threaten to send your cowboys after me," said Jesse.

"You're as goddamn bullheaded as I am, Jesse," said Goodnight. "And you're right on both counts. I didn't figure you'd accept my bargain with Romero any more than I would in your position, and I didn't think you'd commit an outrage against the sheepmen."

"I never knew you to go around Robinson's barn before if you could walk straight through it instead, Charlie. So spit it out. Why the hell did you ride fifty miles to see me?"

"Not to see you. I figured I knew where you stood. I came to see Mattie." Goodnight hesitated, looking at Mattie. "Mendoza passed the word about that Hunter woman along the Canadian. Made her sound like a cross between a longhorn cow and a cougar, with the worst traits of both. Reckon I wanted to see for myself if that female critter they're talking about is the same little Mattie Corley I knew back in Pueblo."

"You came to see if Mattie Hunter was the same girl you knew, Goodnight, and the answer is no," said Samuel, straightening up. "She speaks up to men with no respect for their sex or her own. She puts herself forward with no thought of a woman's proper role. She makes a pet of a filthy animal and grubs in the garden like a field hand—I've actually seen dirt under her fingernails—and she brags at the supper table of spreading ferret dung among the vegetable plants to keep the rabbits from eating them."

He shuddered and folded his arms, his eyes burning with condemnation. "She doesn't belong in a drawing room anymore."

"We don't have any goddamn drawing rooms in the Panhandle, Hunter," said Jesse furiously.

Mattie threw her head back and started laughing in

spite of the tears that rolled down her cheeks and splashed on her bodice. "Dear God, what Jubilee has dreaded the most has happened. Folks are talking about me."

CHAPTER 17

It wasn't the Mexicans with their flocks of sheep that fretted Jesse as the heat broke and the leaves on the cottonwoods turned golden in the fall of 1877; it was news of other herds drifting into the Canadian. The cattle market had fallen over the summer and the buyers were offering ruinous prices in Dodge City. Cattlemen opted to hold on to their herds over the winter in hopes of higher prices in the spring, and news of free grazing in the Panhandle was music to their ears and salvation to their pocketbooks. Jesse ordered Red to move the line camps another ten miles in every direction and sent Squinty and Jubilee to meet incoming herds and either buy them or turn them back from land he and Mattie controlled. He bought cows ready to calf and pairs—cows with baby calves—when he could because he paid no more for them than he would a steer and he got two for the price of one. The calves had no market value, but they would when he was ready to sell them. He had Jubilee rig up a hammock in the back of a wagon and he rode out with Jot Gunter to survey more land and exercise the options he and Mattie already owned. Throughout the fall, the Hunter Ranch grew larger and the number of head carrying the Bar H brand increased. The smell of singed hair and blood hung over the valley as the cowboys feverishly branded each new addition and castrated the male calves, holding back only the few Jesse planned to use for breeding.

Jesse's own holdings grew little. He had already spent most of his first year's salary on land, and he had none left to buy cattle. But he could wait. He would burn the Flying MJ brand on any mavericks he found on his land every spring and fall and let his herd increase. And he would buy more land when he could. In the meantime he would build up Mattie's ranch. Let the other cattlemen squat on free grazing land. He and Mattie would own theirs.

As November neared, Jesse hobbled on crutches, enforcing his will on the newly hired cowboys by character and his reputation as a hard man rather than by physical strength. He allowed no drinking, gambling for money, or fighting on ranch property, and fired anyone who disobeyed. He paid Red one hundred dollars a month and the regular cowboys seventy-five, making them the highest-paid hands in the Panhandle, so few risked losing a job for an illicit bottle of whiskey or hand of cards. Samuel found no one to drink with, so he drank alone.

Still, Jesse's troubled mind found no rest. More than his broken leg, more than the threat of other cattlemen squatting on land he wanted, more than the frustration of managing a ranch from his bed or from a hammock in the back of a wagon, it was thoughts of Mattie that stole away his peace. Wherever he was, she was not. In a house of only six rooms, she was as elusive as a prairie mirage that

A TIME TOO LATE

always seemed to recede into the distance whenever he drew near.

"Jesse, may I speak to you a moment?"

Dressed in another of those loose Mother Hubbards he'd noticed her wearing almost daily, this one a heavy cotton of navy blue trimmed in green braid, Mattie stood just inside his bedroom door as if she was afraid to venture farther. He drank in the sight of her as though she was water and he was a thirsty man. Her hair, now grown out to shoulder length, was loosely pinned up at the back of her head, and he wanted to feel the fine silk of it curling around his fingers. Her skin glowed, and he wanted to warm his hands against the softness of her breasts. Her eyes looked more golden than usual, and he wanted to find himself reflected in their depths.

The ache in his heart exceeded the ache in his healing bone.

He watched a delicate tint of color wash over her cheeks as she caught a glimpse of his bare thigh. His cast was shorter now, just below the knee, but his pants, the same ones Mattie had cut off him, gaped open nearly to the groin. During the day he laced them up with rawhide strips, but not when he rested.

He tossed the edge of his blanket over his leg, suddenly desperate not to frighten her away. "Come sit down, Mattie."

She crossed the room and sat in his chair, idly shuffling the papers that lay on his table.

He levered himself up and leaned against the headboard, feeling dried, cracked places inside of him begin to soften and heal. "Come sit on the bed, Mattie. It's more comfortable than the chair."

She glanced at him, then looked down at the floor. "That wouldn't be at all proper."

Her prim tone flicked him like a rawhide buggy whip. "We've been through a stampede, lice, and a broken leg together, Mattie. We even faced down Charlie Goodnight together. Don't you think that entitles me to at least be treated like a friend?" He clenched his fist as he stared at her bent head. "Look at me, damn it!"

She looked up at him, and he caught his breath at the haunted expression in her eyes. She didn't answer, but then she didn't need to; her eyes were eloquent enough. He wasn't a friend; he was a temptation, a transgression, a threshold beyond which her honor forbade her to step again.

He relaxed his fist at the same time his heart twisted. "Mattie, are you afraid of me?"

"No, Jesse." He barely heard her whispered words.

"I was drunk that night, Mattie." He felt the shame of his confession. The fact that he had only kissed her, not violated her body, did not console him. He was no better than Samuel, preying on her to satisfy his own lust.

She straightened her thin shoulders, and he was reminded of a guilty child who would not allow a playmate to take all the blame in her place. "But I was not drunk, Jesse, and neither were you at the river."

Their eyes locked together and he remembered the sleek feel of her wet body, icy water and hot flesh, the sweet taste of her mouth as she opened it to him, innocent and untutored in such a kiss as he asked of her. Too honest to deny her memories, she wordlessly shared them with him, and he felt her wonder of them as if it were his own. He also felt her regret.

"Do you want me to leave, Mattie? Red can take my place. He's a good man."

"But not as good as you?"

A smile twisted his mouth. "No, not as good as me."

She laced her fingers together, and he saw her knuckles turn white from the pressure. "I—we need you, Jesse, but we must not"—she moistened her lips—"we must not step outside the bounds of propriety again."

"I'll not touch you again, Mattie, and give you no reason to fear me, but I cannot bear to be at odds with you any longer. And we must not be." He waved his arm toward his open window through which the sounds of cattle, horses, and men floated like the faintest notes of a symphony. "We are bound to the land, Mattie, and to each other. We cannot go back to what we were."

"Don't you think I know that?" she cried. "I have changed and I'm not comfortable with it. I am not at odds with you as much as with myself. I would not fit in Pueblo anymore, but I don't altogether fit here either. I hate the flies and the heat and the dirt and listening to the lonely howl of the wolf at night. I am not one with the land as much as I am a prisoner of it. And of myself." She swallowed and tilted her chin up. "I am expecting a baby, Jesse. That is what I came to tell you."

Jesse wished that longhorn cow had broken his neck instead of his leg. Dead, he couldn't feel pain.

"Jesse, you didn't have no call to come with us. Me and Jubilee and Hank Wilson and the other boys can chase them poachers off our range as well as you can." Red's voice was punctuated by the rhythmic thud of horses' hooves.

"You best listen to Red," said Jubilee. "You mess up that leg, you gonna be limping till you goes to your grave."

"Comes to any hard riding, you're gonna fall ass over elbows out of that saddle. Man can't stay on a horse with a broken leg and only one boot," added Red.

"If Squinty can ride with a wooden leg, I can ride with a broken one," said Jesse, concentrating on following the tracks of hundreds of head of cattle and at least a dozen horsemen.

"I'm used to it," said the squint-eyed cowboy. "You ain't."

Jesse ignored the comment. "How many cows in that trail herd, Squinty?"

"I reckon about three thousand, maybe thirty-five hundred. Hard to count cows when a man's looking down the wrong end of a Winchester. That trail boss was more interested in asking questions than answering them. He didn't rightly believe I was a cowboy for anybody, much less that he was trespassing our land. Near busted a gusset laughing when I told him that. I think he suspicioned I was a rustler looking over the lay of the land. Even asked me if I worked for Dutch Henry."

"That's why I brought Hunter along. No trail boss with gumption would believe that a high-toned rustler like Dutch Henry would allow Samuel within a mile of his camp. His standards are higher than that," replied Jesse, tightening his grip on his saddle horn.

"You're hanging on to your saddle like a greenhorn, Jesse. Why don't you go back? Maybe I'm not as good at tracking as you, but a man would have to be blind to miss this trail and I ain't blind. Go on back, settle Miss Mattie down. Lordy, but she was beside herself when you climbed on that horse. Thought she was gonna have a conniption right there in front of the plaza."

"It's been damn near three months since I broke it, Red. It's time to take off the cast anyway," replied Jesse. "Mattie will survive her patient getting off his sickbed." Survive better than if I had stayed at the plaza where I might have said something hurtful, he thought. And I have no right to say anything at all. She isn't betraying me by having Samuel's baby; it only feels that way.

Jesse heard the cattle before the other men, a feat he knew owed as much to concentration as to keen hearing. He held up his hand to stop the band of riders behind him. "Anybody got any doubts about what we're about to do? The trail boss either moves his herd down the Canadian off our range, or we refer the disagreement to Mister Colt and Mister Winchester to settle." He directed his question to the one cowboy he didn't know as well as the others.

Hank Wilson pushed his high-crowned hat back off his forehead so his eyes wouldn't be shadowed by its brim when he talked to Jesse. "You sure as hell can't call in a sheriff to serve no papers on them, can you? Reckon that leaves it up to us."

Jesse studied the other man. Wilson had run a one-horse outfit just east of Hunter property. With only a few hundred head of cows and the market below cost, he had jumped at the chance to sell out when Red offered him a good price. Jesse wasn't surprised. Times had changed in Texas. The huge herds of wild Texas longhorns that used to roam free for the roping after the war were all under somebody's brand. Now a man needed money to buy a starter herd, and money to increase it. Hank Wilson had no money. All he had was a dream, and the low cattle prices put paid to that.

"How long have you been in this country, Wilson?"

Hank spat a stream of tobacco juice on the ground. "Been here since Seventy-five. Came in with the buffalo hunters that summer. Did a little hunting, but didn't last long. Man has to learn to live with a powerful stink to be around buffalo hunters much, and I got a sensitive nose. I made a few dollars, though, and bought some cows. Figured I'd squat on the public land for a while. Then Red comes along and tells me only every other section is free and I'm squatting on a couple that belong to Mattie Hunter, and would I like to sell my cattle or move them. Didn't take me long to make up my mind. I was tired of my own company, so I figured I'd hook up with this outfit. Eat someone else's cooking for a change."

Jesse didn't altogether trust him yet. "A man who has owned his own place might go to considerable risk to put together a stake to own one again. Might even throw in with another outfit to share the profits in the event of a fight."

Hank rubbed his grizzled chin. "I might take offense if anybody else said that, but I heard you was a hard man and liked to know who was coming up behind you."

"Particularly when I'm about to ride into a stranger's camp with only five men."

Hank pointed his thumb at a rider sitting on a gray gelding a short distance away. "I figure there's just four of us. That fellow ain't worth shooting."

"That's Samuel Hunter," remarked Red.

Hank shrugged. "I figured it had to be, but he don't get out and about enough for us new hands to know him from Adam. I had heard he had a close acquaintance with strong drink, and judging by his slack face, he's been renewing the friendship today."

Jesse's fingers tightened around his saddle horn. He could hardly bear to look at Samuel. "I'll take care of Mr. Hunter."

"Then you better gag him. He appears to me to be the type who lets his mouth run away with him when he gets to drinking. That kind gets good men killed," said Hank.

Jesse didn't reply. There was nothing to say.

"McDade! I hear the cattle!"

Samuel's yell caught Jesse by surprise, and he spurred his horse over to Samuel and grabbed his arm.

"Keep you mouth shut. Causing a stampede by yelling is no way to get acquainted."

Samuel swayed as he struggled to free himself from Jesse's grip. "I have no intention of becoming 'acquainted' with any more members of the lower orders. Knowing you and these rude individuals you've hired is sufficient."

Jesse backhanded Samuel off his horse. "In the cattle business, Hunter, the only lower orders are the men who think they're better than the cowboys who ride for them. Out here a man is respected for what he does, not who he is. Climb back on your horse, keep your mouth shut, and back up whatever I say. And when we ride into that camp, you take off your hat, or at least raise the brim. That lets the other man know your hand isn't near your gun. Saves a lot of misunderstandings. And if the trail boss is standing, we get off our horses, too, so he doesn't feel we have the advantage. This is range etiquette, Hunter, and it's a damn sight more important than which fork to use at Sunday dinner. Your hostess won't kill you for bad manners, but this trail boss and his men just might. Do you understand me?"

Samuel rubbed his cheek. "You struck me, you bastard."

"He's trying to tell you how to keep from getting yourself killed, you dumb jackass!" exclaimed Red.

"No, I'm not," said Jesse. "I'm trying to keep him from getting *us* killed."

He raised his arm and waved to the small group of men around a chuck wagon, then rode toward them, holding his horse down to a walk. Galloping a horse into a stranger's camp might be misunderstood. He tipped his hat to the tall man standing by the campfire and awkwardly dismounted, hanging on to the saddle to take the weight off his leg. "I'm Jesse McDade from the Hunter Ranch."

The trail boss, whiskered and dusty, extended his hand. "Figured you must be when I saw the fellow with the peg leg riding with you. My name's Phelps White. I ride for George Washington Littlefield. Looks like you better sit a spell, McDade, you and your men. Didn't expect to see anybody in this country."

Jesse shook hands, liking the feel of the hard callused hand. This was a man who worked beside his men. He gingerly lowered himself to the ground and accepted a cup of coffee from White. "You're a surprise, too. Trailing a herd south for the winter?"

White hunkered down beside Jesse. "Nope, just got through trailing up from there to Dodge. Everybody else had the same idea, I reckon, because there's more cows than a dog has fleas there, and prices are rock bottom. I figure I'll winter the herd here, try again next spring."

"That's wise. No point in selling a herd at a loss. And there's plenty of free grass in the Panhandle—long as you move your cows about twenty miles farther south."

White's eyes narrowed. "Why should I do that?"

"Because your herd's eating Hunter grass. Mr. Samuel Hunter"—Jesse pointed his thumb toward a glowering Samuel—"owns this grass and the water on it for the next twenty miles up and down the Canadian and a fair piece of land on each side."

White stood up. "I don't see no cows on it, so I figure this grass is free for the taking, McDade."

Jesse didn't get up. Standing, his balance was too precarious. Sitting, he could concentrate on his shooting—if it came to that. "You misunderstand, White. I said Hunter 'owns' the grass, and what he doesn't own, I do. We have the deeds to prove it."

"And you're trespassing," said Samuel. "If you don't get off my land, I shall be forced to order my men to throw you off."

Phelps White's face lost all amiability. "It ain't good manners to threaten a man, Hunter. Ain't very smart either, not when you're outnumbered better than two to one."

"I have more men I can call," said Samuel.

White jerked his head, and six cowboys standing by the fire moved closer. "You better damn sure have a loud voice, Hunter, because I don't see but five of you in any direction, and I can sure as hell see a long way in this country." He spat toward the fire. "And who I do see don't scare me. A cripple, a nigger, a man with a broken leg, and judging by your smell, a drunk. That don't leave but one good man."

Using his one good leg, Jesse got up and grabbed Samuel's arm and squeezed until the man's face turned white and he groaned. "Mr. Hunter isn't from Texas, so he naturally has bad manners. We have more than fifty men on the ranch, an unequal fight however you count it, and I don't think you want to kill us over a slight misunderstanding. The rest of my men wouldn't take it kindly. I'm not accusing you of trespassing. There's no way you could know this land's taken except"—he paused for emphasis—"except Squinty told you. So if you would just trail your herd south another couple days, there will be no hard feelings on either side. If you run low on chuck, send one of your men upriver to the first big plaza you see. That's headquarters, and we can give you enough to see you through the winter. Or you can ride over to Fort Elliot and buy from the sutler there, but we're cheaper and a lot closer."

White nodded. "I'm obliged, McDade, but I don't know that I'll take you up on that. I don't want to be beholden to a man who buys free grass and isn't neighborly enough to let a fellow trail his cattle across it. This is open range. I don't think Mr. Littlefield would approve of closing it off."

"You and Mr. Littlefield can squat on free grass until hell freezes over, White, but not on Hunter or McDade property. I'll tell anybody else the same."

"Then you better do it, because we ran across a man named John Ray a couple days back. He and a couple of men are looking for a ranch location for Bates and Beals from up in Colorado. And there'll be more coming. You can't hold the Panhandle against all comers, McDade."

"I'm not planning to, but I will hold what I own and I'll respect the other man's rights as long as he respects mine."

"You sound like one of them sodbusters, McDade. Are you against free range?"

"Not at all—as long as it's not my range other men think is free."

CHAPTER 18

Winter came and with it, the snows. The Canadian froze over and so did the spring in back of the plaza. The cowboys chopped holes in the ice so the cattle could drink from the river, and rode for miles to locate pasture blown clean of snow where the animals could graze on the rich brown grama grass. The men grew gaunt and so did the cattle. The cowboys assigned to the line camps miles from the plaza suffered from frostbite and bad coughs, and Jesse rotated them every two weeks so Mattie and Jubilee could dose them with a cough syrup made of whiskey and molasses. Beards and long hair were the fashion of the day as all the men sought some protection from the icy wind. Jesse caught Mattie feeding Baby some of their hoarded grain and gently forbade it. She cried, but obeyed.

She was learning to survive.

As the New Year dawned the weather cleared and Jesse rode to Charlie Goodnight's to beg Molly

Goodnight to attend Mattie during her confinement around Easter time. It was while he was gone that Samuel Hunter hired Clint Murray.

The first inkling Mattie had of Samuel's deed was when Jubilee knocked at her door. "Lordy, Miss Mattie, you best come to the kitchen. Your husband done hired a new cowboy and Jesse ain't gonna like it none."

Mattie opened the door and gestured at her belly. "I'd rather not, Jubilee. It's not seemly in my condition to be greeting strange men."

"It ain't gonna be seemly when Jesse gets back neither," said Jubilee grimly. "I knows that Clint Murray and so does your husband."

"I don't recognize the name," said Mattie, yawning. She was so tired, so awkward, and still frequently ill. She had no energy for Samuel's intrigues, or Jesse's tempers for that matter. She only wanted to sleep until Easter.

Jubilee drew himself up to his full height. "He was not received, Miss Mattie."

Had Mattie the energy, she would have laughed at his disapproving tone. "Mercy sakes, Jubilee! Most of the people on this ranch wouldn't be received in Pueblo. Imagine Squinty or Red at a dinner party discussing the treatment for screwworm. Or Danny explaining to Mrs. Thatcher why he didn't want stallions in a remuda."

"This ain't no time to be funning, Miss Mattie. I don't like this atall. It ain't natural for Clint Murray to show up at the front door when we is in the middle of the wilderness. There's something not right about it, and there's something not right about him."

Mattie yawned again. "I'll talk to Samuel, Jubilee, but I doubt I'll change his mind." She waddled to the kitchen, feeling like a fat, uncomfortable duck.

Samuel rose from his chair, a welcoming smile on

his face. She didn't trust the smile, but it was better than his usual sneer of distaste whenever he chanced to notice her. "Mattie, my dear, come meet Clint Murray, an old friend from Pueblo and our newest employee."

Clint Murray was nearly as tall as Jesse, with a slim build and neatly trimmed chestnut hair. His cleanly shaven face looked odd to Mattie after so many weeks of only seeing hirsute men, but his features were handsome enough, even though she thought his nose a bit too long and eyes a peculiar color between brown and green and not the most attractive shade of either. His clothes were typical of any cowboy: Levi's pants, flannel shirt, and heavy vest, although they looked cleaner and newer than most.

He pushed back his chair and smiled, holding out his hand. "Mrs. Hunter, I'm honored to finally meet Samuel's wife. He used to speak of you often. I regret that our paths never crossed until now, but I confess that my former profession was not a respectable enough one to allow me entrance to most homes."

"What was your profession, Mr. Murray?" she asked, controlling a shudder when his lips brushed the back of her hand.

He released her hand. "I was a gambler, and I am ashamed of it. Your father convinced me of my error in choosing such a disreputable living, and I'm proud that I have chosen a more upright one." His eyes flickered to her belly, then up again. Some expression surfaced in his eyes, but sank beneath their green-brown depths before Mattie could identify it.

"The Colonel done that for sure," interjected Jubilee. "Run you out of Pueblo like a dog for trying to ruin Mr. Hunter. I don't believe you've changed none either. Leopards don't change their spots, and neither does gamblers."

"Shut your mouth, nigger!" shouted Samuel, rising from the table to face Jubilee.

"Please, Samuel!" Mattie cried. She looked toward Jubilee, pleading without words for the ex-slave to please not pick this particular time to act like a free man.

Clint Murray caught Samuel's arm. "No need to get angry on my account, Samuel. Your family retainer is only looking out for your best interests."

Jubilee looked horrified. "I ain't his retainer. I is Miss Mattie's and I is looking out for *her* interests."

Clint Murray nodded. "And you should be. She is lucky to have such a champion, but you needn't concern yourself. I no longer have any desire to fleece men at cards."

Mattie folded her arms over her belly as though to hide it from his gaze, then felt foolish. "You are most forthright, Mr. Murray, but I must warn you that Jesse—Mr. McDade—does not allow gambling or drinking on Hunter Ranch. I don't know that he would welcome a gambler even if reformed."

Murray looked at Samuel. "You don't understand, Mrs. Hunter. Your husband has already hired me."

"Is that a fact?" asked Jesse, appearing suddenly in the doorway, his eyes immediately fixing on Clint Murray.

"Jesse! We didn't expect you home so soon," said Mattie, finding a relief in his presence that she was unable to explain except that she felt safer when she saw him stroll into the kitchen.

"Three days is long enough to be gone—maybe too long," he said as he peeled off his yellow slicker and hung it on a peg beside the door, followed by his hat. His hair hung past his collar in thick waves that glimmered in the lamplight like the blue-black wings of a crow, and his cheeks above his heavy beard were ruddy from the cold wind. Mattie wanted to warm them with her hands.

A TIME TOO LATE
271

Jubilee handed him a cup of coffee. "He done hired a gambler, Jesse."

Jesse nodded his thanks and pulled out a chair. "Sit down, Mattie. You've got no business standing up." His eyes examined Clint Murray. "I do the hiring, contrary to what you may have heard, and I don't need another cowboy—not in the middle of winter. And I wouldn't hire a gambler at any rate."

Samuel doubled up his fists. "I have hired Clint, McDade. I took the liberty of examining the contracts drawn up by the Colonel and can find nothing that states specifically that I cannot hire a man if I choose."

Jesse dropped into a chair beside Mattie. "You laid hands on my papers without my express permission?" At Samuel's nod, he shook his head. "I will have to kill you one day, Hunter."

"Jesse!" exclaimed Mattie.

He flashed her a quick grin. "But not today. The ground is too frozen to dig your grave. Stay out of my room and out of my papers, though, or I might change my mind."

"Those are ranch papers, McDade, and I own the ranch."

"But I'm the manager," Jesse reminded him. "And I handle the money."

Mattie pushed her chair back. Her head was pounding and she was feeling feverish and slightly nauseated. "Please, no arguments. Jesse, Mr. Murray seems to be sincere in his intentions to reform." She wasn't certain of that. She wasn't certain of anything these days except a sense of foreboding.

Murray inclined his head in Mattie's direction. "Thank you, Mrs. Hunter. Samuel told me you were a charitable woman."

Jesse cocked his head to look at her, and stiffened at her pleading look. He rubbed his hand over his chin.

"All right, Mattie. No arguments. Mr. Murray, you may stay, but I won't pay you. I only pay men that I hire and who know their job—and you don't. Your hands are soft and white as a woman's. You haven't been herding cattle."

Samuel lunged for Jesse, but Clint Murray grabbed his arm. "I'll agree to your terms, Mr. McDade, until I learn my job. Samuel anticipated your objections and has agreed to pay me from his private funds until I prove myself. I hope that is satisfactory with you."

Jesse's eyes darted to Samuel, then back to Murray. "It's not."

Mattie clutched the edge of the table and pulled herself up. "I cannot endure another shouting match, nor another test of wills between the two of you. Please continue your disagreement out of my hearing. I'm much too tired to listen to it, I'm afraid."

Jesse half rose, reaching for her, but she pushed him away. She knew her eyes were yellow as a cat's, yellow as she felt, as if she were smoldering, ready to singe anyone who came near her.

"Please excuse my wife, Clint," said Samuel. "Women in her condition can't seem to keep their minds on anything but their bellies."

She hurried out of the kitchen and barely made it back to her bedroom before her nausea overcame her. Finished, she replaced the lid of the chamber pot and collapsed on the bed. She would cry, but it would only tire her more, and would not sweeten her husband's acid tongue. She wondered how much of her sickness was due to her pregnancy and how much to her own self-hatred, how much of her awkwardness was due to her girth and how much due to Samuel's remarks about her misshapen body.

She realized she had not asked Jesse if Molly Goodnight would come when the baby was due.

★ ★ ★

Two weeks later the blizzard hit, and Mattie stood in her bedroom clutching a blanket around her shoulders and peering through cracks in the shutters. The wind blew with such force that the snow appeared to be falling horizontally rather than vertically. Jesse strung a rope between the two smaller adobe houses where the cowboys slept and the plaza so that no one would be blinded and lose his way. Buffalo dung and wood burned in all the fireplaces, but the chill wind blew in through shutters and beneath ill-fitting doors, causing lamps to flicker and men to shiver. Leon developed a rattle in his chest that shook his thin body with deep hacking coughs each time he breathed. Frantic, Mattie and Jubilee first gave him the cowboys' remedy of whiskey and molasses, then made a tent over a pan of boiling water and forced him to breathe the hot steam. They fed him a rich beef broth and the last of the canned peaches. Jesse, Mattie, and Jubilee took turns carrying or holding him, since he seemed to breathe more easily when he was sitting upright. Finally they prayed.

Samuel did nothing except enjoy Clint Murray's company.

Whether it was the whiskey, the steam, the broth and peaches, the love, or the prayer, after three days Leon recovered. Thin, frail, with translucent skin and purple-smudged eyes, he regained his spirits but not his robustness. He tired easily and lay on Mattie's bed or in Jesse's lap listening to stories, his expression more solemn than it used to be. The cowboys whittled him toys out of whatever piece of wood they found, sang him songs, and told outrageous stories about others like themselves. Leon smiled a thank you for each offering, but seemed more interested in looking through the shutters. When the wind fell, and Jesse felt it was safe to ride out to check the cattle without danger of getting lost or freezing to death, Leon finally roused from his limp condition.

"Mama, snow stopped. I go see Baby now."

Mattie smoothed the little boy's lackluster curls away from his face. "It's too cold, little love, and you've been sick."

"I *not* sick!" He coughed experimentally to prove it, careful not to try too hard lest the act become real. "I go see Baby. Baby miss me."

Mattie looked helplessly toward Jubilee, who was shoveling pancakes onto a huge platter. "You quit pestering your mama, Leon," he said. "She done tole you it's too cold."

Leon looked up at Mattie. "Mama, please." Without warning tears overflowed his eyes and rolled down his thin cheeks.

Mattie turned to the man beside her. "Jesse, will you see about Baby for Leon?"

Jesse rolled a cigarette, the first of only two he would smoke, since everyone was running out of tobacco. He glanced across the table at Hank. "We'll have to find the herd first."

Hank swallowed a forkful of pancakes. "I suspect somebody will ride in today or maybe tomorrow with word."

"What do you mean, find the herd?" asked Mattie.

"Cattle drift in front of a snowstorm, Mattie," explained Jesse. "They may be a hundred miles south of here, I just don't know. We'll be weeks rounding them up and chasing others back north that drifted onto our range. Jubilee, make up sacks of jerky, beans, and flour for everybody. Enough for ten days. After breakfast, all you men saddle whatever horse you can catch and ride out. Hank, take another man and check the line camps. Make sure everybody is all right. Red, take six men and start clearing our range of other men's cattle. I'll take everyone else south with me. Eat up and saddle up."

Mattie bundled up in a fur-lined coat of Samuel's and stepped out the front door to watch the men prepare to leave. A light wind blew from the northwest over a landscape checkered with drifts higher than her head, alternating with patches of bare frozen ground. The sun, reflecting off the snow, threatened to make men blind or at least leave them with red, swollen eyes. Horses, feeling wild and free after a week of not being ridden, reared and pitched when each felt a man's weight. The crisp air rang with curses, and Red spurred his horse in a tight circle, then turned him south for a fast gallop just "to take the pitch out."

Mattie laughed as Danny, one of the best riders among the cowboys, sailed over his mount's head and landed in a snowdrift. The snow did nothing to muffle his cursing and several cowboys turned red with embarrassment that the young wrangler would use such language in the presence of a lady.

"Best go in the house, Mattie," said Jesse, keeping a short rein on his own horse. "The men can't cut loose if you're listening."

She smiled at him. "You mean I have not heard the worst?"

He smiled back, his teeth glistening white in contrast to his black beard. "Believe it or not, they're holding back."

Red rode in from the south, his horse at a dead run as he skirted snowbanks. "Jesus H. Christ, Jesse, you best come see. A bunch of goddamn cattle drifted into that mesa 'bout half mile from here. Three hundred head best as I can figure without counting. And Miss Mattie, Baby was with them."

"Goddamn it to hell, Red, did you have to tell her?"

Mattie gripped his stirrup, hanging on with both

hands. "Tell me what, Jesse? What's wrong with Baby? What does Red mean?"

Jesse's eyes held a frustrated look of sympathy. "I told you, Mattie. When a snowstorm hits, cattle try to get away. They drift like leaves blown by the storm, and like leaves, any obstacle will stop them. They will keep bunching up, climbing over one another, smothering those on the bottom while those on top freeze. Cattle don't have any goddamn sense or they would have walked around that mesa and kept drifting south."

"Oh, God!" screamed Mattie, and started running, her heavy belly and the deep snow holding her to an awkward stagger. She stumbled to her knees, her whole body jarred by the impact. She heard a curse and felt Jesse's hands circle her upper arms and pull her up.

"Go back to the house, Mattie. Now!"

She fought him, twisting and kicking. "No! I have to see Baby. He might not be dead."

Jesse picked her up and held her high against his chest. "No! I'll go see. You can't walk that far in your condition."

She pounded his chest, hearing his stifled grunts with each blow, until she finally tired and let her body go slack. "I have to see him for myself, Jesse. If you won't take me, I'll go alone. I can't just take Red's word that he's dead. I'll always wonder if Red was mistaken, and poor Baby is lost. He's so tame, like a puppy, that he won't know how to survive. I didn't save him when he was born to desert him if he's dead."

"You best take her, Jesse. She ain't gonna rest easy if you don't. It's not comfortable to spend your life wondering." Red dismounted and walked over. "You mount up, and I'll hand her up."

Mattie saw the pulse beating in Jesse's temple.

"That's no sight for a woman to see—or anybody else who hasn't seen it before."

Mattie cupped his chin, feeling the silky beard caress her palm, and turned his head toward her. She felt the arms that held her suspended tremble, and knew he was as powerless to deny her as she was to free herself from his grip. "You cannot protect me, Jesse, not against the death this land brings. I cannot survive in ignorance even if knowledge is ugly."

"Trust me, Mattie," he whispered.

"I do, Jesse. That's why I'm asking you to take me."

When he slipped his arm from beneath her knees and let her feet touch the ground, she knew she had won.

Later, when she beheld the stiff legs and frozen bodies, the eyes open and coated with ice, had walked the line of corpses, had touched the dead calf she had called Baby, Mattie knew the land indeed had no mercy for the young, the weak, the infirm, or the ignorant. She knelt in the snow and cried for the helpless and the innocent, and when the first spasm tore through her belly, she prayed for forgiveness. She knew better now than to pray for mercy.

"Jesse," she whispered, bending over to hug herself as a giant fist seemed to squeeze her womb. "Jesse, help me."

Jesse crouched down beside her, tilting her chin up to look at the face she knew was twisted into a grimace. His other hand pressed against her iron-hard belly, where muscles tightened in another pain worse than the first one, worse than any she remembered from her first labor.

"Jesus," he breathed, then looked at the cowboys who milled around the dead cattle, grieving as only men who lived their lives beside animals could grieve. "Red, over here! Mattie's having her baby."

Mattie heard the exclamations, felt the hands that lifted her onto Jesse's saddle, but all was happening at a distance. All of her mind, all of her endurance, all of her skill as a woman was concentrated on her body and the labor it must survive.

Suddenly she wished Aunt Patty was waiting at the plaza for her. She needed a woman's help.

Jesse kicked open the front door and carried Mattie into her bedroom. Laying her on the bed, he stripped off her coat and boots, then gripped her hands. "Rest easy, Mattie. I'll get help."

She rolled onto her side and drew her knees up, her face blank and blood frozen on her lower lip where she had bitten it. "There's no help, Jesse."

"Rest easy," he repeated as he left her, striding through her door, pushing past the cowboys that crowded together in the hall, their hats in hand, their faces helpless. They could all pull a calf if a cow had trouble dropping it, but none knew how to help a woman.

"Is she birthing?" demanded Jubilee, coming out of the kitchen holding Leon.

"I want Mama," announced the little boy, sensing that his mother, like Baby, was lost.

Jesse took Leon and hugged him. "Your mama is resting, so Danny is going to play with you in the bunkhouse. Maybe he'll teach you how to play his mouth organ so you can surprise your mama when she wakes up." He jerked his head toward the young wrangler whose face was whiter than any snowdrift.

He passed Leon to Danny. "Keep him with you until it's over." He sighed when the door closed behind the two, one only marginally older than the other, then turned to Jubilee. "Where's Samuel?"

Jubilee's broad nostrils flared. "Him and that gambling man is in the kitchen drinking coffee and grinning at each other like shit-eating possums."

Jesse brushed past the darkie and into the kitchen. Samuel and Clint Murray sat side by side, their heads close together and conversing in low voices. Neither looked up until Jesse slammed his fist in the middle of the table.

"Samuel, Mattie's having her baby and she needs help. Go see what she needs or wants."

Samuel reared back in his chair, his face turning pale as if all the blood in his body had suddenly disappeared. If Jesse hadn't known better, he would have thought the man was ill.

"Have you lost your mind, McDade?" he demanded. "No gentleman except a doctor would approach a woman in childbirth until the bloody, disgusting business is over."

Jesse heard murmurs from the listening cowboys in the hall, like the buzzing of angry wasps, and knew Mattie also could hear her husband's voice. He leaned across the table and grabbed the front of Samuel's shirt, jerking him out of his chair. Deliberately and with purpose Jesse drew back his other hand and slapped him once—twice—three times. He saw Clint Murray leap out of his chair, then drop back when Jubilee pressed the barrel of his Winchester against the gambler's skull.

"You son of a bitch," said Jesse, punctuating each word with another blow. "You put that baby in her, and you're telling me you're too goddamn good to help her get it out." Suddenly he flung Samuel backward. "Take your friend and get the hell out of here. Nobody in this house would let you touch Mattie now. Go wait out the birthing in the shed in the corral. You belong with the cow shit."

He watched, fists clenched, hoping Samuel defied

him so he could finally beat him to death. He didn't plan to waste a bullet.

Clint Murray tugged his vest down, then took Samuel's arm, gently directing him toward the backdoor. "You'll regret this, McDade, you and your nigger. I won't forget."

"Neither will I, Murray," replied Jesse softly, his eyes never leaving the pair until the door closed behind them. He turned to Jubilee. "We have to help Mattie. Go help her get into bed."

Jubilee backed away. "I can't do no such of a thing, Jesse. I is a nigger. I can't undress no white woman. It ain't proper."

"This is Mattie, Jubilee. You've known her all her life."

The ex-slave shook his head. "Don't make no difference. She be ruint if folks ever heard. It ain't proper, and you knows it."

"Do you think it's proper for me?" demanded Jesse.

Jubilee nodded. "It ain't proper, but it's right."

Jesse turned toward the door, then glanced back. "You'll have to help with the birthing. She doesn't have anybody but us, and it would shame her if I asked Red or Hank."

Jubilee glanced down at his hands, and Jesse knew he was looking at their color—the blackness that defined and separated him from the pale-skinned woman lying in the room down the hall.

"It doesn't matter, Jubilee. The color, I mean. I don't think anybody takes much notice of it. I see a friend, and Mattie sees family. What do you see?"

Jubilee rubbed his hands together and straightened his shoulders. "I reckon I sees a man." He cleaned his throat. "And I reckon you best be helping Miss Mattie. You call me when you needs me."

Jesse nodded and walked back down the hall. Cowboys leaned against the walls, smoking cigarettes

A TIME TOO LATE

or just looking at the dirt floor and being quiet. He didn't consider for a minute reminding them that the cattle came first.

He closed the bedroom door and leaned against it. He had stripped the clothes off dozens of women—could do it so smoothly they hardly knew they were being undressed—and he was suddenly nervous. But the other women—quickly loved and quickly forgotten—had never shared a soul with him.

Mattie turned her face toward him. "Jesse?"

He walked over to the bed and sat down beside her, gently smoothing her damp hair away from her face. "I'm here."

"Did you find any help?"

He nodded. "Me."

She laughed even as her face twisted as another pain squeezed her. "Oh, Jesse, do you ever tire of seeing me in such unattractive fixes? Bleeding hands, lice, sweaty and fly-stung, now with a swollen body. But one day, Jesse McDade, you'll see me beautiful."

His hand trembled before he could stop it. "I've already seen you beautiful, Mattie Hunter. In the back of a wagon, in a river, leaning over me when I hurt, and now."

Her eyes closed and he realized she didn't believe him. An untidy woman was a slattern. She still saw herself through others' eyes and not her own. She still separated her body from her spirit.

She insisted on undressing herself, struggling to remove her clothes while huddled under the cover of a voluminous nightgown, but allowed him to bathe her face and arms. The morning passed into early afternoon, and her body writhed with nearly continuous contractions. Sweat damped her gown and Jubilee came running when her soft moans turned to screams.

"You figure that baby 'bout ready to come?" asked

Jubilee, taking over wiping her face while Jesse held her hands.

Jesse sucked in a breath. "God, I hope so."

He slid his hands up her calves to the back of her knees and pushed them up and apart. Mattie whimpered in protest, but he ignored her. He had taken too close account of her modesty already and had not examined her before. He didn't know one damn thing about delivering a female, but he hoped to hell the process didn't differ too greatly from pulling a calf. At least he was familiar with a woman's body—probably too familiar to be considered a Christian man—but this wasn't any woman's body. This was Mattie.

He closed his eyes, delicately touched a tiny round head, and opened his eyes to watch Mattie's daughter being born.

When it was over, Jesse McDade, who hadn't cried since he closed his grandmother's dead eyes, felt the tears run down his face as he wrapped a blanket around the still body of a tiny child who would never hear her mother's voice.

Mattie struggled to sit up, her eyes moving from the silent bundle to Jesse's face. "I killed my baby, didn't I? My willfulness killed my baby."

Jubilee wiped her face. "No, Miss Mattie, that child been dead long afore you seen them dead cows. God knowed what he was doing when he made you willful. You would've sickened and died yourself if you hadn't birthed her when you did. I thanks God for sending that blizzard."

"We'll have to bury her this afternoon, Mattie," said Jesse.

Her eyes were pale brown, as if the gold that reminded him of sunshine had darkened into night. "I don't want her buried in a dark place, Jesse. I want her grave in the sunlight."

He nodded. "On the cliff behind the plaza, Mattie. I promise."

"I don't want her to be cold either."

"I'll wrap her in my buffalo rug, Mattie. That will keep her warm. And I'll build her a coffin."

"Where you gonna find lumber?" asked Jubilee, his black skin looking slack and old, and his eyes older still.

"We have four wagons, Jubilee. One of them gave shelter to Mattie on her journey to this land. Its wood can give shelter to her daughter."

Mattie stood beside the open grave. She could see the ax marks where the cowboys had chopped a hole in the frozen ground a full six feet deep so that her daughter would rest safe against the beasts that scavenged the dead buried in shallow graves. The coffin, a scant two feet long and a foot wide, its lid already nailed shut, rested on a cradle of ropes that would be used to lower it into the cold ground. A cross, also made with lumber from the wagon, stood at the head of the grave, the name Amy Hunter and the date, January 18, 1878, already carved in its weathered surface.

No one knew when Amy Hunter really died, and it didn't matter. What mattered was the day those who would have loved her gathered to say good-bye.

The cowboys, all but Hank Wilson, who stayed at the plaza with Leon, stood in silence behind Mattie, their heads uncovered to a wind that blew strong and bitter from the north. On the other side of the grave, Samuel, drunken and maudlin, leaned in the shelter of Clint Murray's arm.

Mattie, her female parts bound up with clean rags she had stored away for just such purpose, stood alone. She wanted it that way. Of all those gathered to mourn, she was the only one who was not a stranger to her daughter. She had shared her body with the tiny creature, nourished her, felt her fragile movements, brought her forth to be wrapped in a buffalo robe and buried in a windswept land.

Jesse stepped to Mattie's side, his eyes red-rimmed from tears. "For a time unknown to us, we shared our lives with two ladies. We are not privileged to know Amy Hunter as a woman grown because her destiny lies somewhere beyond our ken, but for a brief moment we knew her as hope. She reminded us that life renews itself in woman and that man by himself is incomplete, just as life without death is incomplete. We mourn a daughter we never knew. Let us comfort the mother who loved her."

He stepped back and nodded to Danny, who blew on his mouth organ to warm it before beginning to play. As the mournful notes of an unfamiliar tune rang out, Mattie watched Red and Jubilee lower her daughter's coffin. She stood alone and felt the tears drench her cheeks until the wind numbed her wet face.

When Jesse began to fill the grave, she raised her head to look at Samuel. She searched for some remnants of feeling for the fair-haired, slight young man she had married, and found none, not even hatred. Silently she closed the door on the memory of her courtship and early marriage. That Mattie had been young and foolish and in love with love. The Mattie who listened to the dull thuds of frozen clods of dirt hitting her child's wooden coffin realized she felt nothing for the man she was bound to for life, and couldn't afford to be foolish. She was eighteen years old and life stretched out before her like the arid plains upon which she stood.

She turned her face from Samuel and looked toward the Canadian, frozen as was her heart. But spring would come and thaw the river, the land would turn green with new grass, and her heart would began to beat again. She would renew her life and endure, and never again let a man make her feel unclean because she was a woman.

So help her God.

CHAPTER 19

But fate or perhaps Jesse's capricious God decreed otherwise. Spring came, the Canadian thawed and ran bank to bank in a red torrent for weeks, the prairie greened up, and the bawling of newborn calves echoed through the breaks and across the semiarid pastures north of the river, but Mattie did not thrive. Weakened by the trek to the Panhandle, the strain of facing the hardship of ranch life, a difficult delivery of her stillborn daughter, and a chill contracted at the baby's funeral, she fell victim to a lingering fever. Jesse brought Henry Hoyt—a doctor now working on the LX Ranch as a cowhand for lack of enough patients to support his practice of medicine—to examine her, but none of Hoyt's prescriptions worked, and Mattie finally refused to see him. When not confined to bed, she most often sat in a high-backed chair Hank had made of cowhide stretched over a framework of horns selected from the cattle that died during the blizzard, her feet propped on a matching footstool. Called

"Mattie's chair," and placed near the kitchen window where she could look out at the cottonwoods and the bubbling spring behind the plaza, or listen to the cowboys as they ate in shifts at the long table she had bought from Mendoza, she whiled away the months of 1878 waiting for her body to heal and her melancholy to pass. She instinctively knew one had much to do with the other. Her monthlies had not resumed after her delivery and she sensed that whatever force governed her flow of blood also contributed to the fits of tears that dampened her pillow at night, and other times, to the passive uninterest in the men and events of her isolated world. She concealed both her tears and her lack of interest behind a mask of proper womanhood while she waited in an agony of patience for her body and mind to work in harmony again.

Her behavior fooled everyone but Jesse.

He wrote her father.

September 1, 1878

My dear Mattie,

I have received this day a letter from Jesse McDade informing me of your failing health and of his concerns that you will not survive another winter in that godforsaken land. Your confinement and its tragic consequences bear out his opinion. A gently reared lady is not predisposed to survive such a harsh climate and primitive conditions. I regret that I did not follow my paternal instincts and forbid you to accompany Samuel to Texas. I failed in my duty to you on that occasion because a father bears the responsibility of protecting his daughter from her own foolishness if her husband lacks the gumption to do so. I will not fail in my duty again. Therefore I have directed McDade to hire a suitable woman companion to furnish the necessary care of your health and reputation, and to dispatch Jubilee, along with several such armed and trustworthy men as may be found within the bounds of Texas, to escort you home. I will meet your caravan in Trinidad, accompanied by a doctor and Aunt Patty, upon receiving a telegram from McDade with the date of your arrival. Good medical care and the amenities of civilization will restore your health, and the attentions and guidance of a loving father along with the delicate conversation of ladies will restore your spirits. You will soon forget your notions of pioneering and find contentment in more gentle pursuits. I believe the library association would welcome your participation in its fundraising efforts.

*Your loving father,
Colonel Andrew J. Corley*

Jesse waited to give her the letter until Samuel and Clint Murray had ridden off to the tiny settlement of Tascosa that was growing up around one of the few plazas Jesse had not been able to buy. Ostensibly the two men were planning to purchase enough provisions to last until Jesse drove a herd to Dodge City in October and could return with supplies. Mattie knew Samuel and Clint were more likely to buy whiskey at Ira Rinehart's store than flour and canned peaches.

It was one of the many things she didn't care about that year.

She did care about returning to Pueblo. She discovered she cared passionately.

She doubled up the letter and threw it in Jesse's face. "I won't go! And furthermore I do not appreciate your tattling to my father behind my back."

Jesse retrieved the wadded piece of paper and hunkered down by her chair to read it. Finished, he cocked an eyebrow. "What did you expect, Mattie? That I would ignore you like that drunken lout of a husband? That I would stand by doing nothing while you wasted away for lack of a doctor? Or that I would watch you sink further into despair without attempting to save you? Yes, I told your father. I would tell the devil himself, if need be."

Jesse's concern was a tonic more welcome than the concoctions Jubilee had been brewing lately. If there was a foul-tasting liquid she had not drunk in the past few months, it was only because the ex-slave had not heard of it or lacked the ingredients to make it. Still, she had no intention of giving in to Jesse or her father.

"I am not some consumptive miss with no mind of her own. My health is improving and as for my spirit—that is not likely to be improved by "delicate conversation." What on earth would I talk about? The best method for treating lice?"

"It would be an improvement over 'please' and 'thank you,' that is, when you bother to talk at all," he shouted.

Mattie leaned forward in her chair, feeling more alive than she had in nearly nine months. Perhaps the new Mattie conceived on top of that windblown cliff by her baby's grave had needed a gestation period. Perhaps her agony of patience had been the agony of awaiting her rebirth. And now the man most responsible for her delivery was planning to send her away. In a pig's eye!

"Pray tell me where you expect to find a woman to accompany me? Mrs. Goodnight? She is needed by her own menfolk. And who else is there? I haven't seen another white woman in over a year."

Jesse's black brows drew together in a frown, and Mattie felt a rush of exhilaration. "Then go home to Pueblo."

Mattie glared at the man hunkered down by her chair. "I won't leave my daughter!"

Jesse grasped her shoulders. "Name of God, Mattie! Your daughter is dead!"

"I know that, Jesse. I'm not mad. Aren't you always telling me that one must be bound to the land? Amy is one of my bonds. Men bind themselves to the land by challenging it, by investing money and time and work to win a victory over it. A woman invests her heart. I buried a piece of my heart in this land. The rest I have invested in those who live on it—Jubilee, Leon, Red, Danny, Hank, the other men"—her eyes caught his—"and you."

His face took on the hard edges his eyes lacked as he released her shoulders and stood up. "I'll ask you again to return home when I'm ready to leave for Dodge City."

"And if I refuse again?"

"I'll never give you another chance."

October 1, 1878

My dear daughter Mattie,

While I rejoice that your health has improved, I grieve that you will not be returning home. I still believe that would be the best course, as I fear the men around you are taking advantage of your most sweet nature. I must express my sincere disapproval of your nursing infirm men with whom you share bonds of neither blood nor matrimony. Take care that your modesty is not violated by sights inappropriate for a chaste woman. I also see no purpose in your performing such chores as sewing on buttons and mending socks, not to mention turning yourself into a washerwoman, for the benefit of rough men. They can well take care of themselves. As for your pursuit of the culinary arts, it is a proper occupation for a woman to feed the hunger of her family. However, it sounds as if you are running a boardinghouse. It is no part of your duty to prepare meals for every man who happens to work on the ranch or be in the neighborhood at suppertime. That miserable darkie Jubilee hired himself out to cook. Let him do so.

Your loving father,
Colonel Andrew J. Corley

* * *

A TIME TOO LATE

Mattie wiped her hands, smoothed her hair, and hurried to the front door when she heard the horses gallop up. Jesse and the men must have decided to return home rather than spend the night at one of the various line camps. Her smile changed from pleased to polite when she realized that not only did the four men not work for her, but she had never seen them before. A slight young man not more than an inch taller than she and lacking the weight of any more years dismounted and walked up to the door, followed by the three other men whose eyes darted about the plaza and outbuildings before ever looking at her. She noticed that all four rested their hands precariously close to their revolvers, and she drew a quick breath before straightening her shoulders and staring directly into the pale blue eyes of the youth who seemed to be the leader. She could smell the wildness about the four as though it were an actual odor, and knew one should show no fear when confronted by wild animals.

The youth leisurely studied her, his gaze flicking from her hair, damp and curling from working in the kitchen, to the tips of Samuel's secondhand boots that peeked from beneath her gingham skirt. He smiled, and revealed slightly crooked and protruding front teeth that the uncharitable might call bucked. "Is this Samuel Hunter's ranch?"

Mattie hesitated. If these men were acquaintances of Samuel from some of his many trips "on business" to Tascosa or the lawless, disreputable community of Mobeetie, she wanted nothing to do with them. Clint Murray's worrisome presence was sufficient.

"It is, and I am Mrs. Hunter, but I fear we have no need to hire more cowboys."

The youth removed his hat to reveal pale brown hair with a slight curl at the ends. Again he flashed that shy, bucktoothed grin. "We're not looking for work, Mrs. Hunter, but your husband invited us to supper the last time he was in Tascosa. We've come to take him up on it."

Mattie frowned. "Samuel failed to mention his invitation, I'm afraid."

"That's all right, ma'am. He didn't know I'd hear of it."

"I don't understand," began Mattie.

The youth stepped past her. "Samuel Hunter! Clint Murray! Come greet your guests!" He ducked to one side of the door, and his three men took the other.

Samuel appeared, carrying himself with the exaggerated posture that told Mattie he had already consumed several drinks past the point of civility. Clint Murray's taller form appeared at his shoulder, and as usual, he appeared to be more sober, or at least better able to control his body and his tongue. The puppeteer was always more in control than the puppet, thought Mattie resentfully.

"Who the hell's yelling for me?" asked Samuel, peering drunkenly over her shoulder, but not seeing the four strangers pressed against the walls on either side of the door. "Has your voice coarsened along with your temperament, Mattie?"

Clint Murray's snicker grated on Mattie's temper as much as Samuel's question, but before she could retort to either, the four men struck with that lightning physical speed every western man seemed to possess— or at least, every western man whose life had ever depended on speed, which was almost every man she had met since leaving the drawing room.

Guns drawn, they brushed past Mattie and shoved Clint and Samuel back into the house, searching them for arms with the brutal efficiency of men who had performed this same task many times before. Satisfied, the youth holstered his pistol and stepped

A TIME TOO LATE
back. "The boys and me have come for supper, Hunter."

Mattie stepped into the hall. "Who are these men, Samuel? Never mind. It doesn't matter." She turned to the youth. "You, sir, are violating good manners by pushing your way into my home. I would never turn away a man in need of food—it isn't hospitable or customary—but you are straining my manners."

"Shut up, Mattie!" screamed Samuel. "Your unseemly ways will get us killed!"

Jubilee ran out of the kitchen, a revolver clutched in his hand and Leon clinging to his apron. "You gentlemen just stand right there and don't be moving."

The youth's smile had disappeared. "Unless you are faster than William Bonney and his men, you better put the gun up."

"Lordy, Lordy, Miss Mattie," gasped Jubilee. "It's Billy the Kid."

Mattie darted forward. "Dear God, don't shoot, Jubilee. Leon might be killed!" She grabbed the little boy and whirled around to face the strangers. "Please leave my home immediately."

William Bonney smiled at Mattie, then glanced at Samuel and Clint, his smile disappearing. "Your wife has more courage than you do, Hunter."

He turned back to Mattie and smiled again, and she relaxed her tense shoulders. She had already decided that if he smiled, he wasn't dangerous. At least not as much.

"Your little boy isn't in any danger, ma'am. I always hit what I aim at, and I don't aim at babies."

Mattie studied the pale blue eyes of William Bonney and felt a sense of familiarity. Their piercing quality reminded her of Jesse's and Charlie Goodnight's, and she wondered at the choices men made in their lives. "Jubilee," she said, without looking away from Billy the Kid. "Put your gun down. Mr. Bonney will be staying for supper."

Samuel pushed himself away from the wall, his courage—or foolishness—returning with the disappearance of arms. "Yes, Jubilee. Set the table and serve Billy and his men."

Billy's face turned sober. "We'll all eat together, Hunter. I was told that you said one day in Tascosa that no decent man would break bread with a bunch of cow thieves. My men and me take offense at that remark."

Mattie interrupted to prevent Samuel from making any more statements. "If you and your men would care to wash up, Mr. Bonney, there is soap and towels at the backdoor. All the cowboys know to stop there before coming in the house. I expect those who eat at my table to have clean hands and faces."

Billy nodded at two of his men. "We'll wash up in shifts, ma'am, if you don't mind."

Mattie led the way to the kitchen. "I expect you are used to such an arrangement, Mr. Bonney. Your reputation doesn't include letting your guard down. I hope you like wild-plum cobbler. I'm better at lemon pie, but there is a shortage of lemons in the Panhandle."

"I expect to enjoy whatever you serve, ma'am, but you will remember to include bread."

Mattie hoisted Leon a little higher in her arms and turned to see if Jubilee had put away his big revolver and was frying steaks. He was, but she could see that his lower lip was pushed out far enough to step on. "Jubilee, take Leon to my room and stay with him."

"I ain't leaving, Miss Mattie," said Jubilee.

Mattie walked over to Jubilee and pushed Leon into his arms. She felt a cold spot in the middle of her back, as though Bonney and his men were touching her with icy hands. "Yes, you will, Jubilee. I'm certain that Mr. Bonney will agree that Leon is not a party to his disagreement with Samuel, and is too young to witness any possible—arguments." She heard the click of a gun being cocked behind her.

"Billy likes everybody to stay together. He don't think it's a good idea to give somebody leave to be running loose behind his back."

"And I don't recall giving you leave to put words in my mouth, Tom," said Billy in a voice as soft as snow falling in an open grave.

Her legs trembling, she slowly turned around to face the outlaws. "I will pledge Jubilee's good behavior."

Billy slouched in a chair at the head of the table, his pale eyes fixed on the man he called Tom. "Put the gun away. The lady gave her word."

"Jesus, Billy. What good is that?" asked Tom.

Billy didn't move, but he reminded Mattie of a rattlesnake coiling to strike. "It's good enough for me."

Mattie watched Tom avert his eyes from Billy's and holster his gun. Quietly she released her breath and gently pushed Jubilee toward the door, hoping the ex-slave understood she had just offered herself as hostage in Leon's place. She had no doubt that William Bonney would kill her if Jubilee tried to flee or to rescue her. On the other hand, she had no doubt she was perfectly safe if Jubilee did neither.

"I trust sourdough bread with wild-grape jelly will meet your requirement, Mr. Bonney? I've been ill of late and haven't been baking light bread." She was proud that she sounded so calm.

"I heard of your loss, and I offer condolences. I know how losing someone close to you hurts. Sometimes it changes your life."

Mattie tried to remember the stories circulating about her young guest. Something about his employer being shot, and Billy swearing vengeance, she thought. Once she would have been critical of a man's seeking revenge for wrong done him, but that was before she learned that right and wrong often depended on one's point of view. Or others' points of view. No man could afford to be considered weak. Nor any woman either.

"It does indeed, Mr. Bonney, but one still chooses the direction of the change."

Billy didn't reply, but she could sense that he was giving thought to her remark during the supper that followed. It was the strangest company she had ever hosted. While Billy's manners were no worse or better than her cowboys', she couldn't say the same for his men with their silent ways and restless eyes. She had the impression that only the slim boy held them in check.

Billy wiped his mouth on his sleeve and pushed his chair back from the table. "So much for the supper, Hunter. Now I'll accept an apology."

Samuel, whose meal had been more liquid than solid, stared belligerently at the outlaw. "I don't make apologies."

"Samuel, please," said Mattie when she saw Billy's smile vanish. "It wasn't right to disparage Mr. Bonney's honor without proof. Rumors cause much needless harm." Actually she thought the rumors had substance, but unless Samuel saw Billy rustle a cow or steal a horse with his own eyes, she thought an apology was wise. Certainly better than being shot.

"Shut up, Mattie," said Samuel, reaching over and twisting her wrist. "As usual, you're taking somebody else's side against me, and I'll not tolerate it. You look to your own reputation. Do you think no one is talking of your nursing McDade through his broken leg? Or letting him and that nigger deliver your baby when any decent woman would rather have died?"

Billy casually pulled his gun and slammed it against Samuel's temple. "I'm sorry I broke bread with him. I believe there might be some argument about who's

A TIME TOO LATE

decent at this table." He rested the gun on top of the unconscious man's skull and pointed it at Clint Murray. "How about you, gambling man? You feel like apologizing?"

Murray's muddy green eyes were impassive. "I apologize if any words of mine gave offense."

Mattie leaned over and examined Samuel's wound, her hands shaking. She knew now exactly how wildness smelled. It smelled of black powder and blood. But in this land, so did justice. She wasn't certain which she was smelling. She looked up at Billy. "I think you had best go. I can't offer hospitality to anyone who injures my husband."

Billy slid his gun back in his holster and rose, motioning his silent men to do the same. "If he hadn't been your husband, I'd have killed him. I'm obliged for the meal. I'll remember your plum cobbler for a long time."

"How long will that be, Mr. Bonney?" she asked impulsively.

His smile disappeared, but she didn't feel threatened because she saw the expression in those peculiar blue eyes. For a heartbeat she saw a young boy who wished he could turn back from his path. Then the boy disappeared and she found a man in his place. "I reckon that will be until I've used up all the sin I've earned, ma'am."

He plucked his hat off the table and put it on. "Your cattle wear the Bar H brand, ma'am?"

She nodded. "Need I be concerned that some may stray?"

He grinned. "If I ever see any of your cows straying, ma'am, I'll see to it that they find their way back to your range."

"My manager runs a few cattle with mine. His brand is the Flying MJ. Do you suppose those cattle might find their way back home with mine?"

"Your manager is Jesse McDade, the former Texas Ranger?"

"His loyalty is to me now."

"I'm not on the best of terms with Texas Rangers, but I approve of loyalty. It's saved my life a few times." He nodded, those blue eyes seeming to pierce through her skull to all the locked rooms in her mind. "I guess McDade's cows can find their way home, too. It would be a shame to separate pairs."

She looked down at the table, suddenly afraid that Billy the Kid understood much more about her than she wished. "I appreciate it, Mr. Bonney."

He started for the door, then turned around. "I'd be obliged if you would remember that William Bonney played fair and respected women. In case anybody ever asks."

She felt the hair stand up on the nape of her neck and wished his words hadn't sounded so much like an epitaph. "I'll remember, Mr. Bonney."

He gave a quick glance around the large kitchen with its four-cap stove and long table, its whitewashed adobe walls with shelves holding their meager supply of pots and pans, dishes and provisions, the round adobe fireplace in the corner, and the rugs she had woven of rags scattered on the packed-earth floor. She sensed he was memorizing the sight and the sense of it to be taken out and enjoyed when he found himself in a less cheerful place.

His eyes came back to her and he lifted his hat and smiled. "Thank you, ma'am."

She didn't follow him to the front door to watch him ride off. She knew he would leave without bothering any of her possessions on the ranch, and she knew she would never see Billy the Kid again.

★ ★ ★

November 10, 1878

A TIME TOO LATE

My dear daughter Mattie,

Even in Pueblo, we have heard stories of this merciless killer William Bonney. No one with the sense God gave a goose would offer hospitality to a man like that, and your compliments on this outlaw's manners and kindly demeanor toward you demonstrate a woman's foolish trust. I also disapprove of Mr. McDade's teaching you to fire a gun. Although I realize you now live in an uncivilized and lawless place, knowledge of and competence with firearms is most unseemly and leads a woman to believe herself the equal of a man. I pray Mr. McDade does not encourage such a belief, for an independent woman not only is against God's laws, but she is hard and unattractive as well. I fear the company of those wild Texans is having a detrimental effect on your behavior.

Your loving father,
Colonel Andrew J. Corley

Mattie crumpled up her father's letter with shaking hands and added it to the buffalo chips and wood in her fireplace. She could have told him that Samuel's careless words had provoked William Bonney's visit, but such a confidence would only have prompted her father to fire a barrage of missives to Samuel, none of them kind, and all of them guaranteed to disturb the surface calm of her marriage. Better not to mention Samuel at all than to risk stirring up the mud at the bottom of the pond.

Still, the letter hurt, and she resented the hurt.

She wished Jesse was home.

He wasn't. He and several men, including Samuel and Clint Murray, had left several weeks ago for Dodge City, leaving her and Jubilee and Leon and a Winchester rifle at the plaza. But he had been true to his word. He had given her another opportunity to leave the Panhandle.

She had given him a list of provisions instead.

She sat down in front of the narrow little table that served as a dresser and looked at herself in the round mirror hung on the wall above it. Along with most of the furnishings in the plaza, she had bought the table and mirror from Mendoza. She wondered if Mendoza's wife, that quiet woman in the dark somber dress she'd met only briefly before her husband dismissed her like a schoolgirl with no sense, had ever sat looking in the mirror as Mattie was doing. She wondered if Mendoza's wife—and she didn't even know the woman's name—had ever doubted her own existence. Did other women look in mirrors to reassure themselves they were real? Did other woman touch their faces and throats in search of the changes they knew had already occurred inside? Was she turning hard and unattractive as her father said?

Unable to look at herself in the mirror any longer, she unpinned her hair and began to braid it for the night. As she tied a frayed ribbon around the end of the braid, she noticed her hands. She dropped the ribbon. Her palms were callused, the long fingernails she used to buff each day were short and blunt, her cuticles ragged. Clumsily she rose and stumbled to the trunk at the foot of her bed and pawed through it until she found her tiny leather manicure kit, and beneath it—like a flash of sunshine—the yellow silk dress she had worn to the dance at the Thatcher Brothers' store. She wiped her hands on her flannel nightgown, then gently lifted the dress from the trunk and hung it from a peg on the wall by her bed. Picking up her manicure kit, she sat down again at the narrow table and desperately buffed her nails. The reflection of the rich yellow silk gown wavered in the mirror, and hot tears splashed on the table's rough surface.

She wished Jesse was home.

Calluses and broken nails and a silk dress wrinkled like a young girl's creased and useless dream didn't seem as bad when Jesse was there.

CHAPTER 20

Jesse and the men rode in from Dodge City on a sunny November day with three wagons loaded with provisions enough to last until spring. Coffee, sugar, salt, flour, baking powder, dried beans, canned peaches and tomatoes, dried apples, raisins, and prunes, condensed milk, slabs of bacon, new boots for Jesse, more needles and thread, kerosene for the lamps, bolts of plain blue cotton for shirts, ropes, grain, nails, shells for revolvers and rifles, new pots and skillets for Jubilee, a puppy for Leon—and nothing for Mattie.

She stood in the door watching Leon clutch the wiggling mongrel puppy and smiled.

She watched Jubilee count his new pots and felt happy.

She saw Jesse's cold, somber eyes, gray as the mist that sometimes rose along the Canadian valley at dawn, and felt chilled.

"McDade!" Samuel slid off his horse and hung on

to the stirrup for balance, his eyes red as a wild beast's in the firelight. "McDade, pack your bedroll and draw your pay. You're fired."

The cowboys stopped unloading the wagons, dropping sacks of flour and crates of dried fruit on the ground. With only the jingle of spurs to break their silence, they formed a circle around the two men. Dusty and unshaven from weeks on the trail, with leathery skin and white creases fanning out from the corners of eyes used to squinting against the sun and the wind, they made an audience as harsh and uncompromising as the land under their boots.

Mattie stepped away from the door and let it bang shut behind her with a sound like a fired revolver. "Samuel, what are you saying?"

Samuel turned his head toward her, his face twisting into a grimace of indecision, then Clint Murray stepped up beside him and gently touched his shoulder. Mattie flinched as though it was her shoulder Clint had touched.

"Hush your mouth, woman!" ordered Samuel, then licked his lips as though savoring his words. "Hush your mouth and go in the house where you belong. I'll tend to you later."

Mattie looked at Samuel, fancied she could smell the whiskey on his breath, remembered that his hands had no calluses. She walked across the bare, cold earth until she stood beside Jesse, each step taking her closer to her husband and farther away at the same time. "I won't leave, Samuel, and I won't let you fire Jesse."

Clint squeezed Samuel's shoulder but directed his words to Mattie. "You have nothing to say about it. Much as you would like to forget it, Samuel has authority over you. In my opinion he's been far too lenient with you for far too long."

"I do not recall asking for your opinion, Mr. Murray," retorted Mattie. "Nor do I appreciate hearing you voice it without my permission."

Jesse removed his glove from his right hand and flexed it. "Shut up, Murray. Your opinion doesn't count for a hill of beans. Whether Hunter has authority over Mattie isn't the issue here. His authority over me is—and he doesn't have any."

Samuel shrugged away Clint's hand and stepped away from his horse. "I own the ranch, McDade, and I've decided to fire you and turn over the management to Clint. He and I can deal together most amiably."

"I'm aware of how 'amiable' the two of you are," said Jesse, a peculiar note in his voice that puzzled Mattie. "However, that changes nothing. You have no authority to fire me. Colonel Corley hired me and by contract only he can fire me."

"There isn't any such contract, McDade!" cried Samuel in frustration.

"Yes, there is, Hunter. I demanded it. However, I don't keep it with the ranch papers, which accounts for your ignorance. Next time you rifle through my office, perhaps you should be a little more thorough." Jesse curled his fingers around the butt of his revolver. "And lest you think that you and Murray can counter my orders behind my back, consider whether any cowboy on this place would work for either one of you."

"As long as they're paid, why should they care?" asked Murray with a sneer.

Hank spat on the ground, splattering Murray's boot with tobacco juice. "Cowboys ain't servants, Murray. We don't work for just any son of a bitch who can write a draft on a bank. We're particular, and you don't no more measure up to the kind of man we'd work for than nothing. Jesse goes, and we go."

Jesse nodded at the old cowboy. "Thanks, Hank, but I think Hunter and Murray get the drift."

"What do you suppose the almighty Colonel's going to think when I inform him that you're running cattle on his land, you and two or three more of your men. What do you think he'll do when he finds out you're burning your own brand on cattle that belong to him?" demanded Samuel, his face turning red.

"I never brand any cattle but mavericks, Hunter, calves without mothers. Mavericks have always been free for the taking."

"Take more than your share, don't you, McDade? Sounds like rustling to me," said Samuel.

Jesse didn't change expression, but Mattie noticed his eyes and shuddered. She wouldn't want those cold eyes looking at her. "I divide all mavericks found on the public sections of Hunter land with Mattie in proportion to the size of our herds. I do the same with the mavericks on the public sections of my own land. I run both herds over both ranges irrespective of whether it's my land or Mattie's. I am not a rustler, and if you weren't Mattie's husband, I'd kill you."

Mattie smiled. William Bonney had said the same thing. She wondered if Samuel knew how valuable she was as a shield. "I know that Jesse runs cattle with ours, Samuel. It's customary, whether you approve or not. My father knows it, too." Actually she didn't know if the Colonel did or not, and didn't care. "Hunter Ranch is already one of the largest in the Panhandle and we owe it to Jesse McDade. Even if you had the authority, firing Jesse would be a foolish move. I can only believe that alcohol has dulled your senses and an evil influence has weakened your judgment."

Even before she heard the cowboys clear their throats and shuffle their feet and saw their uncomfortable expressions, she felt what little had remained of her world crumble beneath her feet. The destruction that Samuel began with his cruelty on their wedding night she had completed. She had defied her husband, questioned his judgment in public, defended another man, and succeeded in shocking even the men who respected her and hated Samuel.

Samuel's face went slack, then tightened with an anger so fierce, Mattie wondered that one man's body could contain it. Then, without warning, his face seemed to alter as though the heat of his fury had burned away the alcoholic haze and left him staring helplessly at the wreck of his life. He lifted his hand. "Mattie?"

"It's too late, Samuel."

She saw the triumph in his eyes, saw also the relief, and knew he had expected her refusal to forgive him the years of outrageous treatment, had, in fact, depended on it. She had given him a justification for his own weakness.

It was the last thing she ever intended giving him.

She watched Clint Murray put his arm around her husband's shoulder and start to lead him away, and realized she was sick to death of the man and his manipulative ways.

"Mr. Murray!"

Murray turned, and Mattie caught an ugly expression in his eyes and hesitated, sensing that he would make a dangerous enemy. But he was already her enemy, hers and Jesse's, so she had nothing to lose accusing him. What could he do after all? If he abused her, the cowboys would kill him—if Jesse didn't do it first. For once she had not only right, but power on her side.

"Mr. Murray, you gambled and lost. Samuel cannot carry out your wishes and fire Jesse—and that was *your* wish, not Samuel's."

"Mrs. Hunter, you do your husband a disservice. He only wished to save you from the consequences of your unhealthy dependence on McDade. Since McDade's clumsy assistance during your recent confinement, you have been susceptible to his influence.

Need I mention how your father and people of importance would view his intimacy." His eyes dared her to dispute him.

"You son of a bitch!" exclaimed Jesse.

Mattie caught his arm before he could lunge forward. "Please, Jesse. A gentleman does not deign to fight with the lower classes, and a lady, as Jubilee once pointed out to me, ignores them because to her they do not exist. Unfortunately I cannot follow Jubilee's advice in this instance because Mr. Murray does indisputably exist along with rattlesnakes and wolves. But *not* in my house! I cannot horsewhip you off the ranch, Mr. Murray, since my husband pays you for whatever service—or disservice—you do for him, but I will not permit you past my front door again."

"You can't do that, you witch."

Mattie smiled. "I am only beginning to learn what I can do, Mr. Murray. I suggest you not push me into testing my newfound knowledge."

She lowered her eyes and saw Jesse's shadow and her own stretch out across the packed dirt in front of the plaza. She straightened her shoulders, turned, and walked back into the plaza, remembering her father's words: "A man has to stand tall and cast a long shadow."

So did a woman.

"Sorta stole your thunder, didn't she, Jesse?" Hank's question broke the silence left behind by Mattie.

"Miss Mattie just can't help being a lightning rod," grumbled Jubilee in a low voice, new worry lines creasing his forehead. "I hope she don't call no trouble down on her head."

Jesse hoped so, too, but the itchy feeling along his spine told him differently. "Jubilee will clear your belongings out of Samuel's room and leave them by the door, Murray. You may sleep in the tack shed or one of the adobe bunkhouses if you can persuade the cowboys to share their quarters."

Hank spat again. "We don't no more want to bunk with a rattlesnake than Mrs. Hunter does. I reckon he can toss his bedroll somewhere else."

Samuel clung to Murray's arm. "She had no right to throw you out. It's my house." He turned his head to look at Jesse with as much hatred as a man of his nature was capable of feeling. "If anyone's to leave, it's you, McDade, you and that nigger cook—and my wife, if she continues her unseemly ways."

"You're laboring under another misapprehension, Hunter. It is not *your* house. It is the Colonel's house, as you would know if you had read the bill of sale carefully. But even if it weren't, I still would not allow Murray to spend another night there. Mattie just beat me evicting him, that's all. She doesn't happen to like his influence over her husband. I happen not to like him for an entirely different reason."

"It's that whore, isn't it, McDade? The one you found in the alley behind our hotel?" demanded Samuel.

Jesse felt his stomach lurch as he remembered the pathetic creature he'd found lying in the filth and garbage and discarded whiskey bottles that littered Dodge City's alleys. If there hadn't been a lull in the noise pouring out of the flimsy wooden saloons and dance halls and gambling halls into the streets, as if all the drunks and gamblers and men groaning out their lust between the sticky thighs of tired whores had suddenly fallen silent, he would never have heard the woman whimper. He would have walked past the alley with never a second glance at what looked like a bundle of rags. Even the trail of blood splatters that led from the alley back to the hotel wouldn't have caught

A TIME TOO LATE

his attention. Blood in splatters, drops, or rivulets wasn't uncommon in Dodge. A man mostly didn't care unless he was the one bleeding.

But he did hear her, did help her back to a tiny one-room shanty, did find her a doctor, or a man claiming to be a doctor, who said she'd live if infection didn't set in.

He didn't look for the marshal. Not because there was no law in Dodge, and not because what law there was had more to worry about than whether a whore's customer got too rough. He didn't look for the marshal because the whore told him who her last customer was.

Even if she hadn't, the trail of blood would have.

"It's the whore, isn't it, McDade?" Samuel repeated.

Jesse looked at Mattie's husband. "That's part of it, Hunter."

"Aren't you a little high and mighty, McDade? Haven't you ever used a whore?" asked Murray with a sneer.

"I try to leave them in the same condition I find them in, Murray."

Murray shrugged. "We paid her."

Jesse's hand tightened on his pistol and he half drew it before he managed to reclaim the self-control he'd fought so hard for so many years to gain. It was his edge over men like Murray. It prevented his killing a man for reasons of anger or passion or personal satisfaction, but instead enabled him to kill coldly, calmly, and after deliberating all the alternatives. Ultimately that made him more dangerous than other men. Once made, his decisions were not susceptible to change.

Murray saw Jesse cut short his involuntary motion and his lip twisted in derision. "You're like all the other virtuous citizens, McDade. You're not going to kill a man over a whore."

Jesse drew a deep breath. "You're alive because

killing you would mean explaining to Mattie what I saw when I kicked in your hotel-room door. She has no notion such men as you and Hunter exist. I can't keep the world clean for her, but I can damn sure keep her corner of it free of your peculiar kind of filth. So you keep your unnatural acts hidden from her. Mattie's innocence is your protection against me."

Samuel's eyes held their own anguish. "I can't help it, McDade. I've tried, but I can't change."

Jesse searched his emotions for any resembling pity—and failed to find it. "No more whores, Hunter. Abusing women won't change the way you are, and it makes me wonder if there's not more evil than sin in you."

"You're only one man, McDade," said Murray.

Jesse looked around at the circle of cowboys. "There are twelve men here, Murray, plus me as the judge. That makes thirteen, and it's your unlucky number. Now get out of my sight, and take your paramour with you."

He watched them walk away, then leaned over and emptied his stomach of all the bile that had been collecting since Dodge City.

Jubilee lifted a new shotgun out of the wagon and sighted down the barrel at the retreating men's backs. "I reckon you oughts to kill them, Jesse, instead of plucking off their rattles. Don't make them any less pizen."

Red stepped up beside Jesse, his expression that of a man who had bitten into a green persimmon. "Hell, I'll do it, Jesse, if you're worried about telling Miss Mattie. Then I'll leave out of here, and you can tell her I did it over the whore."

Jesse wiped his mouth. "I don't lie to Mattie, and besides, she wouldn't believe you'd kill Hunter for going to a whore any more than she'd believe I'd kill him for the same reason. I don't care how innocent a woman is, she always seems to know about men and whores and overlooks it—or seems to."

A TIME TOO LATE
311

Hank joined them, his eyes crinkling as he narrowed them to look at Jesse. "You're lying by not telling her."

"I'm withholding the truth."

"Not a lot of difference that I can see," said Hank.

Jesse rubbed his forehead. "I know it, but how the hell do you tell a woman a thing like that?"

Hank shook his head, and the other cowboys shuffled their feet and looked everywhere but at Jesse. "Goddamn if I know. Every man on this place walked around for months when Miss Mattie was expecting like we didn't notice her belly was swelling up. If we can't talk to a woman about something as natural as that, how we talk to one about something that ain't natural? Way things stand in the world, I guess you did the only thing you could do, Jesse. But it appears to me that there's something wrong with the world when the only thing you can say to a woman ain't the truth. Goddamn if it don't."

Jesse slapped Hank's shoulder. "Men have been lying to women since Adam for all kinds of reasons, most of them bad. This is one time that maybe we've got a good reason."

"A lie is a lie, Jesse, and I hopes this one don't jump up and bite you on the behind," said Jubilee.

Jesse smiled. "Then I guess you better keep that shotgun handy, Jubilee, because I'm depending on you to cover my behind for me."

"Murray ain't gonna bother Miss Mattie directly. He gonna send Hunter after her, and what you gonna do then?" asked Jubilee. "We all knows the best way to get next to you is to get next to Miss Mattie, and Hunter gots the right to do that."

Jesse turned down the wick in his lamp until it barely flickered, and set it on the floor in the corner behind a blanket he'd rigged up as a screen. He hoped no light shone through his door to give him away, but he couldn't risk the time it might take fumbling in the dark to light the lamp, and he for certain couldn't blunder around without it. Satisfied with his makeshift arrangements, he settled back in his chair in front of his closed door and waited. If Jubilee was right, then Hunter would be walking down that hall toward Mattie's bedroom if not tonight, then soon. And he would hurt her and not just because her flesh wouldn't be receptive, but because only her pain would enable Hunter to perform a husband's duty. His treatment of the whore proved that.

Jesse didn't understand men like Hunter even though he'd spent most of his adult life in the company of men, and thought he'd heard of every way of relieving lust, some respectable and some not. He'd visited whores himself, tumbled a few self-professed ladies in their own parlors, had even on occasion relieved himself with his hand, so he was a damn sight far from being pure. But Samuel and Murray were outside his experience, and not just because their practices were repugnant to him. He had known others of their kind who in no way resembled the two men, so Jesse didn't believe their sexual proclivities explained their sadism toward women. Maybe the two traits coincided more often than not and he was just ignorant of it. Or maybe Hunter and Murray in combination brought out the worst in each.

He just didn't know.

Furthermore he had no way of learning. Even among men, it wasn't a subject for conversation and certainly not for philosophizing. The average man didn't spend much time on philosophy anyway, except that which involved surviving, Jesse admitted to himself. What went on inside a man's head that might account for his actions was not only uncharted territory, it was private land.

Jesse decided it might have been simpler to have shot Hunter and Murray and professed ignorance than to try to protect Mattie from men he didn't understand.

He stiffened when he heard the creaking sound of a leather door hinge and cursed his own philosophizing. He should have been worrying about *what* Hunter and Murray planned to do and not *why* they were doing it. Why didn't matter. Knowing why didn't make that whore's pain any less.

He bolted out of his chair, ripped the blanket down and turned up the wick on the lamp, then picked it up and stealthily opened his door. He drew his gun before he took the few steps across the hall to Mattie's door, then hesitated before reaching for the latch string. With the exception of kissing Mattie, which he had no right to do, he could justify every action he'd taken on her behalf. But if he interfered between a husband and wife, even to save the wife from physical torment, he violated society's strongest law. The marriage bond was sacred. Inside his own home Samuel could do damn near anything he pleased short of killing Mattie and no one would dispute his right to do so. Once Jesse stepped through that door, he forfeited society's approval and respect, maybe even that of his cowboys. Even though they all despised Samuel, Jesse doubted they would approve his invading Samuel's bedroom and pulling him off his own wife. Jesse would be a pariah among his own kind.

He reached for the latch string.

CHAPTER 21

Mattie heard the door hinge creak and calmly turned a page of her book. Although her formal education had ended when she left boarding school, she had discovered a greed for knowledge within herself since moving to the Panhandle that she eased by reading and rereading her small store of books. She had wondered lately if the very isolation of her physical life had not contributed to her greatly expanded mental curiosity, as if her mind sought to journey where her body could not.

But her mind was not the only one starved for the written word. She had learned to her astonishment that every cowboy on the ranch cherished books as much as she. Most owned at least one, and all at one time or another had borrowed from her small library. Although their conversation seldom reflected it, most were familiar with Shakespeare and Milton. They generally dismissed the novels of Mr. James Fenimore

Cooper with the comment that "he don't know squat about Injuns."

Since her infestation of lice Mattie tended to agree with them.

Tonight she was reading *The Merchant of Venice*.

"Were you expecting me, my traitorous little wife?" asked Samuel, blinking his eyes as though the dim lamplight hurt them. Given their reddened condition, Mattie suspected that it did.

Mattie closed her book and laid it aside, then slipped her hand beneath the quilt. "I believe you said this afternoon that you would 'tend to me later.'"

With bare feet, his shirt unbuttoned to reveal a narrow strip of his hairless chest, and his suspenders already dangling loose, he lurched toward the bed with an awkward gait, as befitted a man who smelled like a distillery. "And I will, too, you filthy bitch."

Mattie pulled the pistol from underneath the quilt and cocked it. "Stop!"

Samuel froze, whether from shock or fear Mattie had no way of knowing. "W-what?"

Mattie threw the covers back and got out of bed, her toes curling as her feet touched the cold earthen floor. "I don't believe I care to be tended to tonight, Samuel. I'm much too tired and you're much too drunk."

Samuel blinked again, and Mattie wondered why she had ever thought his eyes angelic. They were glassy, protuberant globes in a face that was bloated more often than not. "You're pointing a gun at me!"

His voice sounded so bewildered that Mattie almost smiled. "It's a Colt Civilian Model Single-Action forty-four, Samuel, or so Jesse tells me, and it's quite accurate at short range. At fifty yards I'm lucky to group my shots within a six-inch circle, but then you're standing much closer than fifty yards, so I should be able to hit whatever portion of you I aim at. At present, that happens to be your belly. Did you hear me, Samuel? I said 'belly.' Do you remember how shocked you were the first time I ever used the word? I was so hurt by your disapproval and so contrite. I'm not contrite anymore. Have you noticed?"

Fury was fast replacing bewilderment on Samuel's face. "Put that gun down, goddamn you! How dare you threaten me? You have forgotten your place."

Mattie raised the gun a fraction and curled her finger tighter around the trigger. "My father was put out with Jesse for teaching me to shoot. He feared I might think myself a man's equal. What do you think, Samuel? Am I your equal tonight?"

"No!"

She smiled. "That's willful male blindness speaking, not your common sense. I am your equal tonight, and we will speak as equals. Are you familiar with Shylock's speech in *The Merchant of Venice*, Samuel? Shakespeare might have written it for women with just a single substitution. 'Hath not a woman eyes? Hath not a woman hands, organs, dimensions, senses, affections, passions? . . . If you prick us, do we not bleed? If you tickle us, do we not laugh? If you poison us, do we not die?'"

"You're mad!" whispered Samuel.

She nodded. "I was mad to have married you, but as Aunt Patty says, I made my bed and now I must lie in it. But not with you, Samuel, not unless you approach me if not with love, at least with respect. I will not be humiliated, degraded, or spat upon again. I am not less than human. I am not filth!"

She stood panting, her hand quivering from the effort of holding the pistol steady. "Get out, Samuel! Get out!"

He stared back at her, anger and fear and stupidity warring together on his face. Stupidity won, and he started forward. "You won't shoot me, you silly bitch."

Her door flew open and Jesse stepped through, his pistol in one hand and his lamp in the other. "But I will, Hunter. Get out of Mattie's room. Better yet, get out of the plaza. Go tell Murray his second plan didn't work. You couldn't fire me and you can't intimidate Mattie." He nudged Samuel's neck with his gun barrel. "Out, and don't plan another attack tonight. I'm barring the front and back doors."

The moment Mattie heard Jesse slam and bar the front door, she sagged to the floor, letting the pistol slip out of her hand. Her skin felt moist and slick all over, and she realized that she had been sweating. She wrapped her arms around herself, closed her eyes, and let the shudders take her.

A few moments later she felt Jesse lift her off the floor as easily as she lifted Leon and lay her on the bed, tucking the quilts around her shivering body. "It's over, Mattie. He's gone. Hush, little cougar, there's no need to be frightened of him."

Her teeth chattered and she grabbed his hand and held on to it until she gradually relaxed. "I'm not afraid of him, Jesse. I'm afraid of myself. Papa warned me that an independent woman was hard and unattractive, and I felt so hard tonight, as if even a diamond could not scratch me."

Jesse sat down on her bed and leaned over, cupping his hands around her face. He stroked his thumbs over her cheekbones, then skimmed them across her lips over and over until she opened her mouth and he slipped one thumb inside to trace once over the serrated edges of her teeth. When she bit down and dragged her teeth over the pad of his thumb and the blunt, short nail, he smiled, his eyes silver in the lamplight. He withdrew his thumb from her mouth and slipped his hands down her throat and onto her chest, and spread out his fingers to warm her skin from the hollow of her throat to the tops of her breasts, and from one shoulder to another. Her breath seemed to stop, then escaped in a soft rush as she licked the taste of him from her lips. His nostrils flared as he caught sight of that tiny motion, and he leaned over to touch the tip of his tongue to the tip of hers.

Her breath escaped this time in a moan.

He lifted his head, his eyes dilated until only a narrow silver rim remained around the onyx of his pupil. "You are beautiful, Mattie. You're incandescent. Your hair shimmers and your eyes glow and you smell of sunshine and wildflowers and your smile warms a man on a cold day." He slipped his thumb between the buttons of her nightgown and traced her breastbone, sending currents of heat that tightened her belly. "Your skin is satin and cream and soft summer air."

Suddenly he jerked his hands off her body and rose from the bed to stride across the room to one of the windows, gripping both sides of its frame like a man on a cross. He threw his head back to stare at the ceiling, his back muscles tense under his shirt. "But it's not your looks that make you beautiful, Mattie, although God knows some days the sight of you tightens a man's gut. It's what's inside you, that damnable courage that draws a man even when he knows better. The woman who survived a stampede and let me pour whiskey over her bleeding hands, who lived through lice and flies and fed an outlaw and won him over, that woman is so fiercely beautiful, she blinds a man to others."

Mattie pushed off the quilts and sat up in bed, hardly able to see him through her tears, not certain she understood him, but afraid she understood him too well. "Do I blind you, Jesse?"

He turned around then, his eyes filled with lonely resignation, and shrugged. "I'm a man like any other."

"Not like Samuel."

His face lost all expression. "No, not like Samuel."

He hesitated a moment and she heard the shutters rattle in the wind that had blown dry and hard throughout the fall. "Would you have shot him, Mattie?"

"I don't know. So help me, God, I don't know." She lowered her eyes to stare at her patchwork quilt. She touched a dark green square. "This is from the train of one of my dresses. And this yellow flannel one is made from a shirt Leon outgrew. The bright red square is a piece of Danny's neckerchief, and the blue one is from the tail of Red's shirt. I think all the cowboys must have holes cut from the bottoms of their shirts because they all brought me material to piece for the quilt. You have two squares: one is a piece of denim from the pants I cut off you the day you broke your leg, and the other is pieced together from the rags I used to wrap your cast. Samuel has a square, too, Jesse. This linen one here made from a handkerchief of his. Of course, being Samuel, he accused me of ruining it anyway when I washed it in 'that dirty river water,' so he donated it for 'my homey little effort.' He's represented in the quilt along with everyone else in my life, so how could I kill him?"

Jesse walked over to the bed to study the quilt. "My two squares are on either side of yours, Mattie."

She lowered her eyes again. "The fabrics complemented one another."

He was silent again, and she could feel his eyes on her. "I guess the quilt is another investment of yours."

She nodded. "I guess so."

She heard him move away, heard the creak of the door hinge as he left. Not until the next morning did she find the heart-shaped gold locket on a yellow velvet ribbon wrapped in brown paper and tied with string lying next to her comb and brush on the narrow little dresser table. More beautiful than the locket was the note written on a page torn from Jesse's tally book:

Mattie,
Sometimes men invest their hearts, too.

J.

She rubbed her cheek against the soft velvet ribbon, then touched her lips to the cool gold locket. "It's too late, Jesse," she whispered to the silent room. "It's too late."

April 1, 1879

Colonel Corley,
Mail service is still erratic due to the difficulty of carriers riding across more than a hundred miles of unmarked prairie between here and Fort Elliot. It is especially dangerous in the winter months, and two carriers were caught in a blizzard and lost their feet due to frostbite. One died anyway. Such incidents do not provide much of an incentive to carry the mail. However, hardy souls do sign on and letters are delivered, although yours of February 15 did not arrive until last week.

In answer to your inquiry, I am not buying up everything in sight, but am continuing to buy land whenever possible, and have contracted for fifty Hereford bulls to be delivered to Dodge City the end of June. We will be the first in the Panhandle to experiment in crossbreeding Herefords with longhorns. I hope to breed a strain that will provide more beef and better beef per animal without sacrificing the strength and hardiness that allows the longhorn to survive almost any climatic conditions and to gain weight on almost any kind of grazing. Goodnight is already ahead of us in this regard, having introduced two hundred Durham bulls onto his ranch in '77. Although the Herefords are more expensive than Durhams, I believe that they are a better animal and are cheaper now and in greater supply than they will be in the next five years. To keep our neighbors from profiting from our bulls—and we do now have neighbors, it being practically impossible to ride thirty miles in any direction without running into another white man— I plan to invest in some of this new-fangled barbed wire to fence off pastures. Many of the other ranchers cling to the idea of free range and are resistant to the notion of fencing, but I believe time and progress are against them.

The winter was harsh with weeks of snow and wind and sleet interspersed with unseasonably warm days. The land has either frozen or burned. Prairie fires have raged around Fort Elliot this past month, reducing the range to a desolate appearance and the officers' quarters to ruin, although one was not responsible for the other except to illustrate how dangerous and how impossible to check is a fire in this mostly uninhabited land. Our own range, which is nearly a hundred miles both west and south of Fort Elliot has so far been spared. I have forbidden the cowboys to smoke cigarettes except at the plaza or in camp. All have taken up chewing tobacco instead, a practice your daughter forbids in the house, saying she prefers men blowing smoke to spitting tobacco juice.

In reply to your question about fresh outbreaks of Indian trouble, it is an unfounded rumor. Several small bands of Comanches, Kiowas, Cheyennes, and Apaches did leave the Territorial Reserves in the late fall of last year, but Charlie Goodnight made peace with the Comanches under Quanah Parker, and the Tenth Cavalry persuaded the rest back onto the reservation. Although the Indians claimed the agency was starving them, I suspect the greater reason for their excursion is the loneliness for a way of life that is gone.

Our greatest danger is not Indians, but those gentlemen who have come to the Panhandle more in search of "climate" than of grass, and who swing a wide loop and carry a ready branding iron. We have had less trouble than most since Billy Bonney has kept his promise to your daughter. Still, we have had some losses.

Sincerely,
Jesse McDade

* * *

Jesse leaned over his saddle, his eyes picking out the trail of the hundred head of cattle and four horsemen. His chest was tight and he could hardly draw breath for his anger. "How long before Squinty got to the line camp, Red?"

"He reckons it took about an hour. If them bastards had been any better shots, I guess he wouldn't've made it at all. Good thing scalp wounds bleed so damn bad. Otherwise they might have noticed they just creased his skull instead of ventilating it. Pretty damn sorry rustlers, I'd say. It'd pay them to be a little more careful if they're planning to make a living in the business of rustling cows. Damn stupid to run off a bunch of cows right under the nose of a cowboy. It's even stupider to shoot a cowboy. Tends to get a man's dander up. Hell, cows is just property, but shooting a man makes it personal."

"They had nothing to lose, Red."

The redheaded cowboy risked a glance at Jesse before turning his attention back to watching the ground in front of his horse. "What do you mean?"

"I was going to hang them for rustling anyway."

"That's pretty hard, Jesse," said Hank Wilson.

"I'm a hard man." The tracks turned into a narrow canyon and he reined in his horse. "Anyone know if this is a box canyon, or is there a way out at the other end?"

Hank pushed his hat back. "It opens out the other end, 'bout three miles or so from here. We come up behind them, they'll just ride out ahead of us and leave the herd clogging up the canyon to slow us down."

Jesse nodded and glanced over his shoulder at the men following him. "Hank, I want you and Samuel and Clint Murray to ride to the other end, get in front of the rustlers, and block their escape. Red, Jubilee, and I will take them from this side."

"I believes I best go with Hank. If them rustlers look to get away, a drunken man might get hisself killed easy as falling off a log," said Jubilee, nodding his head in Samuel's direction. He reined his horse close to Jesse's and lowered his voice. "I gots no objection to you killing him, but I don't want Miss Mattie to feel like she was Bathsheba."

Jesse flushed as he caught the reference. "That was not my intent. I just didn't want two men I'm not certain of watching my back."

Jubilee stared at him with that direct look that read the thoughts behind a man's eyes. "Sometimes a man plays tricks on his own self."

Jesse looked over the ex-slave's shoulder. "Hank, I'll give you and Jubilee an hour to get in place."

Jubilee hesitated, his lined face pensive. "I reckon I spent too many years with the Colonel. I sees crooked places when there ain't any."

Jesse felt a trickle of sweat roll down his back, its path the shape of a question mark. He felt as though his mind had cracked open to reveal an abyss he hadn't known existed. For the first time in his life he didn't trust his own motives.

"McDade! I hear the cattle down the canyon!"

Samuel's yell called Jesse back from a journey into his own suddenly unfamiliar mind. He cocked an eyebrow. He would have thought Samuel was too drunk to hear the faint bellowing.

Samuel swayed and raised an arm. "Once more into the breach!" He spurred his horse into a run, clinging to its back as the animal raced down the canyon, leaving a gritty cloud of sand in its wake.

"Hunter, you stupid son of a bitch!" yelled Jesse as he dug his spurs into the sides of his mount and galloped after Mattie's husband, followed by a silent Clint

Murray. He heard Red echo his own curse, heard the creaking of leather as the others jerked on the reins and pointed their horses after him.

Jesse caught up with Samuel just as the canyon curved and widened, and by then it was too late. They rode into the midst of the rustlers' camp. A crude gate of cedar poles penned the cattle in a narrow, blind canyon that joined the main one like a tiny tributary, and a small fire with three branding irons resting in its heart burned on the sandy canyon bottom. Jesse barely had time to notice either when the first shot came.

Mattie dropped the rag into the basin of bloody water, then picked up the bottle of tequila. "I have to do this—I think. It seems to prevent infection."

Squinty nodded, the lines in his weathered face deeper. "I reckon it does."

Mattie looked at the three-inch furrow that ran along the side of his head. She had shaved the hair on either side, but had not stitched it. She couldn't stitch a wound the width of her thumb and deep as the bone. "It will hurt."

"I reckon it will, but don't let that worry you none. Ain't gonna hurt no more than when the army doctor cut off my leg. We was out of chloroform by then, and it smarted some. He done the best he could, and you will, too. He was crying just like you. He was a young feller and the war just about broke him. He sawed and cursed the Yankees and cried. I think maybe the war was harder on doctors than on soldiers. We could always shoot somebody when we had a mad on, but the doctors couldn't. They just cut and poked and sawed and watched men die. But I ain't gonna die, so you just go ahead."

Mattie poured the liquor over the wound while Squinty clenched his jaw and gripped Jesse's bed cov-

A TIME TOO LATE
ers. "Damn those savage men! Damn them! Damn them!" She wrapped a clean cloth around his head. "I hope Jesse kills them. God forgive me, but I do."

Squinty drew a shuddering breath. "I figure somebody will die if Jesse catches up with them. It's a lot like sticking scarecrows in a cornfield. You got to let the other birds circling your crop know what happens. Can't let anybody get by rustling Hunter cattle, or Jesse would need an army to keep the herds safe."

Mattie's hands shook. "Please, God, keep him safe."

Squinty reached up and patted her shoulder. "Don't you worry none. He'll be fine."

Mattie avoided his eyes as his words roused the guilt that never slept deeply in her mind. She doubted if Squinty was referring to Samuel, and she certainly hadn't been. She touched the outline of the locket she wore under her dress and leaned back in Jesse's chair to wait in silence lest her tongue betray her heart to Squinty and to herself.

"Miss Mattie?"

Squinty grabbed the bedpost and pulled himself upright, and Mattie got up to lean over the bed. "What do you need, Squinty? Another drink of tequila? I'm sure your head must be hurting."

The old cowboy sat on the edge of the bed and lifted his hat off the table. "Hurts something fierce, Miss Mattie, but I ain't never been much of a drinking man, and a bullet that missed anything vital ain't gonna make me start now. I sure would admire you giving me a hand, though. I figure I'll go sit outside on the step."

"Squinty, you shouldn't even be sitting up, much less waiting outside in the cold. Jesse will come back when he comes back. There's nothing you can do to hurry him." She touched the locket again if it were as a talisman.

Squinty stood up and took her arm, swaying a little until he caught his balance. "It ain't cold today hardly at all, Miss Mattie, and Jesse ain't the reason I want to be outside, though I'll watch for him. You see, ma'am, when I lost this"—he pointed to his leg—"I laid up in that hospital for a fair spell, long enough to watch a lot of men die in bed with nothing to look at but walls and a ceiling. I swore then that if I ever got wounded again, I'd never lay in no bed as long as I was able to stand or sit or lay outside. I reckon it's superstition, but seems to me that death can come up on a man's blind side if he stays cooped up in bed when it ain't necessary."

"That's foolishness, Squinty. You said yourself that you wouldn't die," said Mattie.

Squinty patted her arm. "And I reckon I won't this time, but I want to be outside just the same. A man ought to be able to see what's coming for him, whether it's healing or death." He patted her hand. "I'd be obliged now, Miss Mattie, if you was to help me."

She did, even tucking a buffalo robe over his legs as he leaned against the side of the house, but she shook her head when he said she was welcome to sit by him to wait for Jesse and the men. "No, thank you, Squinty, but I'm not so brave as you. I don't think I want to be able to see what's coming." She went back to Jesse's bedroom and waited.

By the time she heard the horses and men, the room was full of shadows cast by the coal-oil lamp. She pushed herself up from the chair and gripped its back until her cramped muscles loosened, then slowly walked out of the room into the hall and found she could force herself no farther. If Jesse was safe, he would walk through the door. If he was not, she could steal a few more seconds of hope by not going outside to greet the men.

Samuel flung open the door and staggered into the

hall. His face was red and his eyes glittered with drunken excitement. "We have returned! And we have vanquished the foe!"

Hank Wilson followed Samuel. He caught sight of her and removed his hat, revealing his grizzled head of hair. "Miss Mattie?"

Mattie laced her fingers together over her breasts. "Yes?"

"Jubilee says you best get some bandages and hot water."

Her breath blocked her throat for a second, preventing speech, and she blindly reached out a hand.

"McDade took a bullet." Samuel's voice held a note of brutal satisfaction.

Mattie swayed, and Hank Wilson leaped to grasp her arm. "He got winged, ma'am. He ain't about to die."

Squinty limped through the door, followed by Jubilee and Red carrying Jesse. A bloody bandanna was tied around his upper left arm and a brand had burned his boot. Fatigue dulled his silver eyes and drew grooves around his mouth. Sweat greased his face and matted his black hair in thick wet curls to his forehead.

She took a step toward him, her arms reaching out before the expression in his eyes stopped her as surely as if he had pushed her away.

"Put him on the bed, Jubilee, and bring me some more rags and hot water," she said, defying Jesse's rejection.

She stepped back to let them pass, then followed the man she had no right to touch into his bedroom.

"He ain't hit bad, Miss Mattie," said Jubilee. "He's just weary, is all. Would be worse if that rustler swinging the hot branding iron had hit him somewheres 'cept on his boot."

Red's voice chimed in. "But we got the herd back,

Miss Mattie. And hanged three of them bastards from a cottonwood tree."

"Shut up, Red!" Jesse's voice was a hoarse snarl. "That's not a fit subject to speak of in front of a lady."

"Well, it didn't hurt the cottonwoods none, Miss Mattie," said the cowboy, looking flustered and uneasy.

"Red!" said Jesse in warning.

"Hush, both of you," said Mattie, untying the bandanna and letting Red strip off Jesse's blood-soaked shirt. She clapped her hand over her mouth to hold back the scream. The bullet had torn through the muscle, leaving a vicious-looking, seeping hole on either side of his arm. Bruising and swelling had already begun, and the arm looked mangled and beaten.

She looked up at Red. "I'm glad you hanged them. I wish I could bring them back to life so you could hang them again."

"Too bad you didn't watch them die, Mattie," drawled Samuel. "It was my first hanging and I found it—interesting."

If Samuel's voice turned her cold, the expression in his eyes set off chills. He had enjoyed it!

Blindly she rose and stumbled toward the door. She heard Jesse's muffled curse and felt hands grab her shoulders.

"You just take yourself to bed, Miss Mattie," said Jubilee. "Hank and Red and me can take care of Jesse." He guided her into her room and onto her bed, pulling a blanket over her shaking body.

She heard the door close behind him and rolled off the bed and fumbled the lid off her chamber pot. She vomited until her stomach hurt, then curled up on the dirt floor. She had rejoiced that three men died most horribly. Dear God, she had become the hard woman that her father had prophesied.

"Mattie?"

His voice was soft but hoarse and sounded as if he were tired beyond bearing.

She sat up and wiped her mouth on her sleeve. "Go away, Jesse."

He limped over to her, his arm bandaged and hanging loosely by his side. "Are you well, Mattie?"

She peered up at him, hardly able to see his silver eyes in the pale moonlight that poured through her open shutters. "Oh, God, I'm so ashamed."

"It's range law, Mattie."

She shook her head. "No, it's vengeance, and it doesn't taste sweet at all."

"They rustled cattle and tried to kill Squinty. They knew they would be hanged if we caught them. They expected it."

She laughed, the sound absorbed by the adobe walls and dirt floor. "You don't understand. It's not the cattle. It's not even Squinty." She drew a breath. "They shot you, Jesse. They shot you."

She heard his breath catch, then whisper out in a gentle exclamation: "Dear God." He lifted one of her hands and kissed her palm.

She watched the door close silently behind him, then turned her head to stare sightlessly out the window at a distant sky that offered beauty without mercy and questions without answers.

CHAPTER 22

The summer of 1879 passed in a succession of heat and fire as the prairie burned to the south of Hunter ranch. The smell of burning pastures hung over the land, and the sun rose and set in a burst of crimson as a haze of smoke and dust diffused its rays. Herds of antelope, flocks of wild turkeys and quail, rabbits, prairie dogs, coyotes, wolves, and all manner of other creatures flew and ran northward before the flames.

And no cowboy slept.

The cattle, smelling the fire, milled in uneasy bunches, threatening to join the other beasts in a desperate flight north. Jesse and the other men rode unceasingly, their faces gaunt and their throats dry from the overheated air. The Canadian lay between the fire and the herds, providing a natural firebreak, but cattle didn't understand such a subtlety, so June passed in a desperate fight between cowboy and animal as Jesse fought to hold the herds on Hunter land.

A TIME TOO LATE

But other animals besides antelopes and turkeys passed through Hunter land. Herds from South Texas trailed over its rich grassland in spring and early summer, leaving behind a legacy more deadly than desolate, burned prairie. In late August and early September Mattie's cattle began to die—first by tens, then by hundreds, until more than a thousand head lay stinking upon the prairie, food for scavengers and maggots.

"Texas fever?" asked Maggie, clutching a handkerchief drenched with lilac water over her nose with one hand and holding tightly to her horse's reins with the other as she gazed at rotting carcasses and swallowed the bile that rose in her throat with each breath of lilac-scented stench.

Red shifted uneasily in his saddle, his glance flickering between Jesse and Mattie. "Yes, ma'am, that's what it is. I knew it right off when I found the first cow down with fever and losing weight faster than a snake shedding its skin. But don't you worry none, Miss Mattie. You go on back to the house and Jesse and me will take care of things."

She laughed. "Don't worry? A thousand head have died in less than a week and you tell me not to worry? Dear God, Red, what should I be worrying about if not this? And how do you and Jesse plan to take care of things?"

Red's darting glance finally rested on Jesse. "God Almighty, Jesse, get her out of here. It ain't fitting to talk about this in front of Miss Mattie."

Jesse rolled a cigarette and cupped his hands around a match to light it. He'd eased his ban on cigarettes when the fever hit, and Mattie suspected it was because the burning tobacco masked the scent of sick and dying cattle. He blew out the match and dropped it in his pocket. "That's for Mattie to say, Red. This is her ranch and her cattle."

Samuel's name hung unspoken in the hot, dusty air.

As it should be, thought Mattie. "There's no one else, Red."

"Why are the cows dying, Jesse?"

Leon, looking older than his three and a half years, stood by Mattie's side, waiting for an answer to his question. He accompanied her everywhere, a tall, thin child whose babyhood lay in his past, and whose somber eyes saw and judged in a manner that often disconcerted her, as if a man's mind were locked inside his still-immature boy's skull.

"Why are the cows dying, Jesse?" Leon asked again.

Jesse drew deeply on his cigarette. Mattie knew he wasn't debating whether to answer Leon's question as much as he was debating *how* to answer it. "I don't know, Leon," he finally said. "The cattle from South Texas give the fever to ours, but I don't know how. The trail herds aren't sick, but when they pass close to our herds, our cattle die. They even leave the grass infected. Let our cattle graze on pasture the trail herds have walked over, and they die. Cold weather kills the fever, but by that time a man may be knee-deep in dead cows."

Mattie forced herself to look again at the dead and dying cattle that dotted the flat plains. A few yards away a cow raised its head, its emaciated body resembling a hide-covered skeleton. As she watched, the animal's eyes became fixed in its skull as Texas fever claimed one more victim wearing the Bar H brand. The scene blurred as she felt tears coat her eyes. It was as if Baby were dying over and over again.

She turned to Jesse. "Stop them, damn it! Stop those herds from crossing our land."

Jesse nodded, his eyes the color of flint and just as hard. "I plan to, but this will be different than buying somebody's herd or chasing them off our grass. It's a Winchester quarantine, Mattie. If we can't talk the trail bosses out of crossing our range on their way to

A TIME TOO LATE

Dodge, we'll have to shoot. There's likely to be dead cattle and dead men. I wanted you to see why before I kill a man."

"What if I say no?" she asked.

"I'm not asking you, Mattie, but I'd rather you didn't set yourself against me."

She felt a instant's resentment, then dismissed it. Men like Jesse never asked permission to do what had to be done. She glanced once more toward the fly-specked corpses. "Then tell the cowboys with the trail herds what they will face. I don't wish to hurt men who do not understand what they will be very sure to meet. Simply tell them they will never pass through Hunter land in good health. Then be certain that they don't."

She gathered her reins and mounted her horse, ignoring Red's shocked expression. Jesse merely touched the brim of his hat. She chose to believe that he was saluting an equal.

She felt no such assurance a month later when she faced a dusty, whiskered, leathery-faced trail boss in charge of a herd from Fort Worth.

"What's a little lady like you doing out on this bald prairie so far from home?" he asked, leaning his forearms on his saddle horn and turning his head to spit tobacco juice on the ground. "And with a young'un, too. You lost, ma'am?"

Mattie felt herself at a disadvantage. Not only was she riding astride, a most unladylike thing to do since a good six inches of her boots showed beneath her skirt, but she was miles from the plaza, on the very edge of Hunter land, with Leon perched on the saddle in front of her and no one to watch her back. She did not feel Jesse's equal now; in fact, she felt like a weak, foolish woman.

"I'm Mrs. Mattie Jo Hunter, and this is my ranch."

"Pleased to meet you, Mrs. Hunter. My name's

Jameson, Bill Jameson." He smiled at her, revealing a gap between his two front teeth that lent a sibilance to his words. "So this here is your range."

A peculiar tone in his voice made Mattie uneasy. "Yes, and I must ask you to turn your herd aside and take the Western Trail into Dodge."

The trail boss laughed. "The Western Trail is a good hundred miles from here."

"Actually it is farther than that because you will have to backtrack. You can't cut across country because it's LX land for several miles to the east of me, and although Mr. Beals and Mr. Bates aren't presently in residence, I don't believe they would appreciate your driving sick cattle over their range."

The trail boss strangled a comment, one Mattie felt sure was unseemly, before clearing his throat and speaking. "My cattle are not sick. Take a look at them. You've never seen a healthier bunch of longhorns."

Mattie didn't bother looking. "My cattle are now dying of the fever caught from the last Fort Worth herd. Don't hope that you can convince me otherwise, and don't hope that you can cross my land. I will not permit it."

The trail boss tipped his hat back, glanced around at his cowboys who had ridden up to gawk at the first white woman they had seen since leaving Fort Worth, then turned back to Mattie. "I don't mean no disrespect, Mrs. Hunter, but I reckon I'll be driving my cows straight north from here. I can't afford to lose no time turning back south far enough to bypass both the LX and Goodnight's place before I turn east. Goodnight's plumb unreasonable about cattle out of South Texas. Can't figure why. The old man drove enough cows north in his day. I guess prosperity makes a man overbearing. Anyhow, I ain't about to cross swords with Goodnight, so I reckon you best move out of the way, you and your boy, and let me by."

"Are you saying you will respect the LX and Mr. Goodnight's property, but not mine?"

Jameson straightened up and spat on the ground. "I wouldn't put it that way, Mrs. Hunter."

"Just how would you put it?"

"You being a woman, it's likely you don't understand what this trail driving is all about. It's about thousands of head of cattle in Texas that we need to drive to the railhead in Dodge City. It's about free grass and open land in the Panhandle so we don't have no gates to open, no sodbusters with their shotguns shooting at our cattle instead of taking money for any damage to their corn crops, and plenty of grazing for our herds while we're on the trail. This here is free grass I'm standing on, and it don't matter what kind of piece of paper you and Jesse McDade are holding."

"You've heard of Jesse?"

He spat again. "I've heard tell of you, too, Mrs. Hunter. You tend too much to a man's business and McDade backs you up. I don't see McDade anywhere, so I'll tell you what I would've told him. The stockmen in the rest of Texas don't like you folks in the Panhandle trying to shut us out of free grass on our trail drives, so I'm breaking through your quarantine. I'm blazing a trail right through the Panhandle to Dodge City and I'm picking your land to cross. You got water and plenty of grazing and you ain't got a lot of friends. Everybody calls you 'that Hunter woman' and they don't generally say it with much respect. If you're gonna butt into a man's business, then you can't expect folks to treat you like a lady. Riding in here in your sunbonnet won't change my mind."

Mattie clenched her reins until her fingers hurt, felt her face turn red with humiliation and anger. She drew a deep breath and decided she was more angry than humiliated. Perhaps a lot more. "So you're crossing my land because I'm a woman, but no lady, and you think I'll let you get away with it."

Jameson shook his head. "That ain't the only reason. Goodnight's got seventy-five armed cowboys, and he won't hesitate to shoot my boys full of holes. The LX might be pretty near as bad. I hear tell that neither spread is any bigger than yours with any more men, but they ain't run by a woman. Jesse McDade's tougher than boot leather, but you ain't. Couldn't be. You're a woman. I figure you're too soft to enforce a Winchester quarantine, and you and McDade being tighter than two ticks on a dog, I reckon you're gonna slow him down some. You're the weak spot in the quarantine, Mrs. Hunter, so this is where I'm breaking through. Nothing personal, ma'am, but if you're gonna act like a man, you're gonna have to be as hard as a man."

Time and space fell away, and Mattie was again on the cliff above the plaza, listening to dirt falling on her daughter's coffin, and pledging that she would never be shamed because she was a woman. She shook her head to clear away the memories and picked up Leon. Awkwardly she shifted him around her body until he rode in the saddle behind her, his arms clasped around her waist. Now her hands were free, and her body between Leon and the men facing her.

"You are set on your course, Mr. Jameson?" she asked, loosening her sunbonnet until it hung free down her back. She didn't want its shovel brim cutting her field of vision when she needed to see more clearly. Fortunately the sun was straight overhead, so she needn't worry about being blinded by it. She heard one of the cowboys suck in a deep breath when her bonnet fell loose and the sun gilded her hair. She had accepted her own beauty since the night Jesse had given her the locket, noticed its effect on men, and discounted its importance. Beauty alone never achieved anything of lasting importance. She smiled to herself. But sometimes beauty achieved a short-term advantage for its possessor. It distracted the trail boss and his men long enough for her to pull Jubilee's Winchester out of the scabbard hanging on the saddle under her skirts.

She levered a shell into the chamber and raised it to her shoulder. "Mr. Jameson, you will turn your herd, or I will shoot you and as many of your men as possible before you return my fire. If I am killed, it will change nothing. The shots will draw Jesse and my other men in this direction, and you will die from their fire. You were most unlucky to have chosen the Canadian River breaks as your path onto my property. The shallow canyons and gentle rises will trap your herd—and you—and my men will block off your escape and commence a turkey shoot. Jesse thought that only a fool would take this route and be trapped. It's difficult to flee when you have three thousand cattle, and you can hardly leave them when they are the whole reason for this foolishness." She glanced quickly from side to side to be certain that none of Jameson's men were edging behind her. "But you see, Mr. Jameson, when a woman acts like a man, she has certain advantages. Years of my sex quietly observing yours has taught women that there isn't any foolishness of which a man isn't capable. To be fair, a woman is just as capable, but she has long lacked the opportunity to be foolish on such a grand scale as a man. In other words, I was not convinced that a trail boss might not someday take this route—particularly when my men are spread out along the boundaries of the rest of my ranch. This is the only way across, and I have been watching it for several weeks"—she stopped and bit her lip until it ceased trembling—"ever since I sat and watched my cattle die from Texas fever!"

"You ain't gonna shoot me," said Jameson, nudging his horse toward her.

Mattie sighted along the barrel. Jesse had cautioned her to always aim for the body. A wounded man was more dangerous than a grizzly bear, particularly a man shot by a woman. Jesse was probably right—he usually was—but Mattie knew she wasn't hard enough to kill a man. Shoot him, yes. But not kill him. Her transformation from pampered, protected lady into strong, determined female wasn't complete. Perhaps it never would be. Perhaps there would always remain a softness, a delicacy, inside of her that would always prevail over her impulses.

Perhaps.

Or perhaps not.

She squeezed the trigger.

Jameson jerked back in the saddle and slapped his hand over a crimson star burst that erupted from his chest just below the shoulder. Mattie saw him mouth words, but the Winchester's discharge had deafened her. She felt Leon squeezing her waist, knew he must be terrified, but put aside his fear and her guilt for bringing him along and turned the Winchester toward another man. She should stop—give the other cowboys a chance to back off—but she couldn't. Violence had a way of accelerating time and reactions while slowing down thought and judgment. She wondered if Jesse ever felt this way—as though he were two separate persons, one watching the other and helpless to stop him.

She saw the cowboy on Jameson's right pointing his Colt at her, saw his finger tighten on the trigger, saw his excited, confused eyes, knew he also was two separate men—and wondered if one would be sorry if the other killed her.

"Jesse!" she cried.

Had her horse not shied, Mattie would have been

dead. As it was, her targeted cowboy's bullet grazed her upper arm, leaving a streak of fire. She jerked her own trigger in shocked reaction and watched in horror as the cowboy grabbed his head and toppled off his horse. Somewhere behind her she heard another Winchester and saw another man slide from his horse.

"I reckon that's enough!"

Mattie jerked around in the saddle to see a man who looked to be a few years older than Jesse sitting on his horse and holding a Winchester rifle. A brown silky mustache and beard barely streaked with a lighter color between yellow and silver covered his chin and upper lip, but didn't disguise the strong jaw and wide mouth that looked as though he might be a man who smiled easily. He wasn't smiling now, though, and the wide-set hazel eyes under thick brown eyebrows held no humor.

Jameson pressed his bandanna against his wound. "What the hell do you think you're doing, Miller?"

The man he called Miller held the Winchester steady on the remaining three men. "I reckon you underestimated the lady, Jameson. She meant what she said. I think you best look to your health and that of the other boys instead of trying to shoot Mrs. Hunter. It ain't polite to shoot women anyhow—even if they do have the drop on you. In fact, it's those kind that you best walk around. Now, I want you to plug the holes in your various hides and turn that herd around."

"Goddamn it, Miller, you're one of my men! What are you doing on her side?" demanded Jameson.

Miller nudged his horse up beside Mattie's. The hazel eyes glanced at her briefly, but Mattie felt warmed by their gentle expression. "It never set right with me, Jameson, picking on Mrs. Hunter's spread. First place, Jesse McDade's meaner than a snake when somebody crosses him, and in the second place, I don't like gossip about a decent woman."

"She shot me, goddamn it!" yelled Jameson. "You call that decent?"

Miller cocked a thick eyebrow. "I can't fault a woman for defending her property. It doesn't make her indecent, just shocks the fool out of a stupid man—like you. Next time you better listen to gossip with a grain of salt. Any woman who faces down Charlie Goodnight, then feeds supper to William Bonney and comes out on the best end of that deal, isn't somebody you want to confront."

"That isn't all she's done," began Jameson.

Miller fired a shot in the air, stopping Jameson in midsentence. "I believe we've had enough idle talk. You best be about the business of turning that herd before McDade shows up."

Uneasiness flashed through the trail boss's black eyes and he gathered his reins in his uninjured hand. "I won't forget this, Miller."

Miller sighted down the gun barrel at him. "You apologize to Mrs. Hunter before you leave."

"What?"

"You best if you know what's good for you. You shot a woman, and not one of them ladies of the night. Moreover she had her boy with her. I figure your chances of getting out of the Panhandle without being hanged aren't very good. Maybe an apology will keep your neck from being stretched."

Mattie leaned over the saddle. "For God's sake, leave it! I don't want anyone else hurt. I won't send my men after you, Mr. Jameson. As you said, if I'm going to act like a man, then I have to be prepared to accept the consequences. You just remember next time you gossip about that Hunter woman, you tell folks I'm hard. Maybe if they know it ahead of time, I won't have to shoot anybody again—and no one will shoot me."

Jameson nodded at two of his uninjured cowboys.

"Patch up those boys and get to riding. I want them cows ten miles away from here before dark." He pulled off his hat and looked at Mattie. "I ain't gonna apologize, Mrs. Hunter, not even if Miller shoots me. I reckon we each did what we had to do."

Mattie nodded. "That's true enough, Mr. Jameson." She watched him ride off toward his herd, watched the cook pack his chuck wagon and hitch up his mules, then slumped over the saddle. She felt herself lifted off her horse and settled into a pair of strong arms on a different mount. The arms didn't belong to Jesse, she knew, because the smell was different. It was still leather and horse and man, but it wasn't Jesse. She heard a man's deep, slow voice, not as husky with controlled passion as Jesse's, but pleasant nevertheless. She listened.

"What's your name, son?"

"Leon."

"You gonna be able to ride that horse without your mama holding you on if I lead it?"

"Yes, sir." Mattie heard the high, childish voice crack. "Is my mama dead?"

The man chuckled. "I believe it'll take more than a bullet's scratch to kill your mama."

Mattie opened her eyes to see Miller's hazel eyes studying her. "I'm fine, Leon. My arm just stings a little."

Her rescuer smiled, and Mattie decided her brief first impression was right. His mouth was meant for smiling. "Glad you're feeling a little more perky, ma'am, seeing that your men are riding up fast, and I suspect the one in front on the black horse is Jesse McDade."

Mattie stiffened and clutched the saddle horn to pull herself more upright. "It is Jesse!" She waved her uninjured arm. "Jesse!"

"No need to fall off the horse getting his attention, Mrs. Hunter. I figure he could pick you out in a crowd."

She heard the dry tone in his voice. "What do you mean?"

Miller shrugged, the hazel eyes somber. "Can't hardly miss that gold hair, can he?"

She turned back to see Jesse jerk on his reins, almost pulling his gelding back on his haunches. She sensed that Miller meant more than what he said, that intuitively he recognized the bond between her and Jesse, but she didn't care. Wordlessly she held out her arms and felt herself scooped out of Miller's arms and into Jesse's. She felt the shudders course through the strong body, the tremors that shook his arms, and the pounding of his heart against her breast.

His eyes were glittering silver and yearning as he clasped her chin and turned her face up toward his. "Mattie, sweet heaven, I—" He closed his eyes for a moment while she heard him struggle for control. "I heard the firing and thought you were dead."

"Lord have mercy, honey chile, what was you doing?" demanded Jubilee, riding up to pat her shoulder. "Why didn't you tell nobody where you was at?"

"Near scared Jesse out of seven years' growth, Miss Mattie," said Hank.

Mattie heard Jubilee's question and Hank's remark, but ignored them as she would the buzzing of a fly. Time was slowing again, and she seized it to share with the man holding her. Too soon she would have to remember who she was—who he was. But not now.

She touched Jesse's mouth shyly, felt him kiss her fingertips. "How did you know where I was?"

Jesse's chest heaved as he caught a deep breath. "I knew."

"She called you," drawled Miller, rolling a cigarette. "Just before that cowboy shot at her. Guess she thought she was going to die."

His words speeded up time, and Mattie resented it. "He couldn't have heard me," she said.

"Probably not," agreed Miller.

Jesse examined Mattie's arm, his lips clenched together until white lines appeared around his mouth, then looked up at the other man. "Who the hell are you, and what happened out here?"

"Jesse!" exclaimed Mattie. "Mr. Miller came to my assistance."

The other man lifted his hat, revealing hair the same silky brown and pale streaked color as his beard. Mattie decided the odd gray-blond streaks denoted experience rather than age, as though he had ridden farther and harder than most men in the same amount of time. "The name's Tom Miller, ma'am. We never had the chance to be properly introduced."

"How do you do, Mr. Miller. You have no idea how pleased I am to meet you."

Jesse pressed her head against his shoulder. "The polite exchanges can wait, Mattie, until I hear Mr. Tom Miller's story."

Mattie tried to relax and to recapture the private moment between her and Jesse, to call back his total attention, but it was already too late. Tom Miller described her confrontation with Jameson, and she watched as Jesse's face first lost color, then flushed red. She touched his cheek. "It's all right, Jesse. It's over and I'm fine."

He jerked away and flashed her a glance from eyes darkened to granite. "It isn't over. Jubilee! Come take Mattie home. The rest of you get your Winchesters out. We're going after Jameson."

Mattie clutched his arms. "No, Jesse!"

His eyes reflected an anger so deep and cold that she despaired of reaching him. "Jubilee, take her."

She released his arms and sank her fingers into his hair, pulling his face down to hers. She pressed her mouth close to his ear as though whispering to him, but instead bit down hard on his earlobe. He jerked, and she lifted her head until she looked directly into his eyes. "Listen to me, Jesse. I gave my word to Jameson that he could leave safely, that you wouldn't come after him. My word has to mean something in the Panhandle, just as yours does."

The cold in his eyes gradually gave way to warmth, and he nodded. "All right, Mattie."

"And I want you to hire Mr. Tom Miller."

Jesse lifted his head to look at Miller. The two men studied one another while Mattie waited, puzzled at their expressionless faces. "I think Mr. Miller might be happier working on the LX, Mattie. I don't need any more men at present, and he appears to me to be a man who wouldn't push in where he wasn't needed."

"Jesse, that ridiculous. We always need good men."

Tom Miller lifted his hat to Mattie. "Mr. McDade is right, Mrs. Hunter. I reckon I might be uncomfortable on your ranch. I do like to be where I'm needed. I'm a top hand, a wagon boss, and you've already got one. I never did like being second best."

"I'll send a note along to the LX manager along with you," said Jesse.

Miller nodded, then looked at Mattie. "It's been nice, Mrs. Hunter. Maybe next time we'll meet under pleasanter circumstances."

Mattie watched him ride off, wondering if she had truly seen an expression of regret in those hazel eyes, and if she had, what it was he regretted.

CHAPTER 23

First called Hidetown because it was a buffalo hunters' camp, then renamed Sweetwater after the creek that flowed close by, the Panhandle's first settlement finally adopted the name Mobeetie when the government refused it a post office because Texas already possessed one town named Sweetwater. Although Jesse doubted that any of its citizens had ever heard of the expression "a rose by any other name would smell as sweet," it was nonetheless the town's guiding philosophy—at least so far as its name change was concerned, since Mobeetie was an Indian word for Sweetwater. Other than that, he didn't see that the settlement had much use for philosophy, there being more important matters to occupy most of its inhabitants, namely gambling, drinking, and other more intimate activities involving women with names like Crazy Horse Lil, Frog Mouth Annie, Diamond Girl, and Poker Alice. Although there were legitimate businesses such as Tom and Molly O'Loughlin's restaurant, a laundry, a barbershop, a general store run by Rath and Hamburg, a pool hall, and two hotels, they were outnumbered by saloons, gambling establishments, and dance halls. Other than a few wives of businessmen and of officers and enlisted men at Fort Elliott located a mile away, Mobeetie was a man's town. Respectable women were scarcer than hens' teeth.

Beautiful respectable women were scarcer than that. When Mattie Jo Hunter rode down its dirt street in March of 1880, the news spread as though blown by the wind across the plains. Men, mostly young, unwed, and woman hungry, poured out of Mobeetie's business establishments to lean against frame buildings, check horses tied to hitching posts, peer at distant Fort Elliott as if it might have disappeared overnight, gather in conspicuous groups to converse in quiet tones of subjects none of them remembered later. Bullwhackers checked the harnesses on their teams, freighters lackadaisically loaded wagons or rearranged sacks and crates, cowboys lolled self-consciously against the wooden posts that held up the porch of J. J. Long's general mercantile store while clerks and proprietors of Mobeetie's respectable businesses found a variety of reasons to leave their counters on some outside errand. Soldiers from nearby Fort Elliott, both white and Negro, stood in solemn groups as though on parade.

For a one-street town of cottonwood pickets holding raw frame fronts against the wind, Jesse thought it was quite a turnout. If any of Wheeler County's five hundred inhabitants were absent from Mobeetie on this blustery afternoon, he figured they must be dead. Otherwise they'd be drinking in the sight of Mattie Jo Hunter mounted on a buckskin gelding and wearing a navy-blue wool riding habit as though she was cool, clear springwater.

Mattie rewarded Mobeetie's covert adulation by

nodding and smiling at every man daring enough to tip his hat as she rode by. Soon men whose heads hadn't been bared to the sun in years were lifting their hats as though they had belatedly discovered the brims were scorching hot. It was a display of respect and admiration.

It was also a display of curiosity.

Mattie knew it, too.

Her gloved hand trembled slightly, and the smiles she bestowed on the crowd demonstrated as much defiance as gratitude. She was "that Hunter woman," confusing and contradictory, respectable and unseemly, desirable and untouchable. Men admired her beauty but eschewed the woman behind it. In a frontier society a woman was either a whore or a helpmate who serviced men in one capacity or another. That she might be neither was far beyond the average man's understanding. That she might be married, yet still be independent of her husband was beyond their comprehension. That her husband was worthless, if not worse than that, did not alter their judgment of her behavior. She might step from a woman's traditional role from necessity, but not from conviction. It was quite all right for her to shoot Bill Jameson, but as Jesse had heard one cowman say, "she ought to be apologetic about it, by God."

Mattie reined in her horse in front of Mark Huselby's hotel, which Jesse noticed was as crowded with men as every other building in town. Perhaps more so. Huselby's was the meeting place designated by Charlie Goodnight in the notes cowboy couriers carried to every rancher and settler in the Panhandle whether he owned one cow or thousands. Goodnight planned to organize a Panhandle stock association, and the old man, by God, intended that everyone should come. As best Jesse could tell, everyone had. He nodded to Goodnight and Bugbee, Nelson, and Cresswell, as well as W. C. Moore, manager of the LX, and another man representing the T-Anchor.

"Jesse, glad you saw fit to come."

Goodnight's voice boomed out over the quiet tones of the other men, and several turned from staring at Mattie to stare at Jesse. He was respected and occasionally feared, but he knew respect and fear had little to do with why the other cowmen were gawking with open interest at him. It was because of Mattie. Jesse McDade, after all, was her man, if not in the biblical sense, then in every other way that counted.

"Charlie," Jesse replied, dismounting and handing his reins to a waiting cowboy to lead to the livery stable. "I'm not brave enough to refuse a summons from you."

Goodnight nodded without smiling. The stock grower seldom smiled. "Don't have to be brave, just smart enough to know we're gonna have to look out for ourselves. There's thieving going on in this country. That ain't even counting the fact we stockmen have to do something to stop those southern herds bringing Texas fever into the Panhandle."

"Mattie and I agree with you," said Jesse, looking over Goodnight's shoulder in time to see a tall cowboy lifting Mattie off her horse. "Excuse me, Charlie." He brushed past Goodnight's massive shoulder, his eyes intent on the stranger.

Pushing his way through the crowd, Jesse stopped at Mattie's side, his shoulder barely touching hers, and recognized the stranger. Jealousy churned his belly. "Miller! What are you doing here?"

Tom Miller, clean-shaven except for a thick mustache and with a fresh haircut, boots polished, and clothes brushed free of range dust, nodded at Jesse. "I rode in with the LX folks to attend Goodnight's meeting. I run a few cows, so I reckoned I ought to come, too. I was just telling Mrs. Hunter how I hoped to file

A TIME TOO LATE
on some land, start a small outfit before you bigger boys grab everything."

"I told Mr. Miller that there might be a few sections to the north of us that are still free grass," said Mattie, tilting her head with its ridiculous little hat to look up at the other cowboy.

Jesse felt a fist clench inside his chest as the gesture bared Mattie's throat for Tom Miller's perusal. "I think Mr. Miller might be happier with land down around the Yellow Houses. I hear there's good grass there." Jesse didn't care if there was or not. The Yellow Houses area was at least one hundred twenty miles from Mattie Hunter.

Miller shook his head, his eyes meeting Jesse's. "Not enough water down there to my notion. I had in mind a little piece of land along the Canadian just to the east of Hunter Ranch."

Jesse's felt his nostrils flare just as they had when he was an Indian fighter and scented Comanches. "Mattie, best go say hello to Goodnight. The old reprobate looks down in the mouth about you ignoring him."

Mattie turned and smiled at Goodnight. The crowd parted to let her through, and Jesse watched the gentle sway of her hips in the riding habit. Damn if he knew what trunk she salvaged it from, but he was glad she hadn't cut it up for quilting squares. Of course, she looked as out of place in this dusty, windswept town with its raw, ugly buildings as a rose in a dung heap, but she was beautiful nonetheless. He wondered if every other man was as hard-pressed to control his lustful thoughts as he was.

"Mrs. Hunter looks mighty fetching in that outfit," remarked Miller.

Jesse whirled around, Miller's words flicking the raw places inside himself. "Shut up, Miller! I don't permit any loose talk about Mattie."

Tom replaced his hat. "Nothing loose about what I said. I told her myself that she looked fetching." His eyes bored into Jesse's. "Did you tell such like?"

Jesse swallowed and looked away. He hadn't. Hadn't because he didn't trust himself anymore. He couldn't be casual with Mattie. If once he complimented her, and those golden eyes grew soft as velvet, he would go on and on, whispering things best left unsaid, touching her in places best left untouched—and she would not turn him away. He knew that as surely as he knew the wind would blow tomorrow. The bond between them was growing strong, tighter, drawing them closer together, until one day neither would be able to tell where one left off and the other began. All that saved her was his silence and his honor—and he had little enough of that. If he were a decent man, he would quit, leave Hunter Ranch for good, leave Mattie in peace.

He felt sweat trickle down his back in spite of the chill March wind. But he couldn't—not if it meant leaving her to the likes of Tom Miller. His lips stretched in a grimace. Ordinarily he would have liked Tom Miller. He was an honest man, a good man who stood up for Mattie against his own outfit's guns. But he was also the first man Jesse had met besides himself who saw Mattie for what she was: a passionate woman who was any man's equal, yet possessing a softness that was purely feminine. The recognition was in Miller's eyes. Jesse had seen it the day Miller rescued Mattie from Jameson's camp.

Jesse didn't trust Tom Miller any more than he trusted himself.

"I think you better not count on claiming any land close to Hunter Ranch," said Jesse.

Tom turned to watch Mattie talking to Goodnight. "I would be a safe neighbor."

Jesse also turned to watch Mattie. "I don't know that."

Tom rocked back on his boots, his thumbs hooked in the waistband of his Levi's, a casual man, a man as placid as a mill pond—and just as deep. "I broke wild mustangs for a while before I took up herding cattle for a living. I'd rope the mares, gentle them to the saddle till they were tame as dogs, brand them for their new owners. But sometimes a young mare recognizes only one master no matter what brand she wears. One day the mustang stallion will come calling and she'll leave no matter if she has to tear down the corral to do it and hurt herself in the bargain. It doesn't do any good to own a mare like that because she'll always turn back if she can."

"We're not talking about mares."

Tom smiled. "I reckon we aren't talking about land either, are we?"

Jesse didn't return the smile. "You remember what I said." He walked toward Mattie, but felt the other man's eyes on him all the way.

He grasped Mattie's elbow. "Let's go inside out of the wind. I reckon Charlie's ready to start the meeting anyhow."

Goodnight nodded and turned his ponderous head to glance about at the men remaining in front of the hotel. "I guess everybody's here who's coming."

"Not Samuel," said Mattie in that clear, cold voice Jesse noticed she always used when speaking of her husband. "He and Clint Murray rode with Jesse and me, but they dawdled along the way."

Goodnight's piercing eyes turned in her direction. "Then he'll represent the Bar H?"

Jesse watched her draw a deep breath. "No, Jesse and I will."

Goodnight squeezed her shoulder in the first warm gesture Jesse had ever seen him make. The old man wasn't known for expressing approval in any manner. Later, seated beside Mattie in the drafty hotel, its air cloudy with tobacco smoke and gritty dust blown in between cracks in the plank walls, Jesse wondered if Goodnight meant his gesture to be one of approval as much as one of encouragement. God knew, Mattie was in need of encouragement. She was the only woman in a roomful of men, and was pointedly ignored by her husband, who sat on the opposite side of the room next to Clint Murray. Jesse longed to hold her hand, or slip his arm around her shoulders, or kiss the quivering lower lip that gave away her vulnerability. Instead he sat beside her, his hands resting on his thighs, fingers digging into his own flesh to keep from touching hers.

Mattie felt ten years old again, sitting with her father as he met with other bankers, merchants, railroad men, stockmen, and miners to map out the future of Pueblo. She had been admired, patted, complimented, given candy and toys, and generally made over by all—who then politely ignored her presence. All his business associates had sympathized with the Colonel's recent loss of his wife, but thought his habit of allowing his motherless daughter to sit by his desk playing with dolls during business hours was decidedly odd. It distracted a man, having a young girl in the room, one railroad entrepreneur told the Colonel. Kept him concentrating on watching his language and his drinking instead of his business.

Looking back, Mattie thought that might have been her father's intention rather than his loudly avowed need to always be available if she suddenly missed her mother and needed comforting. Certainly he had never hesitated to send her away if her presence was inconvenient to him. And he had made some of his most astute—and financially beneficial—business arrangements during the year between her mother's death and

A TIME TOO LATE
353

her own eleventh birthday, when she had asked a visiting banker if buying up property along a proposed railroad route without informing the sellers about the proposed railroad was a nice thing to do. Her father had promptly ejected her from the meeting.

She felt as invisible now as she had then: present, but nonexistent. Except to Samuel, who she noticed glaring at her when he was not whispering to Clint Murray. She frowned. Samuel acted too submissive toward Murray, fawning over him as one might expect a suitor to do. Over the past year—since Mattie had forbidden Murray from staying at the plaza—he and Samuel had become a twosome she felt was unhealthy in some obscure way she didn't understand. More and more she sensed that Murray posed a threat to her, but in what manner she was unable to say. She and Jesse controlled the ranch and its profits, made the decisions with little interference from Samuel, and rendered a yearly accounting to her father. Still, she sensed that Murray was a spider spinning its web and waiting with unnatural patience for her and Jesse to stumble into it.

She shuddered.

Spiders were carnivorous.

Jesse caught her involuntary movement and reached for her, his hand hovering just above hers for an endless time before he clenched his fist and drew back. "Are you cold?" he whispered, his eyes silvery as though a fire burned behind them.

On the contrary, she felt inexplicably flushed from the roots of her hair to her toes. And restless—such restlessness as she had never before experienced—as though she was a child again waiting for Christmas morning and a wondrous present. More and more often she felt restless around Jesse, caught herself reaching to touch him, experiencing shameful changes in her body in his presence.

She crossed her arms over her breasts. "I'm quite

comfortable, thank you." An invisible woman, she settled back to listen to Charlie Goodnight address the meeting.

The tall cowman faced the gathering. If anyone doubted Charles Goodnight intended to bring order to a disordered land, his words quickly dispelled that notion. "In spite of the efforts of such men as Jesse McDade in looking out for the best interests of the Bar H and his own place, and the work of Cap Arrington of the Texas Rangers, the toughs control this country. There's mighty near as many men swinging a wide loop as there are honest men. We've all been hard hit by losses. Our cattle drift before the snows and worthless thieves gather them up on the south plains and drive them into New Mexico Territory before our own men catch sight of their hooves and horns. There's more of our cows sold under altered brands around White Oaks, New Mexico, than a man can shake a stick at. Conditions are such that it's time for the better class of people, ranchers and settlers, to get together to have a better organization and understanding. Every man eighteen or older who has one cow or ten can join, and the association can hire inspectors to watch the railhead for rustled cattle. Any man guilty of illegally branding or handling stock shall be brought before the law—now that we got a court here at Mobeetie in Wheeler County and an honest man in Judge Dubbs. Can't say much for the rest of the county officials."

Mattie smiled. She had heard rumors that all Wheeler County officials except Judge Dubbs had been living with prostitutes at the time of their election. Whether the rumor was true, she couldn't say, but Goodnight, who already despised Mobeetie as a foul nest of thieves and gamblers, obviously believed it.

"The first thing we best do is track down who's responsible for stealing our cows and selling them in

A TIME TOO LATE
355

New Mexico," continued Goodnight. "We best hire a man and send him over."

W. C. Moore, manager of the LX, stood up. "I think we all know who's guilty in New Mexico, and that's Billy Bonney. I say let's call on Judge Lynch to take care of him. A taste of hemp will settle up these rustlers better than the courts."

Mattie rose and faced Goodnight. "We can't be certain Mr. Bonney is guilty of rustling our cattle. I dislike Mr. Moore's remark."

Goodnight looked uncomfortable, either because she had spoken up in the meeting or because she defended Billy the Kid. Mattie didn't care one way or the other. "Now, Mattie, when Bonney left Tascosa, he rounded up a considerable number of cows that didn't belong to him. And I've heard tell he's selling Panhandle beef to the army through a middleman in White Oaks. This association ain't about to tolerate that."

"But do you have proof?"

"We'll get it, Mattie, don't you worry about that. I'm not about to have any lynch law," said Goodnight. "We'll levy a fee against the stock each member owned and hire us a responsible man."

"Maybe Mrs. Hunter could tell us something about Bonney," suggested Moore. "I don't recall hearing that any Bar H cows have been run into New Mexico. Nor any of Mr. McDade's either. I heard about your arrangement with Mr. Bonney. Maybe it went further than you want to admit, Mrs. Hunter. You and McDade got sizable herds for folks that started out the same time as Mr. Beals and Mr. Bates of the LX. Maybe Billy Bonney is selling cows other places besides White Oaks."

Mattie heard Jesse make a strangled sound as he leaped from his chair to face Moore. "You son of a bitch!"

She seized Jesse's arm before he could draw his gun. "If you are calling me a thief, Mr. Moore, perhaps you would care to explain why you're called Outlaw Bill Moore. Perhaps you'd care to explain how you've stocked your ranch up by Coldwater Springs. Perhaps you'd like to explain your habit of marking calves but not branding them during the cooperative roundup, knowing full well that honest men look at the marked ears and assume those calves are also branded."

Bill Moore's eyes, as gray as Jesse's but lacking that man's forthrightness, grew cold. "It's a custom for a cowboy to claim a few mavericks."

"You've claimed more than a few, and everyone knows it, even if Mr. Beals and Mr. Bates don't," said Mattie. She whirled around to face Goodnight. "Perhaps we'd best clean our own houses before we talk of cleaning someone else's."

Goodnight's eyes were as cold and piercing as a chill wind off a snowbank, thought Mattie as the cowman looked at Moore, but spoke to her. "Our rules will be enforced no matter whose neck we drop the loop around, Mattie. But we will investigate Billy Bonney. We've lost too many cows."

Mattie straightened her shoulders. "Then the Bar H will pay no levy to send someone after him. He's treated me fair, and I shall not be a part of tracking him down."

"Mattie, he's a thief," said Jesse in a low voice.

"My wife is distraught," announced Samuel, sounding for once as if he was sober. "A compliment from a man like Bonney who is reputed to charm women has turned her head. I apologize for her taking up this august body's time with her hysterical accusations and pronouncements. Mr. Moore, I trust you will overlook her comments."

Moore nodded his head, but Mattie doubted he had forgiven her. She didn't care. He was as much a thief as Billy—more so because he stole from his employers. No one had claimed Billy was anything but loyal to the men who hired him.

"Sit down, Mattie," continued Samuel. "You are creating a scene. The Bar H has no intention of refusing to fund a hunt for Bill Bonney."

"Samuel!" cried Mattie. "You can't do that! He hasn't harmed us."

"Perhaps I should escort you upstairs to one of Mr. Huselby's hotel rooms until you regain your composure," said Samuel, straightening his coat and starting toward her.

"Damn poor behavior on the part of that Hunter woman," Mattie heard a cowman behind her whisper to another man. "Mind you, my wife gives me what for at the drop of a hat, but she don't do it in public. Even if Mattie Hunter is right about Bill Moore, it's not her place to say so."

Mattie's faced burned and she bit down hard on her lip before speaking. "I will *not* be escorted anywhere, Samuel. I will speak my piece the same as any other rancher."

"You're a woman!" exclaimed Samuel. "Not a rancher! You don't have any right to express an opinion about this business."

"My wife owns a brand of her own," said Goodnight. "I hope you're not suggesting Mrs. Goodnight hasn't any right to an opinion. I doubt she'd agree with you."

Samuel bowed. "Your gracious wife has the decency not to appear at this meeting. In fact, I doubt that a woman has a legal right to attend."

"We haven't formally organized," said Goodnight. "We don't have our constitution and bylaws. I figure we could do that at a later meeting if enough decent people are interested in continuing."

"I did understand from your remarks that any *man*

eighteen or older can join this association," said Samuel. "My wife, in spite of her pretensions otherwise, is not a man. Therefore I suggest in the interests of a productive meeting that I remove her from the premises."

"Hunter, only a low-down bastard would talk about a woman that way," said Jesse. "Make any more such comments, and I'll remove you from the premises."

"Excuse me, Mr. Goodnight," said a low, pleasant voice from the back of the room. "Might I suggest that we accept Mrs. Hunter as an honorary member in view of her actions to prevent southern cattle from crossing her range and infecting our herds with Texas fever. In doing so, she also protected the grass of several ranchers to the north and east of her, ranchers sitting right in this room."

Mattie saw several of her neighboring ranchers nodding their heads in sheepish agreement. She smiled at Tom Miller, then turned to face Goodnight. "I appreciate Mr. Miller's words. It seems he is making a habit of being kind to me, but I am afraid that I have no desire to be accepted by this association if it means returning evil for good. I cannot support hunting down Billy the Kid."

Jesse cleared his throat. "I stand by Mrs. Hunter. I won't have a hand in a manhunt for Bonney. I speak as owner of the Flying MJ and as sole manager of the Bar H. All other reforms and proposals we will support, but not this one."

Goodnight looked at the two of them from under his heavy brows. "Are you setting yourself against the other ranchers? Some folks might see that as a renegade act."

"I cannot dictate what others think or see or believe," said Mattie, hearing her voice shake and despising herself for it. "If you gentlemen will excuse me." She swept from the room, stopping only in front of the cowman who had remarked on her poor behavior. "Please give my regards to your wife."

She stepped outside the hotel into the cold wind and leaned against the building, where she was joined by Jesse. "Why did you back me up?"

He pulled his sack of Bull Durham tobacco out of his pocket and rolled a cigarette. "Because I wasn't about to shame you in front of people. You're both right and wrong, Mattie. Billy Bonney has kept his word to you, and I am included in the deal. Had I been at supper that night, I would have refused his offer, but I wasn't. You accepted on my behalf, and I'll always support you. You ought to know that by now. But Bonney is a murderer and a thief and he's stealing from our neighbors. Maybe not as much as they claim, but enough. To those men in there, maybe even to Goodnight, we've lined up on a murderer's side against them. And that's wrong any way you look at it. On the other hand, those same men know that Mattie Hunter and Jesse McDade keep their word, and whether they acted like it or not, they approve. But it's an eye for an eye. They'll remember we went against them and they'll remember why. I don't know which will weigh more heavily with them, but I do know they'll call for a reckoning one day."

"When we've used up all the sin we've earned," said Mattie. Jesse gave her a startled look, and she leaned her head back and smiled. "It was something Billy Bonney said when I asked if he would ever change."

In January of 1881, the Panhandle Stock Association was formally organized during a three-day meeting in Mobeetie's brand-new courthouse. A constitution and bylaws were adopted and officers elected. Membership was open to any man eighteen or older who owned or controlled stock. Articles XII and XIII allowed for an honorary membership of a nonstock owner on recommendation of any member. Mattie was so recommended by Jesse McDade, Tom Miller, and Charles Goodnight and was elected. Samuel Hunter and his representative Clint Murray cast the two dissenting votes. Mattie laughed when Jesse returned from Mobeetie with news of her election. The Association had taken her at her word. She was not required to pay dues, so she did not contribute to the further cost of hunting down Billy Bonney when he escaped from the Lincoln County, New Mexico, courthouse on April 28, 1881.

On the other hand, Mattie had no vote on Association business.

On July 14, 1881, Billy the Kid used up all his sin. Pat Garrett, assisted by Panhandle Stock Association detective John W. Poe, tracked Billy to Fort Sumner, New Mexico, and shot him to death in Pete Maxwell's darkened bedroom.

He was twenty-one years old.

And so was Mattie Jo Hunter.

CHAPTER 24

With Billy the Kid dead, the Stock Association focused its attention on the quarantine of Texas cattle as losses continued to mount. O. H. Nelson and T. S. Bugbee, who had bought the Shoe Bars, posted losses of two hundred thousand dollars, while Mrs. Goodnight lost nine hundred seventy-five out of a thousand head. The Matadors lost five hundred head a few days after passage of a herd of South Texas cattle across their range. Everywhere in the Panhandle, the smell of dead cattle blew on the wind. The Winchester quarantine begun by Mattie and Jesse became the official, if extra-legal, policy of the Association as six heavily armed members patrolled the southern edge of the Panhandle to turn back herds. The Bar H contributed one man to the joint effort and Jesse continued to assign his own men to guard Mattie's and his range independent of the Association. They lost no cattle to Texas fever the disastrous summer of 1881.

But it was not Texas fever that preoccupied Mattie that summer, it was the death of Billy the Kid. As she sat alone in Jesse's bedroom office in late July, idly turning the pages of the ranch's ledger book, she grappled with reasons as to why his death should so affect her. She had known him less than four hours, yet had formed such an attachment that two years later she had defied Charles Goodnight and the Stock Association on his behalf. When Jesse had told her Billy was dead, she had wrung him dry of details until she could almost feel the startled young man's confusion as he stumbled into Pete Maxwell's dark bedroom calling out *"Quien es?"* She could feel the oppressive heat of the July night, smell the warm earth of the adobe house and the slow flowing river that ran nearby, see the indistinct figure of Pat Garrett standing by Maxwell's bed, hear Billy's last moan as Garrett's bullet drilled his heart.

Why?

I'd be obliged if you would remember William Bonney played fair and respected women. In case anyone ever asks.

She nodded as Billy's last words to her echoed in the room, and the light-haired specter with the bucktoothed grin smiled one last time and disappeared into one of those rooms in her mind and closed the door behind him. He was forevermore a part of her life, perhaps more hers than the dark-haired señorita who mourned at his grave, because he gave Mattie Hunter not his body, but his epitaph.

Besides Jesse, he was the first man who admired her worth.

A woman would always forgive such a man his sins.

Mattie lifted her head to gaze out the window at the distant Canadian, a rusty-colored ribbon of sand-choked water, and at the breaks that marched in rugged, grass-tufted gullies and hills toward the flat Llano Estacado to the south. The heat, already oppressive at barely eight o'clock in the morning, embraced her like a sweaty lover, and the dry earth smell of the adobe plaza clung to her nostrils.

Pushing back Jesse's chair, she stood up. Her heart beat in irregular strokes and she pressed her hands against her breast to calm it. She would not die, as Billy did, with the smell of dry earth and river water in her nostrils—alone.

Nor would she live any longer that way.

She had earned better.

She walked into her bedroom and stripped down to a pair of her abbreviated pantalets; a corset cover, which she had discovered did nicely as an abbreviated chemise; and a pair of thick cotton stockings. She pulled on a blue three-button shirt styled like a man's but with red piping down the front placket and around the collar and cuffs. The suspenders that held up the Levi's she had ordered from Mobeetie in a boy's size were embroidered with plum blossoms done in silk thread. Mattie deemed trousers more practical on the range, particularly when she rode a stock saddle, but she saw no reason to deny her femininity. She had no desire to be a man—only to be his equal.

After pulling on her boots, which were made by a boot maker in Dodge City to replace Samuel's old pair, she braided her hair, pinned it on top of her head, then tied on a high-crowned Stetson with a long, narrow scarf of thin muslin. After facing off Jameson, she had decided that a sunbonnet's shovel brim restricted her vision during certain times when she least needed it restricted. This might very well be one of those times.

She walked into the kitchen, head held high and prepared for battle.

Jubilee set his coffee on the table, his brow furrowing up and his lower lip pushing out in disapproval. "What you fixing to do in them britches? Iffen you think you're going out to ride guard, you just put it right out of your mind. You done been shot once, and I ain't 'bout to allow you to tempt the Good Lord again."

Mattie walked to the gun rack that she had asked Hank to build after she caught Leon with one of the cowboys' rifles and removed Jubilee's Winchester. "I'm not riding guard. The men have that well in hand."

"Then what you fixing to do?"

"I'm going to find a home place, Jubilee. Will you fix me a sack of provisions, please, enough for at least three days? I doubt I'll be gone that long, but I do not desire to have to depend on my hunting ability for food."

Jubilee folded his arms. "You gonna do no such of a thing."

Mattie bounced a box of shells for the Winchester in her hand as she looked at him. "Be sure to include a canteen of water, Jubilee. And I'll take your bedroll. I don't want to use my good quilts on the prairie."

The ex-slave's face took on a stubborn expression. "You ain't taking my bedroll 'cause you ain't going."

"I'm a grown woman, Jubilee. I wasn't asking permission."

"There's lobos out there, Miss Mattie, and cow thieves."

"According to the Stock Association, the king of the rustlers is dead." She heard the bitterness in her own voice and wished she had not revealed so much.

Jubilee sucked in a breath and grew still as he studied her face. "I been waiting for this ever since Jesse come home and told you about Billy the Kid getting hisself killed. You been real quiet with your moping, like you allus are when you're studying on doing something foolish. I rues the day that young no-account tough rode in here and you stood up to him. I wish he'd slapped you down like he done to Hunter 'cause you been acting reckless ever since. Telling off trail bosses like that Jameson, fighting with the Stock Association, standing with Jesse against your own husband—"

"Did you expect me to allow Samuel to fire Jesse?" she interrupted.

"He couldn't fire Jesse, and Jesse knowed it. All you did was draw attention to yourself. I ain't saying you done wrong, but Lordy, Miss Mattie, you ain't doing right in the eyes of other folks neither. There's two kinds of right. There's what you *know* is right, and what other folks *see* as right, and they ain't always the same thing at the same time. I knowed slavery was wrong, but white folks didn't see it that way for a long time. Lots of them still don't see it thataway now, so I'm real careful about standing up for myself. I does it, and you should, too, but I don't wave a red rag in a bull's face whiles I'm at it, and you best not do it either. The world don't change very fast, Miss Mattie, and you acting like a man ain't gonna change it any faster."

"I do what I have to do and I'll accept the consequences, Jubilee," she replied. "And I have. I've been shot just as if I was a man."

"And you'd be dead same as any man iffen you hadn't gotten the drop on them 'cause you was a woman and that trail boss didn't believe you'd shoot."

"Then he was a damn fool!" snapped Mattie.

"That's no kind of language for a lady, Miss Mattie."

Mattie sat down at the table and began to load the Winchester. "You forget, Jubilee. I'm not a lady anymore. I'm that Hunter woman. I want to build a house of my own, not live in one that somebody else's dream built. This is Mendoza's house, and will always be no matter how long I live here. Billy died in another man's home. I refuse to do the same. I'll build a new headquarters for Hunter Ranch, with a main house that doesn't smell of mud bricks."

Jubilee got up. "You done lost your senses, Miss Mattie. It ain't safe and it ain't proper to be riding off 'cross that prairie all by yourself."

She rose and picked up the Winchester. She felt such a need to be herself that she actually thought she might shoot Jubilee if he insisted for another instant in seeing her as anyone but Mattie Jo Hunter, a woman in no man's image. "When I die, do you know what I want for my epitaph? 'She did what she had to do and she respected herself.' I have to do this, and what others think is proper has nothing to do with whether I respect myself. Now, will you fix my provisions, or shall I?"

"So I packs her up some coffee and a coffeepot, a skillet, tin plate and silverware, jerky, a loaf of bread wrapped in a dish towel, beans and bacon and dried apples. I even tied my own bedroll to the back of her saddle, Jesse, and all the time she was looking at me with them eyes like Eve's—like she knowed something men don't—and talking about what she wants on her tombstone and how she don't want to die in somebody else's house like that Billy the Kid. It gave me a turn, hearing her talk like that. I wished you'd swallowed your tongue afore you told her about how that worthless murderer was shot."

Jesse wished he had, too. Most of all, he wished Billy Bonney had not possessed a single streak of decency, and that the miserable little bastard had never met Mattie. But it was futile to wish. Billy Bonney was another emotional investment of Mattie's, but Jesse didn't believe for a minute that his death had sent her rushing off by herself on some harebrained search for a home place, even though that was the reason she gave Jubilee. Mattie knew the ranch nearly as well as he. She had ridden over it, checking the herds with him, discussing how many head to drive to Dodge in the spring and fall, watching the roping and branding, although never roping a calf herself. She knew exactly where she was going—and so did he: a large flat plain protected from the north wind by a small mesa. A creek cut under a bluff a few hundred yards to the south, and a tiny spring-fed pond shaded by cottonwoods drained into it. But neither the creek nor the pond was the main attraction for Mattie. It was a huge cottonwood tree, the largest Jesse had ever seen, that stood midway between the creek and the mesa. She had dismounted and leaned against its trunk and listened with closed eyes to the wind's music in its leaves while he had watched entranced by her expression.

Jesse shifted his weight in his saddle. It was less than a day's easy ride from the plaza. She would be there before dark, sitting under that cottonwood tree and waiting. She had to know that he would come after her, that he would not entrust her to another man. The question was: Did she know for what she waited? Did she journey to seek a home place, or to discover what he already knew? That home was only to be found in the company of one another, and such a home could never be purchased by either. They only had squatter's rights to each other's lives and as long as Samuel Hunter lived, that is all they would have.

He gathered his reins and looked toward the west. Once he could have gone alone after her and brought her back untouched, but that time had passed when he knelt in the river with her. Once he could have gathered several men and gone after her, secure in the knowledge that their company would hold him to his honor. That time had passed, too. He was nearing the end of the path upon which he had first ventured when he met Mattie in her father's office four years ago. Now neither decency nor honor nor society's censure held any meaning for him. He was riding to claim Mattie, and only her innocence would save her.

"I'll bring her back, Jubilee. You keep an eye on Leon. Since he learned to ride by himself, and Danny let him help with the horses, he's been an independent cuss."

"Lordy, Jesse, what's gonna happen to him if Miss Mattie dies out on that prairie by herself?" asked Jubilee, wringing his hands.

"She's not dead, Jubilee. Don't you think I'd know it if she were?"

Jubilee turned his eyes away from Leon's distant figure, and Jesse found himself caught by the ex-slave's direct look—the one that had always seen too much. "I reckon I knows that. You planning to take anybody with you to search for Miss Mattie?"

"No," said Jesse, not evading the other man's eyes.

Jubilee sighed and looked away. "I reckon I knew that, too. I seen this coming, you and Miss Mattie, and I figured a long time 'bout what to do."

"And what did you decide?"

Jubilee was silent, a lone black figure under the enormous, sun-bleached blue sky. The cattle dotted the brown grama-grass prairie, occasionally swishing their tails to swat away the flies, occasionally lifting their heads to stare at the two men who so earnestly stared at them. This herd was different from most of the others on Mattie's ranch. Their bodies were more stocky than rangy, their hides mostly red with white faces, their horns shorter than one generally saw in Texas. They were the crossbreed—Hereford and longhorn—symbol of a changing land as much as the barbed wire that now enclosed many of Mattie's pastures.

Jubilee spread his arms to encompass all that he

saw. "You done this, you and Miss Mattie together, and I can't undo it iffen I tried. I can't undo what's between you neither." He turned to look at Jesse again. "Sometimes what's right is wrong at the same time. You go on after Miss Mattie. I ain't gonna stop you 'cause this old nigger can't judge whether the right or the wrong of it is stronger. But it's too late, Jesse. Ain't nothing gonna change that."

"God, but don't you think I know that?" asked Jesse.

"Figured you did. Figure Miss Mattie does, too, so git along with you."

Jesse hesitated. "I guess it wouldn't be seemly to say thank you."

Jubilee twisted around in his saddle to look at him. "I ain't giving you my blessings, if that's what you think."

Jesse nodded, accepting the full weight of the old man's disapproval, and spurred his horse toward the west, toward Mattie.

He crossed her trail two hours later and followed it, easing his horse into a mile-eating lope. The sun preceded him in the west, sinking toward the horizon in a bloodred burst of light. The sky darkened to a deep indigo, saved from utter blackness by the full moon that rose to shed its pale, pale light and cast his shadow upon the grass, a dark silhouette racing before him. He met no one on the vast, flat prairie, and felt himself the only man in creation. He spurred his horse into a gallop, trusting luck to help the animal avoid the prairie-dog holes. He was riding toward the only woman created for him, and he was late.

He rode onto the little plain and saw the gleam of her beneath the cottonwood tree. She sat on Jubilee's blanket in her bare feet, drinking a cup of ice-cold springwater and waiting.

He jerked on his reins and leaped from his horse,

suddenly angry. "Damn you, Mattie! Where's your Winchester? Why did you sit there like you were safe back in the plaza with a dozen men to guard you?" He reached for her, dragged her up by her arms. "I could have been anybody! What in the hell were you thinking of?"

She blinked and rested her hands on his chest. "I wasn't thinking—I did all of that this afternoon."

His breath caught at the expression in her eyes. "What did you think about, Mattie? Building a house like you told Jubilee?"

She smiled. "I thought about that, too."

He felt his arms tremble, and his voice when he spoke was hoarse. "And what else did you think about?"

She stepped closer, and he let go of her arms to catch her around her waist. "I thought of all that Billy Bonney said—about our being a pair, and it being a shame to separate a pair. He didn't disapprove when he said it, Jesse, but acted as if it was natural."

Jesse's laugh sounded shaky to his own ears as he slid his hand around to Mattie's back, stroking her while she stood quietly accepting his first touch. "Mattie, an outlaw's approval—"

What else he might have said, he forgot as she pressed her fingers over his mouth. "Hush, now. He was an honest man—at least to me—and his death taught me how fleeting time is."

He kissed her fingers, then shuddered as she lifted her arms around his neck and leaned against him, her head tilted back to look at him. He swallowed. "Mattie, if you're standing here with me because you're afraid to die, and think grabbing at me will save you, that's a mighty poor reason for tempting me past what little self-control I've got left."

She smiled again, her eyes bright with self-knowledge. "I thought at first that my running away had something to do with being afraid to die. And it did—a little. I didn't lie to Jubilee about that. But I didn't tell him all the truth either. I ran away to be myself—Mattie Jo Hunter—not some woman that others made up and call by my name. And I waited for you to come."

He undid her suspenders and let them fall to the ground, then slowly pulled her shirt out of her pants and slipped his hands beneath it and the thin undergarment she wore. Her flesh was warm and satiny and firm. "Why now, Mattie?"

He heard her catch her breath as he pulled her shirt over her head and his fingers clumsily untied the ribbons of what he now recognized as a corset cover. But she wore no corset and his golden locket, warm from the touch of her skin, lay nestled between breasts gleaming luminous in the moonlight. His own breath caught at the sight of her beauty and the sound of her words.

"Because it was time, Jesse, time to meet like this. We've earned the right to sin."

He lowered his head to kiss first her lips, then her breasts, hearing her chaste gasp as that sensitive flesh first knew the feel of a man's mouth. He pressed her backward onto the blanket and, with shaking hands, stripped off the rest of her clothes, then his own. There would be no barriers between them tonight—neither cloth nor pretense. They had come too far together to hide from each other. He made no effort to conceal his arousal, and she made no effort to conceal her curiosity. Tomorrow would be soon enough to practice concealment—when the world and regret rushed in.

CHAPTER 25

Mattie suffered no regret in the months that followed, or none that Jesse could see. Each time his hunger overcame what little remained of his honor and he crossed the hall to her room, she welcomed him into her bed, holding nothing of herself back, granting him his every sensual wish. For the first time in his life he was free to enjoy his sexuality with a woman he had not paid, seduced, or persuaded, and found his hunger for Mattie went beyond simply plunging his rigid flesh into a warm, tight, submissive female. Each time he sank into her heated body, he wanted to touch her soul. Each time he explored her body with hands and mouth until he left no part of her untouched, he wanted to brand her with his tenderness.

He counted honor well lost for Mattie.

"Jesse?"

He propped himself up on his elbow in her bed and leaned over her, laying his hand on her breast and smiling when her own hand came up to press his

A TIME TOO LATE
373

tighter against the sensitive flesh. "What, Mattie?"

"Why wasn't I told? Are all women ignorant of this, or am I the only one?" She gripped his hand, her eyes glorious with fulfillment and the brilliance of an intelligence she no longer disguised. "This pleasure. Do all women feel it?"

Her question startled him, and he considered for a moment kissing her instead of answering. But this was Mattie. He never demeaned her by lying. "I've never lain with anyone like you before, only saloon girls and lonely widows and loose women. None of them ever came apart in my arms as you do."

"Why do you suppose that is?" she asked.

He lifted his hand and smoothed back a tendril of hair from her cheek. "They weren't whole women. Maybe they weren't because I never cared before, and they didn't expect me to. Maybe because their circumstances taught them to hold back in self-defense. I don't know. But you're a whole woman, Mattie—body and mind—because I think for a woman, pleasure starts in the mind."

She pressed her hand over his heart. "And a man? Where does his pleasure start?"

He closed his eyes for a moment while he faced a truth about his sex. He opened his eyes to look down at her. "It begins and ends in his body"—he lowered his head until his mouth hovered above hers—"until a woman makes him whole."

He kissed her, and felt as though he and Mattie existed in a place where time had stopped. But time never stops, and the world never stands still merely because two people wish it. Even as he moved over her and found his wholeness within her, he admitted the terrible knowledge that they were walking down a path that led to a reckoning.

Because nothing had changed.

She could never have him, and he could never claim

her, but they belonged together just the same. This was their time for however long it lasted. And it could not last. Jesse knew that even if Mattie denied it. Each day brought him closer to the end of his purpose on Hunter Ranch. Each day brought him closer to the end of his five-year contract with the Colonel.

Mattie felt the melancholy seize Jesse, and it frightened her. But the thought of learning its source frightened her more. Like a child holding her hands over her ears to avoid hearing what she did not want to hear, Mattie clutched him tighter, steadfastly ignoring her sense that time was speeding up.

She would not let it.

The rest of the summer and into the late fall, Mattie threw herself into building a home place under the giant cottonwood tree where she first lay with Jesse. Her house was a talisman against the future, and a symbol of the bond between her and Jesse. A bond that was now complete.

She hired stonemasons from Pueblo to lay the foundation of her new headquarters, and Mexicans from Tascosa to build a bunkhouse and storehouses of adobe. She had nothing against mud-brick houses; she just had no intention of living in one again. She would forever associate the smell of adobe with the death of Billy Bonney, but that didn't mean the cowboys did. They seemed not to mind at all, but the fact that Mattie did not coerce them into making mud bricks the way she coerced them into hammering nails in her new house might have something to do with their preference for adobe.

She ordered lumber from Dodge City, and soon wagons loaded with sweet-smelling oak and walnut rolled into Tascosa and from there to the building site. With clenched jaw she paid eighty-five dollars a thousand board feet and decided that not all the thievery in the Panhandle was committed by rustlers stealing cows. According to her estimates, the freighters had cost her the equivalent of a small herd and hadn't heated a branding iron to do it.

She sent word to Mobeetie, Tascosa, and Clarendon, the third of only three Panhandle towns, that she needed carpenters. She was surprised at the number who rode into the plaza. She wouldn't have thought there were that many carpenters in cattle country. Deciding that a man who could build a horn chair and a gun rack could build a house, she put Hank in charge, and although he muttered about quitting, he organized work crews, shanghaied any cowboy who couldn't get a saddle on his horse fast enough to disappear toward the herds, and put them to work roofing the three-story house, and kept down the fights between the carpenters from Mobeetie and Tascosa and those from Clarendon, called "Saints' Roost" by the cowboys. Clarendon, established by a colony of Methodists, allowed no alcohol, and its residents tended to be a bit more staid than those from the other two Panhandle towns. Hank complained that he "had to hide liquor from one bunch and watch his language with the other."

Mattie raised his salary twenty-five dollars a month for "aggravation."

The building continued throughout the fall and into the winter as the weather remained mild with grass along some stretches of the Canadian "greening" in February of 1882. It was not mild on the rest of the high plains, as Mattie knew. Cattle from Wyoming and Montana began their yearly drift south before the storms toward the Panhandle, and Jesse sent out men to herd them away from Hunter and McDade land. Other ranchers whose grass had been eaten clean by drifting cattle in the winter of '80–'81 found their ranges threatened again. What began as vague talk and piecemeal efforts in 1881 had become by late spring of

1882 a cooperative project by Canadian River ranchers: a two-hundred-mile barbed-wire fence to stretch across the Panhandle from east to west, a drift fence to keep northern cattle off the rich grazing.

Mattie wanted no part of it.

A buffalo hunters' camp, then a post town growing up around Fort Elliott, then a trading center for the eastern Panhandle supplying everything from "a dime ring to coffins and from drugs to hardware," Mobeetie had many reasons to exist and prosper.

Tascosa had but one: cattle.

Nestled in a grassy timbered area on the north side of the Canadian River next to the mouth of Tascosa Creek, with the rugged canyons and arroyos, mesas and knolls of the breaks to the east and west of it, the town lay one hundred thirty-five miles west of Mobeetie in physical distance and a world away in social amenities. In the spring of 1882 Tascosa had no bank, no newspaper, no school, no doctor, and no church. It manufactured no products for shipment to the outside world. Its courthouse was a four-room adobe house rented from Jack Ryan, saloon owner and provider of liquor, gaming, and less savory entertainments, and its jail was such that no decent man would lock up a hog in it. Its post office was in James McMasters's store, and mail came by hack from Mobeetie with what one resident pundit called "uninterrupted irregularity"—if the driver didn't lose his way, bog the hack in quicksand crossing the Canadian, or run his horse to death.

In spite of denials by its permanent citizens—and they perhaps numbered between two and three hundred, including the Mexicans who built their plazas there before it was a town—Tascosa's sole purpose was to supply the ranches that surrounded it. It was a cow town without being a trail town even though the only easy crossing for many miles up or down the Canadian lay within its boundaries. With the land all around it claimed and the Winchester quarantine in effect, no herds passed through Tascosa unless they belonged to one of the adjacent ranches.

But the cowboys did.

Mattie had heard that one cowboy had remarked that "if you've got any life left in you, head for Mobeetie or Tascosa." Mobeetie was lively, but Tascosa was more playful, and when the play turned deadly, Tascosa had its own Boot Hill.

Court was held twice a year, in the spring and fall, and the town was crowded with cowboys, nester ranchers, freighters unloading goods, and other hangers-on. Mattie knew that most had no business with the court, but came to town for the horse races and shooting contests that customarily took place during the court session. Many came to witness Temple Houston, the young, handsome, and flamboyant district attorney, who, it was said, could draw his pearl-handled revolvers faster than Billy Bonney ever thought about.

But it wasn't justice or horses or shooting contests that brought Mattie to Tascosa in late May. Neither was it her purchase of yard goods for curtains for the new house, now painted and polished and sparely furnished while she waited for her father to arrive from Pueblo with her own furniture.

It was cattle.

She had merely taken advantage of the carnival atmosphere of the court session to invite a few men to dinner.

Resplendent in a princesses dress of mandarin yellow silk over which she wore a sleeveless polonaise of ivory white India cashmere embroidered with green, yellow ocher, and Egyptian red arabesques around its border, Mattie knew she was an exotic creature. Add a white rice straw hat whose turned-up brim was wreathed with yellow roses, and a Mandarin-yellow parasol trimmed with a cluster of flowers, and she knew she deserved the slack-jawed, bug-eyed silence that greeted her when she stepped outside the Exchange Hotel on Tascosa's Main Street. The fact that the dress was five years out of date and had been packed away in a trunk most of that time, and that the cashmere had a yellow tint it did not originally possess was unimportant. Tascosa had never seen her like since its beginnings in 1876, and Mattie doubted it would again. She meant to create an impression of beauty, wealth, breeding, and respectability. Judging from the reactions of all who observed her—from Mrs. Russell who had helped her change clothes in one of the Exchange Hotel's bedrooms, to the small girl playing in the street whose grubby hands had shyly and just once touched the colorful embroidery on her polonaise, to the cowboys loitering in front of the saloon next who plucked off their hats and held them over their hearts as they caught sight of her—she had succeeded.

The Panhandle Stock Association was another matter.

Not that it was not an official meeting of the Association that she faced in the hotel's dining room—if two long tables in an adobe room could be considered a dining room—there being present only representatives of several Canadian River members: the LE, LIT, Turkey Track, the LS, the Bar CC, and Mattie's old enemy, the LX. But official or not, Mattie knew that whatever she and Jesse said would be known to all other association members almost before the two of them could saddle their horses for the ride home. Gossip in the Panhandle traveled faster than a prairie fire whipped by the wind, and she suspected that her dinner party would generate more talk than news that the state of Texas had traded three million acres of Panhandle land to a syndicate in exchange for a new capitol building.

"Mattie, your ranchers are stuffed with food and drink and about as amiable as you can expect them to be," said Jesse, touching her arm.

She turned around and took a deep breath. "You don't think they will listen to me, do you?"

He shook his head. "No, but they need to know where you stand."

She entered the mud-plastered adobe building and walked swiftly to the dining room. She stood at the end of the table and glanced at the assembled men. They rose from their chairs and looked back at her, respectful expressions in their eyes. They would look the same at a blind old woman, a shy young schoolteacher, a matron with six children, she realized. They didn't see Mattie Jo Hunter; they saw woman in the abstract.

"Gentlemen, please sit down, and thank you for accepting this invitation from Jesse McDade and myself to join us for dinner."

"The dinner was adequate, Mrs. Hunter, but I wouldn't have come all the way from Leavenworth for a meal," said W.M.D. Lee, partner in the LS, and a man reputed to be harder than a tenpenny nail and careful with a dollar. Also, a dangerous man to cross.

"And why did you come, Mr. Lee?" asked Mattie.

"Your reputation precedes you, Mrs. Hunter. If you wish to talk to the other ranchers about a matter of mutual concern, as your invitation stated, I concluded my concerns were at risk. Except in the matter of the quarantine, you have not been noted for your support of ranching interests."

"Perhaps our definition of ranching interests differs, Mr. Lee."

He nodded without smiling. "I wouldn't be a bit surprised, but what particular interest concerns you this time, Mrs. Hunter?"

"I wish to address the issue of the drift fence." She drew a deep breath and momentarily closed her eyes against the memories of frozen cattle stacked against the foot of a mesa because they could not drift farther. "I do not believe it is a good idea. Cattle stopped by this infernal fence will either freeze to death or graze the pastures north of it to the ground. Neither is desirable. One condemns dumb beasts to death, and the other destroys grazing and puts our neighboring ranchers in No Man's Land out of sorts. And the cost of building and maintaining such a fence is exorbitant. I believe two hundred and fifty dollars is the average cost per mile to build it, plus a line shack every eighteen miles, plus salaries for cowboys to ride fence and keep it in repair. I have better use for my cowboys."

"I believe you got yours building a house," said Hank Cresswell of the Bar CC, a twinkle in his eye.

Mattie smiled. She liked Cresswell. He was one of the early Panhandle ranchers who hadn't sold out to British syndicates as the LIT and the Turkey Track and several others had. "They hadn't much to do after fall roundup, Mr. Cresswell. I don't believe in idle hands on a ranch. They generally end up in Tascosa holding a deck of cards or a bottle of whiskey, and either will ruin a good cowboy."

She heard several of the ranchers chuckle, but saw more eyes growing impatient than amused, particularly Lee's. They might respect her as a woman and admire her competence as a rancher even though it made them uncomfortable, but they still held rigid expectations for womanly behavior, the principal one still being that a real lady didn't speak her mind at a business meeting. A silk dress didn't make a real lady out of Mattie Jo Hunter.

She hurried on. "I have already stated my objections, so it should come as no surprise to you gentlemen that I will not contribute to the building of the drift fence. The Bar H will not be part of your cooperative efforts."

A man stood up. "I represent the LIT, and I have a word to say."

The man wasn't Gus Johnson, manager of the LIT, so Mattie supposed he was a syndicate man sent to observe the meeting. "Certainly, sir," she said.

"Am I to understand, young lady, that you won't support the drift fence because you feel sorry for the cattle?"

Mattie flushed with anger. She despised being called a young lady, as though she was still a child who should be playing with dolls. "You misunderstand me, sir."

Jesse rested his hand on her shoulder, stilling any further angry words. "Mrs. Hunter's concerns are valid ones. This drift fence and others like it you have already built across your ranges will be death traps during a severe winter."

There was mocking laughter from the doorway. "We all know you'll back up any fool notion Mattie Hunter has."

Mattie watched Jesse's face turn pale and his eyes darken to pewter as he recognized the voice of the man taunting him. She looked toward the doorway where Clint Murray stood by Samuel.

"I don't recall your receiving an invitation to this dinner, Murray," said Jesse. "You aren't a rancher. You own nothing more than your horse and the bedroll you toss on Mattie Hunter's storeroom floor."

"Mr. Murray is here at the host's invitation," said Samuel, removing his hat and nodding to the other men. "I apologize for failing in my duties as a host, gentlemen. In fact, had I not already been in Tascosa on other business and recognized my wife's horse at the livery stable, I would not have known of this dinner."

"It seems the stable hands know more of what should be Mr. Hunter's business than Mr. Hunter does," added Clint Murray, disapproval heavy in his voice.

Mattie gasped at the lies told by the two men. She had informed Samuel of the planned dinner the same day she had sent notes to the other ranchers. "That's not true!" she exclaimed, looking around the room. Its male occupants looked both disapproving and embarrassed. It was obvious that they believed Samuel. And why not? thought Mattie. A proper husband would not deliberately lie about his wife's behavior. That Samuel might lie to humiliate her simply would not occur to the assembled men.

"Fortunately I arrived in time to hear my wife's remarks," continued Samuel. "I do not wish you gentlemen to assume her opinions are mine. I will be glad to support the drift fence. We cannot allow womanish sentiment to endanger our pastures."

Jesse's cold voice cut through Samuel's unctuous tones. "Mattie and I propose that we let the cattle drift and charge for our grass—one third of each brand that crosses our range."

"That sounds a lot like cow stealing, Jesse," said Cresswell, his eyes flickering between Jesse and Samuel. "We already levy a drift tax."

"Which is not often collected, and doesn't go to the individual ranchers in any event. My proposal will reimburse our loss of grass and also encourage the ranchers in the northern plains states to change the way they handle cattle, Hank," replied Jesse. "Instead of drift fences, we should be talking of how to manage our herds now that barbed wire is putting paid to open range."

"McDade doesn't have any pastures of his own to speak of north of the Canadian," said Murray. "And we have already heard Mr. Hunter deny that McDade speaks for him. It seems to me that listening to him is a waste of time."

Samuel held his hat against his breast, his blue eyes as earnest looking as Mattie had ever seen them. If she hadn't known better, she would have believed her husband sincere. "As I said before, I intend to help build the drift fence, so it appears all you gentlemen wasted valuable time in the mistaken belief you were attending a social function hosted by me when in fact it was nothing of the sort. I am deeply embarrassed at washing my domestic dirty linen in public, but I feel strongly that my fellow ranchers deserve an explanation even at the expense of my appearing foolish and unable to control my wife." He spread his hands in a gesture of helplessness. "Mr. Murray tells me that I am too lenient where my wife is concerned, and I fear he is right. For lack of a husband's firm guidance, Mattie is meddling in ranch affairs again with the connivance of McDade and in full support of his radical notions."

Mattie twisted away from Jesse's restraining hand and stalked toward Samuel. She saw lips move as several men whispered to one another, knew others were clearing their throats and shuffling their feet, but she heard nothing. She existed in a world without sound, a world without purpose except that of forcing Samuel to recant.

She stopped less than a foot from him. "I would ask you not to humiliate Jesse and me like this, Samuel. For God's sake, don't lie! Tell the truth!"

He tugged on his vest, his eyes sorrowful. "But I am, my dear, although I wish I was not. I am shamed that I have to reveal you and McDade as the charlatans you are. I am shamed that I must reveal McDade as a man who dances to your tune."

Without thought of propriety or of the careful facade she tried to maintain to conceal from outsiders the utter disgust she felt for Samuel, Mattie drew back her hand and slapped her husband with all the strength she had. Samuel rocked backward, and Clint Murray caught him before he fell. Murray's muddy green eyes gleamed with an expression of satisfaction he didn't bother to hide.

Mattie barely heard several exclamations of shock and disapproval as she realized that once more Murray had baited a trap with Samuel, and she had sprung it. No rancher, even Hank Cresswell, would listen to a woman who slapped her husband in public.

Feeling utterly weary, she turned to face the assembled ranchers. "If it is truth my husband wants, then it is truth he shall hear—and in public, since he involved you gentlemen in our personal business." She straightened her shoulders. "I wish to inform you that Mr. Hunter has no authority to spend any of the Bar H's funds. By his contract with my father, who holds title to the land, Jesse McDade has total control over all funds. There will be no contribution to the drift fence from Mr. Hunter unless he has private sources about which I know nothing—and I don't believe he does. I invited you to dinner so we might discuss this project. However, I find there is nothing to discuss. I will not support a drift fence. You gentlemen may adjourn to the Equity Bar for brandy and cigars because the dinner is over."

"Are you setting yourself against the membership, Mrs. Hunter?" asked the man representing the LIT.

"Not quite. The proper question would be—am I setting myself against the membership *again,* and the answer is yes. I didn't agree to hunting down Billy Bonney, and I don't agree to this, and you gentlemen be damned."

She gathered her parasol and reticule and walked from the dining room and the hotel, her head held high and her back straight. Her skirt brushed over the wooden floor with the sound of fallen leaves. Outside, she walked across the street to stand on the wooden

A TIME TOO LATE

sidewalk in front of James McMasters's store so she would not have to speak to any of the ranchers as they walked out of the hotel.

Fences.

There were fences all around her, and the strongest one was not of barbed wire. Dear God, not at all. The strongest fence was the world's notion of how she should act, and she had broken through it once more. But not unharmed. That was the way of the world's fences. One never escaped unharmed.

He saw her across the street in front of McMasters's store, twirling that ridiculous parasol and holding her head as proudly as if she were standing on her own veranda and had not just been publicly humiliated and defeated. Mattie had won the battle of the drift fence, but at the cost of any influence she might have had in the Stock Association. The other ranchers might not like Samuel—and Jesse knew most of them didn't—but they disliked even more a wife's siding with another man against her husband. They disliked that almost as much as they did the other man.

He crossed the street and stepped on the wooden sidewalk. "Mattie?"

She glanced up, her face solemn. "I forgot your advice, Jesse. You said never let an opponent goad me into losing my temper. Do you remember?"

He nodded. "When we bought the plaza from Mendoza."

"That was the real beginning, wasn't it, Jesse? That was the first time we stood together fighting for something we both wanted. You never expected me to stand in your shadow, and you never walked in mine. That's why I forgot myself when Samuel made that remark about you."

Jesse looked down at her, filled with the melancholy

he knew she feared so much as well as the anger of a man ridiculed unjustly. "Don't brood about it, Mattie. Samuel's never been my greatest admirer."

"But none of the other ranchers listened to you either, Jesse."

He nodded, bracing one arm against a wooden post that supported a tin roof that extended over the sidewalk, and staring across the street at Henry Kimball's blacksmith shop. "Some of them aren't admirers of mine either."

"Because of me," Mattie said. He saw her fingers tighten around the handle of her parasol until her nails lost their color. "I cost you in ways I hadn't considered before."

He gave her a sharp glance, but said nothing. He had never lied to her and would not do so now. He had always known that a man who stands behind a woman who speaks her mind in public might be misunderstood.

He saw her swallow as though to rid herself of unpleasant words before she continued. "Jesse McDade, whose courage and determination and foresight and strength and blood—never forget the blood—has built a ranch second to none, is ignored by the very men who should respect him the most.

"Because you are my man," she whispered.

"Mattie. . ." he began.

"Your judgment, your competence, your manhood have been attacked by a man who lacks all those traits, and no one came to your defense. Except me. And my action is hardly likely to win you anyone's regard, is it, Jesse? Quite the contrary. The ranchers might believe that you stand behind me not to support me, but to hide, that you might not be my shield as much as I am yours."

He was conscious of heads turning to watch her, of faces pressed against the windows of the mud-brick buildings, of men loitering in doorways. One could follow the trail of gossip about her dinner party just by counting the number of men who suddenly found the porch of McMasters's store more interesting than whiskey and cards. That Hunter woman was at it again.

He saw her cheeks burn as she laid her hand on his arm and whispered to him. "Please, Jesse, take me home and lie with me."

Surprise temporarily lifted the shadows he felt. "You've never asked me so forthrightly before—not even the first time."

She met his eyes. "We so often speak without words, Jesse. I come to you, or wait for you to come to me. But today I need to be forthright. Today I need the words."

He lowered his arm and straightened to face her. "Why today, Mattie? Why are you asking today? To pay me back for the ragging I took from Samuel? Are you offering me your body like you would offer candy to Leon when he's been hurt? Because you feel guilty? Guilt is not a good enough reason to lie with me."

He heard the bitterness in his questions and felt ashamed. Mattie had never traded her body to him for an imagined favor, and he cheapened her with his questions. If anyone should feel guilty, it was he. He should never have touched her and should turn away now. Samuel defeated her, but Jesse McDade gave him the weapon.

Mattie shook her head. "I'm asking you because I'm afraid you've finally counted the cost and decided that I'm not worth the loss of other men's regard. I'd rather know it now than to lie awake waiting for a man who never comes. And—" He heard her voice tremble. "And because I want to give you my heart in words. I've given it to you in a hundred different ways in your arms, but never with words until now. And I have to,

Jesse."

Jesse felt sick. "No, Mattie, don't do this. Don't humble yourself—not even to me."

She smiled. "Even on my best day as the ladylike Mattie, I was never very good at humility, Jesse."

"Then why, Mattie?" he demanded.

"Because a woman can give her body out of a sense of duty—as I did with Samuel," said Mattie slowly. "But she gives her heart of her own free will. Only then is she a whole woman."

Jesse drew a deep breath and lifted his hand to stroke her cheek with calloused fingers, then turned away to stare across the street again. Dear God, he should refuse her. They had lived too long in stolen time as it was, and she was more vulnerable than he.

But he couldn't—not yet. He had one more dream before he gave her up. Surely they had earned one more dream.

Jesse turned his head to look at her. "You strip me bare and flail me raw with your words until I'm near to breaking."

Her eyes closed briefly, and he saw her shoulders relax. "Then you're not turning me away?"

He laughed, a sound without humor. "I'm not strong enough, Mattie."

She nodded and silently he took her arm and escorted her back across the street to the Exchange Hotel, where Mattie could change back into riding clothes and back into that Hunter woman. The sandy soil upon which Tascosa was built seemed to shift beneath Jesse's feet as though the town itself was as impermanent as the time he had with Mattie, and the land waited to take back the adobe buildings and swallow up their inhabitants.

Suddenly filled with an urgency he could not explain, he hurried Mattie along, waiting outside the hotel with an impatience he could hardly conceal, and not until they rode east, leaving Tascosa to disappear into the sun's dying light, did his strange anxiety leave him.

Five miles before they reached Hunter land, Jesse turned north and rode across the flat prairie until it sank into a shallow depression of perhaps a hundred acres enclosed on three sides by the horseshoe loop of a small creek. A one-story house built of cedar logs faced south from near the top of the loop, surrounded by young cottonwood trees that had grown from switches stuck in the ground and watered. Two corrals, several storehouses, and a bunkhouse stood to the west of the main house.

His dream—the product of his own sweat and sleeplessness and hope—and he felt unsure and nervous as a young boy showing off for his best girl. "What do you think of it? Does it suit you?"

"It's a lovely headquarters, Jesse, but it looks almost deserted in the moonlight, as though it was waiting for someone to claim it."

Jesse dismounted and lifted Mattie off her horse. "Welcome to the Flying MJ," he said, pulling her into his arms, until not even the moonlight could find an inch between them through which to shine. "Lie with me here, in that log house, on my own land. It's fitting, Mattie, because every stolen hour I spent over the last five years building every rude structure you see, I shared with an image of you. You were with me on the riverbank when I chose only the straightest cedar and cottonwood for the house. You watched while I laid the wooden floor and sanded it until it was smooth as satin to the touch, and then polished it until it gleamed. I knew how much you hated earth floors and didn't want you to suffer one in a place I built."

He took off her hat, tossing it on the grass, and began removing pins from her hair until it tumbled over his hands and down her back. "Did you ever wonder about my brand, Mattie?"

He watched her swallow, her head tilted back to leave her throat as vulnerable to his mouth as were her trembling lips. "I always wondered why you reversed your initials."

He smiled and bent his head until his mouth nearly touched hers and her breath warmed his lips. "I didn't. The initials are ours. Even a whole man needs a hopeless dream."

CHAPTER 26

By the time the Colonel reached Tascosa, he was out of bourbon and out of patience. The last six weeks he had spent traveling across its empty spaces had done nothing to change his opinion of Texas as a land of heat, flies, dirt, freighters whose profane talk and thieving ways should earn them all a place in hell, and the most treacherous river he had ever crossed. Who would ever have thought that the Canadian's shallow water hid quicksand that would mire two wagons full of Mattie's household goods? And that was a supposed safe crossing.

And the towns—if one could dignify two such rude clusters of buildings as Mobeetie and Tascosa by calling them towns. Neither had a single brick street or a decent brothel. Such feminine companionship as they offered had been well used by freighters, cowboys, gamblers, and other disreputable sorts. The Colonel hoped he was a cut above such company and resigned himself to a celibate stay in Texas.

His only bit of luck was meeting a sober, reasonably presentable cowboy who agreed to guide him to the Bar H.

"So you're Mrs. Hunter's father," remarked Tom Miller, taking a sip from the only beer the Colonel had seen him drink in the hour they had spent in the Equity Bar, a disreputable drinking establishment of mud brick that boasted it was Tascosa's finest. The Colonel shuddered at what the lesser saloons might be like.

"You have heard of my daughter and her husband, Samuel?"

Tom Miller braced his elbow on the Equity's fine mahogany bar, one of the saloon's few amenities as far as the Colonel was concerned. "The Bar H is one of the biggest ranches in the Panhandle, although there's talk that Goodnight's spread might be a mite bigger. Hardly any way a man can keep from hearing about it even if your daughter didn't own it."

"So you can guide me to her new house?" asked the Colonel. "I understand there are no roads in this benighted land."

"Oh, there's roads. There's the Tascosa–City Trail and the trail from Tascosa to Mobeetie. That's a hard one to get lost on. There's a powerful number of empty whiskey bottles flashing in the sun between here and there. Man might be in danger of being blinded, but I don't think he'll lose his way. But there's no road to the Bar H, leastwise not what you're likely to think of as a road. More like a path full of wagon ruts from when Mrs. Hunter was freighting lumber out to her place."

Miller set his empty glass on the bar and wiped his mouth on his bandanna. "If you're ready, Colonel Corley, we can still make five miles before dark. I heard Mrs. Hunter's house was finished, and I reckon she might be wanting those twenty wagons of furniture."

The Colonel swallowed the last of what he judged to be an inferior brand of whiskey and followed Miller out of the bar onto Tascosa's sandy Main Street and its two-block business district. He shuddered with distaste. With its buildings of mud brick, the town looked as if the earth had vomited it up on the Canadian's sandy bank. The glass windows and occasional tin roof did nothing to improve its dun-colored appearance, and he would be glad to be out of it.

"I suspect you're right, Mr. Miller. Women need their gewgaws to keep themselves occupied."

Miller adjusted his hat so it shaded his eyes. "I reckon Mrs. Hunter has enough to do without worrying about gewgaws. Helping Jesse McDade run a spread the size of the Bar H keeps her pretty busy. I hear they got near eighty men working for them. That's a sizable operation."

The Colonel felt uneasy at the tone of certainty in the other man's voice. "Young man, you're surely misinformed. My daughter is a lady. Ladies do not involve themselves in business. That's what I hired that arrogant McDade for. If he needs any help, there's always my son-in-law."

"Colonel, I don't think you know your daughter any too well. And no offense, but I don't think you know Samuel Hunter at all."

The Colonel felt exactly like he used to feel on a moonless night during the war when familiar landmarks were merely darker silhouettes against the night. He was lost in a strange darkness in a land he knew well. "You are presumptuous, Mr. Miller. I raised my daughter practically alone after my wife's death. I know her very well. She's a spirited miss, but knows what's proper. She would no more give orders to rough men than she would show her ankles. It's unthinkable."

"Begging your pardon, Colonel, but what's proper

where you come from might not be smart in this country. It's not always possible for a woman to wait for a man to give the orders, and sometimes when men give the wrong orders, a smart woman goes against them instead of going along. She gave some of the other ranchers what for at dinnertime, and she and Jesse McDade rode out of here like the devil was on their tails. If you get a move on, maybe we can catch up with them."

The Colonel heard the wind suddenly rattle through the Equity's red-and-white-striped awning, then whirl away down the street in cloudy funnels of sand. It seemed an ominous sign to him. "Mattie rode off alone with Jesse McDade? In front of the whole town?"

"McDade will watch out for her," said Miller, turning left and walking down Main Street. "Let me get my horse from Mickey McCormick's stable, and we'll be ready to start if you can get those freighters out of the saloons, and if any of them are sober enough to drive a team."

The Colonel grabbed Miller's vest and whirled him around. "Just a minute, young man!" he began, before freezing into motionlessness at the feel of Miller's gun barrel against the middle button of his waistcoat.

Miller shook off the Colonel's hand and stepped back, dropping his gun back in his holster as he did so. "Don't ever grab a man from behind in Tascosa, Colonel. It's liable to get you a plot in Boot Hill with a good view of Main Street. If you look over your shoulder at that little knoll to the southeast, you can see it from here."

The Colonel tugged at his waistcoat, then gently patted the sweat from his forehead with a handkerchief, glad that he had confined his reaction to sweating. When Miller first gouged his chest with the barrel of that Colt, the Colonel had very much feared he might shame himself by losing control of his water. A sorry spectacle that would have made: Colonel Andrew J. Corley pissing his trousers.

"I'll remember that, young man." The Colonel despised himself for the tremor in his voice.

Miller stood panting. "Sorry I scared you."

The Colonel started to deny it, then saw the good-humored apology in the other man's eyes. He shrugged. "Any man who doesn't feel some discomfort finding himself at the wrong end of a gun is a fool, sir."

Miller took off his hat and wiped his forehead on his sleeve. "Scared myself, too, Colonel. I reckon that's the first time in near two years I've drawn a gun on a man. I felt you tugging at me, and I didn't have time to do any figuring. I just drew and turned. It's a habit a man gets into 'cause it might save his life. It's like I heard a cowboy tell a dude once: 'I may carry my gun a long time and not need it, but when I do need it, I need it bad.' I'm real sorry, Colonel. I'm not usually so quick. Now you were asking something about your daughter."

The Colonel tucked his handkerchief back in his waistcoat pocket. His heart was still beating too fast, but he was calmer, and oddly enough he wasn't angry at the laconic cowboy who he suddenly noticed was older than he looked. There had been a time in the goldfields of Colorado when he and Jubilee might have shot a man before they thought. But that had been years ago, and he was too old for this kind of confrontation. At his age, he fought his battles using his wits and his money.

He won most of the time.

"What did you mean about my daughter?" asked the Colonel.

"She gave the ranchers hell over the drift fence—"

"No! No! I am not concerned with some minor dispute over fencing. I want to know if my daughter rode off *alone* with Jesse McDade!"

Miller was silent, studying him until the Colonel felt like boxing the younger man's ears. "If you're worried about your daughter's good name, Colonel, there ain't a man in the Panhandle that would bother a woman who don't want to be bothered. It just ain't done. Besides, if somebody tried it with Mrs. Hunter, Jesse McDade would hang the man on the spot if your daughter didn't shoot him first. Mrs. Hunter is mighty handy with a Winchester."

"What!" exclaimed the Colonel, pulling out his handkerchief and wiping his face again. "Oh, I knew that reprobate McDade had taught her to shoot, but I'm certain you're exaggerating her proficiency. Shooting at an empty whiskey bottle setting on a fence post isn't the same thing as shooting at a man. Mattie is too soft to ever do that."

Miller's hazel eyes crinkled at the corners as he smiled. "Don't want to ever misread a woman, Colonel. I'm surprised a man your age don't know that. Best not judge your daughter too fast. She asks questions and thinks, then acts the best way she can, and it isn't always the way a man acts. Like that drift fence."

"Damn it all, man, you keep talking about a fence when I'm worried about my daughter's reputation. A married woman simply doesn't ride off with a man not her husband. Folks will call her loose."

Again the Colonel felt Miller's unblinking stare and thoughtful silence before the lanky cowboy rubbed his jaw and spoke in that slow drawl. "Let's amble toward the livery stable and get our horses. We caught folks' attention when I drew down on you, and I'd just as soon not stand here in the street and make the local people any more curious than they already are. I don't much want to talk to the sheriff either, if anybody happened to think to mention to him that I drew a gun. Not that I think anybody bothered. Best place to be in

Tascosa when the guns come out of holsters is behind a door until the shooting stops. Then it's time enough to worry about the fact a man's not supposed to be wearing his gun in town in the first place. There wasn't no shooting, so folks will go about their business if we let them." Miller slapped the Colonel's back. "So let's just walk on down the street real friendly like. Folks already got enough to talk about, what with Mrs. Hunter telling off the other ranchers, without her pa making a fuss, too."

The Colonel felt himself flush as he glanced up and down the sandy street. Every building, whether it was the Russell Hotel or Scotty Wilson's restaurant or the Equity Bar, seemed to have more people, mostly men, standing outside staring curiously at them than could possibly be inside their mud plastered walls.

The Colonel straightened his shoulders and walked purposefully by Miller's side. "Now, young man, I think it's best if you told me about Mattie and this drift-fence business."

Miller glanced sideways at him with that same thoughtful, unblinking gaze that so disturbed the Colonel before. He knew before the young cowboy started talking that he would not like what he was about to hear.

He didn't.

Mattie awoke with the heat of the sun laying down a pattern of light across her legs and the heat of Jesse McDade's mouth laying down a pattern of kisses across her naked breasts and belly. She stretched and twisted, feeling her breath and the beat of her heart begin to deepen and lengthen in slow, hot concert with every touch of Jesse's mouth, every stroke of his tongue. She knew now the melody of their bodies: the slow, gentle prelude that merged without pause into faster, undulating rhythm, then into a crescendo that blended all thought, all sensation, all feelings into a single haunting note that gradually died away, leaving only the echo of memory.

Jesse rose above her, all moonlight and midnight with his silver eyes and black hair, the companion to the sunshine and daylight of her yellow eyes and pale hair. But if the moon was cold, Jesse was not, she thought as he joined with her in a rush of white-hot heat that first softened, then melted her around him, drawing from him a gasp that was her name just as his body contorted, then flooded hers with its pulsating heat.

She clasped him with legs and arms, the sun holding the moon, until she remembered that sun and moon only seldom shared the sky at the same instant, but followed one another as day follows night through an endless progression of time. She pressed her face tight against Jesse's until she had wet both their cheeks with tears.

Jesse braced himself on his elbows and grasped her face with his hands, stroking away the tears with his thumbs. "Did I hurt you, Mattie?"

The heat in his silver eyes was cooling just as his body was, and she cried out when she felt him slip from inside her. "Nothing changed, Jesse!"

He didn't answer, kissing her instead, because there was no answer and she knew it. She felt his masculine flesh rising and hardening again, and her own softening and arching against him, seeking another joining.

Jesse gently rolled away instead and laid his hand between her breasts, pressing her back against the bed. "The sun's up, Mattie. We have to go. I've kept you far too long as it is, and Jubilee will have my head for risking talk."

Mattie pushed his hand away and sat up, her body

heavy and molten and frustrated. "Damn Jubilee and Samuel and the whole world."

Jesse pulled on his pants and turned to look at her. "Your eyes look as vicious as a cougar's."

She leaped off the bed to face him, her long hair whipping about her head. "And damn you, too, for giving me up every morning like you had no right to me."

Jesse picked up his shirt and pulled it on, his eyes darkening with those shadows she dreaded. "I have no right to you, Mattie. Have you forgotten?" He crossed the few feet separating them and grabbed her shoulders. "Don't you think it galls me every time I leave you? Don't you think I've thought about killing Samuel to have you?"

Mattie shrank back, smelling the violence in him as if it were a bottled scent. "Killing Samuel?"

He pushed her away and clenched his fists. "But I won't, so you needn't fear me. I have just enough conscience left not to kill a man. I've taken you away from him. I won't take his life, too." He reached out, his hand seeming to move of its own volition, and stroked her cheek, then he trailed his fingers down her throat to finally touch her golden locket. "You wear my heart, Mattie. That's the best that I can do."

Blindly Mattie began to dress, resenting each article of clothing that concealed her from his eyes. How far she had come from the old Mattie who would never have dreamed of standing naked and proud in front of a man, never dreamed of touching him and watching his body change, and who certainly never dreamed of feelings so deep they transcended any thoughts of decency or convention. The old Mattie might not have believed that the woman one man didn't want should be freed for the one man who did. But the new Mattie believed it, and so help her God, there had to be a way.

She turned to make the tumbled bed, but felt Jesse's hands seize her arms. "Leave it, Mattie. When I come back to this house, I want to find the bed as it is so I can remember us the way we were last night."

She nodded and licked away the tears from her mouth before leaning her head against his shoulder and tilting her face toward his. "Kiss me, please, Jesse. One last time."

"One last time," he agreed, bending toward her. "Because once we ride out, we can be seen for miles on that flat prairie."

She threaded her fingers through his hair and pulled his head down until she could taste his mouth.

His taste remained until their horses neared the new headquarters and Mattie saw the heavy wagons crowding the ground in front of her house. Until she saw the tall, white-haired man on the covered veranda leaning on a walking stick and glaring at her. Then she tasted only ashes.

She spurred her horse into a gallop, feeling her heart beating in cadence with its hoofbeats. She was twenty-two years old, and she was afraid to face her father.

She jerked on the reins and tumbled off her horse to rush up the wide, wooden steps to the veranda. "Papa! I didn't expect you so soon."

The Colonel's eyes bore into hers, and she stiffened. "That's obvious, young lady, else you would have been here to greet me."

Jubilee pushed by the Colonel, his face a black mask behind which his feeling hid. "I done told your daddy that you and Jesse musta stopped by one of them nester rancher's for the night. I done told him there weren't no need to work hisself up into a fit."

"Hush your mouth, Jubilee," said the Colonel. "Mattie doesn't need a nigger to talk for her." His face suffused with blood and he pounded his stick on the porch. "Where have you been, Mattie Jo Corley?"

Mattie heard a man's footstep behind her and sensed it was Jesse before he spoke. "Jubilee, do you think you could whip up some breakfast for Mattie and me? We left my place this morning without eating."

His words, "my place," hung in the air, and Mattie saw her father prepare to swoop on them as surely as a hawk on a rabbit.

So did Jubilee, and his wits were quicker than hers. "Yes, suh, I be glad to—just as soon as Miss Mattie takes the Colonel in the house. His face done got red as fire in this heat. I reckon he ain't used to how hot it gets in Texas. Hottest May since we come here. Wouldn't want him shaming hisself by fainting like a lady in front of all these folks."

In her agitation at seeing her father, Mattie had ignored the cowboys crowding the veranda and the freighters lolling against their wagons, all watching the scandal about to unfold on that Hunter woman's front porch. She straightened her shoulders and lifted her chin, ruthlessly tamping down the child that cowered within her. She had suffered enough humiliation yesterday in Tascosa. She had no intention of suffering it on her own property.

"Thank you, Jubilee, I do believe you're right. Papa, let's go in the house and let these men get on with their work." She pointed a finger at the cowboys. "You men help the freighters unload and carry my furniture in. Jubilee will tell you where things go. We have lived long enough with Mendoza's leftovers. I have no further desire to eat off a cottonwood plank table and sleep on a mattress stuffed with sheep's wool that smells of lanolin."

"Mrs. Hunter?"

A tall, lanky cowboy leaning against the house at the far end of the veranda tipped his hat back, and Mattie recognized Tom Miller. "Mr. Miller, how delightful to see you again. It has been quite some time since we last met." She marveled at how quickly she dropped back into the stilted, formal manners of a gently reared hostess—and how convenient for covering a multitude of sins such manners were.

"More than two years I reckon, since I tipped my hat to you in Mobeetie. You're looking fine, Mrs. Hunter. Guess ranching must agree with you."

"What are you doing here, Miller?" Mattie had forgotten how harsh Jesse's voice always sounded whenever he spoke to Tom. "You looking for a job? We're full up."

Tom straightened and ambled closer to Jesse until less than a yard separated them. "I got a job come next week. I'm riding for the LS brand. I got a bellyful of that British syndicate that bought the LX, and quit. I was paying my respects to a glass of beer in the Equity Bar yesterday when I met Mrs. Hunter's pa. He was looking for a guide, and I was at loose ends, so I offered to show him the way." He turned his head toward the Colonel. "I told you she'd be fine if she was with Jesse McDade. And she is."

Tom's eyes rested briefly on Mattie before moving on to Jesse. "I reckon you were smart to stop at your place instead of trying to make it all the way here, or worse yet, making camp along the trail. Can't expect a lady to roll up in a blanket on the ground."

Nothing Tom had said was a lie, but Mattie sensed he knew the truth was more than what he told. How much of the truth he had guessed, she didn't care to speculate.

Jesse shifted his feet and Mattie heard his spurs jingle. "We appreciate your trying to ease the Colonel's mind."

Tom shrugged. "I did what I could." He turned to the Colonel and held out his hand. "I'd best be on my way. You and your daughter have a good visit,

Colonel. I reckon it's been a while since you've had a chance to enjoy her company."

The Colonel shook his hand. "Too long, Mr. Miller." He turned his head suddenly and Mattie found herself staring into his expressionless eyes. "Much, much too long."

The Colonel tapped his fingers on the ranch's ledger book and felt a deep satisfaction. He had spent two weeks counting physical assets, including wagons and buildings as well as cattle, then another week carefully examining figures and balancing receipts and bills of sale against entries. There had been no hanky-panky with his money that he could find—and he would have found it. The man hadn't been born who could successfully cheat Colonel Andrew J. Corley. Not Jesse McDade, in spite of the man's admittedly brilliant financial management of the Bar H. Yearly profits of thirty to sixty percent on one's initial investment were a tribute to the man's stewardship.

Financially the Colonel couldn't be more pleased.

Personally he couldn't find anything that did please him. His daughter was a beautiful stranger whose golden-brown eyes looked directly at a man's face with no girlish modesty that he could detect, and whose voice held no tender hesitation when she gave orders to rough cowboys. What was infinitely worse than her lack of downcast eyes and air of being in charge was her range of conversation. She spoke of treating screwworm and of cows dropping calves as casually as though she was speaking of taking broth to the sick and of visiting a new mother. When she discussed breeding and castration as though she knew exactly what was involved in each process and did not even have the decency to blush about it, the Colonel found himself reduced to speechlessness.

But more than her indelicate speech, her familiarity with McDade filled him with disquiet. They spoke too much together without using words, and Mattie always seemed to turn toward him as though she was a weather vane and he was the wind. The Colonel curled his hand into a fist. And Mattie refused to discuss the impropriety of her staying alone at McDade's ranch, dismissing his lectures with the remark that he "could think what he chose." Damn it all, that was no kind of answer for a daughter to give her father, and it burned in his belly like a shot of bad whiskey.

Careful to keep his expression bland and jovial, the Colonel turned his eyes to Jesse. His attempts to question that young man elicited no more information than a terse laugh and the comment that he "respected Mattie too much to discuss her behavior with anyone, including her own father." It was monstrous that both acted as though Mattie's behavior was her own business and none of his.

Reluctantly the Colonel dismissed the two sitting in front of the desk and turned his attention to Samuel. His son-in-law was even less satisfactory than he had been five years ago. Samuel seemed almost womanish, for want of a better word, and a petulant whining woman at that. If Mattie was another man's daughter, he wouldn't blame her for preferring Jesse McDade's company to that of Samuel. He might even be tolerant of her slipping into that young man's bed—provided she was discreet. But Mattie wasn't any other man's daughter—she was his—and her body belonged to his spineless, repulsive son-in-law whether he deserved it or not. Other women managed to live blameless lives with unsatisfactory husbands. Mattie could do the same.

"Papa, are you satisfied with the tally of cattle?"

Jesse groaned. "Please, Mattie, don't suggest that we go through that again. If there's a cow on this ranch your father hasn't personally counted and dabbed with red paint, I don't know where it's hiding."

Mattie squeezed Jesse's arm, and the Colonel felt his own chest tighten as he saw the slow smile she bestowed on the younger man. Then she turned accusing eyes on him. "There was no need for you to mark each cow as you counted it, Papa. Jesse wouldn't cheat you by running the same herd by twice."

"Don't be ridiculous, Mattie. Your father has no reason to trust McDade."

Mattie turned her head to stare at her husband, but not fast enough for the Colonel to miss seeing the utter coldness in her eyes. "He has no reason to distrust Jesse either, and it is unkind of you to suggest it."

Samuel waved a languid hand and slipped farther down in the leather couch that sat against one wall of what Mattie called the office. "You're always defending McDade, Mattie. I wonder you haven't learned how unseemly your behavior is."

Jesse half rose from his chair, his fists clenched and his eyes as dark and deadly looking as a gun barrel. "Hunter, I take exception to your remark."

Mattie laid her hand on his arm. "Please, Jesse!"

The Colonel slapped his hand on the desk. "Samuel, I'll thank you not to talk to my daughter in such a fashion. It's shameful."

Samuel raised his eyebrows. "Not as shameful as my wife being out all night with McDade. Riding in the next morning bold as brass."

The Colonel watched red first stain Mattie's cheekbones, then fade away, leaving her face white and cold as a snowbank. "I will not discuss my behavior with a man who spends more time drunk in Tascosa's saloons than on the ranch."

"Mattie! Such talk in front of strangers is disrespectful!"

She turned her cold face toward him. "Who's a stranger, Papa—Jesse or you?"

"I am your father, young woman!"

Jesse reached for her hand, easing his fingers between hers in an unconscious intimacy. "Let it be, Mattie."

The Colonel watched Jesse release Mattie's hand and tried to reject his near certainty that they were physically intimate. It was too horrible to contemplate, a disgrace, a sin. No decent father would consider such a thought.

He resolved to put a stop to it.

Jesse did it for him. "Colonel Corley, if you are satisfied that I have fulfilled the terms of our contract, then it is time to terminate our agreement."

The Colonel nodded. "Past time, I would say."

"Jesse! No!"

Mattie's scream echoed through the room, so filled with grief that the Colonel knew—*he knew*—that she had tossed up her skirts for the silver-eyed, filthy bastard sitting opposite him. No woman could sound like that who hadn't just lost a man. Jesse's gray eyes met his, and the Colonel had difficulty controlling an urge to throttle him. There was no denial in those hard eyes and face, no self-contempt or regret, only an acceptance that his time had run out.

"I believe you owe me a bonus, Colonel."

The Colonel rose to lean over the desk, bracing himself on clenched fists. "You cold-blooded son of a bitch!"

"Bonus!" exclaimed Samuel, rousing himself from his chair. "Don't pay him anything, Colonel. He never once showed me the proper respect."

Jesse glanced at him, his eyes growing colder. "I think I showed you all the respect you earned."

"And my daughter, McDade," asked the Colonel, forcing the words past the bile in his throat. "Did you show her the proper respect?"

Jesse's eyes closed briefly, and the Colonel saw a

A TIME TOO LATE

vein throb in his temple. When he opened his eyes again, they were as devoid of life as a dead man's. "If I respected her less, I would stay."

For a moment the Colonel felt his determination to see McDade off his property waver, a moral weakness that horrified him. Before his sense of propriety could falter again, he quickly wrote out a bank draft, wincing at the six figures involved. Buying back his daughter's respectability was an expensive proposition.

"Here," he said, handing Jesse the draft. "I want you off my property immediately."

Mattie sat clutching the neck of her dress, her face sick. "Jesse is invited to the housewarming tonight, Papa, and I insist that he come. He is our neighbor and I will not shame him by excluding his name from the guest list."

"How hypocritical to hear you talk of shame, my dear wife," remarked Samuel.

Jesse tucked the bank draft in his pocket and walked over to Samuel. "I've waited five years to do this, Hunter, and I'll have my way if the Colonel whips me off the place for it."

Samuel shrank back in the chair. "What are you saying?"

Jesse leaned over and sank his fist in Samuel's belly, then jerked him out of the chair by his shirt collar and landed a blow on his face. By the spraying blood and the sound of bone cracking, the Colonel decided that Jesse had just split his son-in-law's lips and broken his nose. Furthermore the Colonel decided he wouldn't do anything about it.

Jesse picked up Samuel's limp body and tossed it over his shoulder. "I'll deposit him in the bunkhouse for whatever cowboy has the stomach for it to patch him up. It wouldn't be fair to ask Jubilee to do it since your former slave has wanted to beat hell out of him at least as long as I have." He stopped by Mattie's chair.

"I'll be at your party. Will you save me a dance?"

"She certainly will not!" said the Colonel.

Mattie rose, holding her back as stiff as though she was strapped to a board. "I shall dance with whom I please, and it pleases me to dance with Jesse."

"I'll claim you tonight, then," said Jesse, and swiftly left the room.

"He just laid hands on your husband, and you promised him a dance? What kind of a woman are you?"

Her eyes were as direct as a man's. "A hard one, Papa. And now we have business together, a matter of your signing over the deed to my property. Your investment has been paid back with interest."

"This matter had best wait until Samuel is able to join us," said the Colonel, sitting back down at the desk and meeting his daughter's cold eyes.

Mattie's smile held neither warmth nor amusement. "Samuel has had little to do with this ranch in the past, Papa, and I intend that he have nothing to do with it in the future. Sign the deed over to me."

"Samuel is your husband, Mattie. You cannot exclude him from the deed."

"I intend to divorce him, Papa."

The Colonel rose up with a shout. "You'll do nothing of the kind. A divorced woman is no better than a prostitute. In fact, to most folks that's what she is. I'll not have a daughter of mine called a whore!"

Mattie paled. "I'm already a whore, Papa. I sell myself for propriety instead of money every day I remain married to Samuel. I cannot do so any longer."

"This is because of McDade, isn't it? You want him, don't you? Do you think he'll marry you if you're free of Samuel? Do you, Mattie?"

"Yes!"

"He won't, you foolish girl. No man buys the cow if he can get the milk for free. And Mattie, as a man I can promise you that most milk cows are the same. McDade can find any number he wants. He won't need a woman who's shamed herself." He shook his head. "You'll get rid of Samuel, but you won't get your silver-eyed man."

Mattie touched a gold locket she wore around her neck as she looked up at him. "Yes, I will, Papa."

Her eyes held no doubt at all, and the Colonel felt a growing desperation. "Divorce is against God's law, Mattie. Don't you fear God?"

Mattie's laughter chilled him. "I fear God, but I've noticed that his laws often favor men."

The Colonel sank back in his chair. First adultery, now blasphemy. If Mattie didn't so resemble her sainted mother, he would let her go to perdition. However, she was his daughter, his only flesh and blood, and it was his duty to save her from herself. It only remained to outmaneuver her—which meant striking at both her pride and her woman's feelings. If she had any that didn't lie between her legs.

He leaned forward. "Sit down, Mattie, and listen to me. If you refuse to answer to a higher moral argument, perhaps you are enough of my blood to appreciate a more tangible loss. If you divorce Samuel, you will have to show cause, a humiliating prospect, and you will find the scales of justice weighted against you. You will lose at least half of your property, this Bar H Ranch."

"No! I built this ranch—Jesse and I. It's more mine than Samuel's."

Her eyes were wild, and the Colonel derived a certain satisfaction in confirming what he already suspected: Mattie loved this arid, flat land and the stinking beasts wearing her brand more than she should. Sentimentality had no place in business.

"Then I'll buy out his share," she said. "The ranch accounts will support such an investment."

Her words caught him by surprise. His daughter was more astute than he had realized. He would not underestimate her again. "A wise man would accept your offer. Samuel is not a wise man, but a vindictive one. I would bet my fortune that he would sow this land with salt before he would sell to you. Or else he would sell it to some British syndicate, and you have no love for the syndicates."

"How do you know that?"

"Young Tom Miller told me about your distasteful confrontation with the other ranchers over the drift fence, and I believe it was a syndicate man who most humiliated you."

"No, Papa. It was Samuel—and I slapped him."

He raised his eyebrows. "An unforgivable response on your part, but Miller didn't tell me that. It appears he is more clever than I thought, telling me just enough to make your behavior sound reasonable—outside of the fact that it was not your place to speak at a business meeting. But to continue our discussion. There is always a cost we must pay to gain what we want, Mattie. In your case, freedom from Samuel will cost you half the Bar H." He hesitated, then plunged on. "And Leon, of course."

"What!"

He winced at the anguish in her eyes. "Oh, I'm afraid so, Mattie. No judge would give a man's son to a whorish woman."

Her hands clutched her skirt, twisting it into knots. "I won't give Leon to Samuel! I won't give my son up!"

"Then you must give up McDade."

CHAPTER 27

The dress still looked as elegant as when she had first worn it to John Thatcher's party, its ivory, pale yellow, and deep gold silks as stunning as ever. The garlands of green leaves embroidered around the neck and the edges of the square court train were still as brilliantly green and the spray of silk forget-me-nots as fresh as if the intervening five years had not happened.

Time had altered not the dress, but Mattie.

She no longer looked the gaunt young girl starving from lack of a husband's attention, but a woman well nourished by a man's touch.

If I respected your daughter less, I wouldn't leave.

"Damn your respect, Jesse!" Mattie cried out to the four impersonal walls of her bedroom. "I'd rather be your whore!"

She sank down on the stool in front of the dresser her father had brought from Pueblo and stared into her mirror at the reflection of the heart-shaped locket that dangled from the yellow velvet ribbon around her neck. If she weren't more watchful of her thoughts, the feelings she had so carefully locked away after Jesse's defection and her father's frank words would burst free, and she would drown in her own tears.

"Miss Mattie?" Jubilee pounded on her door. "Miss Mattie, you in there? Your guests done been arriving since sunset. Your papa's 'bout to have a conniption downstairs."

She touched Jesse's locket just before she opened the door. "You needn't raise your voice, Jubilee."

The ex-slave's face was a mask of disapproval. "I reckon I did, too, Miss Mattie. I heared what you said about being a whore 'fore I was halfway up the stairs, and I figured I best make some noise to take folks' minds off what they mighta thought you said."

"I doubt I said anything that folks aren't already saying for themselves."

Jubilee glowered at her. "What folks 'spect they know and what they know for certain is two different things. You go down them stairs and act like you ain't done nothing wrong, and everybody gonna start wondering iffen maybe they was wrong in thinking the worst. But keep hiding up here, and let folks keep talking down there, and you'll be ruint."

"Has Jesse arrived yet?"

Jubilee clasped her arm and shook it. The ex-slave had changed, too, thought Mattie. Five years ago he would never have thought to touch her so. "What you planning now, Miss Mattie? I sees that wildness in your eyes all mixed up with hurt like you fixing to cut off your nose to spite your face. Ain't you and Jesse caused enough talk? You gots to leave it be now."

"Has Jesse arrived yet?" she repeated.

Jubilee sighed. "Not more than ten minutes ago. He's all feathered out like a peacock in black britches and a pearl-buttoned shirt and fancy black vest. He and your pa are circling each other like a couple of old tomcats, but ain't neither one of them clawing yet."

"My father be damned!" exclaimed Mattie as rage burst out of its locked room.

Jubilee shook his head. "You hush up now, Miss Mattie. Your pa didn't make the world."

She felt tears gather in her eyes and blinked them back, fighting to control herself. "But he agrees with it, doesn't he, Jubilee?"

Jubilee gently blotted her eyes with his handkerchief. "I reckon your pa believes the way he was raised, Miss Mattie."

"But you were raised the same way. You always lectured me on how a lady should act."

Jubilee tucked his handkerchief back in his pocket. "I was raised a slave, Miss Mattie, and told how to act and think and allus to do what I was told—a lot like you was raised. Sometimes a slave did something that made him feel free—like stealing a watermelon or taking a rest when he was supposed to be working. But he always knew it wouldn't last, and he'd go back to being a slave. When I seen you and Jesse reaching for each other, I knowed it was wrong, knowed it was more sinful than stealing a watermelon, but I knowed how joyful being free is when you is a slave beforehand and still a slave after. Ain't nothing changed, but you had yourself a time of joy that all the whippings in the world can't take away from you."

"Could you go back to being a slave again, Jubilee?" whispered Mattie, feeling despair trembling behind its door.

Jubilee looked at her from sorrowful eyes. "It ain't the same, Miss Mattie, 'cause you ain't never been freed. You just stole a little time, that's all."

Mattie touched the locket again. "It was more than that, Jubilee."

He patted her shoulder. "I knows it was, Miss

Mattie, and the Good Lord is going to take that into account on Judgment Day. Now you just go on downstairs to your party."

Mattie squared her shoulders and shut her door behind her, shutting in those wayward feelings that had already weakened her: rage and despair and sorrow. "You don't understand, Jubilee. It isn't a party. It's a wake."

Jubilee's eyes locked with hers. "What are you fixing to do, Miss Mattie?"

She smiled even though she felt her lower lip tremble. "I'm going to make a grand entrance, Jubilee. I'm going to laugh and dance and no one will know that I don't have a heart anymore."

"And what else is you gonna do?" asked Jubilee, following her down the stairs.

"I'm going to bring Jesse McDade to his knees. I'm going to throw his damn respect back in his face. I'm going to know why he's leaving me!" She walked down the stairs, ignoring Jubilee's whispered admonitions to "let it be."

Dear God, she couldn't.

She posed on the landing, Mattie Jo Hunter in her yellow silk dress and Jesse McDade's locket around her neck, and waited until she saw her guests began to turn their heads, waited until conversation began to die, waited until the only sound was the rustling leaves of the giant cottonwood tree in the front yard—hers and Jesse's tree. Then she descended the last few steps, her eyes never leaving the figure in the fancy black vest who leaned with one elbow braced against the stone fireplace opposite the stairs. If she had still possessed a heart, it would have been stirred to pity by the look of agony in those silver eyes. If she had still possessed a heart, its kindly nature would not have allowed her to walk with graceful sliding steps to within reach of his arms, then veer away as though blown by a capricious wind to greet a man standing a few feet away.

"Tom Miller! I'm so pleased you could come. I have not yet thanked you for playing guide to my father. Had you not shown him the way here from Tascosa, he might yet be wandering around the prairie hopelessly lost." She shot her father a look that plainly said how much she wished he was doing exactly that and smiled when she saw him flinch. "If I might persuade our musician to play a waltz, perhaps a dance would suffice as a thank you." She hoped the piano player from Mobeetie Jubilee had hired could play something besides tunes more appropriate to the saloon in which he ordinarily worked.

Fortunately he could, and as the delicate notes began Mattie caught up her train and turned to a bemused Tom Miller. "Shall we dance?"

Tom clasped her hand and waist and whirled her around the large living room in time to the music. "That was as slick a job as I've ever seen, Mrs. Hunter."

"I'm sure I don't know to what you refer, Mr. Miller," she replied, observing Jesse's clenched jaw and killing eyes. She had been right in assuming that dancing with Tom Miller would utterly infuriate Jesse.

He squeezed her waist and turned her so her back was to Jesse. "Oh, I figure you do, Miss Mattie. You couldn't have put Jesse McDade in his place any better if you'd planned it—which I'm pretty sure you did."

"Mr. Miller! You presume—" she began, but his steady eyes defeated her. She swallowed. "You're right, of course, and I'm sorry I made you a part of it."

He smiled, that good-natured smile of a man comfortable with himself that always so surprised her. "I was handy, Miss Mattie, and I got to have the first dance with you. As many men as there are here tonight, and as shy of womenfolk as the Panhandle still is, I reckon I'm just lucky to be able to have a minute with the prettiest woman in Texas." He shook his head when she started to protest his absurd compliment. "No, it's true. There's plenty of women might be as well put together, but I don't believe there's another honest enough to 'fess up to using one man to hurt another."

She flushed until her face felt painfully hot. "I'm sorry."

He squeezed her hand. "You already said that. No need to say it again. I just wanted you to know that I'm a hard man to lie to, but a forgiving man when the lies come from hurt and not from meanness."

She closed her eyes and stumbled, her knees suddenly going weak as the doors in her mind suddenly burst open. "You know about Jesse and me."

He slid his arm further around her waist to hold her up. "Steady, Miss Mattie. Don't give way now. Just hang on to my hand tight as you can until you stop shaking and find your pride. I figure if you don't have anything else left, you got that."

She took a deep breath, clutching his hand until her fingers ached. "Why are you being so kind, Tom Miller?"

"I reckon that's my business, and you don't need the burden of knowing it. Now, while I'm feeling so full of saintliness, and since the music's stopped, I'd best let you go to McDade."

She caught a note of bleakness in his voice that matched the prairie in late summer when all the color had gone. "But you don't want to, do you? You don't like Jesse and you don't approve of us."

He grasped her elbow and gently turned her to face him. "I came to steal a dance with Mattie Hunter, not to judge her." He touched the single flower pinned high on one shoulder strap. "Forget-me-nots. I reckon I won't forget you, Miss Mattie."

A TIME TOO LATE
417

She suddenly realized that without the mask of his smile, his hawk-nosed countenance revealed a strength of character she had overlooked before. "You're an unusual man, Tom Miller."

He smiled. "I'm a patient man, Mattie Hunter, and steady. I generally get what I'm after in the long run."

"And what are you after?"

He glanced over her shoulder toward Jesse. "Same thing as most men, I guess—a reason to freeze my gizzard in the winter and bake my hide in the summer. A woman to love, and a family," he added softly, his eyes coming to rest on her.

She felt tears prickle her eyes. "I hope you get them, Tom."

He didn't smile. "Maybe I will, or maybe I won't. Have to wait and see, but like I said, I'm a patient man." He touched his forehead in a brief salute. "Good night, Mattie Hunter. Thanks for the dance."

"Good night, Tom Miller. And thank you."

He grinned, and turned and walked away—a calm man, a steady man, a man who had gentled her mind.

"Mattie."

She didn't need to turn to know it was Jesse. His scent, even his footsteps on the polished oak floor gave him away as surely as his husky voice that always seemed to arouse nerves she never knew she possessed. If she never saw Jesse McDade after tonight, she would hear his voice in the rumble of the thunder, the roar of the Canadian at full flood, the pounding hooves of a thousand stampeding cattle—all the deep sounds of the plains heard first in the blood and bones.

"Mattie, look at me."

Slowly she turned, and lost herself in his silver eyes.

"I'm humbled if that's what you had in mind when you danced with Miller," he said.

"He's a good man, Jesse. I should not have used him so."

"Then why did you?"

"To hurt you. To hurt myself."

He held out his hand. "Dance with me."

She looped up her train and took his hand, shivering as she felt his arm circle her waist. "I'm sorry, Jesse."

His eyes closed briefly as if her apology hurt him. "I should have told you, Mattie, before I terminated my contract. I had planned to, but your father dogged my footsteps in the name of protecting you."

She felt a pain in her chest where her heart used to be. "Then you would have left even if my father hadn't caught us out?"

He nodded. "Yes."

"Why, Jesse? What more could you want than what you already have here? We built a ranch together—a wonderful ranch—from a single herd. We have such ideas, such plans for the future."

"We built *your* ranch from *your* single herd. I was just your hired hand, Mattie, the same as Hank or Red or Danny."

"You were never a hired hand to me, Jesse, nor to anyone else."

"Maybe that was true in the beginning, when all of us were working to settle this country and build our holdings, but the Panhandle is changing. The foreign investors are buying up ranches damn near as fast as they can take inventory and get the owner's signature on the dotted line. The original ranchers, folks like us, are selling up, and the nester ranchers are being squeezed out. Cowboys who were always free to brand a few mavericks during roundup to build up their own small herd are being called rustlers now. There's even talk of declaring their brands illegal and confiscating their herds. A cowboy—*a hired hand*—would never have a chance to build anything for himself. That's the other drift fence going up, Mattie, and it's one that will keep the cowboys and small ranchers out of their share of the Panhandle. I'll never be able to influence the direction of change in the Panhandle as long as the other ranchers and the syndicates see me as just another hired hand. I found that out at the meeting in Tascosa. And you'll never earn anyone's respect or have any influence either as long as I'm your man."

"Damn respect, Jesse! And damn the Panhandle!"

He smiled wryly. "Is that why you hired that itinerant painter from Tascosa to paint murals on the walls and ceilings of this house, Mattie? Because you hate the land? I think you must love it or you wouldn't have all the landmarks of your life here on the walls. Jubilee standing by the chuck wagon and the plaza in the dining room. A view of the Canadian River Valley on the wall by the fireplace. Our cottonwood tree by the staircase. Leon and a longhorn calf that looks very much like Baby by the front door. We're all there, Mattie, all your cowboys. And the ceiling looks like a pale blue Panhandle sky with a few clouds drifting overhead. And the veranda on all four sides of the house so you can step out of any door and watch the land change with the seasons."

He shook his head. "No, Mattie, you can't damn all this, and I can't have folks saying you've taken up with the hired hand. It's time I built up my own ranch. The next time we meet, we'll be equals."

She knew then that even if she could divorce Samuel without losing Leon and the ranch, Jesse would still leave. If she were free, Jesse would wait to claim her until his worth was equal to hers. Jesse McDade would stand in no woman's shadow.

Damn all men and their pride!

Her shoulders drooping with weariness, Mattie confronted Samuel in the flickering light of a single coal-oil lamp. "Whatever you want can wait until tomorrow, Samuel. And I'll thank you not to enter my bedroom again without knocking."

Samuel's face looked more battered and swollen than it had earlier in the evening when he had casually told their guests that he had been thrown into a stack of fence posts when his horse had shied. She supposed it was as good a story as any. And certainly Jesse's fist was as hard as a cedar post. If the guests, all ranchers and cowboys, disbelieved him, they were too polite to say so.

"This is my house now, Mattie, and I'll go where I wish," replied Samuel, his hairless chest looking flabby without his shirt. Flesh sagged over the waist of his trousers and his bare feet made sweaty, slapping noises as he walked across the hardwood floor toward her.

"What do you mean, *your* house? I don't recall your driving a single nail or wielding a single paintbrush. In fact, I don't recall any help from you."

Samuel shrugged. "I don't do menial labor, my dear. That is for hired hands, of whom we have one less. Your Jesse McDade is gone. The Bar H is mine now."

"The Bar H is not yours, Samuel! Even though I have to share ownership with you by law, don't think it is yours. You haven't earned one acre of it."

He smiled. "Your father signed the deed over to me this afternoon."

Mattie doubled over as though he had hit her in the belly. She fought for air. "My father wouldn't do that!"

"The Colonel felt as though your independent behavior needed to be curbed. I believe he called it 'unseemly,' and encouraged me to exercise my husbandly duties with a firmer hand. I have decided he is right. I desire more respectful, more submissive behavior from you, and I have your father's blessings to exact it."

A TIME TOO LATE

Mattie straightened, hatred of Samuel mixing with her father's betrayal to unleash a rage she had never felt before. "You can go to hell, Samuel. You and my father both. As for my behavior, your own abuse of me has long since destroyed any moral authority you once had." She took a step toward the door. "Now that we've settled that, please leave. And for heaven's sakes, if you plan any more nocturnal walks about the house, put on a robe. We do have several guests staying overnight because it was far too late for them to begin their journeys home after the housewarming. I wouldn't want the sight of your nakedness to frighten the ladies."

"Clint said you'd be stubborn."

She felt a shudder of revulsion at the man's name. "What does Clint have to do with us? And when did you see him? Papa threatened to shoot him if he set foot on the property again. I should have listened to Jubilee when he tried to warn me about Clint and had Jesse shoot him years ago."

Samuel grabbed her arm and whirled her around. "You bitch! You just won't understand, will you?"

Mattie's hip slammed into her dresser, knocking over vials of perfume and bath oil. The scent of magnolia and violets choked her. She gasped and swung her fist, crying out in pain when Samuel seized her wrist and twisted it. His swollen lips curled away from his teeth, and she smelled his breath, fetid with whiskey and the odor of canned oysters her father had brought for the housewarming.

"Samuel! Let go of me!"

He twisted her around, forcing both her arms behind her back and holding her wrists with one hand, ripped her nightgown from neck to hem with the other. "So I have no authority over you—no *moral* authority. Perhaps it's time we talked of *physical* authority. And remember, you forced my hand."

"Stop it, Samuel!" she cried.

He jerked one side of her nightgown below her breasts, then the other, effectively pinning her arms still encased in voluminous sleeves against her sides. With a dexterity she believed had long since been sacrificed to abuse of whiskey, he folded up the skirt and tied the torn ends tightly around her chest. He shoved her backward onto the bed.

"A trussed chicken, my dear, if a particularly unappetizing one. I wonder that McDade finds those fat breasts so appealing. Or does he just throw your skirts over your head and go after it as I used to do? Anything to finish the unpleasant chore."

His red-streaked eyes focused on her bare breasts, and Mattie rounded her shoulders and tried to turn over to protect her vulnerable flesh. He slammed one hand against her shoulder, pinning her to the bed, while he clawed at her gold locket with his other. "What is this, my dear?"

She shrank from his touch as though he had dipped his hands in excrement while she sought to distract him. "It's a locket, Samuel. Even a man as drunk as you should be able to recognize a locket."

He smiled at her and twisted the ribbon, cutting off her breath and holding her immobile. "McDade gave it to you, didn't he? Don't bother to lie to me. I saw you touching it tonight. Every time you looked at him, you touched it—caressed it as though you were caressing his body. I don't approve, Mattie. I don't approve of my wife wearing another man's gift. It's unseemly."

His fingernails scratched her throat as he tightened his grip and jerked repeatedly at the velvet ribbon until it broke. She heard the locket hit the floor as she gulped mouthfuls of air to relieve her burning lungs. "Did I frighten you, my dear? Was I too rough?"

Before she could find the breath to defy him, he pressed the bruised, abraded skin that circled her throat, and she gasped in both pain and revulsion. "You're free of him now, Mattie. You're my wife again, and you'll learn to behave as a wife should. Beginning now."

She had been sickened by Samuel's humiliation before, but when he stood up beside the bed and unbuttoned his trousers, exposing himself, she thought she might die of it.

"No!" she cried, and rolled off the bed. Scrambling to her knees, she heard him utter a word she had never heard before. She knew it must be filthy—as filthy as what he was about to do to her.

"You stupid bitch!" he grunted as he seized her hair and pulled her halfway to her feet.

She saw his fist coming and welcomed it. Unconsciousness was better than a waking nightmare.

When she awoke, she used the tattered remains of her nightgown to scrub herself, then bundled it up along with her bedding and threw both in the corner. Tomorrow she would burn them. Tomorrow she would scrub her bedroom with lye soap, scrub every surface that Samuel had fouled with his touch. Tomorrow she would ask Jubilee to nail brackets on each side of her door. Never again would she sleep without a stout wooden bar across her door. Never again would she sleep without a pistol beside her bed.

Pulling on another nightgown, she knelt on the floor and picked up the gold locket, wiping it clean of Samuel's touch with her own hair. Tomorrow she would string it on a gold chain and wear it again—not in defiance, but in resolution. Samuel would not— could not—break her. Only a woman without self-respect allowed herself to be broken by a man less worthy than she. The locket was more than a symbol of Jesse. It was a symbol of the woman she had become—a woman of self-respect.

She rose and walked to the window, pushing aside

the curtains to watch the leaves of the cottonwood gently stir in the wind. Tomorrow would come, and the day after. The seasons would pass, but her reckoning with Samuel would come and she would be ready. She had her cowboys, loyal only to herself, seven hundred thousand acres and the will to hold them—and Jesse. The bond held. She sensed it. Whether they ever lay together again, she was not done with him—nor he with her. As surely as she wore his locket, there would be another time.

CHAPTER 28

Jesse turned back before he had covered half the distance to his headquarters. You're a goddamn fool, McDade, he thought. Don't ride back to her. Let it go. Nothing's changed. All you'll accomplish is to dirty her more. Soon there won't be a man or woman in the Panhandle who won't know that Mattie Hunter is lying with you. If you can't claim her in the daylight in front of men, don't sneak into her bed at night. Don't shame her more.

He rode on toward Mattie's house. He could do nothing less. He could not leave her thinking that he'd given her up as well as his job. He couldn't give her up if he damned them both to hell. At least in hell, they would be together.

Tying his horse to a cedar on the little creek below her headquarters, he walked the rest of the way, avoiding the corrals even though his scent was familiar to the horses. Silently he walked across the veranda and reached for the door, knowing that it would be unlocked. No one ever locked his door. It was rude and insinuated that one's neighbor was untrustworthy. He acknowledged that in the present circumstances, that was true, and felt a moment's shame that he had so forsaken honor and decency. But neither could he let Mattie think he had betrayed their bond.

The door opened, and the Colonel faced him in the dim moonlight. "I knew you'd come sneaking after my daughter, you son of a bitch. I knew it when I saw the two of you dancing. Mattie looking up at you with her heart in her eyes and all the hurt in the world besides, and you so damn stiff and formal while all the time your hand is crawling all over her back and waist like you were gentling some mare so she wouldn't buck when you mounted her. I paid you a king's ransom this afternoon and listened to you blather about respecting my daughter, and it all meant nothing next to the heat between you two. So I've been waiting for you with my shotgun. Now, back off the porch, McDade, and start walking. I don't want to rouse the house by shooting you here. I don't want to shoot you at all, to tell the truth. Competent men are damn rare in this world, and it's a shame I have to kill one. You are competent, McDade, and my appreciation for an honest job done is having a terrible time with my heartfelt desire to blow your head off. I don't suppose I could buy you off with more money?"

Jesse shook his head, his eyes not leaving the Colonel's blue ones. "I earned my bonus according to the contract between us. Mattie has nothing to do with that. And, Colonel, my feelings are not for sale."

The Colonel grimaced. "Damn it, man! I haven't shot anybody since the war—unless you count a claim jumper in Colorado, and I don't—and I'm out of practice." He raised the shotgun until its barrel pointed at Jesse's heart. "But I guess once you learn how, you don't ever forget."

"I reckon you best put down that shotgun, Colonel," said Jubilee, a dark silhouette among the shadows in the open doorway. "Lordy, but you ain't any better with a gun than you was five years ago when I left with Miss Mattie. Now me, I'm considerable better. I got my pistol pointed right at your stubborn old head, and it's cocked and ready to shoot. That shotgun ain't. I figures that I can kill you 'fore you can cock that shotgun and kill Jesse."

Feeling like a fool, Jesse jerked the shotgun out of the Colonel's hands. If he hadn't been so obsessed with Mattie and his gut so torn up with guilt and hunger, he would have noticed the gun wasn't cocked before now. "Thanks, Jubilee."

The ex-slave nodded. "I didn't do it for you. I done it for Miss Mattie. Someday she may forgive her pa for what he done to her, but not if I lets him shoot you."

"Jubilee! Don't you understand? He's taking advantage of my daughter!"

"I knows what he's doing—knowed it a lot longer than you, Colonel—and I knows it ain't all on his side. But we ain't gonna talk about it on the front porch where anybody with a window open upstairs can listen. We be going to Miss Mattie's office before there's any more talk. Jesse, you step inside here and light the lamp that be on that little round table."

Jubilee backed into the house, pulling the Colonel with him, and Jesse followed, striking a match from his own box and lighting the lamp, smoking up the globe in the process. He was surprised to see his hands shaking.

By the time he and the Colonel were seated side by side in front of the desk, he had regained control of his body.

But not of his mind.

He had been caught about to commit a dishonorable act. The fact that it was not the first time was beside the point. He had no defense, no excuse. By all rights, the Colonel should shoot him. Jubilee should shoot him. Hell, if he were any kind of a man, he'd shoot himself. But then Mattie would be at the mercy of Samuel with only an old darkie to protect her.

Someday she may forgive her pa for what he done to her. . . .

Jubilee's words, barely heard while his mind was busy coping with the realization that the Colonel wasn't going to shoot him, struck Jesse like the kick of a horse. He leaped up and grabbed the Colonel by his lapels. "What did you do to Mattie? What was Jubilee talking about on the porch?"

The Colonel wasn't Samuel and he smashed his fist in Jesse's belly, then shoved the younger man backward, following up his surprise attack by grabbing Jesse around the waist. Jesse sprawled on the desk with the Colonel on top of him. The two men rolled off, landing on the floor in a heap of thrashing legs and fists. In between trying to get his breath back and avoiding the worst of the Colonel's blows, Jesse allowed that Mattie's father was damn sure full of piss and vinegar for a man his age.

Jubilee ended the fight by emptying a can of tobacco in both their faces. "I believes that iffen Miss Mattie weren't in a fix, I let you two fight until you kilt each other. But she is—"

"And it's that bastard's fault!" wheezed the Colonel, grabbing the edge of the desk and pulling himself up.

Eyes tearing from the finely ground tobacco, Jesse slumped back in his chair. "I still want to know what you did to her."

Jubilee sat down behind the desk, his pistol held loosely in one hand. "He done signed over the ranch to Hunter."

At first too stunned by Jubilee's words to believe what he was hearing, then too sickened by the

Colonel's expression of triumph to disbelieve, Jesse wiped his eyes on his sleeve, not certain whether his tears were from tobacco or rage. The old man knew how much Mattie loved this ranch and he was using that love to bring her to heel. Jesse wondered if the Colonel knew or cared that he was stealing his daughter's self-respect in the bargain.

"Did you used to tear up her dolls before her eyes and lock her in a closet when she was a little girl, Colonel? Did you force her to crawl on her knees whenever she wanted a new dress? Did you talk about her as if she was the village idiot, capable only of slobbering and wetting herself? How many times a day did you tell her she was ugly enough to sicken a man?"

The Colonel slammed his fists on the arms of his chair. "Are you mad, McDade? Do you think I'd treat my own daughter in such a foul manner?"

Jesse turned sideways in his chair. "Then why did you give her into the custody of a man who will do all of those things? Why did you degrade her by putting Samuel's name on that deed and not hers? Not that it matters legally—this is Texas, and half this ranch is Mattie's whether her name is on the deed or not—but it matters to her. You're telling her that all her hardship, her sacrifice, her work, her goddamn loneliness for the past five years don't count, that *she* doesn't count." Jesse leaned closer to the Colonel. "But the worst thing, the goddamnedest thing, is that by your treatment of her, you've justified Samuel's belief that Mattie is a worthless piece of shit."

"What about your treatment of her? You turned my daughter into a whore, and you wonder why her husband doesn't respect her?"

Jesse backhanded the Colonel. "You ever call Mattie that again, and I'll kill you, father or not."

Jubilee tapped his pistol grip on the desk. "You is both guilty."

The Colonel stared at him. "Who do you think you are? A woolly-headed judge? You always were an uppity nigger, but you're worse than that now. You're acting like you were equal to a white man—equal to me! Goddamn it, Jubilee, I hardly know you!"

Jubilee stared back at him with that direct look Jesse had seen before. "Colonel, I don't hardly know you either, and I don't think I wants to be a white man's equal iffen you're the white man. Jesse is right 'bout what he said. Miss Mattie is at Samuel Hunter's mercy, and I wouldn't trust a no-'count dog to that man. We ain't leaving this room with things left like that."

He turned to look at Jesse. "But the Colonel right, too. You keep sniffing around Miss Mattie, and she sure enough gonna be a whore. Leastwise folks will think she is, and that's what counts. And don't you go arguing with me, Jesse. You knows what I'm saying is the truth. You keep shaming her long enough and first she gonna hate herself, then she gonna hate you. A woman can hold up her head 'round folks just so long, then she bows it, then 'fore you know it, she's belly down in the dirt with folks stepping on her."

Jesse pushed himself out of his chair and paced the room, finally bracing his hands against the wall and hanging his head between his outstretched arms. His first thought was to take Mattie and Leon and run—to Wyoming or Montana, Arizona maybe. Somewhere they could start over. Like Mendoza, they could dwell in a time too late as long as it lasted. But Mattie was too rare a beauty, too spirited a woman to overlook. They would be found out, and Mattie would still be shamed. Besides, Mattie had invested her heart in this land, and so had he. They would be leaving a part of themselves behind, maybe the noblest part.

Yet they couldn't continue the way they were.

There was no way out.

A TIME TOO LATE
431

Grieving already, he straightened and turned back to the Colonel. "If you will add Mattie's name to that deed and give it to Jubilee to register, *and* transfer the ranch accounts to her name also, I will not"—he caught his breath at the pain he felt—"I will not see Mattie again except as a neighbor."

He could see the Colonel examining his proposition as if it was a piece of quartz and he was looking for gold. Finally the old man leaned back in his chair, his eyes opaque. "I will go you one better, McDade. I will set up an additional checking account for Mattie alone in which one fourth of all ranch receipts will be deposited as a condition of deeding over the Bar H— if you don't see Mattie at all. Being the poor businessman that he is, Samuel failed to take the deed with him this evening, so I may make whatever changes I choose. Try to cheat on our bargain, McDade, and I'll break Samuel, and Mattie will lose this ranch."

"You is a bastard, Colonel!" Jubilee burst out. "Using Miss Mattie like that. I was with you fifty years and I never knowed you to be so blessed mean."

"This heat between them has to stop, Jubilee, and I can't trust their decency!" He gestured at Jesse. "He came sneaking back like the worst white trash, and Mattie had that look in her eyes—like that young soldier running up the hill into the guns. I'm not going to let her ruin herself, and I'll use the weapons I find. That means this ranch, because this parched, flat, ugly piece of land is the only thing she wants as much as she wants McDade."

Jesse rubbed his face, noticing how tight his skin felt, and looked at the Colonel. The other man's eyes held no sympathy or charity. He would do as he promised. Not out of cruelty, but out of conviction born of his age and his station. He would destroy Mattie before he saw her shamed.

And Jesse would betray her before he saw her destroyed.

"Leave it, Jubilee. There's no other choice, and this way Mattie will at least have a fighting chance to prevent Samuel's losing the ranch through mismanagement." He touched his holstered pistol as he looked toward the Colonel. "However, if I learn that you have not lived up to your end of the bargain, I will claim her and take her back to the Flying MJ and be damned to you all. I will not leave her defenseless against Samuel."

The Colonel pursed his lips. "Jubilee will keep you appraised of whether or not I have kept my word."

Jesse nodded, then turned to the ex-slave. "Send me word of her, Jubilee. I trust the Colonel's prohibition doesn't extend to news of her."

"I surely will, Jesse."

Jesse opened the door. "I'll be waiting," he said, and walked out of the office and across the living room toward the front door.

He heard the Colonel's footsteps behind him. "I'll see you off the property."

"And I'll go along to see that you makes it off in one piece," said Jubilee.

Jesse ignored both of them as he stepped off the porch and stopped beneath the cottonwood tree. Their time together—his and Mattie's—had begun here under the moonlight and rustling leaves. It was only right that it should end here. To save what was good between them—to save *her*—he must now turn and walk away, leaving behind his heart and all that he might have been, and taking with him only his memories and what remained of his tattered honor.

He broke off a single leaf from the cottonwood tree and tucked it in his pocket. He'd press it between the pages of a book—Shakespeare, perhaps. The Bard understood unhappy endings.

A TIME TOO LATE

Jesse turned around. Before walking away, there was one more task to be done—one more circle to close—so that the ending might touch the beginning. "Jubilee, you gave her to me once to care for. I'm giving her back to you."

D. R. Meredith's grandmother drove a covered wagon in the Oklahoma Land Rush of 1889. Her father passed along to her tales of Jesse James and the Younger brothers that he heard as a youth in Missouri. Lawmen and outlaws, cowboys and Indians, homesteaders and gamblers were not mythical characters to her, but real people her family knew.

After graduating from the University of Oklahoma, Meredith followed her husband to Texas. Although a prize-winning author of eleven mystery novels, she took a holiday from crime writing to create a duo of historical sagas set in the Texas Panhandle. Drawing on her own family's oral traditions and on tales told to her by children of the early-day settlers, as well as years of research, Meredith has written stories rich in local history and stunning in their portrait of a woman fighting for her place in a man's world of nineteenth-century Texas.

Acclaimed by *Texas Almanac* as one of the state's ten best mystery writers, D.R. Meredith lives in Amarillo, Texas, with her husband and two teenage children. She edits a column on western literature for *Roundup Quarterly,* a publication of Western Writers of America and Texas University Press.

HarperPaperbacks By Mail

ZANE GREY CLASSICS

- [ ] **THE DUDE RANGER**
  0-06-100055-8 $3.50
- [ ] **THE LOST WAGON TRAIN**
  0-06-100064-7 $3.99
- [ ] **THE MAN OF THE FOREST**
  0-06-100082-5 $3.95
- [ ] **THE BORDER LEGION**
  0-06-100083-3 $3.95
- [ ] **30,000 ON HOOF**
  0-06-100085-X $3.50
- [ ] **THE WANDERER OF THE WASTELAND**
  0-06-100092-2 $3.50
- [ ] **TWIN SOMBREROS**
  0-06-100101-5 $3.50
- [ ] **BOULDER DAM**
  0-06-100111-2 $3.50
- [ ] **THE TRAIL DRIVER**
  0-06-100154-6 $3.50
- [ ] **TO THE LAST MAN**
  0-06-100218-6 $3.50
- [ ] **THUNDER MOUNTAIN**
  0-06-100216-X $3.50
- [ ] **THE CODE OF THE WEST**
  0-06-100173-2 $3.50
- [ ] **ROGUE RIVER FEUD**
  0-06-100214-3 $3.95
- [ ] **THE THUNDERING HERD**
  0-06-100217-8 $3.95
- [ ] **HORSE HEAVEN HILL**
  0-06-100210-0 $3.95
- [ ] **VALLEY OF WILD HORSES**
  0-06-100221-6 $3.95
- [ ] **WILDERNESS TREK**
  0-06-100260-7 $3.99
- [ ] **THE VANISHING AMERICAN**
  0-06-100295-X $3.99
- [ ] **CAPTIVES OF THE DESERT**
  0-06-100292-5 $3.99
- [ ] **THE SPIRIT OF THE BORDER**
  0-06-100293-3 $3.99
- [ ] **ROBBERS' ROOST**
  0-06-100280-1 $3.99
- [ ] **UNDER THE TONTO RIM**
  0-06-100294-1 $3.99

**Visa and MasterCard holders—
call 1-800-331-3761 for fastest service!**

MAIL TO: Harper Collins Publishers
P. O. Box 588 Dunmore, PA 18512-0588
OR CALL: (800) 331-3761 (Visa/MasterCard)

Yes, please send the books I have checked on this page.

SUBTOTAL	$ _____
POSTAGE AND HANDLING	$ 2.00*
SALES TAX (Add state sales tax)	$ _____
TOTAL:	$ _____

*ORDER 4 OR MORE TITLES AND POSTAGE & HANDLING IS FREE!
Orders of less than 4 books, please include $2.00 p/h. Remit in US funds.
Do not send cash.

Name _____

Address _____

City _____

State _____ Zip _____

Allow up to 6 weeks delivery.
Prices subject to change.

(Valid only in US & Canada)

HO491

The story continues . . .

Watch for
THE RECKONING
by D.R. Meredith

Coming in September 1993 from HarperPaperbacks.

HarperPaperbacks
A Division of HarperCollinsPublishers